THE MULBERRY FUGUE

THE MULBERRY FUGUE

HEATHER SHAW

First published in Great Britain in 2014 by

Bannister Publications Ltd
118 Saltergate
Chesterfield
Derbyshire S40 1NG

Copyright © Heather Shaw

ISBN 978-1-909813-08-3

Heather Shaw asserts the moral right to be identified
as the author of this work

A catalogue record for this book is available from the British Library

This book is sold subject to the condition that it shall not, by way of trade
or otherwise, be lent, re-sold, hired out or otherwise circulated without the
copyright holder's prior consent in any form of binding or cover other
than that in which it is published and without a similar condition including
this condition being imposed on the subsequent purchase.

All rights reserved. No part of this book may be reproduced or
transmitted in any form or by any means, electronic or mechanical
including photocopying, recording or by any information storage and
retrieval system, without permission from the copyright holder, in writing.

Typeset in Palatino Linotype by Escritor Design,
Chesterfield, Derbyshire

Printed and bound in Great Britain by SRP Ltd
Exeter, Devon

Also by Heather Shaw

Brushstrokes – a collection of Short Stories

'The Marsh, or Hidden Quarter as some have named it, is a world apart, a secret, watery world where the ghosts of smugglers trundle contraband through the mist and Martello Towers hunker down at the gateway to England. For centuries, drainage schemes and defensive walls have secured its fertile grasslands but this is territory wrenched, by the Romans, from the sea, and the battle between earth and water can never be conclusive.

The settlements along the coast stand on the margin where fields become beach, beach becomes sea.'

The Farthest South of Kent by Percival Carr, pub. 1965

PART 1

Fugue – a musical term for contrapuntal
compositions featuring a number of parts or voices

Chapter 1

'The tenors were flat again,' Pru said, gripping the steering wheel, 'in the Rutter piece.'

Heading south-west across the Marsh, the car towed its own shadow. Behind the windscreen, the women's faces were blushed by the setting sun, their hair rosy halos.

'I love the way this road threads between two worlds,' Daphne said. 'On one side,' she waggled her fingers, 'the wide expanse of the sea. On the other, the Marsh, wads of emerald green fields hovering above swamps of water.' She frowned. 'Do I mean wads?' Far off to her right, she caught glimpses of the wind turbines, like pale skeletons of Marsh Witches, rising from waterlogged graves and semaphoring messages to their salt-water sisters. 'The Marsh,' she whispered. 'Gift of the sea.'

'If they don't put some serious work in,' Pru shoved the gear stick from second to third, 'it'll be the Choral Festival disaster all over again. You mark my words.'

'All set for a drama, watery, green and lush,' Daphne said, 'against the backdrop of the wide, wide sky.'

She braced herself as Pru slammed on the brakes just too late to anchor all four wheels behind the white line.

'Whoops,' Pru said. 'Road junction.'

Poor Pru, Daphne thought. A dear, dear friend but absolutely no poetry in her soul and, truth be told, a tad whiffy just now. Such a pity she and Jim indulged in fish on choir practice nights. The reek of chip fat did cling so, especially to that track suit. 'I'm popping the window down a fraction, okay?' she said. She leant the side of her head against the glass, let the coolness seep into her ear and took a deep breath.

'It's these muggy nights.' Pru wiped her hand across her mouth. 'If it's this hot in early May, what's the rest of the summer going to be like? I was only saying to Jim. Not that he takes any notice, threshing about for hours on end. Thank the lucky stars we went in for twin beds.'

'Thrashing,' Daphne said.

'Is it here we turn left? I can never remember. What d'you mean, thrashing?'

'Thrashing, not threshing. Threshing's to do with farming.'

Here they come, Daphne thought, the actors and props in my own drama.

*

The threshing machine in the barn rattles and clanks, the men's sun-browned arms are wrapped around the straw stooks, the barn fills with the heady smell of grain. In the spotlight, centre stage, is Daddy's Daphne, hoisted onto his shoulders, his braces tickling her legs. Everyone calls him 'Sir'. Threshing for goodness he calls it, beating out the chaff. Combining means men from all his farms working together, doing their bit to get in the harvest before the rain.

*

'Now we're lost,' Pru was complaining. 'I did ask you where to turn. I should have got the hang of it after all this time but you know how it is.'

Daphne brought down the curtain on the past. Decades ago now. No sense dwelling on all that, letting regrets clog her throat. 'Sorry, darling,' she said. 'I was miles away.'

'Going over that top G were you, in your mind? You're a perfectionist Daph and that's a fact, not like some we could name. Can we get down here?'

'Now that I can tell you,' Daphne said, 'for rent on Fridays.'

Pru snorted. 'For what?'

'Rent on Fridays. It's what May used to tell the Paying Guests, not the overnight B&B's but the ones who stayed for weeks at a time. Early morning tea you can make in your rooms, she'd tell them, but evening drinks I only do for...'

'Rent on Fridays?'

'Exactly.'

Pru flicked the indicator. 'How many years did you skivvy for May Kulman, before you both retired?'

'Skivvy, Pru?' Daphne stiffened. 'I was the Domestic Manager I'll have you know, with my own flat.'

'Come off it, Daph, love. Mulberry House B&B was hardly the Dorchester.'

'That nice young man from the English Tourist Board gave us three crowns.'

'Each one hard earned by you, no doubt.' Pru's hand abandoned the steering wheel to pat Daphne's knee, leaving a damp smudge on her cotton skirt. 'May Kulman put on you, right, left and centre. Not known for her generous spirit, that one.'

'She was kind to me.' Kind when there was no spotlight. A dark, dark stage and no part at all for nearly grown-up Daphne. There'd been a scowl on Daddy's face, as if he'd wanted to beat the chaff out of her.

The car slewed to a stop. Pru turned off the engine and heaved on the hand brake. 'Here we are then,' she said, 'home sweet home.'

How quickly night claims us, Daphne thought, once the sun has gone.

'It must have come as a terrible shock,' Pru said. 'May Kulman popping her clogs like that. Up north wasn't it? What was she doing there? Did she say anything, before she left?'

'What was that?'

'There you go again, Daph. Where are you this time? With the Mendelssohn no doubt and not a moment too soon. Our beloved leader has over-reached himself with *Elijah*, if you want my opinion. Not that anyone ever does of course.'

Daphne frowned. 'Anyone ever does what?'

Pru propped her chin on her hand. 'I can't for the life of me see what was so wrong with my suggestion.'

'Which was?'

'Some numbers from *Tommy*. Rock opera's absolutely respectable these days. It's the way Elvis would have gone.' She sniffed. 'Had he lived.'

'Lived?'

'Am I blathering on again?' Pru said.' According to Jim, my blathering's reached epic proportions, whatever they are. Not that he's got room to talk, painting butterflies in flight all over that van of his. Very hippy. He'll be sporting a ponytail next'. She turned to Daphne.' Take no notice of me. You've got quite enough on your plate. It is funny though, May Kulman disappearing up north somewhere, only to die on us.'

'She often went up north, after we retired, ' Daphne said. 'Usually on the spur of the moment too. She'd get into that nippy little car of hers and take off. Something to do with a relative I think.'

'But she didn't have any relatives, did she? All on my little ownsome was her war cry. She made it sound like a threat. Anyway, what happens now?'

'How do you mean?'

'To you, Daph. What happens to you, now that May's dead?

Open-mouthed, Daphne stared at her. 'But...' she said.

'You'll have to come down from that cloud you live on.' Pru's voice was gentle. 'You need to know where you stand, if she made some provision.'

'Provision?'

'For you ducky, in her will. You should get some advice. It doesn't bear thinking about. You could be homeless.'

But it wasn't May who made people homeless, was it? That had been Daddy's department. No daughter of mine. Never darken my door. Mummy not looking her in the eye.

'May wouldn't do that to me,' Daphne said. 'Why would she?'

'On the other hand,' Pru said brightly,' she may have left you the lot.'

'How d'you mean?'

'The house. Mulberry House. Who else would she leave it to? Quite right too, the graft you've put in. Who's the executor, d'you know?'

'Executor?'

Pru sighed. 'The person who sorts out the will, sees to the bequests and such.'

'I've no idea, unless it's Dr Carr. May was very thick with him.'

'With Thomas Carr?' Pru reached to start the engine. 'You do surprise me. Rumour has it he likes his women a lot shorter in the tooth.'

'He's a horrible man,' Daphne pulled a face. 'No manners at all. And not even a proper doctor.'

'It's academic dear. Very big in history at the University, so they say. All teeth and no trousers, if you ask me, with the emphasis on no trousers. Not much joy there then.' Pru laughed. 'Now I'd better love you and leave you, ducky. Jim'll be sending out a search party. That or ordering a celebration cake. See you on Monday?'

Daphne scrabbled in her bag for her front door key. 'Can we change that, Pru? The Players are auditioning on Monday, for *The Sound of Music*.'

'Don't, Daph, not again.' Pru said.

The reviewers would recognise her talents, Daphne knew. She could see the reviews in the local paper. Daphne Chiltern's Mother Superior – or whatever she was called - brought depths to the role never before encountered.

'Right up my street,' she told Pru and hummed the opening bars of How Do You Solve a Problem Like Maria?'

'You were so cut up last time,' Pru said, 'when they picked someone else. And the time before that.'

But Daphne wasn't listening. She opened the car door and with one foot on the pavement turned to say, 'Tuesday will be okay though.'

'Is that a breath of wind I can feel?' Pru said. 'Last of the muggy weather perhaps? Nothing lasts for ever in this neck of the woods, does it?'

As Pru's car rounded the corner, Daphne stood with her hand on the garden gate. A knot of fear gripped her. Why hadn't it sunk in before? May wasn't coming back. It was the shock, she told herself. Shock had persuaded her this was only the interval, the end of Act Two. Nervy laughter in the Dressing Room. It is going well, isn't it, darling? Lovely audience? Come the five minute bell and all would be back to normal. May in the wings, waiting for her cue.

At the end of the garden path stood Mulberry House, solidly facing the sea with the brick chimney-stack down its left flank, its terracotta roof tiles and white weatherboarding. And the dear little trellis porch, a bit off centre but what did that matter? For over half a century this house had been as much a player in her life as any of the people whose names were top of the bill.

No light in the porch. No-one waiting inside. Not anymore. Come on Daphne, she told herself. Deep breath. Best foot forward. Improvisation, that's what we need. Look at the bigger picture. Let go of the script and see what happens. All that stuff about an empty house was hardly fair to Nelson, now was it? Turning on a light might be more than the dear pusskins could manage but he was waiting for her, wasn't he?

When all the lights were on in her first floor flat and Nelson's little ginger nose was safely immersed in his plate of sardines, Daphne stared from her kitchen window into the darkness of the back garden. Gripping the edge of the sink, she remembered standing here the last time she'd seen May, looking down on her as she'd left the house and stood for a moment to glance at the mulberry tree before opening the door into the back of the garage.

Daphne couldn't even recall what May had been wearing. If you know something is for the last time, everything little detail is significant, carefully stored in your mind. Accidents rob you of that luxury. Nothing about that departure was any different from all the other times May had gone away. She always had been just this side of impulsive and must have had a life away from Mulberry House, a life Daphne had rarely thought about. Perhaps she should have paid more attention.

Come to think of it, had the trips been longer recently? Last December was it, the first time it had been more than a week? May had written down her mobile phone number but Daphne never used it and the slip of paper had lost itself. No sense in worrying about that now.

She flung open her front door and stepped onto the landing. In the rising wind, Mulberry House seemed to shift and list, straining against its anchorage like a ship of the line, as well it could be with Nelson up here on the bridge.

Time to take stock. It was unthinkable that May would leave her homeless, not after offering her sanctuary. And over the years, hadn't she done her best to repay that debt? Surely she could now claim the house, if only by dint of dusting, by right of hoovering, polishing, cherishing.

She drifted from room to room. Guest bedrooms first, six of them, unused since May had decided to shut up shop. The doors were ajar, the doorknobs clammy in her hand. She perched on the corners of bare mattresses, plumped uncovered pillows, slid open drawers. Now they were nearly hers, these ordinary things, furniture she'd dusted and polished for years, felt like the old friends they were, friends going way back. Along this corridor, the memories jostled, empty shells of the lives that had crossed her own.

- The birdwatcher from the Midlands, overweight in scruffy denims, desperate to spot a Temminck's Stint, whatever that was. He called her 'me duck' and worried about his eyesight, poor man.

- That scrap of a girl, tearful and pleading. Please oh please could Daphne get the stuff off her jeans. Dad said it was tar, Mum would go ballistic.

- The couples having what May decided was a dirty week-end. 'Put them in the back, Daphne,' she'd say. 'A sea view's the last thing they'll be needing.'

May's private rooms were downstairs. Next to the front door was the office from where she kept an eye on things. Folk never missed a trick, she reckoned, not these days. One lapse of attention and the towels would migrate from bedroom to beach, fill themselves with gritty sand and have to be replaced before the due date.

Daphne avoided May's sitting room and bedroom, in the annexe behind the familiar kitchen where rent-on-Fridays drinks used to sidle up against full English breakfast. Anything more than a glance into those rooms would seem like prying. When everything was official, and the house was properly hers, she would enjoy a really good ferret.

In the Guests' Dining Room the tables looked naked without their white tablecloths. Next along the passage was the Guests' Lounge with easy chairs and low tables waiting for tasteful magazines. Daphne stood in the bay window and looked towards the sea. Beyond the road, it would be heaving its response to the wind, edging its waves with white ruffs to suck in the shingle.

'High time we retired,' was how May had put it. They'd leave the house just as it was, she'd said, until things were sorted. That meant her will, didn't it? May wasn't one to hang about. In the year that had passed since then she had surely settled the important things.

The brass rings clattered as Daphne closed the damask curtains. Now in the dimness, the furniture loomed like islands in a shadowy sea. She was enclosed in a world turned new, a place she could make her own. She would transform it into a place of artistry, of theatre, of talent, the talk of the theatrical world. 'Have you seen what Daphne's done with Mulberry House?' the darlings would say. 'You must get down there, lovey. That woman's a marvel.'

Back in the hall, one foot on the bottom stair, Daphne looked up. What a wonderful space this was, airy and high. The resonance would be marvellous. She arranged herself at the bottom of the stairs. Deep breath. Hold the moment. With a generous helping of vibrato, she was delivering the opening notes of *Climb Every Mountain* when the phone in her flat shrilled.

Out of breath from scrambling up the stairs, she lifted the receiver.

'Miss Chiltern? Thomas Carr. You'll no doubt have heard that Mrs Kulman made me executor of her will. I need to speak to you. About your present position in Mulberry House.'

Chapter 2

What would his alter ego have done Thomas wondered as he put down the phone. The legendary and entirely fictitious Sir Dreadnought Stumble was, like Chaucer's perfect knight, of noble birth. Sir Dreadnought embodied all the qualities and flaws of his modern counterpart but when it came to Daphne Chiltern even chivalry had its limitations.

With his spaniel, Nell, snoozing at his feet, Thomas closed his eyes. His usual calming strategy - reciting the dates of British monarchs - wasn't working. If he could reach Richard the Lionheart, 1189 to 1199, all those knightly virtues might provide relief but he kept grinding to a halt with the Empress Matilda.

Matilda and Daphne Chiltern, deluded ladies both. Poor Daphne had little idea of her own limitations. The Choral Society was apparently trying to shunt her into the sidings and Harvey at The Marsh Players hid in the scenery store every time her dandelion clock of hair and flowing draperies tripped into view.

And now this business with Mulberry House. He'd tried to explain the situation gently. Winning the favour of a good lady with adoration and brave quests was hardly appropriate and coming straight out with it would have been cruel. But five minutes trying to negotiate the candyfloss of Daphne Chiltern's brain had been enough to have a bloke climbing the walls. Half an hour listening to her twittering was enough to turn him to drink.

'Are you sure, Dr Carr?' she'd bleated. 'That can't be right. May would have told me. You are quite sure?' On and on it went, the careful modulation slipping through whine into shriek. He stared at the wall, mentally designing a funeral hatchment dominated by a lion couchant reaching the climax of a yawn. In the end he'd had to cut her off. Encouraging hysterics would have done no good, no good at all. However hard it was, she had to face facts. May Kulman had left Mulberry House to a woman called Alison Draper.

'Never heard of her, have we, Nell? he said, patting the dog's head. 'Which calls, I think, for a wee dram of the Talisker.' Nell wagged her tail and padded after him into the sitting room.

Swinging open the sideboard door, he decided it was high time he found a new home for his collection of single malts. The room's atmosphere was tainted, not least by Ingrid's photo still in situ on the sideboard, her embroidery dominating the faux inglenook and the ash-wood furniture that had been her choice. He had married a woman happy to mix the cosiness of an imagined past with the austerity of Scandinavian design. The ghost of their marriage prowled and hovered here, a ghost with little reason to leave him in peace. So why bother with this room at all? In a house this size, he could shut the door. Shut the door and ignore the past.

Thomas inspected the label on the whisky bottle. 'Pungently smoky,' he told Nell. He poured a generous, medicinal tot, slumped into an armchair and fondled Nell's ear. The single malt slid its smoky pungency down his throat.

That wouldn't be the end of it with Daphne Chiltern. With her type, fragility cloaked an iron will. Her head might be in the clouds but her feet were very firmly planted in her own best interests. His grin was rueful. A mess of metaphors just about summed up the lady but that was a very unchivalrous thought.

May Kulman had been another of the same ilk. Acerbic, manipulative woman with her sucked-in, puckered mouth and eyes like raisins pushed into an uncooked pastry face. There was a tang of vinegar about her as if her clothes had been pickled, like conkers hardening up for battle.

He pictured her in his Family History class, hunched under a carapace of clothes. Had he known the end game was about to kick off, he'd never have agreed to be executor of her will. Timing wrong and tactics askew though where the fair sex was concerned, even the best battle strategy was likely to come adrift.

For Sir Dreadnought, preserved at his peak in the aspic of history, it was a complete doddle. His womenfolk were his vassals, taken care of, in all senses.

'What would Sir D have made of The Married Women's Property Act, eh, Nell?' Thomas said. 'Enough, enough. How about a walk?'

The dog barked her enthusiasm and rushed to the kitchen to fetch her lead.

They set off down the drive, along the lane and into the rest of the world. From here to the beach, humanity offered its domestic packets for inspection. First a short terrace of Edwardian villas, then a sprinkling of mean-looking boxes put up in the sixties, each with its accretion of porch, conservatory or block-paved drive. On the corner was the pair of semi's, one shipshape and pristine harnessed to a partner dilapidated beyond repair, the place for Nell to enjoy a good sniff.

Now the street of bungalows, neat little white clones with twin bay windows and double-glazed front doors. Here and there a dormer interrupted the roof lines, a Cyclops eye, a cut above the rest.

And then the beach.

With Nell scampering around him, Thomas crunched across the shingle. The south westerly wind had seen off the day's humidity and under a dark and ragged cloud base the sea was sombre. The incoming tide swallowed the breakwaters.

The white poodle, sniffing at a dead crab, was blessed with the name of Trixie, Thomas remembered. A curly hairdo and large bow gave her the air of a dandy trying out purple this season. Near-by, red pooper-scooper in one hand, plastic bag and the end of the poodle's lead in the other, hovered Adrian Cooper, assistant-owner of Trixie and spokesman for wife Pearl, known in the bar of The Grey Goose as Harbour Mouth.

Nell growled. Thomas called her to heel.

'Pearl says it's very strange,' Adrian announced.

'Good evening, Adrian.' Thomas said. 'It looks like rain, then?' Expecting an opinion on the weather from a man whose wife informed him whether or not he was awake, was optimistic.

'No good will come of it,' Adrian went on, 'not in Pearl's view.'

'And which of Pearl's many wise views would that be?' Thomas said. Keeping a wary eye on Trixie, Nell stirred beside him. 'Stay. Good girl,' he muttered.

'Getting killed like that,' Adrian went on. 'Up north.'

'Which strikes Pearl as the more heinous offence?' Thomas said. 'Extinction of life or its location?'

'Daphne Chiltern. Now there's a thought.' And with that Adrian yanked on Trixie's lead and walked off.

A thought best avoided Thomas told himself on their way back home. But avoiding the lady herself wouldn't be easy, not in a place this size. Perhaps he should consider doing his own variation of Dr Syn, the phantom scarecrow of the Marsh. By day, the respectable university don and tutor of community education courses, by night a hooded figure avenging mankind of the women who plagued them. That would confuse things.

Chapter 3

On a Sunday morning in March, weeks before the drama in which Alison Draper would play a leading role, she got into her car and drove without plan or thought of destination. Surfacing that morning, through layers of sleep, she knew she had to get out of the apartment. Weeks after she'd moved in she was still adrift in the sea of her possessions, not at home in any sense. Even her shoes, always at the top of any agenda, hadn't found a permanent parking place. The line of see-through shoe boxes snaked across the living room floor, their contents proof that standing on your own two feet was more than possible. The heels, soles, shanks and insole linings deserved better. Shoes didn't make you feel a failure, look at you with contempt, exchange you for a younger model.

From Bakewell she took the A6 to Matlock then drove through the gorge towards Matlock Bath. Grey rock faces, looming either side of the road, were still flecked with traces of snow. Above her the cable cars huddled in hibernation.

Mothering Sunday was not the best time to visit Matlock Bath she realised as she stuck the parking ticket on the dashboard. The people walking briskly along the riverside, spilling out of shops, amusement arcades, the waxworks, were all in groups, pay and display families clustered in celebration.

'At last,' Malcolm's mother had cooed, a decade ago now, when they'd told her they planned to get married. 'A chance of grandchildren. Our own flesh and blood.'

Aunt Jude had looked doubtful and wondered if Alison was really sure. Alison had been sure. Tired of feeling on the fringe of life, she wanted to belong, to be part of a family. Jude was a love, the best substitute for parents anyone could have been, but she distrusted adult relationships which involved emotional dependency. How right she had been.

Malcolm's mother had soon become suspicious. 'I hope you're not, you know, using anything,' was her perpetual bleat. 'Best not leave it too long.' Three generations of Draper and Son – Garden Designs and Plant Nursery – demanded a vigilant defence of the bloodline, a bloodline that was now in Alison's keeping. The implication was clear: the Drapers had made her a partner in their business, welcomed her into their family, so the least she could do was ensure its survival. Malcolm's first marriage and child had demonstrated his bloodline capabilities. The subsequent divorce and disappearance of their grand-daughter to foreign climes, had been unfortunate but nothing that couldn't be rectified.

Always at the corner of awareness, drifting over the edges of Alison's vision like the shadow of a branch in the wind, was the child she might have had. The baby's features were clear, blue eyes slanted like Jude's, ears just a shade too large like Alison's own, a mouth lumpy with red gums, a fuzz of egg-brown hair. She played a game of peek-a-boo with her almost-mother, one moment there, the next only a memory.

Had Alison been able to share her feelings with her mother-in-law, how much her own longing for a baby gnawed at her, how hope had been buried by disappointment, would there have been compassion? But the years passed and the mutterings into Malcolm's ear suggested mistakes could still be remedied. There were plenty more fish in the sea.

And now he had hooked one.

A ball bounced out of the play area and landed at her feet. Its toddler owner teetered towards it, hands extended, eyes alight. Alison turned away, letting the ball roll into the gutter. 'Selfish cow,' a man said.

Accurate enough Alison thought, though a tad unfair to cows. She was retreating to the car when her phone rang.

'How are you?' Jude said. 'Sorry love, silly question. You still feel bloody awful, of course you do. Are you busy? Where are you?'

'Matlock Bath.'

'What the devil are you doing there? Anyway, I think you should come over. I saw your ma-in-law earlier.'

'Ex-ma-in-law. What did she want?'

'She wanted me to give you...'

'A house warming gift? Spider plant? Living Without a Man handbook?'

'I popped out for some shopping and there I was, leaning on my trolley in the check-out queue, when Malcolm's mother confronted me.'

'Which ear-rings was she wearing?'

'Ear-rings?'

'Lady Golf Captain pearl studs, butter-wouldn't-melt gold hoops or dangly drops?'

'Droopy things, fighting with the collar of her jacket.'

'You're in for a rough ride with those.' Alison pictured brows drawn together, a grudge-tight lip line. 'So what did she want?'

'To pass on some news.' Jude hesitated. 'Face to face would be better than phone. Can you come over? If you haven't had lunch I could rustle up some salad. I have someone to show round the place first but that won't take long.'

Half an hour later, Alison arrived at the Sheldon Lifestyle Community. Jude wasn't in the Manager's apartment so she tried the communal lounge.

Her aunt was shepherding a skeletal woman with a sour expression on her face and arms clamped over her chest, as if she were refusing a request to borrow her cardigan. 'A visitor,' Jude mouthed. The woman stared at Alison with black, beady eyes.

By the window, the Major was in animated dispute with his chess partner, a matronly figure whose bosom cantilevered ominously over the board.

Three of the other residents, feisty old girls whose take on life Alison always relished, had pulled their chairs into a triangle. They were hunched in discussion, the toes of their shoes touching – black patent courts overlapped by swollen flesh, green designer-trainers, stringy espadrilles.

'We've been trying to decide which woman has made the greatest contribution to the world,' one of them said when Alison joined them.

'And what's the verdict?'

'It's a toss-up, between Marie Stopes and Emmeline Pankhurst.'

'Contraception or the vote,' said the owner of the patent courts . 'What d'you reckon?'

Alison hesitated. Six enquiring eyes waited for her answer. 'I've only taken advantage of one.' she said, 'but I'm not saying which.'

A woman with no children is a freak of nature, she told herself, a woman whose body can't fulfil its basic function. Reminders of her inadequacy were to be seen everywhere she went, splayed, like fat pink frogs in baby-slings, bouncing in buggies or squirming and wriggling in restraining arms. They would stretch tiny, star-fish hands towards the trays of winter pansies in Draper's plant shop and gild the air with chuckles. Phalanxes of pushchairs laid claim to every other street corner, bastions against the world, their tiny passengers disdaining their mums' gossip, staring solemnly past each other, as if no other living creature could possibly be so important.

'Marie Stopes, every time,' the wearer of the trainers was announcing. 'Voting's all very well, but as long as there's fellers around, there'll be rumpy-pumpy.'

'Marie it is then,' they decided.

Jude appeared, offering lunch. In her kitchen, Alison leaned against the worktop. 'You do enjoy running this place, don't you, Jude?' she said. 'This apartment feels like home?'

Jude opened a bag of watercress. 'According to George Bernard Shaw,' she said, 'home is the girl's prison and the woman's workhouse.'

'He must have seen the dump I'm living in,' Alison said. Malcolm had suggested it made sense for her to move out of the home they'd shared. 'Give us chance to sort ourselves out,' he'd said, as if the three of them, Alison, Malcolm and Kirsty were pieces of tangled knitting waiting to be unravelled. After all, he'd pointed out, when he'd bought back Alison's shares he'd have a much bigger stake in the garden centre and the house was on the same site. Husband, home and business, a triple forfeit in a game she hadn't known she was playing.

'Nice top,' Jude said. 'Jade green always was your colour.' She cut up cucumber and slid the slices onto the plates. 'What have you done to your hair?'

'Don't you like it?'

'It makes your face look gaunt.'

Alison hugged her. 'Good old Jude, never one to pull your punches.'

'If it's flattery you want,' Jude's eyes softened, 'you've come to the wrong place. You lived with me long enough to know that.'

Long enough, Alison thought, to have felt the global tail wind of burning bras, to have squelched happily through the mud at Women-Against-Patriarchy camps. Long enough for rampant feminism, dispensed with wise affection, to blunt the edge of a small girl's despair at losing both her parents.

'Help yourself to cheese.' Jude pointed to the fridge. 'I got some of that Yorkshire ham you like, too. It's in there somewhere.'

'I've been thinking,' Alison said as they sat at the table.

'Not always a good thing, thinking,' Jude said. 'Can get you into all sorts of scrapes.'

'It was Matlock Bath that did it. The place was crawling with the good and the fertile. Did you know it's Mothering Sunday?'

Jude held her knife above a wedge of Stilton cheese. 'Of course. That's why so many residents have been taken out for lunch,' she said.

'I stuck it out for an hour or so and then I thought, bugger this. You need a plan Alison. So, on the way here I decided. I'll get a bank loan, find some premises and get going. I'll need to work out a business plan, do some calculations. I may need to sell the flat, find somewhere smaller but...'

'Slow down.' Jude pushed a radish around her plate. 'What exactly are you planning to do?'

'To fight back, Jude, that's what. I'll set up the best Garden Design company this town has ever seen. The Drapers won't last six months without me. They've no business sense and brainless Kirsty hasn't a clue. By the way, what did Malcolm's mother want?'

Jude's grip dug into Alison's arm. 'From what I hear, love, Kirsty's got something far more valuable than business sense. To the Drapers, anyway.'

Alison gulped. 'She's... pregnant?'

Jude nodded.

Alison clenched her teeth. Outside, the branches of the silver birch tree trembled in the breeze. She swallowed. 'If this was a film,' she said, 'the script would demand a close-up as my eyes flooded with tears and the violins did their stuff.'

'Write your own script, Allie,' Jude said softly. 'If you start letting other folks dictate, you're finished.'

'It's finished all right,' Alison said. For some reason, the image surfacing in her mind was of a young woman playing the violin, in a bay window with white, fluttering curtains. Her mother? 'Anyway,' she said, 'why should it make any difference to me? I needn't see the brat.'

'If you stick around while that bimbo's bun rises in the oven,' Jude said, 'you're not the woman I took you for.' She popped the last bit of cheese into her mouth and chewed ferociously.

Alison frowned. 'Run away? Absolutely not.'

'Boudicca would have called it a tactical retreat.'

'And look what happened to her.'

'But she did it on her own terms,' Jude said. 'That's my point. Yes, you need to regroup and come out fighting, but not around here. The answer's plain as a bullfrog on a piano.'

'A what?' Alison smiled. 'Where did that come from?'

Jude patted Alison's hand and smiled. 'Never mind come from,' she said. 'Never mind business plans and calculations. What you need to do is get right away from here.'

Hanging above Jude's bookcase was the embroidery Alison had done in junior school, a fanciful, over-bright butterfly of her own design. She thought of the tussle she'd had with the teacher who'd wanted everyone's efforts to resemble reality, a red admiral or meadow blue. 'You're not wrong,' she said, 'but where the hell would I go?'

Chapter 4

Some miles from the apartment where Alison's shoeboxes meandered across the floor, Felstone could be found on the same OS map. It was a town with few attractions for tourists. Getting there meant a diversion from looking up the crooked spire in Chesterfield, swaying in a cable car up Matlock's Heights of Abraham or hiking over heather-scented moorland. But if the words sherbet lemons conjured up a memory of pocket money hot in the hand and ranks of fat sweet jars winking down from well-stocked shelves, the effort was worth it. Felstone was the home of Prosser's Confectionery where a nasal nostalgia of cough-candy twist, lime bonbons and aniseed balls hovered above the streets.

At nearly midnight, the upper floors of Prosser's factory were in darkness but the windows of the packing and despatch room glowed. The man inside paced along the racks of cardboard cartons. 'Bryn Stanfield,' he chanted into empty space 'Bryn Stanfield.' It was getting easier. Plans to ditch the mess he had made were underway but a new identity needed time and he wasn't sure how much he had.

It felt completely wrong, wearing a suit in here. This wasn't suit and tie country. This was t-shirt and trainers territory, wear what's comfortable. His first minutes in here - could it really be thirty years ago? - had been anything but comfortable. One day the last of school, the next tripping over his feet to keep up with his father.

'I harboured hopes you were university material.' Father's voice had filled the stairwell as they descended from office to factory floor. 'Accountancy, business management, something useful.' At the bottom, Father waited, towering over him in every sense. 'But it seems not.' He shook his head. 'It's your mother's idea to set you on here, lad, so you'd better shape up.'

'I'm starting you in packing,' Father threw open the door. 'You may be the boss's son but begin at the bottom and you'll know what's what.' And with more shakings of head, more despairing sighs, his father had left him stranded on an island of humiliation.

A bouncy, scarlet-lipped woman called Dolly saved his bacon. 'That's told us then,' she said. 'Welcome to the bottom of the heap.' With a grin, she'd held out her hand. 'Best make a start in the kitchen. You'll be needing a cuppa, I reckon.'

Good days they had been in here, surrounded by boxes, sticky tape and pallets. Nobody pointed out his inadequacies, peered at him over the top of reproving glasses, sighed and looked out of the window. If some guardian angel had managed to cancel his birth certificate, wipe out the paperwork that defined him, he'd have been a happy guy.

It was here he'd discovered jazz, Big Band. The foreman, a man whose dark hair and white beard gave him a mix and match appearance, liked Jimmy Dorsey numbers playing all day. Apart from what he called Pop Wednesdays when Duran Duran or Eurythmics were allowed, jazz was on the menu.

'I'm not convinced JD had the right idea about Bebop, young'un,' the foreman would say, 'but you can't fault his creative genius. Get the day off to a good start with *I Got Rhythm* and wind down with *Tangerine*, that's the plan.'

Now, thirty years later and far from the delights of packing and despatching, Bryn was suited, and tied in every sense. But not for long.

He squeezed past the forklift trucks and leant his elbows on a pile of sealed boxes, running his forefinger around the edge of the label. 'Lime Sherbets,' he muttered. 'Very appropriate.'

A new life was waiting. Cowardice was the only word for running away from the financial mess he'd made but cowards always find a way out.

PART 2

'Fugue – from the Latin root *fuga*, meaning flight.'

Chapter 5

Daphne was sitting at her dressing table. 'Enormous demands, Nelson, that's what,' she said. Behind her, the tabby cat sprawling on the summer weight quilt rasped his tongue over his paws. She smiled at his reflection in the mirror. 'Any acting project makes enormous demands on time and energy.'

Over a distance of sixty years, a chasm which had gobbled up status and now predictable tomorrows, the memory of Madame Fornier's voice was pebble-clear. 'Atmosphere, mes petites, always the atmosphere.'

Behind Daphne's closed eyes, the scene appeared.

*

The dance and drama tutor's eau-de-cologne fills the garden room at Chiltern Hall with an aura of pavement cafés, star-spangled nights and Paris Theatres. Fingering a lace-edged handkerchief, a mint imperial sweetening her breath, Madame's only aim is to instil elegance and grace into gawky adolescents. Girls from the village, invited to make up the group, might shuffle and giggle but Daphne knows the real thing when she sees it.

*

Nelson's cough wrenched her back to reality. He choked up a ball of soggy fur.

'Naughty boy,' Daphne said. She grabbed a tissue, scooped up the mess and aimed it in the direction of the waste bin. 'You should take more interest, pusskins. You'll suffer just as much as I will if that dreadful Dr Carr doesn't get this inheritance thing sorted.' She wiped away the beginning of a tear. 'Still, this new part will take my mind off things.'

M.A.U.V.E - that's what Madame had insisted on - Movement, Action, Utterance, Volume and above all else, Energy. But time had swooped away so much, demanding her youthful energy, in payment perhaps for the disgrace she had brought to her respectable family, a family where What The Neighbours Thought was pipped to the post only by The Ten Commandments. Now in short supply, energy had to give way to enthusiasm. 'It's still an E, anyway,' Daphne comforted herself. 'It's the E that matters.'

She placed her hands lightly on her ribcage and breathed slowly, feeling each breath start under her diaphragm and rise to her nostrils. At all costs she must avoid tension, the actor's greatest enemy. She flexed her neck. No use putting her whole self into preparing for audition, only to be undone by tautness in the muscles.

The thing now was, had she made the right choice in going for the part of Mother Abbess? Elsa Shrader, the Captain's intended, offered more in the way of glamour but she didn't come off well did she, and it wasn't a good singing part. No point missing out on *Climb Every Mountain* for the sake of an elegant dress. The Abbess, presumably, was a character like the nurse in Romeo and Juliet, a mature, caring woman who had no trouble recognising True Love.

She eased herself off the stool to position the free-standing swivel mirror in front of the window. That couldn't be a shadow of hair on her upper lip, now could it? It must be a streak of dust on the glass. At times like this, housework took second place, of course.

Dress for success was the watchword. The flowing, turquoise maxi-dress hung beautifully. A fraction too long perhaps but the navy, patent stilettos would take care of that. She'd been right not to hire a nun's habit for the audition. The wardrobe department would see to things after she'd got the part but dear Harvey Trevelian was directing and she needed him to see how well her figure suited long gowns.

She patted her hair. She'd persuade Harvey to let her forgo the wimple. No sense in having a soft corona of snowy hair if the audience never got to appreciate it. Better give it a nice squirt of hair lacquer. The wind did play havoc with the coiffeur. A dab of perfume and she'd be all set.

At the sight of a second spray bottle, Nelson scurried off the bed and headed for the door so only the tip of his tale got the benefit of the lovely, scented cloud that engulfed the room. Silly pusskins.

The time of the audition was seared into Daphne's memory but just to make absolutely sure she dived into her bag for her diary. Arts Centre, 4.30pm, the last slot. She checked her watch. Just time to get to the bus-stop. Her talents deserved a taxi but times were too uncertain for financial adventure.

The Victoria Arts Centre looked like a non-conformist chapel. Daphne remembered Harvey Trevelian saying how ironic that was. Over the decades its various guises – music hall, theatre, cinema – had offered the very enticements distrusted by God-fearing chapel-goers.

For years the poor place had been dreadfully neglected, its windows smashed, its roof pitted with holes. Thank goodness for the Millennium grant and a group of people dedicated to restoration. An up-market entertainment venue was such an asset to a town. She still thought the new glass canopy across the frontage made the building look frowny, but it did provide cover for patrons.

The Millennium Garden across the road was such a lovely place. You could enjoy an interval drink there, or sit and discuss those strange art installations in the exhibition room, and it gave mums somewhere nice to wait for their kiddies to come out of the playgroup.

Harvey Trevelian had been an inspired choice for Warden, a medal-winner in the flair department and so versatile. One minute selling tickets in the box office, the next advising artists on hanging their exhibitions or arranging performance dates with visiting folk groups. According to Pru, who was his second cousin or some such, he'd even turned his hand to sorting out the plumbing.

Am Dram was his first love, of course. So many Players' productions owed him their success. Doing an audition for him was such a pleasure, even when he couldn't see his way clear to offering her the part.

'Where would I be without your front-of-house strengths, darling?' he'd say and his brown eyes would twinkle between the quiff of gorgeous auburn hair and that cute little pointed beard. The Players were so fortunate he'd found time to get *The Sound of Music* off the ground. He'd be there in the auditorium right now with all the gathered hopefuls, his clipboard and red felt-tip pen to hand.

So what was he doing coming down the road towards her? Not only away from where he should be but unlocking his car door and throwing his pink linen jacket onto the passenger seat.

'Harvey,' she yelled. 'I say, Harvey.' What a blessing she'd done so much work on projecting the voice. He half turned, caught sight of her then jumped into the driving seat and slammed the door.

The patent stilettos were not quite up to such a challenge but by slinging the skirt of the turquoise maxi-dress across one arm, Daphne managed to teeter towards him. Her plum silk tote bag slid up to her elbow as she waved her arm aloft.

'Harvey,' she panted when she drew level with him. Clutching the car's wing mirror, she slid to a halt. The tote bag slithered across his windscreen. He glanced up, stared at her and frowned.

'What?' he mouthed.

'Harvey dear, it's me.'

'Sorry?' he said, opening the window. 'How may I help you?'

'It was naughty of you not to wait for me, dear. I'm only a tingy bit late. Those silly buses never manage to come on time, do they?'

'Sorry,' he said again. 'But do I know you?'

'Silly boy, of course you do. The 4.30 audition.' She giggled. 'I've climbed every mountain to get here.'

His frazzled look could only be explained by the day he must have had, poor lamb. Ordinary folk had no notion of the demands made on creative people. It was up to her to be as helpful as possible.

'It's Daphne, she said,' Daphne Chiltern.' She clasped her bag to her chest and beamed at him. 'With your good offices, soon to be known as Mother Abbess.'

Harvey wriggled to get to the pocket of his jeans. He pulled out a crumpled sheet of paper and ran his finger down the list of names. 'I'll be casting Pearl Cooper as Mother Abbess,' he said. He fingered his beard. 'She did a very good audition.'

'But,' Daphne said, 'what about me?'

'What did you say your name was?' He glanced at his list. 'Daphne was it?'

All she could do was nod.

'Oh I see it.' He pointed. 'You are down here but I assumed you'd changed your mind. Your name's been crossed out.'

Daphne stared. Through her name was a line in thick, red felt-tip pen.

The Millennium Garden was aflame with flowers. Daphne concentrated on the labels. Dahlia Babylon Red, Potentilla Gibson's Scarlet, Impatiens. In the wild flowerbed Cranesbill and Mauve Cosmos vied for attention.

M.A.U.V.E Daphne thought, what price Movement, Action and the rest now? She perched on the edge of a bench, donated in memory of someone worth remembering.

It was this turquoise dress that let her down. Why couldn't she get it right? Not for the first time either. Not to get the lead in *Evergreen* last spring had been another setback. She'd hardly been late at all for that audition but she should never have worn her black. It did sap colour from the cheeks and first impressions are so important. Somewhere, in shop, mail-order catalogue or fashion department was the perfect outfit, the one that would sweep her out of programme sales and into the limelight. All she had to do was find it.

There'd be no time to search for it now, not with so much to worry about and The Heiress about to descend. Whatever May had in mind when she left Mulberry House to this woman, it wasn't the friendship she and Daphne had shared. But it couldn't have been friendship, could it?

'I came in here for a breather.' Pru was crossing the grass, red-faced and weighed down with plastic shopping bags covered in that brash mini-market logo. Red, white and blue all had their claim of course, lovely colours but in combination best left to flags.

Pru slumped onto the bench and propped the bags beside her. 'I thought you'd got an audition, over the road?.'

Daphne opened her mouth but couldn't persuade any words to emerge.

Pru said, 'You didn't get it? Oh Daphne love, why do you put yourself through all this?'

'Not quite right for this one,' Daphne said.

'And the last one and the one before that.' Pru put her arm along the top of the bench and squeezed Daphne's shoulder. 'You work so hard at it and for what? They just don't appreciate effort, and that's the truth.'

'Tomorrow's another day,' Daphne said.

'And so was yesterday.' Pru pulled a bar of chocolate from one of the bags. 'A lump of Fruit and Nut, that's what we need.' She tore the wrapper and broke off two pieces. 'Get this down you,' she said. 'Forget the calories. We deserve a treat.'

The sound of someone practising piano scales drifted in the air, wrong notes interrupting the pattern. Next to Pru's foot an upturned wasp zizzed and waggled its legs. Pru kicked it away.

'I shall keep rehearsing,' Daphne said, 'on my own. The acoustics of the hall in Mulberry House are wonderful'.

'Rehearsing what?'

'*The Sound of Music* songs.'

Pru snorted, rearranging the slithering bags. 'Why the hell should you? Why not just forget all about it? You've got the choir.' She crumpled the chocolate foil between her fingers. 'Who got the part, anyway, do you know?'

'Of Mother Abbess?' Daphne hissed. 'Pearl Cooper.'

'That dried up old bat?' Pru hooted. 'Harvey Perkins really is scraping a very small barrel.'

Best not think about that comment, Daphne told herself. 'Every cloud,' she said.

'The silver lining escapes me on this one, Daph, and that's a fact.'

'Well, as we both know,' Daphne stroked the turquoise folds of her dress, 'Pearl isn't up to the mark. She's going to need an understudy, isn't she?'

'You never give up, Daph, I'll give you that.' Pru glanced at the now-dead wasp. 'Better be getting back. Jim'll be wanting his tea.' She scooped up the shopping bags. 'Hey,

I nearly forgot,' she said. 'Have you heard from the odious Dr Carr? About the house?'

Daphne stood up and watched a bee clinging to a dahlia petal. 'Apparently,' she said, 'I'm a sitting tenant.'

Chapter 6

'Talk about it all you want,' Alison said. 'God knows you've spent enough time listening to my troubles.'

'It's weeks ago.' Jude shook her head. 'I should have got over it by now.'

Her aunt's hand, lying in Alison's own, was cold. Alison stroked the long fingers, thumbed the writing-bump on the middle finger, noticed a sprinkling of liver spots. Jude's reaction to the traffic accident was unsettling. Shock and horror were understandable but there seemed to be something else, something Alison couldn't name. This wasn't the Jude she knew, laying down the map and leading the way. This Jude was hiding in a cul-de-sac and avoiding Alison's eye. The no-nonsense aunt who had anchored her to reality for so long had been replaced by a vulnerable woman she barely recognised. This Jude was still in her dressing gown and slippers half way through the morning.

'You've not exactly collapsed in a heap, have you?' Alison said gently. 'Far from it. A tower of strength according to the residents.'

Joan Redcliffe, the woman who lived in the bungalow nearest the Community gates, had beckoned as Alison walked past her garden. Her rigid, clothes-hanger shoulders and rustling dress gave her the air of something newly collected from the dry cleaner's.

'Have you got a minute, dear? It's your aunt. It's not my place to interfere but do you think we could persuade her to take a holiday? She's been wonderful but that frightful accident has taken its toll. Foreign lorry driver I shouldn't wonder. They pay no road tax you know. Did you see the report in the local paper?'

Alison had shaken her head. No point in explaining that a paper with full-page adverts for Draper's Garden Centre was the last thing she'd be opening right now.

Jude's apartment felt musty, as if was a long time since the windows had been opened. The curtains were half-drawn, the room dim.

'I can't seem to get it out of my head,' Jude said. 'All that blood. Two minutes before, I was seeing her out. My palm was still warm from shaking her hand.'

'The woman I saw you taking round, wasn't it, on Mothering Sunday? Pinched in cheeks, heavyknit cardigan? She came again then?'

'She got into that little sports car, zoomed off down the drive then...' Jude winced.

'It was horrible for you,' Alison said.

'Slap into the path of that lorry.' Jude rubbed her temples. 'Silence, as if the world had stopped, then thud, metal grinding, glass smashing. She catapulted through the shattered windscreen. Lay on the bonnet like a rag doll.'

Hoping to side-track the appalling memory, Alison said, 'Tell me what she was doing here.'

'Doing?'

'Well, you were showing her round. She'd been before hadn't she? Was she thinking of coming to live here?'

Jude frowned. 'I'm trying to get things straight in my head.' She got up, went over to the bookcase, pulled out a book and looked at the cover as if she'd never seen it before. 'Did you buy me this?'

Alison stood beside her and took the book. '*Middlemarch*? I got it in Foyles didn't I? When we went to London, the weekend before I went to uni? Your old copy was falling to bits. This one's going the same way. Well, it would be by now. Twenty-two years, can you believe it?'

'She keeps appearing in my dreams, her face all slimy with blood.' Jude took the book from Alison and put it back on the shelf. 'That's just plain stupid because I didn't even see her face, after... after.. afterwards. I was too busy dealing with the residents.' She grabbed both Alison's hands. 'Joan Redcliffe saw the whole thing. She was in a terrible state.'

'She told me how calm you were, getting them all into the lounge, arranging hot tea,' Alison said, 'but she is concerned about how you are now.'

'She turned up at the office one morning the week before and asked if she could make another appointment to look around. You're right, she had been before. The day you were here, was it?'

'The woman with the cardigan? She was driving a sports car you said? What was her name?'

'She'd come up here from the south, wanted to make a new life, before it's too late,' she said. Jude rested her chin on steepled fingers. 'An odd thing to say, wasn't it?'

'What did she mean, do you think?'

'She was renting a holiday cottage, a stable conversion near Ashford-in-the-Water, while she looked around for somewhere permanent.'

'And she liked the look of it here, at Sheldon?'

'There weren't any properties empty anyway. She joked about waiting for someone to... someone to die.'

Jude was sobbing now, deep shudders that scrambled up her throat. 'I'm sorry, s...orry,' she gasped.

'Jude, my dearest Jude,' Alison was fighting back her own tears. For a moment the two of them stood there, arms around each other, then Jude cleared her throat and held Alison at arms' length. 'Enough,' she said. 'This won't slice any wholemeal.'

Alison managed a giggle. The old Jude was re-appearing. 'Won't what?' she said.

'Slice any wholemeal. What we need is a stiff drink. Are you driving?'

'Afraid not. The car went back this morning.'

'A Draper's company car, wasn't it? Time for a new set of wheels then. Exciting. Now get us both a drink, will you?'

'A bullfrog on a piano last time,' Alison called from the kitchen, 'and now slicing wholemeal. Where are these very odd expressions coming from ?'

'That would be telling. By the way, I forgot, a letter arrived for you this morning.'

'These glasses need a rinse,' Alison said. 'A letter? Here?'

'Care of here, yes. Someone who doesn't know your new address perhaps? There's a solicitors' name on the back. Sileby and Frandite. That's not the one handling your divorce, is it?'

Alison came from the kitchen with a tray. 'Why don't you just open it and put us both out of our misery?'

Jude took the envelope from the mantelpiece. 'Well, if you're sure.'

Alison wore her scarlet courts to the solicitor's. Strappy, with ciggy heels and pointed toes, the shoes tapped across the wood-laminate floor with complete disregard for legal gravity.

Flurries of dandruff lifted and resettled on the shambling figure's shoulders as she followed him into his office. Men with flaky scalps ought to avoid wearing dark shirts, she decided. His scuffed Hush Puppies would be at home cosying up to a bar in one of those films that made you glad smell-and-vision never got going. The haze of air-freshener in this corridor may well have been an effort to offset his shortcomings.

He stopped beside an open door and stood aside for her to enter the room. Trying not to breath in, she passed him.

'I should introduce myself,' he said in a tone suggesting he'd rather not. 'Edward Sileby.' He slumped behind his desk. 'Now to the business in hand,' he said, 'Sit down, dear lady.'

Alison side-stepped the chair he wanted her to sit in and went to the window. The room overlooked a small courtyard, grey and featureless in the afternoon light. 'I got your letter,' she said. 'What's this all about?'

The solicitor sighed. 'You are Alison Draper?'

His face hardly inspired confidence though one set of jowls prospering on other people's misery was probably much like another. 'I've brought identification,' she said 'as you asked.'.

'But you are Malcolm Draper's wife?'

'Technically, yes. For the next few weeks, anyway.'

'Ah.' He rubbed his hands together. 'The no-man's land between nisi and absolute.'

A dismal territory, Alison reflected, where wives become ex. The borders are fixed before you get there but the horizon is hidden by your very own black clouds. 'Your letter mentioned a bequest,' she said. 'Who was the testator?'

That flummoxed the pompous ass. Clients were obviously not expected to trespass into legal jargon. He scrabbled for his bifocals and inspected a photocopied document.

'A Mrs May Kulman,' he said.

'Not a testator then, but a testatrix, May Kulman?'

'With a K.'

'Oh dear,' Alison said. 'King Kong had two of those.' And brainless Kirsty has one, she thought, as well as fifteen years less on the clock, her paws on my husband and a bun in the oven.

Behind the desk, bewilderment was verging into panic.

'And this woman's left me something?' Alison said. 'Why would she? I've never heard of her.'

'She, it seems, has heard of you.'

'But you don't know her? Your firm didn't draw up the will?'

He flicked through the pages of the document. 'Indeed not.'

'An inferior effort, obviously,' Alison said. 'So you are...'

'Acting as agent,' he interrupted. 'For the executor's solicitor.'

'Who is the executor?'

Further perusal was followed by, 'A Dr Thomas Carr.'

'Don't tell me - another K?'

He glared at her. 'Only as in Kent, Mrs Draper. Where Dr Carr lives, apparently, as did Mrs Kulman.'

Kent, Alison thought as he started to explain the geography of England in words of one syllable. Kent was where Mr and Mrs Malcolm Draper used to drive their Landrover onto the Dover ferry, lean their elbows on the rail and wonder if the pépinières of northern France would provide some new ideas for a corporate client's atrium. Kent was where the excitement of holidays abroad began, holidays with double rooms. Kent was a separate world.

'What about probate?' Alison said when a highly-trained cough penetrated her reveries.

He glared at her. 'Probate is pending.' He bent over the document and began reading out the relevant sections, enunciating the neatly-packaged legal phrases devised to alienate all but the initiated.

'I don't understand any of this,' Alison said when he stopped.

'It's perfectly straightforward, Mrs Draper.' His tone implied that dealing with mental defection was as much par for the legal course as sarcasm. 'I am empowered to give you these.' He pushed a bundle of keys and documents across his desk. 'The late Mrs Kulman has left you a property, in Kent, namely Mulberry House, Marine Drive, Netherstone, together with all its contents.'

Alison phoned to let Jude know there was nothing to worry about, promising to visit in a couple of days. By then she would decide how this strange legacy would affect her life.

When she did call in, Jude was reading the local paper. 'Have you seen this?' she said. 'Prosser's Confectionery are in trouble. I met Brian Prosser once, at a charity do. He seemed a really nice man.'

It was a relief to see Jude looking better. There was a healthy colour to her cheeks, instead of that worrying pallor, and a hint of the old sparkle in her eyes. After so long a time recalling the accident in vivid detail and constantly dreaming about it, with medication and help from a therapist, the details were becoming to fade.

'So?' Jude shoved her reading glasses on the top of her head and put the paper aside. 'You went to the solicitor?'

Alison nodded, sat down opposite her aunt and began her tale.

'And you're sure it's kosher ?' Jude said when she'd finished. 'All the legal side?'

'The house deeds and keys are in my bag, so it must be,' Alison said. 'I've got it all worked out.' She pulled a clump of papers from an envelope file and spread them on the coffee table. 'I'll put the place on the market as soon possible.'

'Sell it?' Jude retrieved her glasses and folded them on top of the newspaper. 'Without even seeing it? And what about the mysterious May Kulman? Don't you want to know who she was? That name rings a bell, I can't think why.'

'She may be that friend of my Mum and Dad? The one who sent me birthday cards when I was small?'

Jude shook her head.' I don't think so, Alison. Her name wasn't Kulman.'

'I can sort all that out later.'

'But surely...'

'I'm not doing too well on the people front at the moment,' Alison said. 'Plans are safer.' She ran her fingers through her hair. 'I've had the idea for ages, the idea but no capital. Now I can make it happen.'

Jude looked doubtful. 'Make what happen?'

'With any luck I won't even have to take out a loan. Property down south fetches a lot more than it does around here.'

'You're not still thinking of setting up in competition to the Drapers?'

'Why shouldn't I? I owe them nothing.'

'You owe yourself something, Alison and that something isn't revenge.'

'Why ever not?' Alison stood up and went over to the window. The Major's chess partner was bustling down the drive in pink ballet pumps.

'That doesn't deserve even half a flight of stairs,' Jude retorted.

'There you go again. Bullfrogs, pianos, wholemeal slices, what's going on Jude?'

'Old sayings need preserving,' Jude said.

'Even if they don't make sense?'

'Especially,' Jude said, 'if they don't make sense.'

'But where are you getting them from?'

Jude smiled and stared into the middle distance.

'Jude?' Alison said. 'Is there someone new in your life?'

'You could say that,' Jude admitted.

'Does he have a name this man?'

'Who said it was a man? Well yes he does. He's called Peter, if you want to know. I met him at a Labour Party shindig last Christmas.'

'That's wonderful. You're a dark horse. Why didn't you tell me before?'

'You've had enough on your plate with your own worries. As to wonderful, that remains to be seen. But he does want me to go on holiday with him, to the south of France. Says it will help me get over this accident thing.'

'If I can trust him with my dearest aunt, then I agree with him.'

'Don't get all sentimental with me, my girl. Thing is, I shall be gone three weeks, ample time for you to get yourself out of here, investigate your inheritance, and find out something about your benefactor.'

Chapter 7

The demise of the apostrophe? Thomas was in his study, reading a newspaper article. The writer, an academic known for espousing whichever trendy view would get him into print, was not about to put on mourning. Why, he asked, had so tiny a mark caused so much hot air and raised blood pressure? Who would miss the apostrophe if it did the decent thing and dropped into the dungeon of archaic practices? As long as the textual meaning was clear, where was the problem?

'He'll be after a professorial chair at some trendy institution,' Thomas told Nell. He tossed the newspaper into the air and watched its pages separate, flap and waft. Nell darted from under his chair, anchored one page with her paw and wriggled as the rest tented over her head.

Rescuing her from newsprint, Thomas laughed. 'The man's an idiot,' he said. 'You've always thought so, haven't you old girl?' The spaniel thumped her tail against his leg. 'But if I'm to get where I deserve to be,' he went on, 'I may well have to emulate him. Idiocy provides the best path to glory these days.' He folded the paper and dropped it into the bin. 'And glory is what I deserve, is it not?'

Across his computer monitor, screen-saver fish glided in and out of improbably green underwater foliage. Thomas clicked on his Favourite Websites list and then to University Jobs. Somewhere along the academic line, appointments had become jobs, on a par with plumbing, carpentry and the like, an incomprehensible communism of labour.

Several universities were looking to recruit leading international teachers of history, candidates with a strong track record of research and an ability to lead teams of world-class academics. But lead them where, Thomas wondered? Into a labyrinth where specialists in sub-divisions of modern history kept the minotaur of excellence at bay with titbits of current jargon? All the time avoiding the dungeon of archaic practice, presumably.

'Time for the pub.' Thomas decided. The Grey Goose was just the place to reduce his irritation. His fan base Ingrid had called it. Ensconced in its warm fug, in the company of drinkers who conferred on him the courtesy title of Prof and respected his talents, he could forget being adrift on the plains of middle age without the trappings of success to show for it.

Mike, the landlord, pulled a bottle of single malt whisky from under the bar. 'You won't have tried this one,' he said proudly, showing Thomas the label.

This was an old game and one which Mike, poor chap, stood little chance of winning. A single malt that Thomas hadn't tried would be a find indeed. He had three bottles of this particular brand in his sideboard but pointing that out would be churlish. 'Better make it a double then,' he said. 'There's a good crowd in, for a Monday.'

'Fifties and Sixties Quiz Night,' the landlord said. 'Brings in the older punters. Best idea the missus ever had.'

Thomas sighed. As a member of the Pub League Quiz Team, he didn't usually bother with themed quizzes. All he'd wanted was a quiet drink and a game of dominoes. He looked for somewhere to park himself. The empty stool next to George Hessop, the local butcher, was probably explained by the odour-of-carcass that wafted around him.

'Evening, Prof,' George said. 'Park your arse 'ere why don't you?' He popped a crisp into his mouth and brandished the quiz sheet. 'I've already paid up. You can settle with me later. Make a good team, we will.' He guffawed, spraying the table and stool with half-chewed fragments. 'Brains and brawn, like.'

Trying not to think about the fate of his trousers, Thomas brushed the debris off the seat and sat down. 'We'd better file our flight plan, then,' he said.

George frowned. 'Come again, mate? ' The quizmaster called for hush.

Together Thomas and George negotiated uncharted quiz-space. Take-off was smooth with a good tail wind on politics and world affairs. George was surprisingly knowledgeable on the ins and outs of the royal family. But with pop music they hit turbulence.

'Two chart hits for Connie Francis in August nineteen-sixty?' George said.

Thomas shrugged his shoulders. 'No idea, sorry.'

George investigated one of his cavernous nostrils with a podgy forefinger. 'Nineteen-sixty? I'd be goin' out with that blonde bint from the estate agent's. Now what was 'er name? Big knockers. Carol, were it, or Chrissie?'

'History in terms of conquest?' Thomas suggested.

'Come again?' George looked puzzled. 'Now what were those songs?' He upended the bag of cheese-and-onion into his palm and licked up the scraps. 'Got it,' he cried, slapping Thomas on the thigh with the same hand. '*Robot*, that was one.' An asinine grin crossed his face. 'It was our special tune. Georgie Robot. Chrissie called me. Robots go on forever. Get it? '

Wondering how often innocent-sounding lyrics had been put to such a purpose, Thomas stood up.

'You're never leavin'?' George said. 'We've not got it licked yet.'

Thomas picked up the glasses. 'Bitter is it?'

'Don't mind if I do, Prof. Very civil of you.' George licked the end of his biro. 'And some pork scratchings, as you're offerin'.'

When Thomas got back from the bar George was triumphant. 'I knew I'd get it,' he said.

Outside, a sports car roared across the car park. Thomas saw the door of the white MG flung open. A leg appeared, followed by its partner; two legs clad in thigh-length, high-heeled boots. The studied elegance of such a pose, emerging from that make of car, he recognised only too well, favoured as it was by someone he'd hoped never to set eyes on again, Gwenda Gifford.

'You'll know it,' George was saying, '*Everybody's Somebody's Fool* , remember?'

Before this evening Thomas had never heard of Connie Francis's hits, with or without apostrophe. He looked out at the figure approaching the pub door. Gone was the Pre-Raphaelite auburn hair swathed around her face. Purple-streaked spikes now. Very far from vulnerable.

'How could I ever forget?' he said to George 'Won't be a mo.'

Summoning Sir Dreadnought, he headed Gwenda off in the hallway.

'Tommy,' she purred, peering up at him from under black lashes. 'Long time no see.'

Had she always simpered? She still used the same perfume. Cheetah was it called? Thomas shuddered to remember how he'd sniffed out its trail. From Junior Common Room to Psychology Department, coffee shop to library he'd trotted after the scent of her like a trained bloodhound. For the year since she'd finished her doctorate and left his life, even the sight of its slinky bottle on shop shelves made him sick to the stomach.

'No need to look like that, darling,' she said, sidling up to him.

'Look like what?' he said.

'A frightened rabbit.' Her eyes were green slits. 'What's the form?' she said. 'Shake hands or throw ourselves into each other's arms?'

Thomas backed away.

'Oh dear,' Gwenda sniggered. 'Formality it is then.'

Thomas looked down at her extended hand. Did she expect him to kiss those scarlet-tipped fingers, still covered in the rings he recalled only too clearly? Every part of her had always been festooned with jewellery. She'd been his glittering prize.

He shook her hand so firmly she winced. 'How's Duncan?' he said.

'Out to grass, darling.' She pouted. 'Somewhere or other.'

Poor sod, Thomas thought, husband in name and bank balance only. 'You wanted to see me?' he said.

In the sky behind her, a sky-writing plane coughed out trickles of white smoke. Low pressure in the oil canisters, perhaps, or an inexperienced pilot.

'Return to the wetlands without looking you up, Tommy?' Gwenda said. 'Unthinkable. After all,' she wriggled her shoulders, 'I owe my doctorate to you, now don't I?' Her hand slithered through his arm. 'Such a generous gesture but no more than I deserved after all.' The spikes of her hair quivered above her sneer. 'The truth and I haven't always been the best of friends, as you well know Tommy, but I did have to think about that one, saying I was with you when I wasn't, the night your wife died.' Her smile was triumphant. 'The suicide verdict was very convenient, wasn't it? I still wonder if I did the right thing.'

Thomas swallowed a surge of bile. Whatever it was she wanted he'd have no option but to go along with it. He couldn't afford to cross her.

Now she was trotting ahead of him. 'I said to Lydia,' she gestured towards the car, 'we must look up Tommy. You remember Lydia, don't you?'

Nodding his agreement was best. Her acolytes had been much of a muchness. Women's friendships were unfathomable, one day, giggling phone conversations late into the night, the next, tears and recriminations. 'How long are you here for?' he said.

Gwenda turned and prodded his chest with a long fingernail. 'Well that, darling rather depends on you.'

Leaning on the open car door and with Lydia as witness, she explained. A job was coming up, Midshire University. Social Psychology, some lecturing but mostly research into the function of risk in modern societies. Just up her alley. He could see his way to put in a word for her, couldn't he? For old time's sake? Professor Hartman was still a friend of his, wasn't she? She ran a finger under his lapel. Her voice dropped to a whisper. 'You know how these things are done, Tommy darling, don't you?'

He knew. She knew. However the verb was conjugated it amounted to the same thing. If not placated she could be, would be, dangerous. Hating the satisfaction on her face, Thomas heard himself promise to do what he could.

In the sky, the pilot had failed in his efforts to achieve the shape of a perfect heart. Instead of a confession of love, the message read I O U.

Thomas took a deep breath. Stumble was very much in the ascendant. Where was Dreadnought when he needed him? 'William I 1066 to 1087, William II 1087 to 1100,' he recited. By the time he got to King Stephen, another bloke with serious woman trouble, the MG was a tiny white speck in the distance.

Chapter 8

Daphne stood across the street from the row of shops set behind the colonnade of columns, a setting largely unchanged since Victorian days. Sadly, the greenery framing George Hessop's window looked a bit tired but the butcher had never been strong on detail. The mini-market with its gaudy shop sign spoiled the effect as well. Only the frontage of Mr. Jenkins's grocery summed up the elegant shopping experience customers could expect.

Once inside, she looked at the old photos displayed beside the door. Here was Mr Jenkins's father fixing up Coronation bunting across the shop front in nineteen fifty-three and his grandfather taking delivery of eggs under a wall advert for Lifebuoy Health Soap. The message was clear, tradition counts.

There was quite a queue. 'Sorry about the wait, ladies,' Mr Jenkins called out. 'I'm on my own today. Young Brian's taking a sickie.'

How very good, he was, Daphne thought, keeping up with modern expressions. She watched his long fingers select a wedge of cheese, admired the hint of moustache bristling under the patrician nose. Thank the good lord for men like Mr Jenkins, so different from that dreadful Dr Carr. Put him right out of your mind, she told herself, him and his silly notions.

Mr Jenkins was a real man, kind and noble, the only proper grocer in the county. Only a grocer of genius could have kept this place going in the face of all the competition from common mini-markets. Only a man of discernment could mix mahogany counters with a modern freezer cabinet and come up smiling. In the shadowy interior of his shop, the dark wood shelves housed every foodstuff a civilised household might require. He was so understanding about one needing an account, and self-service was a vulgar expression best forgotten. Savouring the aromas of Stilton cheese, coffee beans and a hint of parsley, she smoothed her skirt. You couldn't go wrong with accordion pleats.

On the noticeboard were advertisements for Fair Trade products and locally-sourced vegetables along with a poster about the Chopin Festival in Rye. How very apt. Mr J was a man of the classics, of minuets, of flute concertos and piano nocturnes.

The woman in front of Daphne was enquiring about large amounts of smoked salmon. 'Party is it?' said Mr J. 'I'll fetch the order book.' He came out from behind the counter and headed past Daphne to the stock room.

'I need a word with you, Miss Chiltern,' he whispered in Daphne's ear.

Was he looking in the direction of the Chopin poster? She couldn't go with him of course, he was a married man, but it did no harm to dream of sitting by the windows in the concert hall, looking out as the sky darkened and the stars gathered. Chopin's music would float into their souls, romantic and expressive, a million miles from that dreadful American racket Pru liked so much. In the interval they would find a table with a pink cloth and carnations in a glass vase, drink cocktails and ignore the hubbub around them.

By now Daphne was the last customer in the shop. She and Mr Jenkins were alone.

'You wanted a word?' she said. The poor man looked almost bashful. It would take all his courage to ask her to go out with him. Her refusal would wound but she'd make it gentle.

He stroked his moustache and avoided her eyes. 'I'm sorry to mention it madam,' he said, 'but could you see your way clear to settling your account in the near future?'

Daphne stared at him. She found herself gesturing wildly towards the Chopin poster. 'You do admire him, don't you?' she said.

'What's that?' Mr Jenkins said. 'Oh the posh music festival. No way. My wife's into all that classical stuff but not me. I'm more of an Elvis man myself.'

'You're in Chinese mode then,' Pru said. 'I like the kimono top.'

Daphne's finger traced the golden dragon embroidered on her sleeve. 'You've got to make the effort, haven't you?' she said. ' Can't just throw on any old thing.' Poor Pru, she thought, bursting out of that navy blue fleece with its fortnight-old egg stain. Not much sign of an effort there.

'You're being really brave,' Pru said, 'under the circumstances.'

They were reading the tea-leaves, sitting opposite each other across the Regency drum table in Daphne's sitting room.

Pru blew a tendril of grey hair away from her eyes and peered into her cup. 'Could this be a kite?' she said.

Daphne looked out of the window. The sea didn't seem sure what sort of mood to be in.

'Come off it, Daph,' Pru complained, 'you're not concentrating.' She set down the cup in its saucer. 'Not that I can blame you, what with this house thing hanging over you.'

'Sorry, darling. What did you say?'

'Still, at least you're secure in your flat. She can't put you out, this woman May's left the house to?'

The Heiress, Daphne thought, the unknown woman who had stolen her inheritance. She'd been cheated, cheated out

59

of what should have been hers, again. But this time, she was here in Mulberry House, not The Southern Moral Welfare Hostel having a last cuddle.

*

She's holding her baby, feeling his grip on her finger, his warmth, his heartbeat. He has his father's hair, like dark feathers cupping the tiny head. How can she bear to give him up? But his name is on the Removals List because she's no better than she ought to be, little better than a prostitute, they've told her. She's waiting, waiting for the respectable couple to come and take him away. The teddy she's made for him stares up at her with glassy eyes.

*

Pru was pushing her cup across the table. 'A kite I thought. What d'you reckon?'

Daphne swallowed. 'That means a holiday,' she said. 'How exciting.'

Pru stuck out her bottom lip. 'You've hardly looked.'

'The tea leaves are such lovely colours aren't they?' Daphne said. But tea leaves too were best forgotten. The only place to buy those round here was you-know-where. Never again would she set foot in that man's shop. It was mini-market tea bags from now on, even if she had to keep a pair of scissors in the caddy to cut the corners and empty out the contents. Her cheque was in the post and that was the end of stuck-up Mr Jenkins.

'You could do more than snatch a quick peek,' Pru was saying.

Daphne sighed. Pru could be tiresome at times but she was a good sort.

'I can't see unless I hold the cup at arm's length,' Daphne explained. 'St. Anthony hasn't found my reading glasses yet. Rushed off his feet, I shouldn't wonder.' She narrowed her eyes. 'Oh a kite, no question. ' She beamed at Pru. 'The money path last time, and now a holiday. Where was it you're wanting to go?'

Indignation creased Pru's forehead. 'Gracelands, Memphis, Tennessee,' she recited. 'As you well know.'

'Well now, that's where you'll be in...' Daphne counted on her fingers as she checked the leaves stuck to the side of the cup. '...about six months by my reckoning.'

'Oh my goodness,' Pru was panting. 'I've gone all dumbstruck. Six months did you say? That'll make it December. It'd mean missing the choir's Christmas concert but I could take his card. Save postage. Postage to America's getting dreadfully expensive.'

'Whose card?'

'Daph,' Pru protested, 'I'm hurt you need to ask.

Daphne watched her grope in her Elvis Presley shopping bag. Her passion for the vulgar pop singer was incomprehensible.

Pru fished out a screwed-up ball of tissues and dabbed the corners of her eyes.

'He still gets cards, then?' Daphne said, 'in spite of being...?'

'The King will never die,' Pru insisted. 'Pete Jenkins was saying so only the other day.'

Daphne raised her eyebrows. 'Pete?'

Pru nodded. 'Purveyor of fine food and wine, as it says on his shop front. He's such a friendly man. Only too willing to cut off two ounces of mild Cheddar for my Jim. We always have a good long natter.'

Daphne shuddered. 'Very kind of him I'm sure,' she said. She pointed to Pru's cup. 'Did you see the needle and thread?'

'Really? Are you sure?' Pru's grin set her chins awobble. 'That means a sincere wish granted, you mark my words.'

An occasional fib couldn't matter, Daphne told herself, not if it helped a friend. 'Not a doubt of it,' she said. 'Gracelands here you come. What about Jim though?'

'What about him?' Pru said. 'Your turn now.'

Daphne picked up her cup in her left hand and drained it into the slop basin. Her coral pink nail varnish had been an inspired choice for this afternoon tea party, a nicely subtle contrast to the Crown Derby crockery. She covered the cup with the upended saucer, turned it over and closed her eyes. 'One, two, three,' she said as she rotated it clockwise.

'Now,' said Pru, 'what's in store for you?'

'Nothing like Gracelands in December, anyway,' Daphne said.

Pru looked up. 'Which Astral House did we pick today?'

Daphne frowned. 'Happiness, wasn't it,' she said. 'The birds flying near the sun?'

'So, where does the turkey fit in?' Pru wondered. 'There's a turkey in this cup of yours, plain as the nose on your face. Look.'

'That means someone is behaving stupidly.' Daphne snatched the cup. 'I don't think so.' If anyone was behaving like an idiot, it wasn't her. She wasn't the one getting ideas about Mr Jenkins. 'That's never a turkey's beak,' she said. 'More like a walking stick with a curved handle.' She wriggled her toes. 'That means I'll be taken care of in a difficult time.'

Pru looked doubtful. 'If you say so,' she said. 'But those are definitely scissors. Look, under that head.'

'A dark-haired man, perhaps?' Daphne murmured picturing a fuzz of dark hair.

'Could be, Daph but don't forget those scissors,' Pru pointed out. 'More disappointment could be on its way.'

Chapter 9

'No roses round the gate then,' Alison said when the taxi bumped to a stop in front of Mulberry House.

The driver eased himself out of the car and waddled to the boot. Puffing with the effort, he heaved out Alison's suitcase and dropped it onto the pavement. 'Mrs Kulman preferred trees, I reckon,' he said.

'Did you know Mrs Kulman?' Alison said.

'Comes in from the continent you know,' he said, looking towards the sea. 'The rain. Just the one bag is it? You'll not be staying long then.'

A slammed door, a revved engine and a squealing of tyres left Alison alone, facing the rendered garden wall of Mulberry House. Behind her, beyond the road and a low fence, the sea whispered and lapped up the shingle. Squawking gulls, silhouetted against the sky, wheeled and circled above her. It was getting dark.

Why, she wondered, hadn't she considered what this would be like? Across the networks of travel, in trains, buses and taxis, from a landscape of moorland and dales, to this wide-skied, open flatness, the situation had remained unreal. The house had been an idea, a refuge. But now, the dim shape was waiting to confront her, a property which, for some undiscovered reason, was a stranger's legacy.

Alison grabbed the handle of her suitcase. She would go back home right now, put the wretched property on the market, take a holiday, buy some clothes, have fun.

But taxis weren't exactly ranked along the kerb nor was there a bus stop in sight. To the right of the house gleamed a row of stuccoed bungalows, like a curving string of square beads in pastel colours. To the left, tattered RNLI posters obscured the windows of a narrow, Georgian building.

The gate to one of the bungalows creaked open and a small white poodle trotted out followed by a man carrying a dog lead. When he saw Alison, the man's mouth tightened and his eyes slitted with consternation. Scooping up the poodle, he scurried away.

'The natives are friendly I see,' Alison told her suitcase. She dug in her handbag for her mobile. But whom could she phone? She needed a bed for the night but options were limited. Trudging back along the coast road to book into a hotel did not appeal and the strung-bead bungalows showed no sign of hospitality. Anyway, now she was a only a step away from Mulberry House, curiosity had sneaked up on her.

'I'll just stay one night.' Alison decided, 'if there's anything to sleep on that is.' House and contents the solicitor had said but what did that mean? She opened the gate and stepped into the garden. The taxi man had been right. There were no flowers. Of the mulberry tree, after which the house was presumably named, there was no sign. She'd been imagining an orange-brown trunk with wide, sinewy crevices in the bark, twisty branches, pale green leaves and fruit with sweetness oozing from claret-red clusters. All she could make out were stunted Monterey pines straining away from the harshness of a marine climate towards the comforts of home.

And so they faced each other, Alison and Mulberry House. Set back from Marine Drive, on a corner plot, the house offered white, weather-boarded walls for inspection while Alison's was an appearance crumpled by recent emotional turmoil and creased by today's travel. The house's asymmetry was pleasing. On the left, two dormers sat above multi-paned, ground floor windows with the third above a porch, formed from ivy-covered trellis, around the front door. To the right of the front door was what looked like an extension to the original building. She craned her neck to look up at the steeply-pitched roof of terracotta tiles stretching between brick chimney stacks. 'How long have you been here?' Alison said under her breath. 'And why are you mine?'

If the house voiced an answer, it was drowned by a screeching of gulls. Alison glanced behind her. Was someone watching? Lights twinkled from the bungalows, then, one by one, disappeared as curtains were drawn against the strangers of twilight. Alison shivered. Needing to escape from the confines of the walled garden, she left her suitcase, retraced her steps and crossed over to the beach.

Under the expanse of darkening sky, with only the sea and wind for company, it was easy to imagine she was entirely alone, the only mortal being in the world. This is where existence began, she thought, on the beach. Life forms crawled out of the salty water and crossed this margin of land and sea. In the gloom, she fancied she could picture them, waterlogged ancestors of humanity, scuttling up the beach to establish a new order.

And every damned one of them had Malcolm's face, smugly escaping the boredom of a childless marriage to be rescued by a fertile blonde named Kirsty.

Alison stamped on them. First with one brown loafer, then the other, then both together she jumped on them, crunching her vision into the shingle. Let them get out of that if they could. Hemmed in by family obligations and tired business prospects, they were the ones with no choices. Her own future was as wide as the horizon. She could choose to sell up or to stay. Here, in a place where nobody knew about her past failures, she had a chance to build a life of her own. She had a mysterious legacy to solve, an unusual house all to herself and the sea on her doorstep.

Arms flung out, the taste of salt on her lips, Alison spun round and round, a kaleidoscope of sea, beach and sky whirling with her. But something caught her eye, something in the sea, weird, unnatural. She stared. How long had it been there? Surely it was a trick of the fading light, an optical illusion, this monster rearing from the sea? Dark against the horizon, it thrust itself above the waves. A vengeful Neptune bent on destruction, his green eyes flashing into the dark?

'Now you really are getting fanciful,' Alison said aloud.

'Eerie isn't it, especially at dusk?' The man was behind her. How had he got so close without her hearing him? Had he materialized, like the sea monster? Alison wheeled round. The spaniel sniffing at her ankles was real enough.

'I'm sorry if I frightened you,' the man said. 'Here, Nell,' he called to the dog then turned to Alison. 'You were ...'

'Behaving like an idiot?' she suggested.

'In a world of your own, anyway.'

The dimness cloaked his features but the smile in his voice wasn't sneering.

'First time you've seen our wreck, I take it?' he said.

'Wreck? What sort of wreck? Don't tell me that kind of thing still goes on here.'

'Oh don't worry, it's nothing to do with luring ships to their fate.' He bent to fasten a lead to the spaniel's collar. 'Something much more prosaic, and more recent.' He pointed to the rearing shape. 'You can only see it at low water. It's a section of Mulberry Harbour, one that didn't make it to the French coast.'

'Now you've completely lost me,' Alison said, watching the spaniel investigate a string of seaweed.

'Concrete pontoons. 1944, the Normandy landings?'

'Oh I see.' Alison laughed. 'Thank the lord for that. I'd got something very different in mind. And the green flashes?

'Marker buoys. At sea, green is the colour of danger.'

'A different world,' Alison said.

She could feel him looking at her. 'Indeed,' he said. Then, calling the dog's name, he wished her goodnight.

Alison looked back at the sea monster. Prosaic was the word. Mulberry House had been named after a wreck. Extremely appropriate, she thought, and suddenly more manageable. It was time to use her key.

The house, her house, looked benign, warmly shadowed, silent and empty, a shelter from the wind and darkness. The key slid easily into the lock but the house was neither silent nor empty. Someone was in there. Someone who was trying, with spectacular lack of success, to lend an operatic flavour to the upper registers of *Climb Every Mountain.*

Alison squared her shoulders, turned the key and peered round the door.

'The resonance can't be bettered.' The voice lingered over the vowel sounds as if they were an endangered species. 'The stairwell is the only place for singing.'

The elderly woman who stood at the end of the hall, with one naked foot resting on the bottom stair, was tiny, a wren of a woman wearing what might once have been a sexy black nightdress.

'My name is Daphne Chiltern,' the woman announced. She sniffed. 'We h..h..haven't met before but I'm sitting very comfortably thank-you.

Chapter 10

In the bedroom of her flat, Daphne's fingers trembled as she pulled the black nightdress over her head. 'That's it then, Nelson,' she said. 'Exit stage left.' She slipped her arms into her silk robe and stroked the leaves, embroidered in shades of sage and moss green, across the front, beautiful workmanship that would never date.

'We'll need more than the overture to get rid of The Heiress,' she said, popping the nightdress back into the drawer, 'but there's plenty more where that came from.' Nelson eyed her greenly, stretched out a forepaw and with an air of indifference licked his foot.

'I know,' she told him, 'rehearsals for that little scene down there have already taken up far too much of our time but you can be proud of me.' She reached to tickle him under his chin but he arched his head out of range. *Climb Every Mountain* may not be your favourite,' she admitted, 'but the performance took the wind out of The Heiress's sails, didn't it?' Recalling the astonishment on Alison Draper's face, she giggled. 'Particularly the aspirated-h on haven't, and that as I recall, Nelson, was your idea.' She beamed at him.

She sat on the dressing-table stool and rooted in the drawer for her dry-skin cream. Next time she had a moment, she really must have a sort out. Toiletries and cosmetics did get in such a mess if you didn't keep tabs on them but she'd had so much on her mind lately. Whatever had May been thinking of, bequeathing the house to that dreadful woman? And who did she think she was, arriving, unannounced, on the doorstep in her creased, unco-ordinated outfit and hedgehog coiffure?

'Speechless she was,' Daphne said. 'Scurried through the first door she came to. No backbone, you'll be thinking, Nelson and quite right too.'

Watchful of catching his claws in his crochet blanket, Nelson followed the tip of his tail into a preferred position and ignored the ritual going on behind him. Daphne had found the jar she needed. She pushed up her sleeves and started to slap cream onto her elbows, in a practised routine.

'No sense in letting things slide,' she said. 'Life goes on.' It was a disgrace, that woman being here. Not that she could make any real difference, of course she couldn't. Daphne drew herself up and peered at her reflection in the mirror.

Now for her face. The Heiress might be slim and young enough to be her daughter, but her complexion wasn't anything to write home about and her diction was dreadful. No respect for proper articulation, none at all.

With strokes emphatic and circular, Daphne applied cream to her cheeks, chin, forehead and neck. No-one was going accuse her of letting herself go.

Nothing could alter her right to stay in her flat, could it? Changes were bound to be afoot though. 'And we don't take kindly to changes, do we Nelson?' she said over her shoulder. But Nelson, drifting into sleep, was not inclined to count fifty strokes of the tortoise-shell hairbrush through tresses that had once been thick enough for a hundred.

Leaving the bedroom door ajar in case Nelson needed her, Daphne crossed the tiny hallway to her kitchenette. Yes, she had remembered to close the window. She was about to close the door again when the empty milk bottle on the draining board caught her eye. How very tiresome. Putting it out would mean going downstairs and an unrehearsed encounter with The Heiress was not on the programme for this evening. It would have to wait, at least until she heard the wretched woman go to bed.

She wandered into the sitting room. Things had gone very quiet downstairs. What could The Heiress be doing? Pricing up May's ornaments? Counting the silver? Putting her feet up on the buttoned Dralon? It didn't bear thinking about.

'We can do without all this, can't we, Mother?' she asked the photograph on the mantelpiece. In her silver frame, squeezed between an unfinished piece of embroidery and a cluster of seashells, Mother said nothing but then she didn't need to. Bristling against the stripes of a post-war beach deckchair, her best polka-dot silk pulled well down over her knees, she gripped her handbag as if she were about to hurl it in the face of such an outrage. The world is full of trouble, she was informing Father's Leica 1A camera, but only the feeble go under.

Feeble or not, cocoa would be welcome, Daphne decided, half-and-half cocoa with two spoonfuls of brown sugar. But that would mean running the tap and The Heiress might take advantage of the knocking water pipes to creep upstairs. Best do without and keep alert for this stranger within the gates.

The thing now was, how to stay awake? It had been a tiring day. Dame Maggie Smith herself would have found the long wait in the wings exacting, not to mention the performance. And what a performance, improvisation woven into rehearsed material to maximum effect. Daphne sighed. If dear Harvey Trevelian had been on hand, never again would she be relegated to front of house.

Daphne yawned. It was no good. She would have to disturb Nelson and go to bed, after she'd taken the milk bottle down of course. The milkman would be annoyed if the bottle wasn't waiting for him on the step in the morning. Such a coarse man, slouching around with his shirt hanging out and using language decent people shouldn't have to hear. Moonlighting as a taxi driver too, according to Pru. Daphne looped the belt of her robe round her waist, popped into the bedroom to tell Nelson where she was going, fetched the milk bottle then ventured out of her flat onto the staircase.

The wind was well into its stride. External weatherboarding might be the very devil to maintain, Daphne reflected as she tip-toed downstairs in the dark, but its woody grunts did mask internal noises. Even knowing these stairs as well as she did, it wasn't easy to avoid the creaks. One hand hovering over the place where the newel post ambushed unwary fingers with splinters, the other hand clutching the milk bottle, with a naked toe she felt for the bottom stair. So far, so good. No sight, nor sound of The Heiress.

Daphne wrestled with the wind for mastery of the front door. Had she settled the bottle firmly on the doorstep she might not have stooped to readjust it. But stoop she did, giving the wind the opportunity to insinuate itself into her robe. The garment unfurled. Silk sails billowed round a diminutive mast of goose-pimpled flesh. Daphne stepped backwards into the hall. A pennant of silk belt whipped around her. The front door slammed shut, trapping the belt. Daphne was pinioned. Outside, the milk bottle toppled off the step and shattered onto the path.

'What the hell is going on?' In an arc of light, The Heiress appeared in the hall. Spread-eagled, like a cartoon character, against the front door, Daphne groaned.

'Oh it's you,' The Heiress said. 'Not sitting quite so comfortably now then?'.

Chapter 11

Bryn was driving the silver-grey Porsche. Behind tinted windows, he stared ahead, his knuckles white on the steering wheel. The tang of the life he was leaving hung over the town, liquorice and blackcurrant. When he reached the motorway junction he relaxed, took a deep breath and muttered, 'That's that then. So long Felstone. Yours truly bows out.'

Heading south, he stayed in the middle lane, tapping the steering wheel to the tempo of Scott Joplin on the CD player and reassuring himself that the Sainsbury's carrier bag and a grey rucksack were still on the seat beside him. At Junction 8 he left the motorway and drove to Hemel Hempstead Motors.

'Mr Stanfield?' The salesman nodded at the car. 'Nice motor. Cash sale, if memory serves. We inspected the vehicle on ...' he consulted the computer screen, '...two weeks back. Owner a Mr Prosser. Expecting is she?'

'Sorry?' Bryn said. 'Not with you, mate.'

The salesman grinned. 'That's usually when deluxe becomes practical, when the little lady's expecting. Can't get a kiddy's seat into a Porsche.'

Bryn shrugged his shoulders. 'I'm just the hired help.'

He'd arranged the deal some time back. Once he'd made the decision to do a runner, his fake persona took over with a strength of mind his real one found hard to believe.

'Couldn't bring himself to be here I s'pose,' the salesman went on. 'Mr Prosser, I mean? Parting of the ways and all that. Best come inside. Can't hand over all those readies in the cold light of day. Follow me. Got authorization and all the right paperwork, have we? '

Half an hour later, with the now-bulging rucksack rumpling the shoulder of his made-to-measure suit, Bryn strode away, swinging the carrier bag and whistling *Maple Leaf Rag*.

After downing a half in The Rose and Crown, he peeled off his suit in the Gents and changed into jeans contoured with creases, a rugby shirt and anorak.

Emerging from the pub into the sunlit High Street, he spotted a rubbish bin and deposited the Sainsbury's carrier on top of a segment of congealing pizza. With an imitation of the American salute, more enthusiastic than accurate, he announced, 'That's the last bloody suit I'll ever wear.'

No more standing around in poncy men's outfitters, with bootlicking twerps getting off on wielding a tape-measure and asking personal questions. No more squirming at the tone in Sylvia's voice as she wondered whether the pinstripes might help 'in the height department, darling.' But wife Sylvia wasn't here, was she? Here, he was a refugee from doing the right thing. He'd danced to other people's music long enough; it was time to play his own tune.

Syncopate the rhythm, that's what he'd do. Displace the beat. Lou-IS Arm-STRONG, Char-LIE Par-KER. Jazz rhythms. Strong beats made weak, weak strong. No-one knew where he was. He had more ready cash than he'd seen outside a bank. He could do what he wanted, go where he liked. Beyond the moment of escape from the cage of car and suit he'd made no plans. Plans weren't his thing. Not anymore.

In the window of a coffee shop, a poster advertising a Steam Railway Bonanza triggered a long-buried memory.

'The Romney Hythe and Dymchurch Railway is the smallest public railway in the world,' Bryn could hear his father saying. They'd been sitting in a station buffet somewhere or other, waiting for the connection to Hythe. The twelve-year old Bryn, daunted by the prospect of a whole day alone with his father, was licking sugar crystals from a jam doughnut.

What a pompous old boy Father had been, communicating nothing but facts. He'd sat there that day, British Rail tea steaming on the table in front of him, propelling gobbets of information round the pipe clamped between his teeth. 'Her Majesty was there in 1957, at the R. H and D, March 30th.' The mug was lifted carefully to thin lips under the stiff moustache. He removed the pipe, took small sips of tea. When the mug was back on the table, he patted his moustache with the starched handkerchief Mother had folded into the tweed breast pocket before they'd left that morning. 'Five coaches and a van,' he went on, 'hauled by locomotive Number eight, Hurricane. Driver, George Barlow.' He'd nodded at Bryn and smiled in a put-that-in-your-pipe-and-smoke-it sort of way. And then came the pièce de resistance. 'Duke of Edinburgh and the royal youngsters took turns on the footplate.'

It had smelt sooty, the railway, like chimneys. The locomotives, belching smoke, reached only to Father's shoulder and the coaches were small enough to make him stoop to get in. What a day they'd had. The down train from Hythe followed the line of the Military Canal for the first mile or so and then the track crossed low-lying marshland with the view of the sea hidden by a high wall.

Even Father's gobbets about Martello Towers and the Napoleonic threat hadn't spoilt the thrill of it all. Hanging out of the window, Bryn had felt the sea air tighten the skin on his cheeks, had drawn in his breath as loco smoke snatched away his view of the trackside and when he'd licked his lips, he tasted a mixture of salt and soot.

They'd gone as far as Dungeness, sat on the shingle and eaten cheese and pickle sandwiches, washed down with ginger beer. An old guy in long, rubber boots had told them all about the lighthouse. Bryn had been so intrigued by his wobbly false teeth that he'd forgotten to notice Father's face, on the receiving end of information for once.

That was a good day, in the end, Bryn thought as he finished his coffee, possibly the only one Father had ever organised for the two of them, a day to wrap in memory and bring out when required. Like now. It was required now all right. His own world, or rather his old world, was about to go belly-up. Not that he'd be there to see it.

He pulled out his MP3 player and soon had Kenny Davern, playing with Humphrey Lyttelton. He thought about the CD cover with Kenny and Humph leaning on a brick wall with some other guys, gripping pints of ale. Humph was wearing an anorak over red trousers which had seen better days.

Bryn put in the earpieces of his player and surrendered to the lazy tempo of *Jackass Blues*. And somewhere between Martin Litton's piano trills and the sob of the alto sax, the image of a house came into his mind, a house by the sea, weatherboards, brick chimneys and a garden full of scrappy pine trees. Bed and Breakfast. He and Father had stayed there, he remembered. The old guy with the wobbly dentures had rambled on so long they'd missed the last little train and had to call a taxi. 'Not even a toothbrush between us,' Father had told the landlady, sharp-nosed and suspicious. But she'd let them stay.

The next track was *Of All the Wrongs You've Done To Me* but all Bryn could hear was the hissing of the sea on the beach and the creaking of weatherboard walls. And with the memory of those sea sounds came what Charlie Parker had called an epiphany, a moment of revelation. Bryn wasn't washing dishes at Jimmy's Chicken Shack in Harlem or trying to think up variations on standard chord changes, as Charlie had been; Bryn was following his nose along your standard English High Street, but an epiphany it most definitely was.

He would go to The Marsh, buy another motor right now, not a see-what-I-can-afford status symbol but a vehicle he'd be happy to call his own. He'd take his time getting there, meander a bit, call at places he'd never had time to visit. The past could drift off to where it belonged. Time enough, when he got to The Marsh, to start sorting things out.

Cash transactions were obviously part of the scenery for the owner of Quality Used Cars. Swathed in cigar smoke and hunched over the racing pages, he was only too happy for Bryn to look around.

Bryn walked up and down the rows of vehicles.

'Nice set of wheels that one,' the cigar smoker said when Bryn stopped beside a two-tone truck. 'You know what the adverts told us, Ford pickups are built tough.'

'Sounds good to me,' Bryn told him and within an hour of arriving at the back-street car lot, he drove away in a brown and cream, 1978 Ford pick-up truck with 140,000 miles on the clock.

Chapter 12

The extra Faculty meeting, arranged at short notice and very near the end of term, fell on a day when Thomas had planned to stay at home marking exam papers. Which would involve the lesser ordeal, he asked himself, wading through adolescent speculations about England in the Age of Chivalry or professorial twaddle in a room clotted with hot air?

Sir Dreadnought Stumble would have had similar dilemmas of course, responsibilities to his manorial tenants and obligations to his liege lord, though not, perhaps, on the same day? But unlike Sir Dreadnought, bound by Sumptuary Laws to the wearing of garments costing no more than six marks, Thomas could indulge himself in designer jeans and a cashmere sweater. One thing they did have in common was that personal status symbols, whether a knight's finely tooled broadsword or Thomas's Classic Jensen Interceptor Convertible had to be left, outside official buildings, in the care of others.

'Take your pick, Dr Carr.' The guy who checked parking permits, among a plethora of other duties, indicated the wide choice of empty spaces. 'Some of your Faculty colleagues haven't arrived yet.'

Thomas waved his thanks. The university was quiet. Students whose exams were over had gone down and most academic staff were busy with holidays or research projects.

With time to spare before the meeting, he went into the rose garden. A woman was sitting on one of the wooden benches, her face held up to the sun, her eyes closed. Dark hair, loosely tied at the nape of her neck hung over her shoulders. The long, floral skirt and top cinched in at the waist with a silver belt was familiar.

It was Cordelia Hartman.

'Your nose is shiny,' Thomas told her.

Without opening her eyes she said, 'Good morning to you too, Tom. I wondered how long it would be before you turned up.'

'I hadn't planned to be here at all today.'

'Lucky break for you then, isn't it?'

No pursuit had been necessary with Cordelia, no pretence at will-she-won't-she? A mature, attractive woman with no obvious hang-ups. 'I'm up for it, if you are,' she'd said at some academic conference or other. 'My room number is on the list in the foyer. No strings, though I prefer conference monogamy.'

For a while, respite from the chase provided an alluring distraction. She was refreshingly direct and had no inhibitions about listing her requirements in what she called the pleasuring department. Beyond that she made no demands. Her presence had added spice, a reason to attend a whole series of conferences and seminars, all of them adding nicely to his CV. A dozen or so delightful encounters brought their mutual explorations to a natural end and they'd parted without rancour.

Thomas sat beside her. 'What brings you here?' he said.

'A paper on artificial metals.' She opened her eyes and smiled at him. 'Bruce is collaborating with a guy in the physics department.'

She'd described her husband as her rock, Thomas remembered, a rock to which she was secured as insurance against choppy waters.

'I came along for the ride,' Cordelia said.

'Nothing to do with me then?' Thomas teased.

'Never gave you a thought, darling,' She stretched her arms behind her and cupped her hands on the back of her head. 'Well, not till last Thursday anyway.'

On the other side of the hedge a lawnmower stuttered into life. 'What happened,' Thomas said, 'last Thursday?'

'Someone called Gwenda Gifford happened,' Cordelia said. 'Or rather her application did.' Her look was quizzical. 'And what do I find? Your name, Tom, nestling in the list of referees.'

And so my castle is besieged Thomas thought. I'm surrounded by the enemy intent on destruction. The slim chance that Gwenda might have lighted on another target had vanished. He folded his arms across his chest and attempted a grin. 'That's naughty of her,' he said. Was it Nemesis flailing the chain mace inside his chest?

'She didn't get your permission? That's her out of the running then.'

The lawnmower's whine was getting louder.

'Well.' Thomas hesitated. A vision of Gwenda's spiky hair crossed his mind and the toxic look on her face when she'd thrown down the gauntlet. 'I did say...'

Cordelia laughed. 'Don't tell me, one of your conquests calling in the favours?'

'She's a bright girl. I said I'd put in a word.'

Cordelia raised her eyebrows. 'You didn't supervise her doctorate did you?'

'Social psychology's not my field, of course, but one chapter in her thesis was on the effect of matrilineal succession in hierarchical societies. I had a very small input. It was more a case of pointing her in the right direction.'

'And at the right people?'

The lawnmower stopped as he replied. His voice detonated into the silence. 'She's an able young woman.'

'No need to shout, Tom.' Cordelia shrugged her shoulders. 'Ms Gifford's qualifications are not in doubt. Her CV is most impressive.'

Thomas clenched his fists to stop his hands trembling. If Gwenda got what she wanted, he was in the clear. 'You'll appoint her then?' he said.

'You should know better than to ask that, Tom.' Cordelia stood up. 'It's not just my decision anyway.'

She was looking down on him. 'She'll get her chance along with the rest.'

'But she is on the short list?'

'The best man will win.' Cordelia wagged her finger. 'Or woman.'

He'd forgotten how tall she was. Standing beside her, their eyes were level. 'I haven't asked you about your own work,' he said.

'I'm having a go at fiction,' she said. 'God knows how long I've analysed the significance of literature in history. So now I'm writing the stuff.'

'Genre?'

'Literary who-dun-it,' she said, 'about an academic who murders his wife.'

Thomas grabbed for the arm of the bench. Cordelia put her hand under his elbow and frowned in concern. 'Are you okay Tom? You've gone as white as a sheet.'

He forced a laugh. 'Too many wee drams and not enough sleep I expect. I'll be fine.'

Cordelia slipped her bag onto her shoulder. 'You make sure you are,' she said, holding up her cheek for a kiss. ' It's been good to see you, Tom. We must catch up sometime. Now I must find that husband of mine.'

Guilt was an unpredictable beast, Thomas thought as Cordelia walked away, one moment passant, the next as rampant as it gets. And the size of it was completely out of proportion to any misdemeanour its prey might have committed.

Sir Dreadnought's motto translated as 'No Enemy Shall Prevail'. The enemy laying siege was only too obvious; but what if a second enemy, in the shape of Cordelia, was on the gallop to provide re-enforcements?

Now you're getting paranoid Thomas told himself. Cordelia hadn't met Ingrid and knew almost nothing about her. A good dollop of academic verbiage would take his mind off his troubles. He left the garden and strode across the campus in search of light relief.

The Dean of the Arts and Humanities Faculty had mastered the full range of facial expressions. Within the few moments it took him to greet Thomas and several other colleagues, it segued through hail-fellow-well met, smooth charm and bonhomie. Now, Thomas saw, it had settled into concerned mentor as, head on one side, the Dean gave his full attention to whatever was troubling the guy from American Studies.

'A focus on litter is indeed long overdue, Gareth,' the Dean said, patting the guy on the shoulder. 'And one we will give our minds to a.s.a.p.' He arranged his face to accommodate the demands of leadership and marshalled the troops.

Given the Dean's close rapport with paper clips and photocopying, Thomas expected matters of mundane admin to be the subject under discussion and had come prepared. He sat opposite a window so that his staring out at whatever was happening on campus might be interpreted as deep thought, and his doodling pencil was to hand. It was unusual for so many senior staff to have been summoned. Some crisis in the distribution of staplers perhaps?

The word vacancy came as a shock. Thomas sat up to take notice. The Dean looked serious. The Professor of

Medieval History had, it seemed, succumbed to something nastily medical and would be absent for the foreseeable future.

'At this point in time,' the Dean said, 'we're looking to make a temporary appointment. In due course our stricken colleague may well feel able to re-grasp the nettle.'

A temporary appointment no less, Thomas thought. And whom do we know who could more than adequately fill this vacancy?

'So at the moment,' the Dean went on, 'the vice-chancellor and I agree that it would be sensible to keep the appointment an internal one. Applications are welcome from candidates throughout the Faculty.'

'So not,' American Studies Gareth asked, 'just historians?'

The Dean, grasping his lapels, suggested that an area of expertise in history would be an advantage. 'But,' he cleared his throat, 'in terms of academic endeavour, medieval history might well need some re-evaluation.' He went on to point out that in these days of interdisciplinary focus, input from a wider spectrum would be facilitated with enthusiasm. Interface between areas of study was to be applauded and there was always mileage in thinking outside the box.

'But historians of the medieval period are welcome to apply?' Thomas said.

The Dean's expression registered this as a relevant question 'Indeed they are, Dr Carr,' he beamed. 'Indeed they are. And I have every expectation and hope that senior dons such as yourself will feel themselves able to consider our requirements.'

Thomas grabbed his doodling pencil with both hands, so tightly that it snapped in half. 'Thank-you, Dean,' he said, slipping the pencil pieces into his pocket. 'Thank-you indeed.'

Matters stationery and mundane received due consideration during the rest of the time, as the Dean put it, at their joint disposal. Now that clerical staffing had succumbed to cuts, his secretary was more than willing to assist staff who had misplaced their individual photocopying identity codes.

Thomas, occupied with tunes of glory, heard little of it. A professorial appointment was within sight. His CV ticked the inside and outside of various thinking boxes: an excellent teaching record; authorship of a very successful novel set in the eighteenth century; presenter of a TV series entitled The Rise and Rise of the Tudor Dynasty; publication in several prestigious journals. Surely he was in with a better chance than Gareth from American Studies whose main area of expertise appeared to be an interest in litter.

Let Gwenda do her worst. The temporary appointment here was a matter of urgency and would start at the beginning of the new academic year. Interviews for the appointment she was after wouldn't be held till well into the new term. By that time he'd have made such a success of the position that accusations from such as Gwenda would be put down as the ravings of an hysterical female. She'd be off his back and he'd be ensconced in a temporary professor's chair which, with fortune and medical glitches on his side, might well become permanent. Timing and strategy right for once.

He raced away from the university car park with a roar only the Interceptor could achieve.

He'd take the coast road home he decided, an opportunity to have another look at the Martello Towers along the route. The Friends of Martello Society had been formed as a local adjunct to Geograph, the organisation setting out to photograph every Ordnance Survey grid square. Thomas was an enthusiastic member. There was something about those round fortresses built to repel

Napoleon which appealed to him. Squat and solid, they represented the British bulldog spirit, the we-won't-be-beaten attitude to tyrants.

Some of the towers were in a sad state, crumbling and neglected but others, like the ones in Folkestone, had been restored as holiday homes or visitors' centres. He didn't always approve of restorations that altered a building's original use but in this case it was a fine way to preserve the past and serve the present.

He stopped his car near one of the Sandgate towers which was in process of being restored. Very well too by the look of it. Workmen were taking down scaffolding and dropping rubbish into a skip. If the owner was about, he'd ask permission to take some photos for the Society's magazine. His hand was raised to knock on the door when it opened and Pru Perkins came out carrying a full bin-bag.

Pru was a good sort, straightforward and friendly. He couldn't imagine she'd ever been the sort of woman he'd want to beguile and bed but there was no pretence about her, no duplicity. She'd been good to Ingrid too, seeing to the horses and doing jobs around the stables when his wife had been so ill. But now, her glare was anything but friendly. Napoleon himself might have got a better reception.

She hurled the bin-bag into the skip. 'And what can I do for you, Dr Carr?' she said.

'I was looking for the owner,' Thomas said. 'Would that be you, Mrs Perkins?'

'Jim and I bought this place last year.' She turned away. 'Though I'm not sure why you'd want to know.'

'And you're having it done up?'

Glancing from him, to scaffolding, to skip she said, 'Certainly looks that way.'

Thomas called up one of his best smiles. 'For holiday letting, perhaps?' he said.

'Were you wanting to make a booking?'

'What I was hoping to do is take some photographs, of the renovation, inside and out, if it's not too much of an intrusion.'

Pru stood with her hand on one hip and considered him. 'A sort of favour, you mean?'

'You could put it like that, yes.'

'That's exactly how I am putting it,' she retorted, turning to go back inside. 'And one favour deserves another, I'm told.'

'It there's anything I can do for you in return, Mrs Perkins, I'll be only too happy to oblige.'

He had one foot inside the tower when she said, 'Even if it's to do with Daphne, Daphne Chiltern?'

'Ah....' Thomas hesitated.

'I thought that might make a difference,' Pru said.

She was shutting the door on him. Damn the woman.

'Having second thoughts are you, or even third?' she said, opening the door a fraction, giving him a glimpse of what he might be missing. Thomas could see that the ground floor, which had originally housed food and water for military needs, was now transformed into a modern kitchen-dining room. Fascinating.

'What exactly do you feel I can do for Miss Chiltern?' Thomas said.

'Why don't I show you around, you take your snaps and then we can have a little chat?' Pru suggested. 'I can even offer you tea. There's no power on yet but I'm armed with a primus stove.'

Thomas fingered his camera. A scoop like this would look well under his name in the Society's newsletter and be one in the eye for Adrian Cooper with his maps and lists of dates.

'It's a deal,' he said stepping over the threshold.

'It's quite a challenge,' Pru said as he took photos of the ground floor accommodation, 'finding things to fit around the curvature of the walls. These units,' she ran her hand along the work surfaces, 'are made to measure.'

'Not the sort of thing you can pick up in a chain store,' Thomas said.

'Indeed not,' Pru said. 'The bedrooms are on the next level, with a sitting room at the top.'

'There'll be a fine view from up there,' Thomas said.

'I'll show you.'

He followed her up the stairs, stopping every few steps for her to catch her breath.

'Not for the faint-hearted, these steps,' she said, 'or the overweight.'

'This is wonderful,' Thomas said when they reached the top where a circular observation room had replaced the gun emplacement. 'A three-sixty degree view.'

'Well placed to keep an eye out for greedy men getting above themselves,' she said, leaning her elbows on the ledge below the curve of windows. 'Ever since Boney cast his eyes in this direction, in fact. Looking out is more comfortable now than in his day, of course.'

'Not much comfort then,' Thomas agreed, 'but fewer complications perhaps. They knew who the enemy was.'

Her look was appraising. 'I don't think things change all that much, Dr Carr,' she said. 'Not really. I don't have any trouble identifying the enemy. No trouble at all.'

Before he could get his own enemies out of his mind, she went on, 'Now you take all the photos you like. When you're finished come back to the kitchen and we'll have that cup of tea.'

Half an hour later the two of them sat on stools in the kitchen.

'Thank-you so much, Mrs Perkins.' Thomas said. 'Are you happy for the photos to appear in the Martello Society's magazine?'

Pru put her mug on the worktop and subjected him to another of those penetrating looks. 'Well now,' she said, 'as I mentioned, it's my friend, Daphne, Daphne Chiltern.'

Thomas sighed more loudly than he'd intended. 'I don't know...' he began.

'She's not the easiest of people, I grant you. But she's my friend and she needs help, your help.'

'There's nothing I can do for her, I'm afraid.' Thomas said.

'But you're not afraid, are you, well not about that? You're glad. Glad to wash your hands of Daphne.'

'It's not a matter of hand washing, Mrs Perkins but of hands being tied. I can't alter the provisions of Mrs Kulman's will. All I did was tell Miss Chiltern the position.'

'She was expecting to inherit Mulberry House you know. Well-deserved in my book. She'd skivvied for that Kulman woman for more years than you've had...' she stopped.

'Had what?'

'You didn't even bother to see her, explain the situation.'

Thomas laughed. 'Explaining any situation to Miss Chiltern isn't easy. As her friend you'll recognise that, I'm sure.'

'And a very good friend to me she's been. Daphne has qualities she never gets a chance to show.'

'All the qualities in the world won't alter the position, Mrs Perkins. Mrs Kulman left the house to a woman none of us has ever heard of. But she did make sure Miss Chiltern's position in the house is secure.'

'But not happy perhaps?'

He thought about that one. There was something about the way May Kulman had arranged her affairs that made him think other people's happiness was very far from her intentions. 'No,' he said, 'perhaps not that.'

'Will you see Daphne? Explain.'

'I thought I'd done that already.'

'But not, Dr Carr with as much tact as I know you're capable of, or grace.'

'Grace?' he said.

'It would do me a great favour if you'd let Daphne come and see you.' Pru stood up. 'And I,' she said, 'will come with her.'

Thomas didn't bother with any more Martello Towers. Uneasy for a reason he couldn't quite identify, he took the most direct route home. The euphoria he'd enjoyed had faded. The hopes he'd built up after talking to Cordelia, and the news of a very possible promotion had dribbled down the drain of, well the drain of something or other.

Chapter 13

The sea claimed Daphne, wrapping her in moist satin, sliding over her limbs. Weightless, she floated and dreamed.

For most of the years Daphne had lived in Mulberry House, she'd thought of the sea as a friend she'd one day get to know. She would look at it from her window, watch its changing colours and shapes, hear its changing moods. There'd been so little time then to get acquainted but retirement and a towelling robe had suggested new possibilities.

The woman modelling the towelling robe on the front of a catalogue had been pictured on a stretch of golden sand. Behind her was the sparkling blue sea. Daphne liked the look of the outfit. Here was the chance for a brand new role. A sea goddess would suit her well, though not perhaps in fuchsia pink. But the robe was available in dusky rose and also a beautiful aqua blue.

So it was in an aqua blue towelling robe that Daphne could now be seen crossing the road to the beach every morning, when weather and tides co-operated. Underneath it she wore the very pleasant flowery swimsuit the catalogue had also provided and on her head, a white swimming cap she'd found in the box of things guests had left behind.

'Good idea,' had been May's comment when Daphne mentioned her plan. 'Swimming's ideal exercise for the over-seventies. I may even join you.'

But she never had. Daphne didn't mind one bit. This was a solo, starring role. Leaving the house without a full complement of clothes had been a challenge but a true actress wears whatever the part demands.

Anticipation escorted her across the road, past the board provided for folk who needed information about seashore creatures, sea birds and the Mulberry Harbour, and then to the beach. One arm stretched out for balance, she carefully crossed the knobbly shingle to reach the sandy belt between the pebbles and the water. Breathing deeply she took off her robe and slid her feet out of her turquoise crocs.

Curtain up.

Her entrance was a lingering one. The water lapped her toes, cooled her thighs then circled her waist. Now she was one of the sea nymphs, those shape-changing maidens, mistresses of the waves whose unpredictable moods determined the fate of all who venture into their domain.

The sea was a separate world, her world. Swimming blotted out everything, scenes from the past, present disappointments, fear of the future. The Heiress dare not venture here. Time ticked to a different rhythm unhurried, leisurely. Lazy breast strokes took her from one breakwater to the next then a slow turn and back to where the aqua robe and crocs waited on the shore. She thought of her sister nymphs waving their long, white arms on the other side of the marsh, saw dark silhouettes of gulls against a sky unfurling its blue backdrop, puffy with splodges of white cloud.

'Daphne, hey Daphne.' The voice sliced into the peace. It was Pru, red of face and track suit. Daphne sighed, reluctant to leave her aquatic home.

'I knew it was you, ducky,' Pru said as she watched Daphne slide her arms into the robe, pull off the cap and run wet fingers through her hair. 'I told Jim. She'll be having her dip.' She frowned. 'We'd better get you home or you'll be catching your death. She's arrived then?'

'Who?'

'The woman who's inherited. What's she like?'

'What time is it?' Daphne said.

Pru consulted her watch. 'Ten past eight.'

'Something urgent is it?'

Trudging up the beach, several steps behind her friend, Pru yelled, 'We've never tried Chinese, have we?'

'It's rather indigestible,' Daphne called over her shoulder. She reached the grass verge and waited for Pru to catch up.

'Not food,' Pru panted, 'Horoscopes.' She came to a halt, leaned her bulk on the fencing and shielded her eyes with her hand. 'Is that Adrian Cooper with Pearl's soppy dog?'

Down on the beach Mr Cooper, tugging on Trixie's lead, was getting nearer. A vision of Pearl decked out in a nun's habit slithered into Daphne's mind. 'We'll have some tea, shall we?' she said, starting to cross the road.

'Slow down, can't you?' bleated Pru. She followed Daphne into the house and closed the front door. 'No sign of her then?' She jabbed her thumb in the direction of the kitchen.

Daphne left Pru to make tea in her kitchenette, whilst she showered. She held up her face to the water and let it trickle over her cheeks, taking with it the image of Pearl Cooper smirking at the audience.

'Nice turban,' Pru said when Daphne joined her.

'I'll need to do my hair,' Daphne said. 'When you've gone,' She looked on as Pru fished in each mug with a teaspoon and hauled out the dreadful teabags. 'Couldn't you find the tea pot?'

Pru's glance hovered over the sink where unwashed crockery seemed to have got itself into a tottering pile, then flitted over the worktops. 'Sorry love,' she said, 'but the whereabouts of the tea pot escaped me.'

'It's here somewhere,' Daphne said shrugging her shoulders. She rearranged the towel on her head. 'We'll go through to the sitting room shall we?'

'It was on the telly,' Pru said as the two of them sipped tea. 'Last night.'

'What was?'

'The programme about Chinese horoscopes.'

It was time to have a sort out in here, Daphne though. Her collection of pretty shells and pebbles were all of a jumble on the mantelpiece. Poor Mother in her photo looked like a hostage kidnapped by coastal ornaments.

Nelson, lost to the world in one of the armchairs, had dislodged that pile of things waiting to be ironed. She rescued her best pink silk blouse from under the heap of other stuff and draped it over the back of the sofa.

'I can't for the life of me think why we haven't checked out the Chinese horoscope system, ' Pru said. 'With us reckoning to be experts.'

'Experts?'

'Divinations of the world, ducky.' Pru delved into her Elvis bag and pulled out a handful of papers. 'I printed these out.'

'Sorry?'

'You can't ignore the internet for ever, Daph. It's really useful.' Pru peered at the top sheet. 'D'you think your St. Anthony could spare the time to find my reading glasses?'

Daphne smiled. 'He's busy right now,' she said, 'rooting out my tea pot.'

'You'll be a rabbit,' Pru said, consulting the papers.

'I beg your pardon. That's not very nice.'

'No, no, in the Chinese horoscope. What year were you born?'

'A lady, Pru, does not divulge her age.'

'Nineteen thirty-nine and you're a rabbit, nineteen forty, a dragon.'

'Not a lot to choose between them then?'

'The dragon is lively and charismatic .' Pru turned to the next sheet. 'Sounds promising. Colour yellow.'

Daphne shuddered. 'What a pity. I've nothing against dragons but yellow does nothing for the complexion.' Head on one side she said, 'Though there's a lot to be said for honey yellow.'

'Not much joy if the dragon doesn't run to honey.'

'And the rabbit?'

Pru ran her finger down the list. 'Naturally conservative it says here.' She frowned. 'I'm not sure I'd go along with that. Doesn't go with their reproductive habits, does it?'

'And the colour?'

'Green.'

'Chartreuse I could do at a pinch though I'd team it with something darker. Navy perhaps?.'

'We still haven't established the year, Daph.'

Daphne pushed herself out of the chair. 'I wonder if Nelson needs some breakfast?' she said, prodding the cat. 'Mummy's just checking.'

'That animal is seriously overweight, in my opinion,' Pru said.

'And you'd be the one to know about that, wouldn't you?'

They stared at each other. Pru said, 'Quarrelling wasn't on the cards, or in the tea leaves.'

'Sorry, Pru. I'm a horrid cross-patch.'

'You've a lot on your mind, ducky. The house and all. The whole business sounds a bit iffy if you ask me. How about getting on to Dr Carr again? Go and see him, perhaps?'

Daphne bit the inside of her cheek and winced as she thought of the only scene she'd played with Dr hoity toity Carr, years ago. She'd been waiting for May outside the Menil Institute. He knew his lines of course but she was completely unprepared, dumbstruck.

'Miss Chiltern isn't it?' he'd said.

She was in her red three-quarter coat, she remembered, a mistake if ever there was one. Never let a sale price persuade you against your better judgement. And the black patent bag. Not real leather, another glaring error.

'I've been researching the Chiltern family,' he said.

He wasn't looking at her. Better fish to fry on the other side of the road apparently.

'Interesting,' he said, 'very interesting, from the historian's point of view.'

She fluffed up her hair. It needed cutting. She'd let it go more than a month and that spelt disaster.

'One of the few families in England,' he said, 'with matrilineal inheritance.'

Across the road a some teenage girls were giggling.

'Until very recently.' he went on. 'Your generation in fact.'

What was keeping May?

'It went to the House of Lords, I gather. But you'll know that of course? Had things not been changed so dramatically, it would be you not your cousin...'

'Have you seen May,' she heard her voice saying. 'Mrs Kulman?'

'I left her talking to another of my students,' he'd said. 'She's a great one for talking, isn't she?'

What had May told him? The thought that she had talked to Dr Carr about private things had been horrible.

Pru was looking worried. 'Are you okay?'

Daphne said. 'American isn't it, that word okay?'

Pru laughed. 'Never mind that Daph, love. We need to beard the lion in his den. I'll come with you if you like. I know the old goat quite well, or I did.'

'I didn't know Dr Carr was on your visiting list.'

'I helped out there, with the horses, when his wife was so ill. She was a charming woman. Didn't deserve to be landed with that scumbag. Sinister as the ace of spades under all that smarm.'

'A good reason to steer clear of him,' Daphne suggested.

Pru put her mug on the occasional table and picked up her bag. 'I've often wondered about that evening, the one when his wife died. If only I'd known what was in her mind. She'd got rid of most of the horses by then of course but Midnight was still here. Beautiful animal, lovely nature.'

Daphne slid a coaster under Pru's cup. 'And you were there?'

'I didn't go up there in the evenings, not as a rule but Midnight had been off his feed and I wanted to check on him. I didn't go into the house, more's the pity. Just settled Midnight in his stable and went back to my car. It was a funny thing. She stopped.

'What was funny, Pru?'

Pru stood up and went to stand by the window. 'Well, at the inquest Dr Carr testified that he wasn't at home that evening, that Ingrid was alone, but...'

'But what?'

'But someone was looking out of the kitchen window and that someone definitely wasn't Ingrid Carr.'

Chapter 14

'She's a what?' Alison's dismay pumped through the shop, a place small enough for self-service to mean helping yourself to other people's lives.

'A sitting tenant, I'm afraid.' It was the man from the beach, now identified as Dr Thomas Carr, the executor of Mrs Kulman's will. They'd met beside the tinned vegetables and he'd introduced himself. Mid-fifties, with greying hair and intelligent eyes behind designer glasses, he had the look of a helpful librarian but what he was saying was very far from helpful.

Alison dropped her voice. Her outburst had already attracted far too much attention. 'So I can't get rid of her?'

Thomas added two tins of dog food to the wholemeal loaf in his basket. 'Not very easily it seems,' he said.

'But she's barking mad.' Tell me this is a mistake, Alison pleaded silently, staring down at Thomas's suede moccasins. All I want to be is an extra in the film of life not the lead in some weird cult movie.

'You could say that,' Thomas said, 'though eccentric might be kinder.'

'I'm not sure I do kind,' Alison said. Not any more, she thought. Kind gets you betrayed, walked on, kicked in the teeth. She said, 'And there was I, thinking she was a temporary house-sitter.' She pulled a tin of low-sugar baked beans from the shelf and stared blankly at the list of ingredients. 'Though, come to think of it, the nightdress should have been a clue.'

The corners of Thomas's mouth twitched. 'Nightdress?'

'I opened the front door and there she was at the foot of the stairs.' Alison put back the beans and steadied the pile of tins. 'Decked out in a black lace nightdress and warbling at the top of her voice.'

Thomas's guffaws were loud and long. Alison frowned at this frivolous response but the chortling was contagious and she found herself joining in. There they stood, surrounded by cans of peas and carrots and this week's special offer, shaking with laughter as if fun had burst through its sell-by date.

'We're making a spectacle of ourselves,' Thomas said, crossing his arms over his chest to quell his chortles.

'Nothing like the spectacle of *Climb Every Mountain*,' Alison burbled, 'accompanied by a flurry of lace.'

Thomas took off his glasses and wiped his eyes with the back of his hand. 'What did you do?' he spluttered.

'What my Aunt Jude calls doing a Boudicca, made a tactical retreat. Through the nearest door in my case. I spent the night wrapped in my coat on the sofa.' Alison looked him in the eye. 'You might have warned me, last night on the beach. Didn't you realise who I was?'

Thomas concentrated on his shopping list. 'I did know, yes. I saw you cross the road from Mulberry House but I'm afraid I did a Boudicca myself.'

'And left me to face the music.'

'And the night attire.'

'Don't remind me,' Alison said. 'The spectacle of that lacy lining is impossible to forget. Oh dear, she's not a friend of yours is she?'

Thomas hesitated then put a jar of honey into his basket. 'Allow me to make amends,' he said. 'Come for a drink. Tomorrow evening?' He reached into his inside pocket and held out a card. 'Here's my address. It's only a short walk from Mulberry House.'

'I'd like that,' Alison said. 'Thank-you.'

'Eight o'clock? I'll look forward to it.' He checked the things in his basket against his list, then not quite clicking his heels, he took her hand and said, 'Until tomorrow then.'

At the checkout Alison asked the assistant if the shop gave cash-back. Above a cleavage that could plunge for England, the woman stared. 'Cash-back?' Alison repeated.

The woman twisted round in her chair, unpopping the only fastened button on her uniform overall. 'Told you,' she informed an unseen spy in the darkest reaches of the storeroom. 'It's 'er all right.'

Swallowing consonants was a feature in these parts it seemed. The taxi driver had sounded the same though Dr Carr's voice was much more BBC. Perhaps he wasn't local.

'I'm sorry?' Alison said.

A headful of streaky blonde curls corkscrewed onto the woman's shoulders as she turned back to Alison. 'You're not from round here,' she said. It was not a question.

Alison sighed. And now the rejects gather, she thought, the careless ones who mislay their status, add nothing to the bloodline. God bless the chosen and all who sail with them.

What a load of self-pitying codswallop you do come up with, she told herself. 'No, I'm not from round here,' she agreed. She treated the assistant to a saccharine smile. 'I hope that's not a problem?'

The woman raised her chin. 'Depends,' she said.

On her way back from the shop, Alison ducked under the roadside railing and headed across the grassy verge which bordered the shingle. Screeching gulls wheeled against a sky plumed with wispy clouds. A tonic of a morning Jude would call this one, hazy sunlight, shimmering waves and a frisky breeze. Alison shaded her eyes to look out to sea. The thin dark line below the horizon must be the stranded Mulberry Harbour Thomas had talked about. To her left and right, the beach stretched into infinity, brindled under a sweep of sky. The expanse of it put life into perspective. Apart from the blip of self-pity in the shop, she'd hardly given Malcolm, his bimbo, or babies a moment's thought this morning. It was tempting to imagine this immensity could gobble up human foibles, make anything possible.

But a new foible by the name of Daphne Chiltern was lurking in the house, a foible that had to be faced. Who the hell was it watched you clamber over the hurdle of a broken marriage only to erect another in the shape of a sitting tenant? There must be some way of getting rid of her. Alison turned for the house. She'd find a local solicitor and sort out exactly where she stood.

Back in the house, she turned on her laptop and unpacked the shopping while it booted up.

The internet provided a list of local solicitors. Alison was reaching for her mobile when it bleeped. It was Jude, responding to the text she'd sent last night. Her aunt sounded happier than for some time. She'd be setting out for the airport, within the hour, she said.

'With shadowy Peter?'

'More substance than shadow, I assure you. He's getting our stuff into the car. D'you want me to fetch him so you can give him a verbal once-over?'

'If he's passed your stringent tests, I'll rest easy,' Alison said. 'I'm not sure he'd be that impressed with me anyway, the way things are here.'

'The mad house-sitter?' Jude said. 'When is she leaving?'

'She isn't.'

'Why not?

'Because she isn't a house-sitter, she's a sitting tenant.'

'Says who?'

'Dr Thomas Carr.'

'The executor? D'you believe him?'

Alison leaned on the edge of the sink and looked out of the window. She hadn't bothered with the garden yet, a sheltered courtyard with a gnarled tree at its centre.

'Why would he lie?' she said. 'So far he's the only person round here you'd recognize as normal. The bottom line is, unless I can find some way of getting her out, I'm stuck. Who'd buy a house with a madwoman hovering in the attic?'

'And no sign of Mr Rochester to the rescue?'

'Knight on white charger rescues damsel? Wash your mouth out, Jude.'

Jude laughed. 'Any clues to the mysterious Mrs K?'

'She went in for nautical ornaments, landscapes in elaborate gold frames and velour upholstery. Apart from that, no.'

As they chatted, Alison wandered along the hall and into the sitting room.

'What's the house like?' Jude said.

'The kitchen's nice, cream cupboards and dark, marble worktops.'

'And the rest?'

As Alison began to describe the wide, stone-flagged hall, the study on one side of the front door and the dining room opposite, it was as if the house, like a child desperate for approval, held its breath. Faded, dull and dusty were the words forming in her mind but when they reached her mouth she heard herself say, 'It's light and spacious. The hall leads to the staircase which is beyond a passage dividing the rooms at the front from an annexe at the back.'

'Larger than you thought then.' Jude said. 'And upstairs?'

'The madwoman's flat is on the right of the landing, with its own front door, praise be. Then to the left, three steps lead up to six bedrooms, all en suite.'

'All those bedrooms? Is it a guesthouse?'

'Could have been I s'pose. It's much bigger than I expected and I still haven't explored it all. Poking about doesn't seem right for some reason, so I'm more or less camping out, till I've decided whether or not to stay.'

'But the place is growing on you, by the sound of it,' Jude suggested.

Alison hesitated. 'No,' she said firmly, 'it's a means to an end, or it was. With dopey Daphne installed, the place is completely worthless. Bang go all my plans to start up on my own. Hardly a trouble-free legacy is it?'

'No saving graces?'

Alison looked out of the window, at the froth of clouds hovering over the beach, at the sea, a sinuous, green creature flecked with silvery white-horses. 'The sea views are wonderful, Jude,' she said. 'I can't wait for you to see them.'

'You'll be there long enough for me to visit then?'

Around Alison, Mulberry House waited for her answer, an answer that wasn't ready. 'Well, I'm not sure,' she said. 'I need to see a solicitor, sort out just where I stand.'

'About dopey Daphne?'

'The very same.'

'The person you need to consult is May Kulman's solicitor, He or she might give you some idea of who she was and where you fitted into her life. It'll be the firm who drew up the will. Isn't the name on that?'

Outside, the white poodle man, was standing by the front gate, staring up at the house. Alison twitched aside the curtain. The man scurried away.

'I've no idea,' she told Jude. 'I haven't really looked.'

'I'm not happy with all this, Allie,' Jude said. 'Something about it smells wrong. Have you had a look at the documents, a really good look?'

'I tossed all the papers into my suitcase.'

'Time to get them out then.' Jude had put on her firm voice. 'Sooner rather than later, if I were you.'

Alison made herself a coffee and took it outside to have a closer look at the garden. Cupping her hands round the mug, she stood in the enclosed space looking back at the house. On either end, like pieces from a child's Meccano set, were twin fire escapes, one from the end of what must have been the guest corridor, the other, presumably, from Daphne's flat.

She turned to face the garden. On her right, topped by a sloping slate roof, was a redbrick building with a window and door on one side. She peered through the dirty window and saw a garage, opening presumably onto Ashton Gardens, the road running along the side of the house. To her left, and across the end of the garden, the walls were bearded with thick strands of encroaching ivy.

Uneven paving stones, fringed with weeds, covered the ground and at their centre was the tree, a tree with a tawny creviced trunk and twisted branches. Spears of embryonic fruit clustered between the leaves. A mulberry tree.

'You're here after all then,' Alison said.

Above her head a window opened with a squeak. Alison looked up to see an overweight tabby cat squeeze through the space and land on Daphne's fire escape. He crept down the flight of steps, sat on the halfway landing then leapt onto the garage roof. Alison felt, rather than saw, Daphne hovering with intent.

Back inside, Alison went into the extension. Separate from the rest of the house, with an en suite bedroom and a sitting room, it offered more privacy than any of the rooms upstairs, a camp away from the enemy. It was where she'd decided to sleep for the time being.

She pulled the papers out of the zipped section of her case, perched on the edge of the bed and smoothed them out on her knee. The deeds of the house looked okay but the photo-copy of the will must have been done on a machine running out of ink. The name of the firm drawing up the document was smudged and the signatures were illegible.

All she had wanted was to make this unexpected legacy the means to start again, to be here and then gone. She'd given little thought to the woman who had lived in this house, this inheritance which was proving far from simple. So who was Mrs Kulman and what was her connection with her? The house must hold the answer.

Alison opened the drawer in the bedside table. It was empty. The dressing table drawers held nothing but an unopened box of tissues; the only thing in the wardrobe was an acidic smell, like citrus perfume turned sour.

Chapter 15

The bell tower of St. George's, Daphne always thought, was like three up-side-down ice cream cones slotted one atop the other, waiting their turn for a nice dollop of raspberry ripple. According to one of the B&B guests, having a separate tower was an unusual feature. Originally it had been built on top of the church roof but its weight had been more than the shifting marsh ground could support.

Usually when she was in this part of the town, she liked to pop inside the church to see St. George in his window. Perched up there on his brown horse, lance held aloft, he seemed to be wondering if the virgin who'd caused all this trouble was worth saving, a valid point in Daphne's opinion. Pallid and draped in a nightie that had seen better days, the girl stood with a soppy grin on her face and her hands in the air. The dragon, with his beautiful greeny-turquoise scales and fiery red breath, was much more attractive.

But this morning there were other things to think about. Last night she'd been restless, fidgety, turning over and over in bed much to Nelson's annoyance. Poor pusskins, trying to sleep on his special blanket at the foot of her bed, and there was she tossing around like a boat which had slipped its moorings. By the time dawn peeped under the curtains, Nelson had stalked off, tail in the air, in search of peace.

She could hardly blame him. It wasn't his fault that the question of who could advise her whirled round and round in her head. For decades May had organised anything remotely official. There was always Pru of course. She'd be kind and understanding but she did get the tingiest bit stroppy if you didn't take her suggestions on board.

The fluttering bedroom curtain had put her in mind of that tiered, cotton skirt Samantha, the vicar's wife, had worn to the Carol Concert. Not the best garment for a December evening perhaps and in Daphne's opinion cotton tiers didn't sit well with knee-length leather boots but modern young women had their own ideas. Samantha had been very astute about the importance of soprano voices in a choir in spite of her taste in clothes and the dreadful way everything she said sounded like a question. And she was married to the vicar, one of the few people under forty May had admired.

An hour before the alarm clock was set to jangle, the decision was made. Samantha it would be. Daphne had fallen into a deep sleep.

So here she was, wearing her good navy jacket, brushed and pressed, with her smart pencil skirt fitting snugly over her hips. The right outfit for the occasion was half the battle.

The white bungalow, even with an added loft conversion, dormer window and balcony, hardly seemed fitting for a man of the cloth but the rectory had long since been sold off to a dental practice.

Samantha was wheeling a bike round the side of the bungalow. She smiled at Daphne. 'Good morning.'

She'd gone for the layered look which Daphne thought made women resemble children who couldn't bear to part with garments that no longer fitted so wore them on top of some that did. Her fair hair, not quite caught up in a comb, drifted around her face in untidy strands.

'I do hope you don't have an appointment with my husband,' Samantha said. She dropped a Union Jack shopping bag into the basket on the front of the bike. 'The bishop's collected his underlings together this morning. Tony, being Tony, forgot to write it in the diary.' She grinned. 'What d'you suppose such a gathering is called? A surplus of clerics?' She leaned the bike against the low, garden wall, opened the gate and looked more closely at Daphne. 'You're very sombre in navy,' she said. 'Oh God, you've not come to arrange a funeral have you?'

'I was hoping to have a talk with you,' Daphne said. 'But I can see you're busy. I should have made an appointment.'

'Oh dear,' Samantha laughed. 'I'm not at all the sort of person people make appointments to see. Is it important?'

Blinking away tears, Daphne heard her own voice, sharp and abrupt. 'It is to me.'

'I can see that,' Samantha said gently. 'Hang on, I'll get rid of the wheels so that you can get past.'

'But you're about to go shopping,' Daphne said. Expecting the girl to be at her beck and call was unforgiveable. Just because her own world had gone what Pru would call pear-shaped didn't excuse rudeness. She was about to apologise when Samantha said, 'I know you don't I? The choral society? It's Miss Chiltern isn't it, a friend of Mrs Kulman's?'

Was that how May had seen her, a friend? Daphne wondered. Six months ago she'd have been quite sure May was the best friend she could wish for. But would a friend, a real friend, have left her in this horrible position? 'I worked for May,' she said quietly, 'managing Mulberry House.'

Samantha was ushering her into the front garden. 'That's right,' she said. 'The B&B on Marine Drive. One of Mrs K's many business interests, apparently.' She put her arm round Daphne's shoulders. 'It can't be an easy time for you just now.'

Daphne burst into tears.

'Oh dear,' Samantha said. She plucked a crumpled tissue from her jacket pocket and handed it over. 'You'd better come inside.'

'But...' Daphne's words see-sawed over sobs that wouldn't stop, '...you were on your way out.'

'Just popping to Mr Jenkins for a bit of something tasty, to keep body attached to soul,' Samantha said. She pushed her hair out of her eyes. 'But that can wait. One thing about being self-employed, no-one's clock-watching.' With one hand on the bike, the other under Daphne's elbow, she led the way to the back door. She propped the bike against the wall and opened the door to a wooden building at right-angles to the bungalow. 'We'll be better off in my studio,' she said. 'The sitting room's littered with tea-cups. Mothers' Union Committee last night.' She opened the studio door. 'Park yourself in there and I'll see what I can rustle up by way of what Tony calls restoratives.'

Samantha's studio was alive with colour. Curtains patterned with blue swirls hung at the windows, a large workbench housed a computer and all those gadgets people had these days. Near the window with its view of a neglected garden, were two buttonback armchairs, upholstered in purple and placed either side of a small chest covered with magazines.

Samantha, Daphne knew, was a professional photographer. The walls were hung with her photographs. As Daphne's sobs subsided into dwindling shudders, she went to look at them. What a clever girl Samantha was to capture the moods of the Marsh like this. A winter snow scene shining with frosted fields; the wind turbines, bony against a sky pitted like an orange skin; Becket's church enveloped in mist.

'Did you know,' Samantha said, appearing in the doorway with a tray in her hands, 'that the Marsh churches were built on hummocks of earth to keep away the devil?' With one foot she pushed the door shut behind her. 'Come and sit down.' She elbowed aside the pile of magazines and rested the tray on the chest.

Daphne sat in one of the armchairs and stared at the tray.

'You'll be awash with tea, I expect,' Samantha said. 'Gin's much better in a crisis.' She uncapped the bottle and sloshed gin into two glasses. 'Easy on the tonic, eh? Help yourself to the box of choccies. Grateful parishioners do come in handy.'

'Your photographs are lovely.' Daphne said. The tissue was a soggy ball in her hand. She stared down into her drink. Gin at half past ten in the morning, very naughty. 'Would it be awfully rude to ask if they sell well? I don't really know much about these things.'

'Not rude at all,' Samantha said. 'And no reason why you should know about photography. I don't know a thing about running a B&B.' She reached for the box of chocolates and examined the inside of the lid. 'Coffee cream, I think. I don't usually get a look in with coffee creams. Tony nabs them.' She nibbled the edge of the chocolate. 'I make a living,' she said, 'calendars and such. Just now I'm working on a commission for a book about the Marsh churches, hence my knowing about hummocks and the devil. Now.' She licked her fingers and picked up her glass. 'Fire away.'

And at half past ten in the morning, sipping gin and indulging in a rum and raisin truffle, Daphne did fire away, letting it all hang out, as Pru would say.

'So you see,' she finished, 'The Heiress has arrived and I don't really know where I am.'

Samantha bit her lip. 'Well, in one way you do,' she said, 'and in another you don't. Dr Carr says you're a sitting tenant, which means you know no-one can put you out of your flat, but what you don't know is why Mrs Kulman left her house to a stranger. You're wondering why she did it and, much more important, why she hadn't told you how things stood.' She frowned. 'And from where I'm sitting, the second bit's much worse than the first.'

Daphne felt her mouth drop open. That was it exactly. With Samantha in the lighting box, complete blackout gave way to saturation rig. 'You're the only person to see that,' she said.

'What we need,' Samantha said, 'is a plan of action.'

Nothing in the last horrible weeks was so comforting as that 'we' Daphne thought. She flopped back in her chair and let out a huge sigh. An ally at last.

'I know some things about Tony's churchy people,' Samantha said. 'I'm not supposed to know anything at all, clerical confidentiality and all that, but you can't live here and not pick up the odd detail.' She got up and stood in front of her photos, staring at each one before moving on to the next. 'This helps me think,' she said. 'Now then, let's concentrate on Mrs Kulman. She was here a lot.'

'She came here?' Daphne said. May had called herself a triathlon church-goer, Christmas, Easter and Harvest Festival. Some years she went over to Folkestone for the Blessing of the Fisheries but only if the WI President's nephew was MC or whatever they called it. She'd described Samantha's husband as having a good head on his shoulders but come to think of it, how did she know? Daphne had never thought of May as being pally with the vicar.

But then her memories of May away from Mulberry House were already shadowy. May in the kitchen, eyes screwed over the bill from that dreadful Mr Jenkins, yes; May sitting under the mulberry tree, reading the paper, yes; May keeping an eye from the office, yes. But May in the High Street, May on the beach were dimly lit scenes, fading like a photograph left too long in sunlight. It was as if May hadn't really existed outside the house. Or was there another May, a double who did all the things Daphne's May would never have done? The Germans had a word for it, didn't they? One of those long words that gobbled up your breath before you got to the end of them?

'She took a lot of notice of Tony's advice on financial matters,' Samantha said. She was staring out of the window.

'He was an accountant you see, before he got the call.' She laughed. 'When I first took Tony home, Dad thought I'd do all right there. Reckoned he'd never met a poor accountant.' Her back was to the window now, her face indistinct against the light outside. 'Funny old thing, life. Here we are now, poorer than the mice running riot round the choir stalls.' Her hand went to her throat. 'And happy as Larry.'

'How lovely,' Daphne said.

'Bit of a cheek really,' Samantha went on, 'Mrs K getting Tony's help for gratis.'

'How d'you mean, dear?'

'Freebies,' Samantha said, 'but that's the rich all over, isn't it? It's the way they stay rich, my Dad would say, never paying their bills and hanging on to what they've got.'

'I'm not sure I'd describe May as rich,' Daphne said. 'I never saw the accounts of course. We got by and she was always generous to me, but rich?'

'As Croesus, apparently.' Samantha dropped into the armchair and swung her legs over its side. 'She owned half the holiday lets and chalets in the area as well as Beach View, that whopping hotel further along the coast.'

Daphne gasped. 'She what?'

'Oh God, you didn't know?'

'It seems not,' Daphne said. 'All my own lines off by heart, but the wrong play '

Samantha looked puzzled. 'Play?'

'Theatricals dear. It's in the blood.' Daphne re-crossed her legs and straightened her skirt over her knees. 'Truth to tell...' Her fingers tightened on the damp tissue. 'I'm beginning to wonder if I really knew May at all.'

'And who could blame you?' Samantha said. 'Well now.' Her voice was brisk. 'Let's be systematic. How about the will? Have you actually seen it?'

Daphne shook her head. 'Dr Carr's got it, I think.'

'He's the executor, you said?'

'If that's what you call it.'

'Did he know Mrs Kulman well enough? Well enough, I mean, to have some idea of her thinking, when she decided who was getting what?'

'I don't know.' Daphne hesitated. She had to be careful here. That dreadful man might well be one of Samantha's friends.

'You won't want to ask Thomas Carr,' Samantha said. ' And who could blame you?'

How delicious, Daphne thought, if Samantha proved to loathe the man as much as I do. 'You know him, do you?' she said.

'He came here once to talk to Tony. Something about church history I think. Tony said...' Her face reddened. 'Well, he suggested I stay out of Dr Carr's way, make myself scarce.' She wriggled her legs back over the arm and sat squarely in the chair. 'What about the rest of Mrs Kulman's assets? Who gets those?'

'I've no idea.'

'A will has to be in the public domain, doesn't it? If we knew who she left the other properties to, we could maybe work out why she left Mulberry House to this woman. Even find out who she is? Perhaps her solicitor would help.'

'But I've no idea who her solicitor was.'

'Tony might have made a note of it.' Samantha glanced towards the bungalow. 'But I'm not sure I could go as far as hunting through his desk. Very un-vicar's wife-ish. We'll have to think of something else.' She closed the box of chocolates, screwed the top back on the gin bottle and collected the two glasses. 'Hang on, I remember now. I saw Mrs Kulman coming out of a solicitor's in Rye sometime last year it was. I forget the name, something and Higgles? It's next to that bookshop, the one that always has loads of hanging baskets outside.'

Chapter 16

Thomas rinsed the brush and wiped it on a piece of kitchen paper. He pushed back the chair and admired the coat-of-arms he was painting, the Kingdom of the Two Sicilies, quite a challenge. The gold lion rampant, on the black background of the dexter base, had turned out rather well. Making sure he'd left the paper parallel with the table edge and the brushes neatly splayed, he picked up the water pot.

'Stir yourself, Nell,' he called to the snoozing spaniel. 'Time to get things ship-shape. The lady will be here in thirty minutes. Stand by our beds and all that.'

Not a bad idea, bed. 'Bound to be attached though, isn't she Nell?' he said. The spaniel rubbed her nose against his leg and he patted her head. 'How much attached, that's the question?'

When he'd first heard about her, the idea of a stranger inheriting Mulberry House had been intriguing. The mysterious Alison had been a conceptual theory to be considered with speculation. But now abstraction had transformed into reality, flesh and blood were very different. He pictured Alison's dark hair, the tiny crease of concentration between her eyebrows when she spoke and the way she focused on his face as he'd talked to her in the shop.

He shut his study door and went upstairs to change. By the time the church clock began to strike the hour, he was hovering behind the front door wondering how many life-changes its chimes had announced down the decades. Before the strokes had finished, Alison was there.

You did say eight, Dr Carr?' Her face, flushed from the walk, smiled up at him.

'Your punctuality does you credit,' he said. 'And the name's Thomas.' Giving a mock bow he added, 'M'am.' He held out his hands. 'May I take your coat?' She was wearing pale trousers and a knitted jacket patterned with leaping fish.

'Did you know,' he said, 'that the Japanese believe any fish able to leap a waterfall will turn into a dragon?'

'That's the kind of thing you expect people to know, is it?' she said. 'Like the name of your house?'

'Passelande? King Arthur's horse. People know what they know, don't they?'

He pointed to the sitting-room door. Her hair smelt lemony and shone under the hall light. He hung up her coat and followed her.

'This is amazing.' Alison was admiring Ingrid's embroidery of a medieval knight. 'It's almost life size. And done in so many different techniques. Not just embroidery but appliqué, collage. What wonderful colours.' She took a step back. 'The chain-mail's so realistic I can almost hear it clunking.' She turned to him. 'Do you know the artist?'

'My wife would have been pleased to hear you use the word artist,' Thomas said.

'Would have been?'

'She died, just over a year ago.'

'What a pity,' Alison said.

'Thank-you.'

'What for?'

'For not saying, I'm sorry. Most people do.'

'I meant it's a pity that someone so talented should have died.' Alison looked at Ingrid's photograph on top of the sideboard. 'She was a horsewoman too?'

'Indeed.'

She was frowning. Had he shouted? From her basket in the inglenook, Nell growled softly in her sleep. Calm down he told himself, she knows nothing about you, or Ingrid. Controlling his voice he said, 'You didn't know my wife and to express anxiety over her death could be seen as shallow not to say inaccurate.' He cleared his throat. 'You were sensitive enough to see that. Please sit down. Can I offer you a drink?' Now I'm gabbling, he thought. She'll assume the wound of loss is raw and my grieving not yet done.

Alison said, 'I expect you *can* offer me a drink but that wouldn't tell you whether or not I wanted one, would it?'

For a moment he glared at her, then felt a smile creep over his face. She was feisty. So much the better. 'You're quite right,' he admitted. 'I am a stickler for linguistic accuracy.' His laughter woke Nell who ambled over to sit at his feet. 'They don't call me Prof the Dictionary for nothing,' he said, patting the spaniel's back. 'Do they old girl?'

'They?' Alison said.

'The regulars at The Grey Goose. So, back to the top, as they say in theatrical circles. Mrs Draper, would you like a whisky?'

'Thank-you, I would. But please call me Alison. It's just as accurate as Mrs Draper, more so really.'

'Alison is your given name and not acquired through marriage?' Was it the word marriage that made her flinch? She was gazing at the floor.

'What can you tell me about Mrs Kulman?' she said.

The change of subject was abrupt. 'I'm glad you mentioned that,' he said, opening the sideboard door.

'Wow,' Alison said. 'That's the biggest array of whisky bottles I've seen outside Scotland.'

'Single malts,' he said. 'One of my vices, I'm afraid, along with family history, wargaming and heraldry.'

Alison said she could imagine family history might well involve vice, and even at a pinch, wargames but heraldry?

'You'd be surprised what sirs and their ladies got up to,' Thomas said. He handed her a tot of whisky. 'This is Talisker, I wonder what you'll think of it.' He settled himself in the armchair opposite her and gulped the whisky. Alison was looking round. What did the room suggest to her, he wondered. Whatever it told her wasn't about him, but Ingrid.

She was sipping her drink. 'Disturbing the peace of this elegant room feels like an intrusion,' she said. 'But...'

'You need to ask some questions,' Thomas said. 'You want to know about May Kulman. Of course you do.' Her expression was distrustful. She's weighing me up, he thought, assessing how best to get the information she wants.

She swallowed then said, 'You must have known Mrs Kulman well, for her to make you executor of her will, I mean.'

Thomas lifted his glass and held it to the light. 'Such a wonderful colour, Talisker,' he said. 'The only single malt distilled on the Isle of Skye. Alchemist's gold, Ingrid called it.'

'Ingrid was your wife?'

Mistake Thomas, he cautioned himself, mentioning her name like that. You're under sentence of blackmail, remember. He got up, fetched the bottle and stared at the map on its label. 'Another dram?' he said, pouring one for himself.

Alison shook her head. 'D'you mind my asking you about Mrs Kulman?'

'Of course not. I didn't know her well. She was one of my students.'

'Students?' She sounded surprised.

'I teach Family History, at the Menil Institute in Rye. Have done for years. It's an offshoot really, of my position at the University.'

'A professor?'

He grimaced.' Sadly no, well not yet. Senior lecturer in Medieval History, what there is left of it.'

Alison put her glass on the coffee table. 'Medieval is past, in more than one sense?'

'Indeed.' Thomas narrowed his eyes. 'Modern is the buzz word these days.'

'And modern history starts in...?'

'Fifteen hundred.'

Alison smiled. 'That's more appropriate than fourteen eighty-five is it?'

Thomas laughed. Not just a pretty face this one. 'The Tudor dynasty wouldn't have thought so,' he said. 'Anyway.' He stared at the sideboard. 'I took some weeks off, to....to nurse Ingrid. A colleague stood in for me. When I returned....after...afterwards, May Kulman had joined the class.'

Armoured by chunky beige cardigans, he reflected, her stance aggressive, her comments snide. What had been a relaxed and enjoyable two hours in his week degenerated into an on-going battle. Why the devil had he agreed to be her executor? Perhaps, suggested Sir Dreadnought, if he hadn't been so flattered to be asked, the present mess would have been avoided. Pride before, a fall after.

'And you hadn't known her before that?' Alison was saying. 'I thought this was one of those places where everybody knows what everyone else's grandmother had for breakfast.'

He hesitated. Innocent and ignorant Alison might be and much more attractive than he'd anticipated but it wouldn't do to drop his guard. He said, 'I knew her by sight.'

'How old was she, Thomas, when she joined your class? I'm sorry to give you the third degree but you're the only person I can ask. I'd imagined she was getting on a bit. I thought courses these days were designed to get people into work, not aimed at the elderly?'

He grinned and wagged his finger at her. 'I think you'll find, Alison, that the older you get yourself, the farther away elderly slinks. But if late seventies qualify as elderly, then the word would fit May. Why do you ask?'

'I have to start somewhere,' she said, reaching to pat Nell. He saw the spaniel gaze up with limpid eyes, her head on one side. 'Until very recently I'd never heard of Mrs Kulman. And I've still no idea what my connection with her was. You can't tell me anything about that, can you?'

This ground was safer. 'I'm afraid not,' he said.

Alison picked up her empty glass and twirled it in her hands. 'The solicitor at home gave me a bundle of papers,' she said, 'but I haven't sorted through them yet, beyond checking that I've got the house deeds. What about the other bequests?'

'Others?'

'I mean did she have any other assets to leave? My copy of the will is virtually illegible. If there are other assets, who did she leave them to?' She grinned. 'Sorry. To whom did she leave them?'

'Correct, but ugly.' Thomas reached for the whisky bottle and offered it to her. She shook her head. He went on, 'In the same class as up with this I will not put.'

'Churchill?'

'I'm impressed,' he said, 'impressed and relieved that the education of the young has not been neglected.'

'It's kind of you to include me in the ranks of the young but not in keeping with your reliance on accuracy, perhaps?'

'More gallant than accurate then? But I can give you a few years. To ascertain the exact number would involve inexcusable prying.'

She frowned and replaced her glass on the table. 'I get the feeling,' she said looking straight at him, 'that you're stalling.'

'About?'

'About Mrs Kulman's will. You do have a copy?'

'I do indeed. The probate papers haven't been issued yet but Lynwood authorised me to tell you, and Miss Chiltern, the provisions about the house.'

'Lynwood?'

'Lynwood Higton. Mrs Kulman's solicitor. Apparently his instructions were that the will's stipulations with regard to the house should be conveyed verbally to you and to Miss Chiltern and that you should be given the documents to allow you to take up residence immediately should you so desire.'

'And that Miss Chiltern should know her own position?'

'Indeed.'

Again Alison frowned. 'Is that normal?' she said. 'Without probate being granted I mean?'

Nell was back with him now, nuzzling his leg. He ran his hand along the length of her back and felt her shudder with pleasure. 'I did wonder about that myself but Lynwood seemed to think it was in order. He'd had sight of the death certificate. I imagine there are as many normal situations after a death as there are people to devise them.'

'Hang on,' Alison said, 'if this Higton guy was Mrs K's solicitor, what connection did she have with the Hush Puppies?'

Thomas laughed. 'The what?'

'Sorry, the solicitor who gave me the house deeds.'

'And wore Hush Puppies?'

'Scuffed ones, smelly I shouldn't wonder. Not too hot on anti-dandruff shampoo either.'

'A total disaster then?'

'You've said it. But where does he fit in?'

Thomas shrugged. 'Sorry,' he said, 'I really have no idea.'

'So I'm no further forward,' Alison said. 'Here I am in possession of May Kulman's house and batty tenant, interrogating a man I've only known for a couple of days. I feel as if I'm in a series of flickering trailers for films that will never be screened.'

'Set in Kent's farthest south,' Thomas said, 'with its smuggler heroes and forty-five thousand acres of marshland relying, my father always maintains, on Roman defences.'

'Your father?'

'Professor Percival Carr, an authority on this area.'

'You take after him then?' Alison said. 'Does he live locally?'

'Not for some years,' Thomas said. 'He's currently warming his bones in the south of France.' He took a slug of whisky, staring into the bottom of the tumbler.

'Relying on Roman defences sounds really scary.' Alison said. 'You are joking?'

'Indeed I am not. If the Great Sea Wall is breached, the sea reclaims us all.'

'There's no need to sound so delighted at the prospect.'

Thomas laughed. 'I don't think we need be overly pessimistic,' he said. 'The wall has been rebuilt several times and there are more drains, dykes and pumps on the marshes than there are people. Modern technology has given the Romans a helping hand. History is on our side, or her-story as some of my more militant lady colleagues would have it.'

'Who would not be very happy to hear themselves called ladies?' Alison suggested.

'We all have our crosses to bear,' Thomas agreed.

'And mine,' Alison said, 'goes by the name of Daphne Chiltern. Does she have a story?'

'Oh yes,' Thomas said, 'indeed she does. But then we all have one of those.' He stood up. 'Follow me.'

She picked up her drink and followed him and Nell, into the hall. Beside the picture hanging next to his study she stopped. 'Is this the cover of a novel?' she said. 'It has your name on it.'

'My one and only venture into fiction,' he said.

'Frost Fair?'

'The title and cover illustration are from the painting by Thomas Wyke, *Thames Frost Fair.*'

'It was made into a film, wasn't it, the novel?' Alison said. 'I saw it on TV, a medieval who-dun it, was it?'

'Eighteenth century.'

She looked surprised. 'Well out of your comfort zone then?'

Thomas opened the study door and ushered her inside. 'It seemed a good idea,' he said, 'at the time.'

'You didn't feel like writing a sequel?'

'I'm afraid the writing didn't feel like co-operating,' Thomas said. 'Now then the Chilterns.' He went to the wooden filing cabinet, pulled a sheet of paper from a file and handed it to Alison. 'This is the family crest They probably originated from the Chiltern Hills but the name turns up in the records of various counties. Robert de Cilterne of Middlesex 1296, is the earliest I've come across.'

'It's an interesting design,' Alison said. 'Have you painted it for Daphne Chiltern?'

'Indeed not. Daphne is the last person to want reminding of her family background. This,' he tapped the painting, 'is just a hobby of mine.' He replaced the sheet in the file and closed the drawer. 'Sit down won't you?'

She chose the carver chair beside the fireplace. Now she really was in his territory, Thomas thought. What would she make of it? Pictures of coats of arms on the walls, books arranged in alphabetical order, pens, ink and paints on the gate-legged table.

'What do you think of your inheritance, now you've had time to digest the idea of owning Mulberry House?'

'Common sense tells me to stick to my original plan,' Alison said.

'Which was?'

'To sell the place. I had plans for the capital. Part of me still wants to put up a For Sale board, decamp and leave the house to its fate, Daphne included. I only came down here to...' She ran her finger round the glass rim.

'Do a Boudicca?' Thomas said. 'I'm sorry, that was unforgivably intrusive.'

Alison's expression was wary. 'But perceptive,' she said.

'Only part of you wants to sell up, you said. What about the rest?'

Across the hearthrug she regarded him sternly. 'Is this some kind of test? If I give the wrong answer, will I find it's all been a trick and I'm to take myself off, back up north with my tail between my legs?'

'And if it is a test?'

'The part of me that's crying get me out would cheer.' The tiny crease appeared between her eyebrows. 'But it is only a small part. In spite of everything I might call better judgement, the house seems to be growing on me.'

'Places have a habit of doing that,' Thomas said, 'people too.'

Alison sighed. 'I'm not doing well on the people front at the moment,' she said, 'apart from Jude of course.'

'Jude?'

'My aunt. Her given name is Judith but no-one calls her that, not if they value their life.'

'You have a good relationship with her?' Thomas said.

Alison nodded. 'She was my mother's sister. My parents died when I was very small so Jude brought me up.'

'With advice from Boudicca?' Thomas ventured.

Alison's eyes sparkled. 'Jude's role models have always been strong women,' she said. 'Catherine de Medici or Emmeline Pankhurst helped out when Boudicca was busy dealing with Romans. I grew up assuming women ruled the world.'

'And men were the enemy?'

'Oh no, Jude's loved lots of men. But she believes that dependent relationships are demeaning, to either sex.'

'A wise woman,' Thomas said softly.

'She's very dubious about this inheritance of mine, thinks it may be some kind of trick.'

'Nothing like that. You have the deeds. Mulberry House is yours.'

'Lock, stock and sitting tenant, you mean?'

'Indeed.'

He was helping her on with her coat when she said, 'You never did tell me, about the other beneficiaries to the will.'

Thomas reached to open the front door. 'There is only one,' he said,' a charity which supports single mothers.'

When Alison had gone, Thomas settled Nell into her basket and headed for the stairs. He thought of the way Alison had tucked one leg behind the other when she folded herself into the chair and pictured the knitted fish swimming over the rise of her breasts.

He straightened the painting hanging next to his bedroom door. As soon as his new post was confirmed, he'd put this house on the market. It had been a mistake to stay. Memories drifted like cobwebs in a draught, none of them helpful. From here in his bedroom, where Ingrid never set foot, he could still hear the ghost of rituals from her own room along the corridor, the rasp of a drawer, the clink of the pot lid opening on tiny wads of cotton wool, the top of a jar unscrewed, the pop of the mascara wand. There were smells, too, nail polish, hairspray, perfume.

He leaned on the window sill and watched the shifting cloud images come and go in the sky, a fortress with crumbling battlements, a wood with tall trees covered in feathery snow. One scene rapidly re-formed by the wind as it thrashed through branches and wailed into crannies. Long ago on nights like this, the owlers would be splashing through the dykes, alert for Ridings Officers. The church vestry would reek of tobacco and the pulpit be packed with casks of brandy. Ethelred could impose his tax on every tun of wine entering the country or Edward III charge for exporting sheep fleeces. Whatever rules authority tried to impose, the honest thieves called smugglers won the day. Heroes of the Marsh, their deeds would outlast those of any king.

No historian worth his salt would assume that moral dilemmas were simpler in the past but it was tempting to transport yourself into an age when Marshmen knew where their loyalties lay, when friend was distinguishable from enemy.

Two deaths, two women. One, May Kulman, of no importance to him at all, the other, Ingrid, of less importance than she should have been. They had made their bargain early in their marriage and he'd treated her with courtesy, done his best to conceal his indifference. But the pain on her face as the cancer took hold was clear in his memory, her hollow cheeks, her pleading eyes. Like a fossil imprinted on the rock falls of its time, her emaciated presence held only the suggestion of the person she had been. She had looked him in the eye and said, 'I'm dying, aren't I, Tom?'

He hadn't expected that. Truth had long been consigned to the attic of their lives.

'What's that you always say, darling?' her voice had insisted. 'Something about counsel to a lady? The knight's code?'

'Never give a lady evil counsel,' he'd quoted.

'Well then.'

Whatever his past misdemeanours, he had more than redeemed himself by complying with her wishes at the end. With Gwenda in the picture, that compliance was taking its toll.

A rustle drew his attention to the hedge. Was that a movement? As he narrowed his eyes to peer out, the security light blazed, slicing lozenges of brightness across the garden. The figure on the lawn cast a long shadow over the knot garden.

Thomas unlocked the window, and leaned out. 'Odd time of night to call.'

Shielding his eyes, the man clutched the brim of his fedora hat and looked up. 'I wanted to give you time to settle down after, shall we say entertaining Mrs Draper?'

'What the hell are you implying?'

'I don't deal in implications, Dr Carr. Only facts. Only facts. Turn the bloody light off can't you? '

'How did you get in?'

'Gate was open, pal.'

Thomas knew it wasn't. Downstairs Nell began to bark.

'Setting the dogs on me now are you?'

A gust of wind lifted the fedora from the man's head. Thomas grinned to see its owner scurrying after it, out of sight.

By the time Thomas got downstairs, Nell at his heels, a hammering on the front door filled the hallway. The curve of the spyhole glass probably exaggerated the domes of the guy's cheeks and the twin arcs of his moustache like a pair of duelling pistols across his top lip. But nothing could disguise the brilliant hue of his pink bow tie.

Thomas opened the door on the chain. 'Who the hell are you?'

The man perched his battered hat under his arm and poked the edge of a business card through the gap in the open door. 'Thornly's the name,' he said, 'Gerald Thornly, without an e.'

'A field full of thorns,' Thomas said.

'Say again?'

'What I do say, Mr Thornly without an e,' Thomas snapped, 'is firstly how did you get through my locked gate, secondly do you know what time it is and thirdly...'

'Thirdly, what the dickens do I want?'

'You've caught the general drift.'

'Thirdly then, something to your advantage, to your advantage, Dr Carr as the legal johnnies say. Take a shifty at this.'

The business card slid through the gap between door and doorframe and landed on Thomas's foot.

'Gerald Thornly, as you see, of Thornly Private Investigations. It's bloody blustery out here. If you could see your way clear to inviting me inside, we can get things sorted out nicely.'

'At eleven-thirty at night? I don't think so. Anything you have to say to me can be said when you've made an appointment. You have a phone book in your office, I take it? If people like you have an office. You'll find my number under C for Carr, Dr Thomas Carr that is.'

'No need to take that tone with me, pal. I know who you are, Dr Thomas Carr, executor of the late Mrs Kulman's will. Good pals we were, me and Mrs K. She mentioned you to me, more than once, more than once.' His grin was less smile than leer. 'A great talker, Mrs K. Knew more than you'd reckon, that one. More than you'd reckon.'

Chapter 17

Daphne had never been sure about cochineal. All those little insects dried and crushed for the red colouring, it didn't seem right. She should have checked that humane methods were used but it was too late now. At any moment The Heiress might come back.

Until the wretched woman had arrived Daphne had been pleased with her rehearsals. Mornings were best with the clear light pouring through the landing window, though evening glimpses of the moon made it easier to evoke the ambience of a nunnery. She'd come out of her flat and arrange herself on the bottom stair, one hand on each newel post. The best outfit she'd been able to root out was an old black nightdress bought when she'd auditioned for a part in *Separate Tables*. Its lacy straps and red lining didn't quite provide the right aura for the Mother Abbess character but the swish of it around her ankles took her straight into the role. A deep torso-filling breath and off she'd go. The tune would hover then reach up to resonate round the stairwell. It was impossible to judge one's own rendition but when your ears rang with the trill of the notes, when your diaphragm ached with vibration, when your mouth was round with vowels, you were surely on your way to success.

She'd had trouble choosing between interpretations of the part, Peggy Wood in the film or Lesley Garret in the stage production she'd read so much about? Peggy had the maturity but Lesley was perhaps a tad more elegant? Her own performance would, of course, be recognised as infinitely superior after Pearl Cooper's efforts bit the dust but she'd need to bring something entirely new to the role.

The Heiress, taking possession of her rehearsal space, had ruined everything. Deep despair was all she could expect and for some time it had clouded her world. But then *The Marsh Courier* had arrived.

'Shakespeare for All'. The project's advert had been tucked into the classifieds. Volunteers with an interest in drama were needed. The library had provided a copy of the Scottish Play and her ingenuity had provided the rest. She would keep up what practice she could manage for *The Sound of Music*, that was only right given her commitment to the part. It couldn't be long before Pearl Cooper succumbed to the demands of performance; the call could come at any moment. But in the meantime she had other fish to fry. By the time she got around to letting the Shakespeare Project know she was available to play Lady Macbeth, she'd be well rehearsed.

Blood was essential but tomato ketchup proved hopeless. The colour was good but it was too thick and slid off the knife in globs, not the droplets she wanted. The whole scene would be ruined if the blood didn't look genuine. Real blood would have been best but that meant raw meat, seeping into slimy wrapping paper with the nauseous smell of old coins. And meat meant facing George Hessop, the butcher, a dreadful man who leered at you over the sausages and made a request for one pork chop sound like a smutty suggestion.

It was a good time to prepare her scene. The Heiress had taken herself off some time ago, banging the front door with no thought for disturbing others. 'We don't want her sort of person to know what we're up to, now do we?' Daphne asked Nelson.

On the kitchen window sill Nelson interrupted his personal hygiene routine to stare at the white, cowled robe his mistress was wearing. He yawned widely.

'You might take more interest pusskins,' Daphne sniffed. 'It's time for two birds with one stone. Practice for me, and frights to scare off The Heiress. You'll suffer as much as I will if she doesn't pack her bags and go. She'll never leave us alone. I know that sort, a modern young woman with notions in her head and her legs never out of trousers. What she might do here just doesn't bear thinking about. We've nowhere else to go, you and I, now have we?'

Costume, that was the secret. Arrive at the auditions fully costumed and the director would be so impressed he'd send everyone else home. Not dear Harvey this time. He was far too busy to take on further commitments. The man in charge of the Shakespeare project was an unknown quantity, from the Education Office apparently, probably some young lad who would welcome her guidance.

She pulled the white, surgical gloves over her hands, stretched and pinged them into position. The stains splattered over her fingers were most convincing. Blades clinked and jangled as she scrabbled in the cutlery drawer for the bread knife. With shaking hands she dripped cochineal along its serrations.

'Out, out damned spot,' she whispered. She reached for the torch she'd attached to the cord which usually held her reading glasses. Slung under her throat the beam would throw an uplight on her face, hooding her eyes and making a dark cavern of her mouth.

She pulled the cowl over her head, straightened her shoulders and raised her chin to ensure every inch of four feet eleven was displayed to advantage. Then, with the bread knife soaking crimson poppies into her snowy gown, she glided to the door.

'Beginners to the stage please,' she said. 'And don't forget, Nelson, The Heiress's key in the lock is our cue. Break a leg darling.'

That couldn't be a car stopping outside, not when she was all set. Better just check. Leaving a trail of red drips on the carpet, she crossed the sitting room floor and peered through the net curtain. The window was spotted with rain but she could just make out a tubby little man walking away from a vehicle which hadn't made up its mind whether it was a car or a lorry. It hadn't decided whether to wear brown or cream either. The man looked up at the house, nodded and came along the garden path.

The doorbell rang. Daphne crept down the stairs. Whoever he was he couldn't be allowed to interrupt. It was unthinkable that her performance should be interrupted. Latecomers must wait for the interval. She flattened herself against the hall wall.

The doorbell rang again. Then the letter box opened framing two dark eyes. 'Anyone there?' a voice called.

Daphne held her breath. The letter box snapped shut. She peered through the spy hole. The man had stepped back and was shaking rain out of his hair. Behind him a white Mini sploshed to a stop and Samantha got out, followed by The Heiress. They were heading up the path.

Chapter 18

Earlier that day Alison had heard Daphne moving around her flat but she hadn't emerged so the morning had been quiet. Rain lashed at the windows and dripped off the branches of the mulberry tree. She had spent the time making a systematic search of the house for a sign of anything personal to May Kulman, clothes, cosmetics, clutter, something that conjured up the woman who had lived here.

Nothing. Not a scarf, hairbrush, or rolled up pair of tights could she find. It was just conceivable that the woman had taken all her clothes with her when she went 'up north' but she'd hardly need to take a passport, or any of the leave-behinds most people would own. Apart from ornaments and books in what must have been the public B&B rooms, it was as if the house had seen neither sight nor sound of her.

The house had its documents, utility bills, council tax receipts, home insurance policy, all neatly filed in the study desk. Mulberry House, authenticated by paper but of its owner, or rather its previous owner, there was no trace.

Only a few days ago, Mrs Kulman as a person hadn't featured much at all in her thoughts. Now, the frustration of discovering nothing about the woman was driving her mad.

Alison had told Jude she would make up her mind what to do with the house by the weekend but Friday evening was infiltrating Friday afternoon and still she was dithering.

Before she'd seen Mulberry House, her plans had been definite, sell the property to finance a new business and start a new life. But now she was here, ridiculous as it seemed, the house was tethering her, like a puppy with pleading eyes, waiting for her verdict.

It was impossible to think clearly indoor so after hours of searching, wandering from room to room, running her fingers along the bookshelves or staring at the ever-changing seascapes, she had come out for a walk. The rain had stopped but the air was damp and heavy.

Sell up or settle, settle or sell up? The words pounded through her head as she splashed along the lanes. Above her, The Grey Goose pub-sign creaked on its hinges. She thought about Thomas laying down linguistic law and sipping single malt. What an odd man he was. The two rooms she had seen in his large, comfortable house were full of things, yet empty of life. The precision drained all individuality from his possessions. She had found herself longing for a badly-folded newspaper or a glimpse of biscuit crumbs crunching their way along the wainscot. But the soaked-in muddles of ordinary living had been eliminated. The place could have been a private museum.

He'd behaved very strangely, one moment plying her with whisky and hanging on her every word, the next squirming in his armchair and avoiding eye-contact, as if she posed some kind of threat. When he'd spoken about his wife, it wasn't grief that filled his eyes but apprehension.

Sell up or settle, settle or sell up? How could she deal with Daphne Chiltern? Whatever she decided, how would her plans affect Jude?

The countryside butted against the village here, as it did in the landscape she was used to, but on the edge of The Marsh instead of drystone walls and open heather moorland, the fields formed a patchwork of lush greenery. She thought about being surrounded by water and what

Thomas had said about the Marsh's network of dykes and ditches.

She'd go as far as the church at the end of this lane and not turn for home until her mind was made up. But that was the whole point, where was home?

List the options, she told herself, get rid of the ones that don't appeal or aren't practical, make a decision and stick to it. All very well in theory but theories didn't allow for emotions, especially ones that crept up on you then clung like burdock burrs. The glimpses of her benefactor she'd gleaned were tantalising and made her desperate to know more. What was her own connection with this shadowy figure whose possessions had vanished and could not speak for her?

Alison crossed the gated, wooden bridge over a stream and went into the churchyard where departed citizens of the parish lay in the equality of death, the variable weathering on their gravestones the only difference between them. The small graves brought a lump to her throat. Agnes aged three months, safe in the arms of Jesus, Frederick beloved son, four years, Beatrice, six weeks. And what about all those unrecorded deaths, babies of the poor, who couldn't afford memorials? What was there to mark their short lives?

Some of these tombstones must commemorate smugglers. The two hundred years since a Captain Sebastian Marchant had completed his voyage was marked by a single light-yellow rose lying on the grass in front of his stone. A nineteenth century commander of the Dungeness battery was commemorated with a carved sailing ship, its sails encrusted now with lichen.

The choices these people made had disappeared with them but all their decisions had affected somebody else. Had the naval captain agonised over waving goodbye to his wife each time he sailed away? Had the smugglers thought about what would happen to their families if the Revenue men caught up with them?

She opened the church door and found herself in a nave no more than thirty feet long and flooded with light. She sat down in one of the pews and was pushing her thoughts into the silence when a low bass note thundered from the organ, long and insistent, transforming the tiny church into an immensity of sound. Alison gasped as the resonance barrelled around her, rolling and swelling inside her head. Just as she thought it would go on forever, a melody took over, three or four notes at first, repeated in a simple pattern then joined by lower and higher patterns of sound. A quartet of harmonies soared and descended. This wasn't the sort of music Alison usually liked but the precision, the mathematical intensity of it overshadowed thought. She closed her eyes and let the sound carry her.

When the final note had dwindled, Alison opened her eyes. The organist looked over her shoulder. 'Oh dear,' she said. She swivelled round and slotted her feet into the pair of gold sandals waiting by the foot pedals. 'I didn't realise anyone else was here.' She smiled, a wide-faced grin under a shaggy fringe and mane of blonde hair, most of which had escaped from the bright pink scrunchy perched on top of her head. Dangling ear-rings glittered as she moved. 'Once JSB takes hold,' she went on, pushing a lock of hair out of her eyes, 'I forget the world exists.'

'JSB?' Alison said.

'Johann Sebastian Bach,' the woman explained. 'Wonderful.' She pulled the cover over the organ keyboard then swung her legs across the seat. 'I'm taking the opportunity of having fun with the *Art of Fugue*, after delivering Uncle Sebastian's rose, that is.'

'The yellow Charles Darwin on the sea captain's grave?'

The woman's eyes widened. 'You know about roses, do you?'

Alison hesitated. 'I used to,' she said. 'Was he was an ancestor of yours, the captain?'

'My husband's great-great-great, etc. etc.' the woman said. 'It's the anniversary of his death today. Hence the rose and a chance to run JSB through his paces.' She pushed her fingers through her hair. 'Fugue means flight in Italian. Very appropriate given that you've flown here from somewhere or other. She held out her hand. I'm Samantha Walsh, by the way, well Samantha Marchant too but I usually stick to my professional name. I'm a photographer.'

'Alison Draper,' Alison said shaking Samantha's hand.

'Well, you had to be, didn't you?.'

'I'm sorry?'

'Alison Draper, inheritor of Mulberry House.'

Alison frowned. 'How did you know who I am?'

Samantha laughed. 'The Marsh is the gift of the sea, remember, and populated by news-bearing mermaids. Rumour has it you'll be selling up. I hope you won't.'

'Why not?'

'From where I'm sitting you look like the new blood we need around here.' Samantha dug into her large straw bag and handed over an advertising flyer. 'The summer classes starts next week. Aromatherapy, very relaxing. New students always welcome.'

'Menil Institute, Rye,' Alison read aloud. 'Is that where Thomas Carr teaches?'

'The very same. But there there's lots more on offer than boring family history.'

'I'm not very good at that sort of thing, groups and suchlike.'

'You'll be a Cardamon type then,' Samantha said, 'straightforward but inclined to be detached.' She hitched the bag onto her shoulder. 'I'm a Clary Sage, wise and foolish in equal quantities.' She laughed. 'Sorry. Aromatherapy is my current hobby. It's an ancient art with modern uses, like classifying people. As to being good at things, it's very un-English, don't you think?'

'Nobody likes a smart-arse you mean?'

Samantha grinned. 'You'll do fine,' she said. 'Have you got your car with you?'

'I haven't got a car at the moment.'

'You'd better let me give you a lift back then. I grabbed the Mini before Tony could bag it for his parish visits. He's the vicar, by the way, at St. George's down the road, this place and a couple of others. The days of one vicar one church are long gone.' She led the way outside. 'Can't have you wandering the lanes at the mercy of the Marsh witches.'

'They're worse than the mermaids are they?'

'Definitely.' Samantha took a large key from her bag, locked the church door behind them and pointed to a grubby, white Mini parked beyond the bridge. 'That's me. Hop in.'

Alison dug her fingernails into the sides of her seat as the little car hurtled past The Grey Goose, whizzed round corners and sliced through puddles. Samantha's driving technique owed much to the Mr Toad School of Motoring and did not include keeping her eyes on the road. It was raining hard again now and the wipers skimmed water droplets from the screen.

'Seismic shock round here,' Samantha said, slamming on the brakes at the Give Way sign on the junction with Main Street. 'Mrs Kulman getting herself killed like that. Some place called Bakewell by all accounts.'

Alison's heart lurched. What the hell had May Kulman been doing in her own backyard? She swallowed and said, 'Mrs Kulman died in Derbyshire?'

'Is that where it is?' Samantha stabbed the gearstick in the direction of first gear. 'Whoa there,' she protested as the car lunged forward. 'Bakewell was more of a shock than the accident. Frozen north and all that. Funeral was there too, very odd. Nobody round here got an invite.' She grinned. 'But the biggest shock of all was you, a complete stranger. The whole place is still reeling.'

'Ditto,' Alison said. And there I was, she thought, imagining a clean slate. She pictured the look on the poodle owner's face, remembered the way the woman in the shop had spoken and the taxi driver avoiding eye-contact.

The rain was bouncing off the pavements as Samantha swung the car into Marine Drive and screeched to a halt outside Mulberry House. 'Don't want to worry you,' she said, 'but there's a right old banger parked outside your house and a very odd-looking bloke lurking by your front door. Hunchback by the looks, or is that a rucksack? Do you know him?'

PART 3

Fugue - a period of escape, mental or physical, from one's usual environment.

Chapter 19

It was quiet in the Netherstone charity shop and muggy after yesterday's rain. Bryn hovered by a rack of shirts, enjoying the warm fug of the place, the undemanding atmosphere of second-hand things with nothing to prove. What he needed now was playing-the-blues gear, off-pitch from his old life.

These unambitious shirts for instance. He ran his thumb over the chequered fabric which was rubbed and beginning to fray at the cuffs. Perfect.

'What d'you reckon? Blue or purple?'

The plump, grey-haired woman who had planted herself in front of him wore a grimy tracksuit. Dangling from the hangers she waved aloft, were two floaty dresses, the sort of clobber women wore for posh do's and went from being 'I just had to have it, darling' to 'this old rag' after one outing. Bryn hesitated.

'Not the kind of garment I normally go for,' the woman confessed into his ear. 'Only I thought I'd make a bit of an effort. Can't just throw on any old thing, now can you?'

Throwing on any old thing sounded good to Bryn. He concentrated on the stain dribbling down the curve of her jacket zip. 'S'pose not,' he muttered.

'I've got this friend, you see,' the woman sighed. 'A dear lady but she's always dressed up to the nines. It's depressing.'

She was on his wavelength now. The picture that popped into his mind was of Sylvia, hand on hip in inspection mode. 'Not quite cutting the sartorial mustard today, are we husband mine?' she was saying. Bryn saw her off with a shake of his head.

'Which one do you like best yourself?' he asked the woman.

'I was rather relying on you,' she said.

The man he used to be would have run a mile from no-win questions like this. The new Bryn was aiming to be made of sterner stuff. 'I'd go for the blue,' he said. 'To match your eyes.'

The woman's face creased into a smile. 'Bingo!' She reached to shake his hand. 'I'm Pru Perkins.' Her grip was firm. 'Haven't seen you in here before. I know most of the regulars.'

'Bryn Stanfield,' he said. It was getting easier. With any luck the name would soon be second nature. 'Recent arrival in these parts.'

'From the north perhaps? Not many accents get past me. Where are you staying?'

'Place called Mulberry House. D'you know it?

Her eyes widened. 'Aaaaah,' she said. 'It's you then. You're not very tall it's true, but you're nicely rounded and you don't look in the least bit peculiar.' She beamed at him, thrust the purple creation into the rack of shirts and strode towards the counter, the blue dress wafting in her wake.

He watched her haggling over the price. Nicely rounded? Not in the least peculiar? What was all that about? A connection with Mulberry House, apparently. Something very odd was going on there.

Driving south yesterday, he'd thought of the house on the edge of the beach as a bolt hole. He remembered gable-end windows, a wide entrance hall, and hearing Father's snores trumpeting over the rhythms of the sea in one of the front bedrooms.

It had taken some finding. Vague memories weren't much to go on. There was every chance the area had been re-developed out of recognition long ago. But as he drove through the rain along the coast roads, everything was as he remembered, the same sturdy three-storey terraces, bungalows with rendered walls, Martello Towers built to keep a look-out for Napoleon. The place was almost unchanged, waiting for his return.

And then he'd found it, Mulberry House. It was smaller than he'd remembered but places not visited since childhood had a habit of shrinking.

No-one had answered his ring. He'd been on the point of giving up and looking for somewhere else to stay. The place probably wasn't a B&B any longer, there was no sign up. That sharp-nosed landlady could be long dead and the lady who'd done all the running around too, Miss Chilburn was it? No Chiltern. Fancy coming up with that after all these years.

Standing in the porch, he could swear someone was hovering behind the door, someone who held their breath when he peered through the letter box into the dark hall, someone who chose not to answer the doorbell.

Rain dripped through the trellis of the porch, dribbling down his neck, soaking his shoulders. He'd felt like that photo of the Blues singer, St. Louis Jimmy with his hands drooped by his sides like dangling bags of sugar and his eyes dark with desolation. Finding a B&B shut up couldn't be compared to the troubles poor old Jimmy suffered, but the epiphany that had carried Bryn from the north to the south coast was definitely not doing the business.

And then the car had arrived. Two women ran up the garden path. The younger one, wearing those dopey cut-off trousers women liked so much, held a large floppy bag over her head. The other one, older and much less tousled, pulled up her collar and stared at him.

'Can I help?' she said.

'Do we know you?' tousle head added.

'I stayed here once, you see,' Bryn faltered. 'Years ago. Do you still do B&B?' From the murky depths of his old life Sylvia was sneering that she loved it when he was masterful.

Tousle head frowned. 'B&B? Not for some time.'

The other woman had waved a key towards the door. 'It's awfully wet,' she said. 'We'd better go inside.'

'Alison,' the younger woman protested, 'we need to be a tad careful. Neither of us has ever set eyes on him before. He could be anyone.'

'He could, couldn't he?' Alison laughed. 'Come to that, Samantha, an hour ago I'd never set eyes on you.'

And what about that extraordinary malarkey? Miss Chiltern, no less, alive and very much kicking, though she'd obviously lost the plot, poor old soul. Draped in bloodied sheets, she'd wailed at the bottom of the stairs, her face a white mask. He and the two women had stood there and gawped while a load of weird, historical stuff came pouring out of the old bat's mouth Then the poor soul had run out of steam and collapsed in a heap.

'If you have that effect on Daphne,' the woman called Alison said, 'you can't be all bad.'

Between them they'd managed to get Miss Chiltern up the stairs to her flat and through to the bedroom. Samantha, the younger woman, seemed to know her quite well and stayed until another friend arrived. Come to think of it, that friend could have been the woman who'd just bought the blue dress. He'd only got a glimpse of her last night. By the time she'd turned up, he was putting sheets on the bed in the same room he and Father had shared all those years back.

Where Alison Draper fitted in was a mystery but she was friendly enough and fortunately not the nosey type. The opening bars of his new life had been more Ragtime than Hard Bop but none the worse for that.

Kitted out for the foreseeable future, Bryn left the charity shop and wandered along the High Street, whistling *Maple Street Rag*. A shop sign caught his eye, Dandy Candy. Somebody knew their stuff here. This was how a sweetshop ought to be. In the window, white and dark chocolates, arranged to look like pieces on a chess board, were flanked on one side by cascades of liquorice torpedoes and on the other by wedges of pink-and-white coconut ice. Through the door he could see shelves loaded with sweet jars, and ranks of chocolate bars. Irresistible.

The teenage girl behind the counter had pink stripes in her pale hair. She sat with her back to the shop, cradling a mobile phone against her ear. 'She's a right cow,' she was drawling as Bryn went in.

'Candy is Dandy but liquor is quicker,' he told a display of classy-looking chocolate boxes.

The girl looked over her shoulder, paused mid-sentence and lifted one eyebrow. 'You having a laugh?' she said.

'A line from Dorothy Parker, I think?'

The girl looked him up and down. 'Whatever,' she said.

That's told you mate, Bryn thought. She'll have heard that a thousand times. Heading for the pic'n'mix, he was about to pass the jars, fat and glinting on their shelves, when he stopped. His heart pounded. It was bound to happen. He ought to have been prepared. Every jar was labelled with the familiar red and gold sticker, Prossers of Felstone. Nothing for it but to face them, Cough Candy Swirls, Liquorice and Cranberry Chews, Lime Sherbets. He closed his eyes and heard the machinery that had created them, saw their sugary beginnings, remembered disputes about wrapper designs. Guilt he'd expected but not this horrible sense of loss. He turned away. His taste buds might be pleading, but he couldn't set them loose on Prossers's stuff. Not yet.

'You just looking or what?' the girl said.

It was her hair that decided him. 'Two hundred grams of coconut ice, please.'

With a sigh, she rested the phone on the counter, pulled the tray of coconut ice towards her and reached for a pair of tongs.

If nostalgia had a taste it must be coconut ice, Bryn decided as he made his way to where he'd parked the pick-up. The cloying sweetness and the flakes of coconut stuck between your teeth pointed straight back to childhood Christmases. Whatever else Santa forgot to put in your stocking, the pink-and-white bar in its crinkly wrapper was always pushed into the toe. He used to save it until the end of the school holiday when Mother was agonising over the bathroom scales and the dustbin lid was pivoting on festive waste. Coconut ice could be relied on to sweeten the horrible prospect of another school term.

What now? The day was his own, spreading into whatever he chose to make it. Dungeness then. He found the Tourist Centre and bought a local guidebook and Ordnance Survey map. The road he needed ran close to the coast, beside the route of the Romney, Hythe and Dymchurch Light Railway. A glimpse of the little train was just what he needed.

Chapter 20

Daphne made it to the bus stop with minutes to spare. Her plan to go into Rye had meant missing her morning swim but her marine sisters would understand. After the debacle of Lady Macbeth, she had to get away. Samantha and Pru had advised staying in bed but what could they know about the despair after a botched performance?

Across the road, by that shop she wasn't going to look at, a group of people were waving banners with SOS painted in dreadful shades of red and yellow. Not a good choice, particularly under a dull, grey sky. Yellow needed constant vigilance. Pearl Cooper was one of the number. Polyester slacks were hardly in sympathy with her hips and all that shouting wouldn't be doing her voice any good, now would it?

'Daphne.' It was Samantha. 'You didn't feel like a lie-in then?'

Daphne shuddered. Meeting one of last night's audience was the very last thing one wanted.

'You will sign our petition, won't you?' Samantha thrust a clipboard under her nose. 'We're doing our best to save the local shops being gobbled up by a supermarket mammoth. Pete Jenkins, George Hessop, the mini-market, they're all under threat.'

'What do we want?' chorused the group of protesters. 'Save Our Shops. When do we want it?'

'I'm on my way to Rye,' Daphne said, turning aside. 'To consult the solicitor as you suggested. Here's the bus.' And before Samantha had time to argue, she clambered aboard.

It was naughty of her to sidestep the issue like that she told herself as the bus drew away, especially when Samantha had been so kind. But after the way he'd behaved, being gobbled up by a mammoth was just what Mr Jenkins deserved.

The journey across the Marsh was a favourite even in this misty weather. Jumbles of sheep nibbling away, lattices of drainage channels hidden behind lush greenery, crops ripening in the distance, all framed by the bus window. It reminded Daphne of a storyboard that nice young man had shown her, the one who'd directed *Anglepoise.* Floyd was it? He'd made coloured sketches of each scene to ensure an integrated whole, whatever that was. She'd so enjoyed delivering the charlady's one line, especially when Floyd confided he'd never seen anyone bestow such quirky liveliness on a dustpan and brush. But then she'd always had a way with props, hadn't she?

How would the storyboard of her own life look? The early frames in primary colours, clear and uncomplicated, the later ones muted and more shadowy? And what about the scene in the middle? The crucial scene on which all the others depended?

*

It's a fairground. Loops of coloured light bulbs, hurdy-gurdy music, the smell of candyfloss and hotdog onions. Her life is just hours away from tying itself to Douglas, immaculate fingernails, polished brogues, sexless Douglas who's willing to take on her surname because that's what's required if you set out to marry a Chiltern heiress.

She's escaped the marquee on the lawn, the champers in buckets, the engagement ring in its box, and is out with the village girls, learning to shriek on the rides, going over the top on the Big Wheel.

She's in candy-striped, glazed poplin, over layers of underskirt stiffened with sugar solution, sticky on thighs bare above stocking tops.

On her own in a dodgem car, she's hunched over the steering wheel, clinging on for dear life, bumped and bashed on all sides. Buddy Holly's *That'll Be The Day* throbs around her, electricity sparks red from overhead wires.

A hero in tight, black jeans and flapping shirt, is winging to her rescue, leaping from car to car, to land on her bumper. He's leaning over her, taking the wheel with one hand. 'What's all this then?' he says in her ear. 'A lovely lady all on her own. We can't have that, now can we?'

He's tall, swarthy. Sunburned arms. An anchor tattoo on his wrist. Grimy fingernails. He grins at her, takes control. She's trembling, praying the ride will never end.

And later he's a smoky reflection, behind her own, in the hall of distorting mirrors. Breathing on her neck, hot and tangy, he smells of cigarettes, sweat and spicy aftershave. He's on his break he says. He can't get her out of his mind. His hands are firm on her waist. She leans back into his arms. His caravan is behind the hoop-la stall he whispers.

*

The bus jerked to a halt. Daphne blinked back tears. Best not think of fairgrounds.

The town of Rye always put her in mind of a backdrop for a costume drama, the sort with wigs like piled-up meringue and artificial beauty spots. Delicious. The shop displays were so pretty and every street had a wonderful air of olde worlde elegance.

She found the book shop Samantha had described and next to it a large square building with multi-paned windows either side of the front door. On the wall was a gleaming brass plate: Higton, Balfour and Higton, Solicitor-Advocate.

Daphne gripped her handbag, the serious black leather one as befitted her errand. Her grey tweed suit was rather warmer an outfit than the weather demanded but a solemn occasions called for sober attire.

Was a solicitor's office a public building? Could she just walk in? She looked away and stared at the bookshop window, biting her cheek. She must stop doing that. The place in her mouth was getting sore.

This was silly. Why was she hesitating? She was a mature woman, entitled to look out for herself. What could he do to her, an important legal man behind a desk? Her tongue probed the sore place. Perhaps she should she have rung for an appointment? Of course she should. That's how these things were done. Solicitors were busy people. You couldn't just drop in when you felt like it.

But she didn't feel like it did she? Another day would do. She'd go back home, see if she could persuade Nelson into having a cuddle, then ring for an appointment. The number would be in the phone book, if she could remember where it was.

On second thoughts, it was a pity to waste the whole trip. Why not visit the Art Gallery. It was advertising an exhibition of work by Edward Burra. Had she heard of him?

The first pictures weren't very attractive, dark colours and people not at all at their best. She decided she'd just pop into the next room to see if things cheered up a bit.

This was much better. The darling man had been a theatrical. Look at those costume designs and over there a model of a stage set. Something called *Miracle in the Gorbals* apparently. Wherever the Gorbals were they looked completely dreadful and in dire need of a miracle or two.

Carmen of course was quite a different matter. His sketch for the set showed foreign-looking buildings bathed in blazing sunlight. The costumes designed for Frasquita and Mercedes had wide, rippling shoulders and were tightly fitted over waist and hips before falling to mid-calf, in fringed cascades. What bold expressions he'd given the models. Game for anything these two. They wouldn't have collapsed with exhaustion if an audience didn't appreciate their talents.

Back outside, it was spitting with rain. By the bookshop, Daphne scrabbled in her bag for her waterproof poncho. Its salmon pink wouldn't do the tweed any favours but there were times when colour co-ordination had to take a back seat.

'Daph?' It was Pru.

Daphne frowned. 'Are you following me?'

'Don't be daft.' Pru took her arm. 'Why would I do that? I've come to pick up Jim's prescription. The chemist has a delivery service but the usual woman's on holiday and her replacement is, well, never mind. You don't want to hear about Jim's ailments. Neither do I, come to that, but that's life. One minute you're starry eyed at the altar, the next it's bunions and bilious attacks.' She hesitated, glancing sideways at Daphne. 'Are you sure you're well enough to be out? You had such an awful time last night.' Before Daphne could invent a response she went on,' Are you busy? For lunch, I mean?'

'Not especially, why?'

Pru stopped by an alleyway between two shops and glanced around as if she were worried about being overheard. 'Let's try that new coffee shop,' she said, 'down by the harbour.'

The waitress in the coffee shop was elusive. 'The larger I get the more invisible I become,' Pru said, waving an imperious hand. 'Did you find what you were looking for, in the book shop?'

Daphne drew in her breath. She'd hoped to keep Pru out of the solicitor thing but she had no talent for unrehearsed lies. 'I wasn't planning to go into the bookshop,' she said.

'You were gazing in the window when I spotted you. Very immersed in something or other. You didn't hear me when I first called.'

Daphne re-arranged the sachets of sugar in their dish. 'I was looking for my pac-a-mac.'

'Sorry,' Pru said. 'I don't want to pry.'

'Before that I'd been to the exhibition in the Art Gallery.'

'You came into Rye just to look at some old paintings?'

'If you must know I had planned to see the solicitor.' And out it all came, the visit to Samantha, her suggestion to find out all she could about May's will.

Pru frowned. 'And what did he say?'

'What did who say?'

'Lynwood Higton, silly, the solicitor.'

'I never even got inside the door.'

Pru covered Daphne's hand with her own. 'You should have asked me to come with you,' she said. 'Not that it would have done any good.'

'Why ever not?'

'Because Daph, the solicitor wouldn't have told you anything.'

'Samantha just thought...'

'She's a lovely girl, talented and thoughtful but she really doesn't know much about this kind of thing does she?'

'And you do?'

'Hear me out and you might think so.'

Listening to Pru tell her about the encounter with Thomas, Daphne softened towards her friend. Bossy or not, she was on her side.

'So you see,' Pru said. 'He's agreed to see us. Beard the lion in his den, remember?'

Daphne stared out the window. A couple of rowing boats lay high and dry at the edge of the harbour, waiting for the tide to release them from the mud. Across the empty channel stood one of those abandoned Martello Towers, hardly recognisable under a thick tangle of ivy. 'Was yours like that?' she said. 'When you first bought it?'

'We need to strike while the iron's hot,' Pru said. 'Before he's had chance to get his act together. Are you game?'

Chapter 21

Still whistling *Maple Leaf Rag*, Bryn drove towards Dungeness, a tongue of land thrust at the sea. Unlike his native landscape, punctured by craggy outcrops and walls of rock, this place was open, mile after mile of it, an empty stage waiting for the gig to begin.

After he'd passed the low-level buildings of Lydd Airport, the skyline was dominated by the Nuclear Power Station. It was a towering presence, like enormous building bricks abandoned by the pylon giants that strode away dragging the electricity cables. Bryn laughed. Whimsy wasn't his usual line but nothing about this headland was usual. At any moment a redcoat might emerge from that ruined fort, or an excise man crunch across the shingle in pursuit of smugglers.

He drew up beside one of the lighthouses, a dark column topped by a lantern room with lattice windows. An information board said it had been replaced as a functioning beacon decades back, but was still open to the public by arrangement.

'The present lighthouse was completed in 1961.' The speaker, a round-faced blond lad who looked about ten, was standing beside the pick-up. His arms hung stiffly at his sides. Bony ankles poked out of jeans several sizes too small. Wary eyes glinted behind a huge pair of specs.

'Is that right?' Bryn said.

The boy stared past him. 'I just said so, didn't I?' He left a space between each word as if it needed room to breathe.

'This was the first lighthouse to be built by Trinity House for over fifty years. His Royal Highness the Duke of Gloucester opened it in 1961.'

He's swallowed the guidebook, Bryn thought. That or the lad was a reincarnation of Father. 'You weren't around to see the opening then?' he teased.

Staring at his feet, the boy frowned. 'I was born in two thousand and four,' he said. 'At seven-thirty a.m. on May the ninth, a Tuesday. My star sign is Taurus the Bull which means I am placid but sometimes obstinate.'

'Not a complete bundle of laughs then?' Bryn suggested.

With the toe of his trainer, the boy scuffed a circle in the sandy soil. 'If that's a joke,' he said. 'Mum says to explain that I don't understand them.'

'You live here do you?' Bryn said, 'on Dungeness?'

'I am not allowed to give out personal information, Mum says.'

'Your Mum is quite right,' Bryn told him. 'My mistake. I'm sorry.'

As if he was reminding himself, the boy said, 'People say they are sorry when they have done something wrong.'

'Jake?' A blonde woman was calling from the garden of the bungalow opposite. Under a paint-smeared boiler suit her figure was curvy. 'I've made some tea, if you'd like some.' The boy ran towards her, his gait awkward, as if he was still getting to know his limbs. Bryn followed but stopped at the edge of the garden. It was an amazing sight, full of colour and shapes made not by plants and flowers but by what could only be called sculptures, a metre-high tree made from children's plastic spades in bright colours, a driftwood woman struggling to free herself from a tangle of fishing nets, a huge clock face with shell numbers and tent-peg hands.

'F-and-J.' The woman was beside him, her eyes level with his own, dark grey and smiling from a round face, the mirror-image of the lad's. The breeze lifted strands of her hair and played with them. Bryn looked away.

'F and what?' he said.

'F and J. Flotsam and jetsam.' Her voice was mellow, muted alto sax. 'Made from stuff I find on the beach. Jake helps, when he's in the mood. What d'you think?'

Was this a trick question, Bryn thought, the sort with only wrong answers? 'They're very....' He cleared his throat. 'Sorry, I'm not good at...'

'Don't worry,' the woman said. She smiled. 'If I could find the right words, I wouldn't need to make things.'

'Fourteen ticks for my maths,' the boy called from the doorway.

'Only one wrong today. You've done well,' the woman said. 'Shall we have tea out here?'

'The temperature is twenty-three point five degrees Celsius,' Jake said. 'Warm enough to have our drink outdoors.'

'Bring the tray, will you please?' the woman said.

For several moments, Jake stood, frowning. Then he said, 'I will, after I've done my correction.'

'I teach him at home,' the woman explained. 'It's easier that way.'

Easier for her, or the lad? Bryn wondered. Taking the easiest path was a route he, of all people, could understand.

'Fancy a cup of Earl Grey?' the woman said.

Bryn looked at his watch. 'I ought to go.' Best let her think someone was waiting for him. What he wanted from this place was freedom, a landscape which made no demands. People complicated things.

The woman was smiling at his hesitation. 'Jake and I are fairly harmless. I'm Hannah by the way, Hannah Sherwin.'

'But I might not be,' Bryn said, 'harmless I mean. My name's Brian.' He swallowed. 'I mean, Bryn, Bryn Stanfield.'

'You've more or less passed the Jake test already, Bryn,' Hannah said. 'Three mugs on the tray would clinch it. He won't be long.' She rescued a strand of hair and pushed it behind her ear. Bryn gazed at his feet. If she'd noticed the gaff he'd made over his name, she wasn't letting on. He found himself imagining her in the blue floaty dress.

Jake's progression with the tray was slow and measured. Hannah did not move to help him as the teapot slid from one side of the tray to the other and the mugs clinked. There were three of them. Hannah smiled at Bryn.

'It's polite to offer biscuits,' Jake said to Bryn. The mugs and milk jug lurched towards the edge of the tray as he lowered it onto the picnic table. 'If you like biscuits I'll go and get some. Mum doesn't eat biscuits. Biscuits are fattening.'

'How about some of this,' Bryn said. He pulled the bag of coconut ice from his pocket, grabbed Jake's hand and dropped the bag into it. The lad shrank back, flung the bag on the ground and dashed behind a castle made from beach buckets with crenellated tops.

Bryn left the coconut ice where it had landed and went to examine a mermaid with a doll's torso and a seaweed tail. Best let well alone while Hannah reprimanded the lad. Embarrassing for her, an outburst like that in front of a stranger. What a fuss his own father had made about what he called misdemeanours of manners.

'You will apologise this minute,' he could hear his red-faced father demanding. Useless to ask which took precedence, truth or politeness. When Aunt Edith had asked if her new frock suited her, an honest opinion was evidently not required. It was a lesson he still had trouble with.

But Hannah was not demanding. Looking perfectly calm, she was kneeling a yard from the beach-bucket castle speaking slowly and quietly. After some minutes, Jake's head appeared above the parapet, followed slowly by the rest of him. He stared at Bryn and stepped round his mother, careful not to touch her. Only when the lad had reached the bungalow did Hannah get up and go back to the table.

'Your tea's getting cold, Bryn,' she said. 'Milk?'

Bryn sat beside her and took the mug she offered. 'Yes please,' he said, 'and sugar if you have some.'

She retrieved the coconut ice and put the bag on the table. 'A sweet tooth then?'

' I'm afraid so, yes.'

'Do you have children?' she said. Bryn shook his head. 'If you did,' she said softly, 'would you apologise for them having blond hair or blue eyes? Make excuses for their shoe size or the date they were born?' Her expression was uncertain. 'You wouldn't do that, would you? Those things are beyond control.'

She was looking straight at him. This time he didn't look away. She said, 'You'll be wondering what that's got to do with the way Jake behaved just now. Behaviour can be, should be, controlled. If they're going to fit into the world we've made for them, children have to be taught to behave properly.'

This was a considered speech, Bryn thought, well-rehearsed and often aired.

'Jake lives by inbuilt rules he has no choice about,' she said. 'He's no more able to change them than I am to stop the tide turning.'

'And by offering him the bag of sweets I broke these rules?'

She nodded, sniffed and wiped the corners of her eyes with the cuff of her boiler suit. 'One of his rules is that nobody may touch him. Another is that food touched by anyone else is dirty.'

'Dirty?'

'It's not logical, I know. But unless Jake has taken the food from the supermarket shelf himself, he can't eat it.'

'So my sweets?'

'Exactly.' She shrugged her shoulders and held out her hands. 'There are plenty of posh-sounding labels, all of them created by clever and well-meaning people. But Dyspraxia, Autism, Asperger's Syndrome, are just that, labels. They don't provide a plan of action. He's a little boy tethered to a set of rules which will never let him go.'

'Tethering horses in a field can make their necks sore,' Jake said. Bryn hadn't seen him coming. The lad held two plates in one hand and a packet of biscuits in the other. He sat down, slid two biscuits from the packet and arranged them on the plate so they didn't touch each other. On the other plate was a pink Post-it note with 'offer a biscuit to visitors' written on it.

'Do you think Bryn would like to see my paintings?' Hannah asked Jake.

Jake wiped his mouth with the back of his hand. 'You should ask him, Mum, not me,' he said. 'I can't tell you what he would like.'

'You're an artist?' Bryn said. 'As well as a sculptor?'

Hannah nodded. 'I may look as if I'm doing a spot of decorating but art in various guises is my thing. Sometimes I think that might be an easier way to make a living.' She grinned. 'You're welcome to see my stuff.'

Here we go again, Bryn thought. Nothing was ever straightforward. What exactly did she want from him? Tea in the garden was one thing, going into her home was another. And what did he know about painting and such? He tried to push back his chair but it stuck on the grass. 'Bit dodgy isn't it?' he said, forcing a grin. 'Inviting strangers into your home?'

'Mum works in the studio over there,' Jake said, waving his arm in the air. 'It's not her home.'

'Everyone's a potential customer,' Hannah said. 'Anyway,' she pointed towards the bungalow, 'our security system is very efficient.' Two large geese were waddling towards them. 'Meet Dantë and Beatrice.'

A poncy foreign accent now. Bryn gave the chair a serious shove and got up. 'Another time,' he said. Negotiating the slalom of sculptures, he scrambled towards the gate. 'Thanks for the drink.'

'You're very welcome, Bryn,' she called after him. 'I hope you'll come and see us again.'

You're an idiot, he told himself as he climbed into the pick-up. Now the bloody woman thinks you're scared of geese.

Chapter 22

What to do with the photographs, Thomas wondered? Dozens of them all over the house. Silver frames littered every horizontal surface, Ingrid in evening dress at the Hunt Ball, suntanned in a bikini in the south of France, at Ascot with a huge confection on her head. Always alone, queen of the picture plane. The only other creatures she'd ever allowed to share her limelight were horses. Most of the equine photos were still displayed in what she'd called her den, along with the rosettes, the certificates, the silver cups and all the paraphernalia that defined her life on horseback. From Pony-Club to Olympic hopes, it was all still there, a shrine he was avoiding.

When she was alive, sitting across the table at meals, blowing him a goodnight kiss as she disappeared into her bedroom, he'd hardly noticed this intrusion of images but now everywhere he went her eyes confronted him. Not in accusation, she had little right to that, but in cool appraisal, her head forever tilted with the question, and now what?

'You know Ingrid Ericson, don't you?' someone had said at a party. 'The publisher's daughter?'

And there they were, he with an unpublished novel in the drawer beside a pile of rejections slips, she carrying another man's child, a married man whose position in the government precluded doing the honourable thing.

Like Speyside single malt, she was chill-filtered and light honey blonde, charming and haughty in equal measure. The sight of her mounted on her dressage horse had men drooling. Blonde hair confined in a snood beneath the black riding hat, a figure hugged by the riding jacket, white-jodphurred thighs disappearing into shiny black boots and completely in control of the power between her legs.

A Girl Like You, or something by Queen throbbed through her dressage routine. Midnight, that glossy, black beast, responded to her lightest touch with prancing hooves, surmounted by white ankle supports, delicate as the toes of Scottish dancers between crossed swords.

She was a trophy wife he had been proud to win, an ice-maiden patroness in the tournament of life. Even his father had been impressed by their marriage. 'Your mother would have been pleased,' was the highest of compliments. Dead from puerperal fever three days after his birth, his mother had hovered over his childhood, a ghostly, mythical influence. On his sixth birthday, he'd overheard his father talking about him to one of the relatives summoned to salvage the occasion. 'I'm not sure he'll ever amount to much, poor little chap, especially without his mother here to drag him up to scratch.'

'And here I am, still trying to make the grade, aren't I girl?' he said to Nell. The spaniel barked and stuck her head in the cardboard box Thomas had found to house the photographs. 'The hand that rocks the cradle, or doesn't.'

No cradle had been needed for Ingrid's baby. No-one admitted to cause and effect – riding point-to-point, miscarriage. By then, marriage lines imprisoned them. 'Beastly luck darling,' Ingrid had said. 'But no reason not to enjoy life.' The pact they'd made meant freedom of a sort. Divorce was never mentioned. Failure at anything had never been on Ingrid's agenda and his second novel was simmering in notebooks. That, like the baby, had never materialised.

Time to bury it all.

He shoved the thought of Gerald Thornly's implied threats to the back of his mind, rescued the box from Nell's attentions and folded back the flaps. The Hunt Ball photo he'd leave in the sitting room. No photos at all would look suspicious but the others he scooped up and heaped into the box. He was summoning the willpower to make a start on Ingrid's den when the phone rang. If that creep Thornly was chancing his arm again, a flea in the ear was all he'd get.

'Dr Carr? I'm calling in that favour,' Pru Perkins announced. 'From your drive.'

And under a Marsh mist, billowing and rolling, there she was, phoning him from her beat-up Peugeot. Daft Daphne sat beside her. The pair of them emerged from the car, one bulky as a hay bale, the other diminutive beneath a flapping plastic raincoat, like some other-worldly creature caught in the act of metamorphosis.

'It's customary to send a herald ahead to declare an invasion,' Thomas, on his doorstep, told the pair of them.

'For herald, read mobile phone,' Mrs Perkins said.

The contents of the cardboard box slithered and clunked as he shoved it into the sitting room before ushering the women in to his study.

'I am rather busy,' he said. 'As you see.' He indicated the neat piles of papers covering the desk top and piled up on the chairs, the computer screen with its spreadsheets which he'd abandoned when the mood to eliminate Ingrid had got the better of him. In the midst of all this evidence of crucial activity, they might do the decent thing and depart. 'It's that time of year, I'm afraid. Exams to mark. You know how it is.'

'All the more reason for you to take a break then,' Mrs Perkins said. 'We can't have you overtiring yourself, now can we?' She hooked a heap of papers from one of the chairs, and dropped them on the floor. 'We'll ask Daphne to sit here, shall we?' she puffed as she straightened up.

Daphne Chiltern looked at the chair as if it might bite her. 'We could come back later?' she ventured, folding her mac over her arm. 'Another time, perhaps?'

'That's most understanding of you, Miss Chiltern.' Thomas said, rescuing the exam papers Pru had dislodged.

But the Perkins woman was not to be deflected. 'And I'll perch on the window sill,' she said. 'What a lovely view of the garden from here, and the stables. It's sad to see them without their horses.'

Faced with an opponent who knew much about the art of allusion but little of warfare indentures, capitulation was the only tactic. 'What can I do for you?' he said.

Mrs Perkins stared round the room, at the paintings of coats of arms hanging round the walls, the diagram of medieval combat beside the door, the miniature knight in armour on the mantelpiece. She smiled. 'Discretion always was the better part of valour, wasn't it?'

Outside the door, Nell whined

'Is that your dog?,' piped Daphne C.

'Best see to her,' Pru said firmly.

Reluctant to leave them in here on their own, Thomas wondered about turning off the computer but mind-reader Perkins was on the case.

'Don't you worry about us, Dr Carr,' she said. 'When you get back, everything will be just as you left it.'

But that was no guarantee, Thomas thought as he let Nell into the garden, that everything would remain unscrutinised.

Whatever Mrs P had said to Daphne in his absence had galvanised the woman into speech by the time he got back. 'I'd be very grateful, Dr Carr,' she said, regarding him with soulful eyes, 'for some clarification, the exact wording of Mrs Kulman's will, regarding my position at Mulberry House.'

'Mrs Kulman must have thought very highly of you, to make you her executor,' Mrs P said.

So that's the tactic, Thomas thought. Attack from both flanks.

'Only it just doesn't seem like the May Kulman I knew,' Daphne went on.

'Could you let us have a look at it?' Mrs Perkins said. 'The will I mean?' She put her head on one side and smiled at him. 'It's not that we don't trust you Dr Carr, perish the thought. It's just that Daphne would feel so much easier in her mind, wouldn't you dear? If we could see the genuine article, I mean.' She pointed at his desk. 'In there, is it?'

'Certainly not,' Thomas said, 'it's in the safe.'

'Which will be behind one of those?' Mrs Perkins gestured towards the pictures on the walls.'

Keeping his temper by fiddling with the light over his desk, Thomas cleared his throat and said, 'My copy is safely locked away.'

'And you've lost the key?'

Thomas stood up, rested his elbow on the mantelpiece and glared down at them. Enough was enough. Skirmishes were all very well but they didn't get the job done. 'Forgive me, Mrs Perkins,' he said, 'but your own position in the matter escapes me.'

'I act on behalf of my friend, here, Miss Chiltern.'

'Who is, I take it, unable to speak for herself?'

A flush crept up Daphne C's neck and her eyes narrowed. 'No need to make me sound like an imbecile, Pru,' she said.

Sir Dreadnought would be proud of me Thomas thought. Divide and rule was one of his favourite maxims. Now to press home the advantage. 'Ladies, ladies,' he said. 'Let's not get...' He managed to swallow the words that threatened to spill from his lips - our knickers in a twist. Lifting the miniature knight in armour from its base and holding it in front of him like a shield he said, 'It's not an easy situation, for any of us.'

'How long is it you've lived here, Dr Carr?' Pru said. 'You never had children, did you?'

Diversionary tactics now. He shifted his weight from one foot to the other and back again and said, 'How very kind of you to take an interest, Mrs Perkins. I've been here, that is, my wife and I had the place built about ten years ago.'

'Your poor wife,' Daphne whispered.

'To Ingrid's own design, I believe?' Pru chipped in. 'I remember her telling me about her ideas.'

Her sadly ludicrous notions, Thomas thought. Modern Historical was her word for this ridiculous mish-mash of styles where inglenook, wood burning stove and low ceiling beams sat uneasily beside central heating, insulation and automatic sprinklers. The sooner it was off his hands, the better. He needed to start again. 'Indeed,' he said. 'Ingrid had her own ideas.'

'And very nice too,' Daphne said.

'Weren't you on TV about then? Ten years back? ' Mrs Perkins said, 'It never went into a second series, that Tudor thing, did it?'

Thomas turned his back on her and carefully replaced the knight. 'You were asking about Mrs Kulman's will,' he said. 'Probate is pending, Miss Chiltern, but according to Mr Higton, Mrs Kulman's solicitor, she left instructions that you were to be informed of your own position as soon as possible after the issue of the death certificate.' He went over to his desk, sat behind it and reached into a drawer. 'I can let you have the exact wording of that telephone conversation if you like.'

'You took instructions over the phone?' The Perkins woman was incredulous.

'Confirmed by email, my dear lady.' Thomas smiled at her. 'This is the twenty-first century, after all.'

'I never quite got the hang of computers,' Daphne Chiltern said. 'May used one in the office but I left all that kind of thing to her.'

'Let me get this straight,' Mrs Perkins persisted. 'You got a phone call, followed by an email telling you what to say to Daphne?'

'That's not quite the order of events, Mrs Perkins but no matter.'

'No matter to you, Dr Carr but of considerable matter to Daphne.' She pursed her lips and stared at him. 'So who is this Draper woman, the one Mrs Kulman left the house to? Where does she fit into the picture? Did Mr Higton have anything to say about that?'

'I can't speak for Mr Higton, Mrs Perkins, as I'm sure you'll appreciate' He coughed. As I said, probate is pending but for the time being, I can re-assure you, Miss Chiltern that you are, as a sitting tenant, perfectly secure in occupation of your flat, for your lifetime. With that stipulation, and as you know, the property has been left to a Mrs. Alison Draper.'

'The Heiress,' Daphne whispered.

Poor, silly woman, Thomas thought. May Kulman's death had catapulted her into an encounter with disappointed hopes, no less a battle, perhaps, than his own with a discarded lover and sleazy private detective.

Chapter 23

Daphne refused Pru's offer of a lift home from Dr Carr's house and stomped off down the lane. Better to be on her own right now. She should never have agreed to set foot inside that man's home. Passelande, what sort of stupid name was that for a house? Perched up at the end of the lane, it was as hoity-toity as he was. All that stuff to do with knights and such, cold history with no heart. She wasn't impressed by piles of papers and computer screens either, everything arranged to prove how important he was. Well he needn't think he'd fooled her.

The way he talked to them was horrible, either sneery or glancing over their shoulders as if something much more interesting was happening on the wall behind them. Playing the grieving widower didn't cut much ice either. According to Pru there'd been no love lost between him and his wife.

And what about the way Pru behaved? How dare she imply that Daphne was too stupid to speak up for herself? The whole thing had been so embarrassing and a complete waste of time.

As she turned into Marine Drive the sky felt heavy above her. Reflecting its gloomy mood, her sea sisters wore grey too. Apart from one young woman jogging, the beach was deserted.

Mulberry House stood solid, without sign of life. Someone should sort out this garden. The weeds were having a field day. Not that it was her problem but it did look untidy. She was sliding her key into the lock when the postman came up the path behind her.

'Afternoon, Miss C.'

With the couple of circulars he handed over was a long white envelope with her name and address typed on it.

'Thank-you Gareth.' Best grab the post before The Heiress got her hands on it. She checked the bundle in her hand. 'Nothing for Mrs Kulman then?'

Gareth looked puzzled. 'Well there wouldn't be, would there?'

'I'd have thought some post might still arrive, for a while anyway. Not everyone will know she's passed away.'

'Oh not because she's popped her clogs.' Gareth adjusted the postbag on his shoulder. 'According to the guy in the sorting office, she had her post redirected, couple of months back.'

'Redirected? Where?'

'Sorry love, I haven't a clue.'

Nelson emerged round the side of the house and sat on the path meowing. 'What's going on pusskins?' she said. When she opened the front door, he raced up the stairs, sat by her front door and meowed again.

No post for May. It hadn't occurred to her before, what with everything going on, but there had been no post for May since the day she'd left to go north that last time, weeks and weeks ago. Someone might have informed the bank, the credit card people and such that she had died but where were the catalogues, the magazines she subscribed to? Where were the household bills? Re-directed, according to Gareth, but re-directed where, and why? It was bad enough May getting herself killed like that and cremated goodness knew where, and now this.

In a daze of uncertainty, Daphne let herself into her flat, fed Nelson, put the kettle on and ferreted out the tea bags.

She sipped the hot drink, her thoughts floundering around in a fog. The mug was nearly empty when she remembered the letter. The postmark was blurred and there was no indication of who had sent it. She popped on her reading glasses and slit the envelope open.

Dear Miss Chiltern,
I hope you will forgive me getting in touch. It's taken me some time to find you but the archive of what was once called The Southern Moral Welfare Hostel has recently become available to children adopted from there.

Daphne flinched and bit hard on the inside of her cheek.

There is no easy way to say this but I really do think you may be my birth mother...

Daphne flung the letter onto the floor. What was all this nonsense? She wrapped her arms around herself and rocked to and fro. That dreadful business had all been settled years ago. Hadn't it? They had taken her baby, the respectable couple who could give him everything he needed, everything his pitiable mother could never provide. She wasn't that person any longer, was she? She didn't want to meet that silly girl again, or her offspring.

She poked at the letter with the toe of her shoe. The signature was handwritten but she couldn't read it at this distance, thank goodness. Whatever name he went by, he wasn't that snuggly bundle she'd cuddled for the last time on a cold morning so long ago. He'd be a middle-aged man by now, wouldn't he?

That fat little man was middle-aged, the one who'd turned up the other night, the night of her Lady Macbeth. No she wouldn't think of that.

But he reckoned he'd stayed here before, years back. With his father. His adopted father perhaps? What had Samantha said? 'He's never forgotten you, Daphne and come back to get reacquainted.' Was Samantha in on this hideous plot?

The fat little man who'd turned up here could well be the writer of this horrible letter. He'd come to give her the once-over and then decided to write this. She pictured him hunched over the dressing table on his room, Number 3 at the front, chewing the end of his pen, deciding how best to trap her. He'd have crept out at dead of night to the post box round the corner. Smudged postmarks were easy to arrange. Now he'd be watching, waiting for her reaction.

It was nothing to do with her, nothing. She picked up the letter between fingertip and thumb and managed to slide it back into its envelope. Then, holding it at arm's length she took it into the sitting room, popped it behind Mother's photo on the mantelpiece and rearranged the shells until it was completely hidden.

'Now for a swim,' she said loudly. 'The sisters look in need of cheering up.'

In bed that night, Daphne lay staring up at the ceiling. Lying there in the darkness, without the comfort of colour, she was uneasy. The end of day noises, shifting weatherboards, the murmur of the sea, whispered wind in the branches of the mulberry tree, offered none of their usual comfort, the familiar rhythms of her world, but seemed loaded with menace.

Even Nelson had deserted her, not returning after his evening jaunt or responding to her calls. The future hung over her, with the hostile Heiress and that awful man in the house, a man whose name she was afraid to know.

It was after midnight when she drifted into half-sleep, a state where dreams lent reality to conjured images, people, desires and hopes.

*

She is waiting in the wings of a vast theatre, the dusty wing curtain brushing her right arm. Her floor-length costume, black with red satin lining, hangs from lacy shoulder straps. Beyond her view, the packed house buzzes with unspoken anticipation. Her entrance will be greeted with wild applause; the other actors will stand admiringly, waiting whilst she acknowledges the adoration. Here comes her cue.

But her triumph is interrupted. Before she can go on, each member of the audience must sign a petition to confirm it is Daphne they want to see. The clipboard is wielded by Pearl Cooper.

The buzz of anticipation turns to irritation, to anger. Her audience are refusing to sign. The theatre is emptying. Her fellow actors are frowning, swearing, blaming. Alone on the stage she stares out into blackness.

A spotlight clicks on, motes of dust floating in its beam. It comes to rest on a man in the middle of the front row. He's swarthy with sunburned arms. Even from up here on the stage she can see the anchor tattoo on his wrist. His grin controls her. She's trembling, praying the light will never go out.

But the light dims. The sight of him is distorted, smoke and mirrors. Behind him another figure lurks in the shadows, tubby but with the same dark looks. He raises his finger and points at her.

*

Daphne woke, her heart drumming into the dryness of her mouth. In the darkness she fumbled for the glass of water. She sat up and swallowed a great gulp then turned on the light. At the end of the bed, Nelson was settling himself on his blanket.

Dawn was beginning to return the colours borrowed by the night. This was a new day. Dreams meant nothing. She'd already decided that, hadn't she, when Pru borrowed *Opening the Door to The Dream World* from the library and wanted them to start recording their dreams? The Dream Goddess on the book's cover was dripping with vulgar jewellery and had a very iffy attitude to blue

What she had to do now was put that pointing finger right out of her head. It was a shame the poor man hadn't found his mother but it was nothing to do with her, now was it?

'Better get some more shut-eye,' she told Nelson. 'We need to be fresh for the next rehearsal, now don't we Pusskins?'

Chapter 24

Alison had just confirmed her appointment with Mrs Kulman's solicitor when the landline phone rang in the little office by the front door of Mulberry House. The house was quiet. Bryn had gone out and Daphne hadn't put in an appearance.

'Alison? It's Thomas Carr. How are you this fine morning? Rumour has it there was something of a kerfuffle on your doorstep the other night.'

Alison smiled. 'The news-bearing mermaids have been about their business, have they?'

'News does have a way of getting around, as you know. So, how are you?'

'Polite answer or the truth?'

'Oh dear,' Thomas said. 'The truth then, though not perhaps the whole truth, eh?'

'Fair to middling just about covers it.'

'Might a trip to Rye nudge middling into good? I'd welcome your views on the Edward Burra exhibition at the Art Gallery.'

'I've never heard of him.' Alison said.

'So much the better, a fresh eye. How does two o'clock suit?'

'Should I bring medication for motion sickness?'

He laughed. 'Don't tell me, you've had the Pru Perkins transport experience?'

'Samantha Walsh actually.'

'Both graduates of a bad day at the driving school, I'm afraid. You'll find my own driving technique is far more sedate.'

'Sedate goes with the Jensen Interceptor does it?'

'You noticed my car.' Thomas said. 'I'm impressed.'

'The Jenson was a formative part of my upbringing. Jude fancied Robert Vaughan, in re-runs of *The Protectors*.'

'Well, I should tell you, my Interceptor hasn't solved many international crimes.'

'How disappointing,' Alison said. 'Two o'clock is fine. I need to do some shopping in Rye afterwards so I'll make my own way back.'

'Without a car?'

No husband, no car, Alison thought. A firm's car had made good sense but now the firm no longer had a use for its driver. She said, 'Buses, Thomas. Remember them? See you at two o'clock.'

Thomas and an art exhibition Alison thought when he rang off. What sort of combination would that prove to be? Would he have further comments to make about Daphne's bizarre performance?

At first Alison had seen the funny side of Daphne's antics; now she saw the whole thing for what it was, another irritation she could do without. Opening the front door to the sight of the elderly woman, hooded, draped in sheets dipped in red dye, and chirping garbled lines from *Macbeth* had been more than ridiculous. Samantha's giggles had been infectious and soon they were hooting with laughter.

Bryn had taken it all in his stride. 'It's Miss Chiltern isn't it?' he said when Daphne paused for breath. 'You won't remember me. I stayed here, years ago.'

Daphne had run out of steam then, tripped over her sheeting and landed flat on her back on the hall floor. Looking down at her, a tiny human island in a sea of red stains, Alison thought how small and pathetic she looked.

'What can she be up to?' Samantha said as Bryn gently helped Daphne up. She'd pushed him away and fled in the direction of the stairs.

Things had finally quietened down. Samantha went home to her vicar and someone named Pru arrived to sort out Daphne. Alison had taken a chance that Bryn wasn't a mass murderer, agreed to let him stay, shown him where the sheets were kept and told him to take his pick of the bedrooms. Then she'd settled down with a drink of wine, a magnifying glass and the photocopy of May Kulman's will.

Thomas had been cagey about the will but he had mentioned Lynwood Higton. The internet had come up with Higton, Balfour and Higton, Solicitor-Advocates, whose website gave their address in Rye. Her appointment with Mr Higton was at four-thirty that afternoon.

'That's Samantha Walsh's, isn't it?' Thomas pointed to the bike leaning against the porch.

'She arrived just now,' Alison said, closing the front door behind her. 'She's trying to get some sense out of Daphne.'

'You're a better man than me, Gunga Din,' Thomas muttered.

Following him down the path towards the road, Alison couldn't see the look on his face but his tone was mocking.

The tide was low, the sea navy blue and sluggish, the air humid and heavy. On the beach, three or four adults were trying to control a group of schoolchildren, herding them together like sheep dogs snapping at the hooves of the flock. Bent over clipboards, the children tramped across the shingle with small rucksacks on their backs. Not a fun day out, apparently.

The prospect of a drive to Rye had cheered Alison's morning but Thomas's mood was no longer light-hearted. Banter had been replaced by silence. He was clutching the steering wheel as if it might get out of control. His profile was stony.

How would Samantha's Aromatherapy method classify Thomas's mercurial nature, Alison wondered. She stared out of the car window, counting babies.

One, in a blue buggy, neck craned to follow a window cleaner's progress up his ladder.

Two, transfixed by the colours and shapes in a sweetshop window display.

Three, chubby knees emerging from a sagging nappy, desperately toddling three paces behind a young woman clamped to a phone.

This idiocy had to stop, she told herself. She had more than enough new problems without dragging the old ones with her.

On the outskirts of Rye, Thomas embarked on a history lesson. The cluster of terracotta-roofed buildings and silhouette of a medieval tower spread across the incline, was a Cinque Port he told her. Alison did not interrupt him to say she'd thought Cinque Ports had to be on the coast. Dates followed, twelve something, fifteen something, Edward the something, Elizabeth the first.

'Edward Burra was local then?' she said as they got out of the car.

Thomas glanced at her. 'You've done your homework.' He set off across the cobbled street. 'He was born in London but lived here in Rye for many years. He died in nineteen seventy-six.'

'What's the etiquette of viewing?' Alison said as they went into the gallery. 'Do I cling to your side and wait for nuggets of golden information to fall from your lips?'

His glare dissolved into a concession 'My manner had been less than courteous,' he said curtly. 'You have my apology.' He picked up a leaflet from the desk in the gallery foyer and stared down at it. Without looking up he said, 'Things on my mind, I'm afraid.'

'You sounded more cheerful this morning,' Alison said.

He nodded. 'I did, didn't I?' He thrust the leaflet back with the others. 'We'll do our own thing in here, shall we? Meet up later for a drink in the cafeteria?' He turned away.

Less than courteous? Plain rude I'd call it, Alison thought. Why the hell had she bothered washing her hair, putting on the only dress she'd bought with her, deciding on high-heeled sandals? She'd half a mind to leave him to it, Edward Burra or not but now she was here with an hour or so before her appointment at Higton's, she might as well improve her mind, if that's what art was supposed to do.

The paintings grouped under the title *Danse Macabre* caught her eye. Hung along the length of one wall they depicted a bizarre world of bright colours where nothing was what it seemed. From a distance *The Eruption of Venus* showed a trio of women. Closer inspection revealed that two of the faces were depicted as cogs and wheels and the torso of the third rose up from the surface of a glass-topped table with human legs.

There were bird men with beaks and beady eyes, their clothing an unsettling halfway between fabric and feathers. *Dancing Skeletons* had figures of bone, pink, bright blue, red, cavorting under a white, one-eyed full moon with a sewn-up gash for a mouth.

In any other circumstances Alison might have dismissed this disturbing amalgamation of reality and fantasy as having nothing to say to her. But as life, her life, was turning out to be, these pictures depicted her world exactly though how she'd explain that to Thomas she had no idea.

She need not have worried. In the coffee shop Thomas showed no interest in what she thought of the exhibition but was voluble with his own reaction.

'Disappointment just about sums up my feeling,' he said. 'A remembered enjoyment from seeing the work some time ago, not sustained I'm afraid.' He folded his arms. 'I want to inhabit a painting, feel an integral part, be drawn inside the frame. Vermeer achieves it of course, makes you believe his kitchen maid will turn and ask your opinion of the meal she's preparing. Renoir too. Despite the overdone banality of his boating party, at any moment your own drink might well be handed over.'

Alison stared out of the window. This was pretentious twaddle.

'With this work I feel on the periphery, an onlooker,' Thomas said. 'Not much in the way of originality either. *Skull in a Landscape* is more than influenced by Otto Dix and the wedding one has its origins in Hogarth. He gave Surrealism a run for its money, of course, though the results aren't a patch on Dali. The American ones are strong, credible depictions of butch-looking, dudes would you call them? Big square shoulders and crew cuts.'

'If you do decide to ask me what I thought of the exhibition, you invited me to see,' Alison said, 'feel free to give me a ring.' With furious fingers, she zipped up her bag and stood up. 'Thank-you for the lift.'

By the time she'd found the Georgian building that housed Higton, Balfour and Higton's offices, Alison had started to calm down. Daphne, Thomas, the enigmatic May Kulman, the relationship between them and where she fitted in, were mysteries all. It felt like being in one of Burra's macabre paintings. This wasn't real life, it was an intermission, a pause between the trailers and the main feature, time to visit the counter for a bucket of popcorn and a large Coke.

She'd soon have a full set of solicitors she reflected as she sat in the waiting room, her divorce lawyer readjusting spotless cuffs linked with bling, the scruffy guy who'd handed over documents and keys to Mulberry House and now the unknown Mr Lynwood Higton.

Mr Higton was indeed a different breed of the species. Tweedy of three-piece suit, shirt and hair, he moved across the expanse of his carpet to shake her hand, carrying himself stiffly as if his torso had no knowledge of life below the hips. Thick lenses made his eyes look like grey jelly.

He settled her in a high-back, green leather chair then sat behind his desk. The smell of pickled onions came from a plate with what looked like the remains of lunch.

'Mrs Draper, I was expecting you.' he said.

'Well you would be,' Alison said. 'I made an appointment.'

He pushed his glasses further up his nose. 'Before that, I mean. I quite expected to see you earlier than this.'

'Back to the future you mean?'

'More like intuition,' he said, 'intuition and a certain acquaintance with Mrs Kulman's affairs.' He consulted his computer screen. 'How may I help you?'

'Intuition doesn't go that far then?' Alison said. What was it with the guy? After putting up with Thomas and his moods, avuncular banter was all she needed.

'That may be for me to know and you to wonder,' Mr Higton was saying, 'but it's the client's prerogative to explain her needs.'

'I'm not sure I am your client,' Alison said, 'but I wanted to ask you about this.' She handed him the photocopy of Mrs Kulman's will. 'The heading is indistinct, as you see, but that is your firm's name?'

He peered at the top sheet, turned over and perused the second. 'Indeed so, though the document has obviously led an interesting life since it left this office.'

'Your did draw up this will then?'

Mr Higton examined her over the top of his glasses. 'I am at liberty to say that this firm did indeed draw up the original of this document,' he said. 'In fact I did it myself. Mrs Kulman sat where you are sitting now and was most specific in her instructions.'

'Does liberty extend to telling me how long you'd known her?'

Mr Higton smiled. 'Legal jargon,' he said, 'it creates a fence.'

'For you to hide behind?'

'If necessary, Mrs Draper. We all need a fall-back position. I can, of course confirm that this firm has dealt with Mrs Kulman's affairs since she moved into the area in...' Glancing at the computer screen, he tapped his keyboard, '...the late nineteen fifties.'

'But she had connections with Derbyshire?'

Once more the glasses were pushed further up a nose that seemed reluctant to oblige.

'You suggested,' Alison went on, 'that your acquaintance with Mrs Kulman's affairs are of longstanding?'

'And there's my intuition,' he said, 'don't forget the intuition.'

'I have to admit Mr Higton,' Alison retorted, 'that if I knew what hackles were, mine would be in danger of rising.'

He held up both hands in a gesture of surrender. 'Quite right too. Forgive me. You didn't come here to skirmish with a legal wallah far too much in touch with his inner child. Pax?'

Alison sighed. She should have prepared for this interview, thought out exactly what to say, and ask. Leaving things to chance had been a mistake. She said, 'I'm just trying to find out why a woman I'd never heard of until a few weeks ago, has left me a property in part of the country I've never visited.'

'A very natural endeavour.' Mr Higton said. 'Let me see,' he said, 'how I can assist you. You heard of this bequest from?'

'Edward Sileby of Sileby and Frandite.'

'That would be in Bakewell, Derbyshire?'

Alison nodded.

'Apparently, in consulting them about a number of matters,' he said, 'Mrs Kulman lodged a copy of her will there, along with instructions to contact ourselves in the event of her death. This they did the day after the accident was reported. She had requested that the deeds and keys of Mulberry House be handed over to you with immediate effect.'

'You sent them to Mr. Sileby, before probate was granted?' Is that usual?'

Mr. Higton sighed. 'Not entirely. I did suggest to Mr. Sileby that he may see fit to leave the matter for the time being but he decided otherwise.'

'So you have no idea what Mrs. Kulman was doing in Derbyshire? Or how I fit into the picture?'

Giving up the battle with his glasses, he threw them onto the desk. 'I have no idea, Mrs Draper,' he said, 'no idea whatsoever.'

Chapter 25

When Alison took herself off, Thomas twisted in his seat and watched her make for the door of the coffee shop. Head high, bag gripped under one elbow, the skirt of her burgundy-red dress swishing around her legs, she took her time. She didn't turn and simper, as Gwenda would have done, or, in Cordelia-style, toss him a wave as she left. She didn't let the door slam behind her with the unruffled composure Ingrid would have displayed. She just behaved as if he were invisible.

This was it then, a gargantuan blot on the escutcheon, a stain on one's honour, discourtesy to a lady. But Alison was not a lady teasing and evading before capitulation. Alison was a woman, a woman who had intrigued and delighted him since the moment he'd seen her on the beach. That was his trouble, had always been, women. But he'd scuppered any chance of progress with Alison. Why would she want to spend time with a patronising oaf who hurled out facts like a banner across the sky? And all that pompous nonsense at poor Edward Burra's expense. One of his favourite painters reduced to the status of dauber. The ease with which his mouth had gushed such drivel was disturbing. However fallacious and prompted by ill humour, the invention had its origin in his own mind.

Sir Dreadnought was shaking his head at all this soul-searching. Ladies were delightful creatures, what would we do without them? But they needed to be kept within the confines of their own place.

Thomas looked around him. The unfussy decor in this coffee shop should have been soothing, raw brick walls, saddleback chairs, unvarnished pale-wood tables, but single plastic lilies in imitation cut-glass vases destroyed the effect. What he needed was a roaring wood fire, a retinue of squires reverencing his person, a ewerer to pour water over his hands. The only waitress service on offer here was grudgingly provided by a work-experience lass with inefficient adenoids.

Instead of this menu, fat-free, sugar-reduced, suitable for vegetarians, he should be able to command a haunch of venison, oozing juices into the trencher and washed down with the finest Rhenish wine.

'How you doing, Prof?' George Hessop stopped by the table and slapped Thomas on the shoulder. Biker's leathers, plastered around his bulk, squeaked with every movement. 'You'll be wondering what I'm doing here?'

'I wouldn't have you down as an art lover, no,' Thomas agreed.

'No to art,' George grinned, 'yes to lover.' He nodded towards the woman coaxing the coffee machine into life, a woman, Thomas saw, with charms pneumatic enough to offer bliss to any knight.

'You are in pursuit of the fair lady?'

The vigour of George's nod set off a series of leathery squeaks. 'Not much needed by way of pursuit, mind you.'

'Got someone minding the shop, have you?' Thomas said.

'The shop?' George grinned. 'Not my problem, mate. Not anymore. Haven't you heard? I've sold out, the whole caboodle, to the big boys.'

'The supermarket?'

'The very same. Made me an offer I couldn't refuse.' He leered towards the coffee machine. 'Come the end of the shift, 'er and me are off.'

'Off?'

'On a cruise Prof. Time to see the world.'

'I thought the developers wanted the whole block,' Thomas said. 'Pete Jenkins's place and the mini-mart, as well as your premises?'

'Abbas has got other plans so he was only too happy to let the mini-mart go.'

'And Pete?'

'What's that thing you brainy blokes say? Fate accomplished, is it? Not much Pete could do, not on his own.'

'But it's not what he wanted?'

George shook his head. 'Not so's you'd notice. Don't get me wrong, I'm sorry for the poor guy but life's too short for tradition. You gotta move with the times.'

Moving into modern times was not encouraged by the Tourist Board, Thomas reflected as he walked back to where he'd left the car. Re-enactments, medieval banquets, living history were on offer on every corner. History without the smelly bits. So-called Heritage must be the country's most thriving industry, bland hygienic counterfeits masquerading as authentic experience. What sort of mind-set was it that encouraged this appetite for a sanitised past?

The tang of Alison's perfume lingered in the car. Thomas opened all the windows and concentrated his mind on the upsurge of Heritage. Affluence couldn't entirely explain it. Some medieval knights had been wealthy beyond counting but an image of Sir Dreadnought Stumble taking time off between tournaments to organise authentic Viking banquets or all-in trips to Hadrian's Wall was not easy to conjure.

Historical investigation needed to be professional, cerebral, a matter of the intellect. Based on documents, contemporary accounts, objects, it was biased and open to interpretation but it aimed at warts and all, as close to fact as it was humanly possible to get. Heritage lathered froth on the facts and covered them with chocolate sprinkles, an emotional response to the best bits of history.

Rather a good analogy that. When it came to personal history though, clinging to the best bits was tempting. As it was, if there were any best bits in his own past they were evading him. It was his blunders that were not only coming home to roost but looked set to dominate his life.

The knock on his door earlier that day had changed the sunlit morning – talking to Alison and the prospect of her company – to an arctic landscape.

He'd been getting his lunch, humming Handel, enjoying the patterned strips of light filtered through the window blind, the gold of olive oil drizzling into the salad, when the visitor arrived at his front door.

'Dr Carr.' A tall, auburn-haired woman held out her hand. Striking rather than pretty, wearing a business suit cut to follow the curves. She wouldn't see forty again though she was doing her best to ignore that.

'Anna Bestwood,' she said. 'Thornly Associates. I believe Mr Thornly said twelve-thirty?'

Nothing had been agreed but thwarting an enemy with evasion wasn't likely to diminish the appetite for a fight, especially when reinforcements had been summoned. Thomas stepped outside, closed the front door behind him and headed for the drive. 'What exactly is it that Mr Thornly wants?' he said.

Ms Bestwood kept pace with him, her high heels clicking on the paving.

Thomas split off a sprig of lavender and smelt it, a nosegay against the odour of, well what? He said, 'If Thornly had come himself, I'd be telling him to spit it out.'

She smiled. 'No spitting required Dr Carr. Certainly not in this pleasant garden of yours. Your wife would no doubt agree, were she still here to share her opinion.' She cleared his throat of that little blockage people like her seemed prone to. 'The thing is, Dr Carr. Not medical of course, your title?'

Thomas's listing got to the end of the Normans before he said, 'Were you wanting some academic help? Historical research perhaps?'

She glanced at him with the air of someone sizing up a prize ram. 'Research?' she said. 'Interesting concept.'

They had reached the front gate now. Thomas opened it and stood aside for Ms B. to pass him. 'And you wanted to verify some of it with me, is that it?'

She raised her expertly plucked eyebrows. 'Verify, Dr Carr. Now there's an fascinating word. 'The thing is, certain facts came to light during, shall we say our collaboration with Mrs Kulman.'

'Facts that affect me?'

'You could say that.' Her eyes were derisive. 'The thing is, Dr Carr that Thornly Associates have been put to some expense on Mrs Kulman's behalf and now she has, as Gerald would put it, departed this world.' She flicked some pollen from her skirt. 'You are the executor I believe? Seeing to outstanding debts and suchlike?'

When he'd got rid of her Thomas had gone back into the house and sat at his desk. Lunch was abandoned, Handel silenced. He stared out at the gardener riding the sit-on mower up and down Ingrid's paddock, at the stripes of mown grass, at the empty stables. He listened to the clock ticking, to the thrum of the computer, to a car engine muted by the thickness of his garden hedge. Telling Thornly to submit his invoice to Lynwood Higton would hold him off only for a while, but it did give some breathing space. The implied threats were surely not based on anything May Kulman had known. But insinuations would be meat and mead to the likes of Thornly.

He'd been about to turn off the computer when the email inbox pinged. There were three new messages:

To all applicants for the temporary professorial post in the Faculty of Arts and Humanities. Please be advised that some changes have occurred in the way the appointment will be decided. The Dean asks that you attend an informal meeting at 10.30 a.m. on Thursday 16th of June to discuss the matter. Confirmation in writing is in the post.

Marian Fowler
Secretary to Dean of Faculty

Dear Dr Carr,

Thank-you so much for your submission to our journal. Your photographs and comments on the restoration of the Sandgate Tower are most interesting.

Unfortunately, as Mr Perkins, owner of the Tower, has written and submitted a much fuller account of the process of restoration, including many documents and information not at your own disposal, we feel his submission to be the more suitable for publication. As you may know, Mr Perkins is well known for his expertise on local history and has appeared in print and on TV documentaries about the area.

Please do let us know about any future areas of interest you may be working on.

Yours sincerely.
Joyce Brindley [Secretary, Friends of Martello Towers]

Good boy, Tommy. I'm on the short list. Interview at the start of next term. I've every faith in your further powers of persuasion. Heaps of love and kisses, when you want to collect. Gwenda.

Defeat in triplicate. The end of the woods wasn't even in sight. This is what came of getting involved with women. Damn them all, Ingrid, May Kulman, Gwenda, Cordelia, Pru Perkins, Daft Daphne and now a madam called Joyce

Brindley. Damn the whole monstrous regiment, damn them all to Hades, Alison Draper included. If she thought she was getting in on his act, she had another think coming. He'd half a mind to stand her up this afternoon.

Chapter 26

When The Heiress left the house with what sounded like Dr Carr, Daphne was still in bed. After getting up to feed Nelson and open the kitchen window for him to go out, she'd burrowed under the duvet, rigid as a statue, and kept her breathing as shallow as possible. Like poor dear Ophelia, crowned with nettles and daisies, she was gliding along the river of death. She was the Lady of Shallot, her mirror cracked beyond repair, the drifting boat her last refuge. Above her, the trees bent in sorrow, the sun hid its face and the sky was heavy.

She couldn't control the pictures in her mind, nor stop her tongue probing the throbbing place in her cheek but snuggled like this, with not one tiny part of her risking contact with the world outside the covers, she was safe from The Heiress and That Dreadful Man. She wouldn't even take one peep at the Scottish play costume still lying in a pool of rippled crimson on the bedroom floor, or the surgical gloves skulking on the dressing table like shrivelled pink jellyfish.

A fragment of poetry swam through her mind. Something about disappointment being a worm. She couldn't net the exact quotation or the poet's name but the words were definitely associated with her midnight blue kaftan. Hadn't she worn that the last time she'd gone with May to the W.I? The biscuits had been soggy and Poppy Skeffington from the library had given her *Poems You Might Have Missed* talk.

There had been so many disappointments. By this time the worm had grown into a snake, another snake to slide down on the board of her silly old life. Surely she deserved a few ladders?

Sounds from the real world crept into her flat, muted voices from the staircase, the doorbell, the ringing phone, the front door slamming. Whatever happened she would stay put. The Heiress she had no choice but to tolerate but no way would she set one foot outside her flat whilst That Man was under the same roof.

It had been kind of Samantha to get Pru round here the other night but her friend had wanted what she called the full monty. Apart from suggesting she had felt faint and tripped over her robe, Daphne had been completely unable to talk. The shame of fluffing her lines had overcome her. Skilled acting had been needed to hide what a state she was really in. Still was, come to that. The night had been a torment. Every time she shut her eyes she saw Him, first the dream figure pointing the finger and then the memory of him standing on the doorstep, large as life, going on about having stayed here before. What a stunt to pull.

He was much fatter than in her dream and shorter but that would be part of his disguise, along with the greying hair. She wasn't fooled for one moment. He had come to take his revenge.

Poor dear Ophelia would understand her suffering, though she hadn't had the trauma of being a mother whose baby had been torn from her. Daphne thought about the Sunday trudge down that long drive towards the road.

*

The founder of The Southern Moral Welfare Hostel built his ticket to heaven well back from the sight of respectable people so the girls' ankles are swollen well before they sight the road. The pennies in their hems bang against their legs.

Brickface, as May calls her, got them up at six this morning to sew in the coins. A strong wind was forecast and she didn't want it having its evil way with their skirts. Even a peep of their calves on their way to chapel was likely to enflame inappropriate passions, she said, and hadn't they already ensnared unwary men by getting themselves in the family way?

So come eight-thirty here they are, a crocodile of young women, hemlines respectably weighted, pregnancies ill-concealed under a motley of voluminous garments, waddling down the tree-lined drive behind Miss Bickford.

'Look at her heels, stabbing into the tarmac,' May whispers. 'Digging holes for the unrighteous, d'you reckon?'

Above them the branches sway, the leaves whisper. Most of the girls, a waywardness of wantons, an expectancy of lasses, as May calls them, are well used to whispers.

May is older than most of them. Rumour has it that her husband threw her out when he found she was carrying another chap's child.

Daphne walks with one hand in the small of her back, the other rescuing her hair from her eyes and patting it into place.

'You're fighting a losing battle.' May tells her. 'In this wind.'

But Daphne knows she must look her best; at any moment Luca might show himself, behind the next tree perhaps. Soon he will come to her rescue, her knight in shining armour, and carry her away on his white horse.

'Looking for a visitor?' May says.

*

Someone was knocking on Daphne's front door. She wouldn't answer. Sooner or later whoever it was would give up and go away.

The letter box rattled open. 'Daphne? It's Samantha. Daphne, are you there? Please answer the door. I'm worried about you.'

Samantha had been here the night she'd fluffed her lines, hadn't she? Friendly with The Heiress by the looks of it and talking to That Man too.

'Please open the door, Daphne. If you're not feeling well, I won't stay long but I do have something to show you.'

Was this a ploy or a genuine, friendly offer? After all, Samantha was the only person to show any comprehension of what she'd already been suffering, before this latest ordeal. Speaking to her through the letter-box couldn't do much harm. Daphne put one foot on the floor and then the other. She tiptoed out of the bedroom and into the hall. 'Have you got The Heiress with you out there?' she demanded.

'If you mean Alison, she let me in on her way out,' Samantha said. 'Bryn's not here either. There's nobody in the house but me.'

Daphne called, 'I'm not fit to be seen.'

'What does that matter?' Samantha said softly. 'I just want to know that you're okay. Why not let me in so that I can make sure?'

'You said you had something to show me?'

'Well yes, but making sure you're all right is more important.'

Daphne turned the key and opened the door a fraction.

'Hi,' Samantha said. 'Why don't I make us a cuppa?' She pushed gently on the door. 'You go and put on a dressing gown.'

'The kitchen's a mess.'

'Thank the lord for that,' Samantha said, stepping into the hallway. 'Tidy places make me nervous. This way is it?'

'I hope you don't mind,' Samantha said, ten minutes later. She carried the tray into the sitting room. 'but I've brought you a scented candle. Bergamot and coriander, very good for counteracting emotional fatigue.'

Daphne breathed in the fragrance.

Samantha handed over a mug. 'According to my Dad,' she said, 'every predicament deserves a cup of tea.' She was looking at the red stains dotted over the carpet. 'What the hell's happened here?'. she said. 'You're not hurt, are you?'

'About the other night, when you arrived here with The Heiress and That Man,' Daphne said. 'I don't know what to say,'

'Say nothing and put it in the bureau.'

'I don't have a bureau.'

'Not a real one. Dad again. It's what he does with any situation he doesn't want to think about for the moment. Put it in the bureau. It'll still be there when you're ready for it. ' Samantha smiled. 'Whatever was happening here that night, Daphne, it obviously upset you a great deal. Give it time to simmer.'

'In the bureau?' In spite of herself, Daphne felt a grin crease the corners of her mouth. 'I like the sound of your Dad,' she said.

'Next time he visits, I'll get you to come to tea. You can take his mind off arguing the god-toss with Tony. Now,' Samantha reached into her bag,' I wanted to show you this.' Drawing out a large envelope she said, 'I remembered it when I got home from here the other night.' She glanced at Daphne. 'Are you okay to talk about Mrs Kulman?'

'Is that a photo of her?'

'Not of her exactly but she is in it. It's one of a series I took in Rye earlier in the year, general shots of the town. D'you remember I said I thought I'd seen her coming out of that solicitor's office? It'd be the same day.' She slapped her palm on her forehead. 'Oh god, you went there, didn't you? You were about to get on the bus when I was all caught up with that petition thing.'

Another of my poorer moments, Daphne thought. I wasn't very nice about the shops closing.

'Suggesting you just turn up there was a mad idea,' Samantha was saying. 'Typical of me, tongue wagging before the brain's in gear. But this,' she pulled a photograph from the envelope, 'is intriguing.'

Daphne peered. It looked like a shot of Rye harbour.

'Did you get short shrift,' Samantha said, 'at the solicitor's?'

Daphne shook her head. 'I changed my mind. I didn't think anyone would see me without an appointment.'

'You've got more sense than I have, thank the lord.' Samantha ran her fingers through her fringe. 'I should never have suggested going there. No solicitor worth his law degree would tell you stuff about his clients. They'd get de-frocked, or struck off, or whatever they do to the wrong'uns. But look at this.' She handed the photograph to Daphne and leant towards her pointing at it. 'See there?'

Daphne said 'I haven't got my reading glasses. Anyway, I'm not sure I want to look.'

'I didn't notice it at first.' Samantha pushed hair out of her eyes. 'I was more interested in the composition than the details. But once I got it under the magnifier, I saw her.'

'You saw May?'

'Just there, see. It's Mrs Kulman all right. And look who's she's with.' Samantha's voice rose with excitement. 'The guy with the droopy moustache and bow tie? It's Gerald, what's-his-name, that's who. I only know about him because one of Tony's churchy people was involved in a really messy divorce and Tony had to call him off, or some such thing.'

'Stop, stop,' Daphne said putting her hands over her ears. 'I don't know what you're talking about. I'm all in a muddle.'

'Sorry, there I go again. I'll slow down.' Samantha stood up, moved behind the chair and leaned on the back of it. 'That is definitely Mrs Kulman, yes? Sitting on that low wall by the harbour in cahoots with the man beside her. And that man is...'

'Gerald What's-his-name,' said Daphne. 'Who specialises in messy divorces?'

'Amongst lots of other things apparently, all of them seedy. Thing is, what was she doing with a guy like that? He's a really odious private detective.' Her arm, flung out in emphasis, dislodged the heap of shells and pebbles from the mantelpiece. They cascaded over the gas fire and crashed into the hearth. Dropping with them was The Letter.

'Oh God,' Samantha wailed, 'now look what I've done.'

Together they knelt to sort out the muddle. Daphne reached to hide The Letter before Samantha asked any questions. But Samantha had stretched for it at the same moment. Letter and envelope parted company. Daphne stared down at the envelope in her hand.

'You look terrible.' Samantha sounded really concerned. 'Not bad news, I hope?'

'It's from That Man,' Daphne said. 'The one who arrived the other night. It's a threat.'

Samantha looked down at the letter in her hand. 'What sort of threat? she said. 'Who the devil is he?'

Shudders ran down Daphne's spine. Even her misery couldn't disguise this cruel quirk of fate. Centre stage she was now, about to deliver the best line in Act Three. Movement, the hand to the throat, Action, cradling the empty space in her arms. The best acting was truth in pretence. But this wasn't pretence was it? This was real and nothing in Madame Fournier's bag of tricks had prepared her.

'He's my son,' she whispered.

'Your son?' Samantha said. 'I didn't know you had one.'

It was one of those moments when what was really in your heart spilled out, when the words coming out of your mouth seemed to arrive from another place, an out of control ventriloquy. Daphne took a breath and they tumbled into the room, the individual scenes of her life, running together, merged into the complete drama.

While the sun made its way from early to late afternoon, while the tide reached its height, paused and turned, while Samantha's eyes grew round and her glance never left Daphne's face, the narrative wound its way. From the grandeur of Chiltern Hall it lingered in a fun-fair, touched down in the Southern Moral Welfare Hostel and finally came to rest at the door of Mulberry House.

With the last word, the wind faded from Daphne's sails. She slumped back in her chair. Samantha knelt in front of her and took both her hands. The clock ticked. A shaft of sunlight arrowed Mother's photo, reinstated amongst the pebbles. Outside a single gull screeched.

'All those years,' Samantha said. 'All those years you waited for him, you worked here in Mulberry House and waited for your fairground love. What did you say his name was?'

'Luca.'

'You waited for Luca to come back to you. You never gave up?'

'Something horrible will have happened to him,' Daphne murmured. 'He'd have come otherwise, I know he would. But it has saved me from having to confess.'

'Confess?'

'About his son, about what I did with our baby. I gave him away.'

'You poor love.' Samantha stroked Daphne's arm. 'What else could you have done? Things were very different in those days. Single mothers had little choice.'

'Fate is stalking me, bringing justice.'

Samantha sat back on her heels. 'What makes you so sure the man who's turned up here is your son? Isn't he a bit too young?'

'I just know it's him. Just as I know he's come to punish me.'

'Does he look like his father, like Luca?'

Snatching her hands away, Daphne stood up and pushed past Samantha. 'No, she said, 'no, he does not. He's squat and fat and ugly. Luca was, Luca was wonderful.'

'What does the letter say?'

Daphne stood by the window, folding and unfolding the bottom of the curtain. If she closed her eyes, if she held her breath, all this would go away. She'd cover her eyes, count to a hundred and when she turned round everything would be back the way it was.

'If you don't want to tell me, I'll understand.' Samantha said.

But hide and seek didn't work, not any more. 'You can read it if you like.' Daphne said. Behind her The Letter rustled in Samantha's hand.

'Didn't the man on the doorstep introduce himself as Bryn?' Samantha said. 'That's not the name down here.'

Daphne whirled round. 'Oh he's much cleverer than that, isn't he?' she snapped.' He's using another name, hoping I won't realise.'

'You won't have much faith in my plans, I know,' Samantha said. 'Not after last time but we need to think this through. Work out the best way to find out more about him. Can you be very brave?'

'Brave?'

'We don't know what's going on, either with this Bryn guy or with the other situation, Mrs Kulman's will. I reckon the best plan is to act as normally as possible. Softly, softly catchee monkey as my Dad says.'

'Put it in the bureau?'

'Not exactly. We need to keep on the case, see what happens and find out all we can but act as if nothing's wrong.'

'Acting?' Daphne said. 'Now you are talking.'

Chapter 27

Reluctant to go straight back to the house, Alison went down to the beach when she got back from Rye. It was cooler now and the tide on the ebb, exposing a wide band of sand, sprinkled with tiny slivers of white shells, below the shingle. She took off her sandals, wobbled over the pebbles then stood for a while on the squelchy brink of the beach. When she pulled her feet away, the edges of her footprints disappeared and the hollows filled with water.

How old was she when she'd first seen the sea? Her memory was of standing with her father, at the edge of frothing waves. Her fingers, curled inside his large warm hand, played a game of trying to escape from the cosy cave but each time she flicked one of them into the chilly air, a big thumb quickly folded it inside again. In spite of the scary, heaving mass of water trying to swallow her toes, she knew she was safe.

Other memories of her parents were hazy but their music tethered her to that part of consciousness born before language. Her instinct had always been to distrust classical music. Without logic, she had blamed it for taking them away from her, but, that apart, it reached farther into the emotions than she wanted to go. Trills of violin notes or the steady, persuasion of the double bass released a confusing kaleidoscope of images she could never quite pin down.

She associated the plane crash that had killed them with starting school. Logic, and adult knowledge, told her that the two things were weeks apart, that she hadn't gone to school on that first morning and come home to discover they were dead but memory, that unreliable crutch, insisted this was so. She had never completely lost the dread of returning home to discover someone, or something dear to her, had vanished.

The driver of the van parked outside Mulberry House was on his mobile. 'Mrs Kulman is it?' he said as Alison passed his open window.

'Who's asking?'

'Marsh Computers at your service ma'am. Computer repaired and in working order. Okay to bring it in now?' He glanced at the clip board on the passenger seat. 'Boss says to apologise for the delay, you having a maintenance contract and all. We were waiting for a new disk drive. '

Before Alison had time to reply, he was out of the van and unloading a PC. Following her up the garden path he said, 'Managed without it, have you?'

Alison opened the front door and showed him into the office. 'I've been away,' she heard herself say.

Why hadn't she realised? There was a printer and router box on the office desk but no computer. Had she assumed that a laptop had vanished along with all Mrs K's other possessions?

If the van driver noticed that her squiggled signature had only one letter in common with the name on the invoice, he made no comment. When he'd gone, she plugged in the computer and turned it on. This may well have been the only thing that Mrs Kulman's meticulous disappearance hadn't taken into account. When it had booted up, she'd see if its files offered any clue to what the hell was going on.

'Have you got a minute?' That friend of dopey Daphne was at the office door. The bright blue chiffon dress she was wearing was doing its best to conjure up posh garden parties but the shabby trainers weren't co-operating.

'It's Pru,' the woman said, 'Pru Perkins.' She glanced over her shoulder and lowered her voice. 'I've been looking in on Daphne. Could we go somewhere else, perhaps?'

'Like where?'

'It's just that this room is...' Pru jabbed her thumb towards the ceiling.

'Walls have ears?' Alison suggested.

'We are right under Daphne's sitting room.'

'Kitchen safe enough?'

Pru frowned.

'Guest dining room?'

The two of them sat opposite each other at the table in the bay window. Outside, the pines bent towards them, spindly eavesdroppers.

Fiddling with the sleeve of her dress, Pru said, 'Have you ever thought how much money clothes manufacturers have saved by this three-quarter-length style?' She smoothed down the filmy fabric. 'Hoodwinked, aren't we? On a par with wearing designer labels on the outside of garments, perhaps?'

'Fascinating as this ramble down sartorial lanes may be,' Alison said, 'I'm afraid I have other things to do.'

'Getting rid of Daphne being one of them?' Pru said sharply.

My day for grumpy encounters it seems, Alison thought. First Thomas now this lump of a woman. 'As far as I can see, Mrs Perkins,' she said, 'the boot is most definitely on the other foot.'

'Pru, call me Pru. Everyone does. She expected to inherit this place, you know.'

'And that excuses spying on me, warbling in the hallway, draping herself in blood-stained sheets and shrieking like a banshee, does it?'

Pru frowned. 'Daphne is a little eccentric, always has been. But that doesn't mean she's not got a point. For years she ran this place single-handed, more or less.'

'With the hope of inheriting it?'

'No, of course not. She'd never given it a thought, I'm sure. But once we heard about Mrs Kulman, we naturally expected, well, you know.' She tapped her fingers on the table edge. 'Mrs K always said she had no relatives, and no-one had ever heard of you.'

'And until a few weeks back, 'Alison said, 'I'd never heard of Daphne or Mulberry House and definitely not Mrs Kulman.'

Pru looked sceptical. 'Forgive me, Alison, may I call you Alison? But from where I'm sitting, that does sound more than a tad far-fetched.'

Alison pictured the computer, waiting in the study. She was half-tempted to suggest they might investigate its contents together but that was something best explored on her own.

'I completely agree,' she said. 'The whole situation could have been dreamed up in a Hollywood studio. Does that fit in with the Mrs Kulman you knew?'

'Given to dramatic gestures you mean?'

Alison nodded.

'Not generous ones, that's for sure. I shouldn't speak ill of the dead but tight-fisted just about sums her up, I'd say. Very keen to look after the pennies, not so keen to settle her bills. A byword in the local Chamber of Commerce, according to my Jim. '

'A B&B ranks as commerce does it?'

Pru laughed. 'Not so's you'd notice but a couple of swanky hotels, bundles of holiday chalets, the odd amusement arcade probably fit that bill.'

'She owned all those?'

'Among other business interests apparently, all over the place.'

'A wealthy woman then?' Alison said. 'Does Daphne know that?'

Pru shook her head. 'Not as far as I know. Least said soonest mended. What Daphne doesn't know can't hurt her. She's enough on her plate just now and not coping at all well. I'm really quite worried about her.'

What was it Thomas had said? The remainder of Mrs Kulman's assets, considerable assets apparently, she had left to a charity benefitting single parents. Did Pru know that, did Daphne? She said, 'So who gets the rest of those assets?'

'Lord knows,' Pru said. 'At the moment, apart from Lynwood Higton, only Lothario Carr is in on the act.'

Alison smiled. 'You're not a fan of the good doctor then?'

'Not so's you'd notice,' Pru snorted. 'Far as I can see all historians do is regurgitate other historians. Fat lot of good that is. And he's all teeth and no trousers that one, if you get my meaning. Smarmy's not the word. Why May Kulman dragged him on board is as much of a mystery as socks doing a vanishing act in the washing machine.'

Keen to steer her away from the side-tracks and back to the main road, Alison said, 'Did you know Daphne before she came to work here?'

'No. We met in the local Choral Society,' Pru said. 'In the early sixties. Jim and I hadn't long been married and I was getting used to the place. Joined this and that, the way you do. Jim's local of course but it took a while for people to take to me. My folks came from Margate.'

'Not a million miles away then?'

'Half a mile, a million, makes no difference.'

'Most small places are like that,' Alison said.

'Anyway, I knew Daphne worked here, of course and we were both in the Choral Society but we didn't really pal up till my two had flown the nest. She's not that keen on kiddies. Well people who've never had any often aren't, don't you find?'

Scanning the woman's face, Alison let her voice drift on. There was something obnoxious about nose hair, she thought, like spiders disappearing up the nostrils. Her own mother, had she lived would have been about the same age as this woman. What would the years have done to that slender violinist silhouetted against the light of a long ago bay window? She said, 'Has Daphne said anything, about how she and Mrs Kulman met?'

'Forgive me, Alison but we're at cross purposes here. My concern is with Daphne, yours is for yourself.'

'Can you blame me? The sitting tenant here is a very recent acquaintance and not an easy one. The woman inside my own skin I've lived with for forty years.'

Pru grinned. 'Fair enough.' She glared at the floor. 'Now what is that animal doing in here?'

Daphne's cat had pushed into the room and was nuzzling Alison's ankles, its furry, solid body warm against her feet. 'Corpulent cat with discerning desires,' she said.

'You're about right there,' Pru agreed. 'If you ask me, it's about time Daphne put him on a diet.'

'Eagerly eating fearsome forkfuls,' Alison said. This was the alphabet game Jude had invented for them to play on the way to the dentist, the doctor or anywhere else Alison hadn't wanted to go.

'Sorry?' Pru said.

The cat squeezed himself under the table and clambered onto Alison's lap. He lay curled and purring as she stroked him. 'All I want,' she went on, 'is to find out what connection I had with Mrs Kulman and then decide what to do with this house. Unfortunately for her, and for me, Daphne is part of all that.'

Pru re-settled her bulk against the back of the chair, her expression solemn. 'As far as I understand it, Mrs Kulman and Daphne arrived to run this house as a B&B some time in the late fifties. I've discovered since, that Daphne had fallen out with her family, quite well-to-do folk apparently. Mrs K owned the place and Daphne ran it for her. What the financial arrangements between them were I don't know.'

'And this went on for how long?'

'Decades.' Pru nodded. 'Till just over a couple of years ago when Mrs K decided to shut up shop, so to speak, and the pair of them retired. Daphne has had more time to find the right outlet for her performing skills.'

'Using this house as her rehearsal space, I take it?'

'Mrs K hadn't been seen much recently. Daphne had no idea where she got to.' Pru leaned her elbows on the table. 'Earlier this year, she told Daphne she was going away for quite a while.'

'To?'

Pru pursed her lips. 'Just said, the north, apparently.'

'Which could be anywhere north of the M25?'

'Next thing we know, Dr Posh-boy Carr is telling us she'd been killed in a road accident, somewhere in Derbyshire apparently.' Her eyes narrowed as she said, 'That's your neck of the woods, isn't it?

Chapter 28

Bryn spent the day mooching along the coast. The fish and chip lunch in the pub at the edge of Dungeness was the best he'd ever tasted. Afterwards, keeping well away from Hannah's bungalow, he spent some time wandering around. The atmosphere here was amazing, unlike anywhere he'd ever been. Under a sky that went on forever, it was, according to a guy in the pub, the largest area of shingle in Europe, and still growing. The sense of unchallenged space, an environment existing on its own terms, exactly fitted Bryn's frame of mind. He sat on the shingle between clumps of what looked like curly cabbage, its greeny-blue leaves almost hidden under domes of white flowers.

Just One of Those Blues on his MP3 player provided the right mood with Bruce Turner's alto sax gliding above Johnny Parker's staccato piano notes. Bryn watched a tiny striped spider creep from a sandy crevice and scurry across pebbles whose colours reminded him of honey humbugs, butterscotch toffee and mocha jelly beans. He'd buy some binoculars, he decided, come here often and find out more about the plants, birds and animals that lived in this incredible place.

No smugglers or revenue men interrupted his drive back to the Dungeness entrance gates. Listening to a DJ keep the Radio 2 audience in touch with life, he headed east, found his way back to Marine Drive and parked the pick-up round the corner outside what must be the Mulberry House garage. He was gathering together jacket, map and remnants of coconut ice when he realised he hadn't asked Alison for a front door key. If she, or the weird Miss Chiltern, wasn't there to let him in, he was scuppered.

Wasn't that the tousle head woman pedalling off like the clappers? Good thing he'd missed her. She'd not been at all happy about Alison letting him stay. Whistling *Of All the Wrongs You've Done to Me,* he approached the house.

Knocking brought no response and peering through the letter-box showed only an empty hallway. He went back ten yards down the drive and looked up at the house. In an upstairs window above the porch, Miss Chiltern was peeking round the net curtains. He gestured to the front door. 'Sorry to disturb you but I've got no key,' he called. 'Could you let me in please?'

She glared down on him as if he were an alien intent on taking over her life, then she dropped the curtain and disappeared from view.

Two pub meals in the same day wasn't the way things usually happened but nothing about the last couple of days was usual. An indeterminate time capsule had engulfed him, Bryn thought, and nothing that happened had anything to do with what was going on in the real world.

A quiz was underway in The Grey Goose, a bad-tempered affair by the sound of things. A guy with very trendy clobber and a sizeable, southern plum in his mouth was pontificating about the invention of the photocopier.

'It's nineteen thirty-seven, Adrian,' he insisted to the guy on the table next to his. 'Chester Carlson was granted a patent for a system which came to be known as Xerography.'

Adrian was smug. 'Sorry Prof, but it's James Watt, seventeen eighty. Pearl would bear me out. We saw his machine with our very own eyes, on the Antiques Road Show. I remember the date 'cos I was seventeen when I met Pearl.'

'And now she's eighty?' offered a muffled voice.

The landlord suggested splitting the difference and calling it eighteen-fifty-eight. Several drinkers applauded his maths but plum posh would have none of it.

'Adrian is right in one respect,' he conceded. 'James Watt did invent a copying machine, but it wasn't a *photo*-copier.' He prodded his answer sheet. 'The question asked who invented the photocopier .'

This was great stuff, Bryn decided. Good cheap food and free entertainment. He dunked a handful of French loaf into the last of the vegetable soup and reached for the cheese and relish sandwiches. Outside the bubble that life had become, Sylvia would be burbling about carb counts and calories but he couldn't hear her, could he?

On the way back to what was beginning to feel like home, he listened to Humphrey Lyttelton's *The Onions*, savouring those tiny gaps when the music's heartbeat faltered, momentary doubts before the trumpet weighed in again and the rhythm was restored.

The woman from the charity shop, Pru something or other, was coming down the path from Mulberry House, sporting the very dress he'd championed. It didn't look quite right.

'We're not on the stairs,' she said as he came level with her, 'so it's not bad luck to pass.' A fold of the floaty blue stuff clung to his trousers as she squeezed past him and then was gone, along with its owner. 'Good night to you,' she called over her shoulder.

'Sorry to disturb you,' he told Alison when she opened the door. 'I should have asked for a key.'

'I never thought,' Alison said. 'There must be several sets.'

Her accent was nearer to his own than anyone else's round here but her words were clipped with irritation. She seemed distracted, hair shoved behind rather large ears, dress creased, feet bare. Bryn followed her into the room off to the right, an office by the looks of it. The desk chair had been pushed back, the computer screen glowed on one side of the desk, a laptop on the other, envoys from a world he hoped never to revisit. 'Sorry,' he said again, 'but did you say there must be sets? Of keys?' he said.

She glanced at the computer and then at him.

'I can see you're busy,' he said. 'Sorry.' Third time now. Sylvia would be sneering in disdain, his never-apologise-never-explain father shaking his head in whatever section of the afterlife he'd booked ahead.

Alison was looking round the room as if she was unfamiliar with its habits. 'They're in here probably, the keys, though I haven't come across them yet.'

'Yet?'

She looked at him then, the sort of sizing-up look people give you when they're deciding if you fit the trustworthy category. She looked back to the computer, sighed, then said, 'I think I'd better explain what I'm doing here.'

'Not running a B&B perhaps?'

'Not exactly.'

As she explained her situation, she opened cupboards and drawers. Most of them were empty but one of the desk drawers held a box which rattled when she lifted it out.

'Eureka,' she said handing over the box. 'Help yourself.'

'You sure about that? According to Miss Chiltern upstairs I'm not only short but peculiar.'

Alison's laugh was sardonic. 'She's a fine one to talk.'

'So,' he went on. Not much point in bush-beating. 'You really have no idea why this Mrs Kulman left you the place?'

'None whatsoever.'

'But you dropped everything and came straight here? Without trying to find out more?'

She grabbed the box of keys and clattered it back into the drawer, her face stiff with annoyance.

Now you've blown it, Bryn thought. Overstepped the mark. You'll be out on your ear, sleeping in the pick-up. 'Sorry,' he said, 'shouldn't be poking my nose into your business.'

The tightness in her face relaxed. She flexed her fingers. 'Business sounds far too organised,' she said, 'I've no idea what I'm doing here and as to what I've left behind me in Derbyshire, well.' She stared up at the ceiling. 'Every move feels improvised.'

'That's what I like about jazz,' Bryn said, 'room for improvisation, doing your own thing. Playing at odds with the background rhythms Louis Armstrong called it.'

'Sounds like a recipe for chaos,' Alison suggested.

Derbyshire she'd said? Not too far from Prosser's, which explained the accent. She'd not been in Kent long, apparently. Might she have seen her local paper recently? Put two and two together about him?

He said, 'There is a framework with jazz but it's kept loose.' He twiddled the tag on the key ring, a black metal disc with a small outline of the building and MULBERRY HOUSE embossed in gold. 'You've been more than kind to me, telling me the score, letting me stay. Perhaps I should explain what I'm doing here too?'

'A holiday didn't you say, a return to the place you visited as a child? Where was it you said you come from?'

Brian felt his mouth open, his upper teeth prepare to fold across his bottom lip to form the word but what he heard himself say was, 'I'd rather not tell you if you don't mind.' What was it they used to say as kids? Sticks and stones may break my bones but words? He took a deep breath. 'I'm running away.'

She was staring at him now, surprise spreading over her face as if she'd expected a squishy soft centre but discovered a caramel.

Chapter 29

There was a scene in the film *The Go-Between*, Alison remembered, when Leo, the young lad, climbs to the top of the haystack in the farmer's yard. It's a pivotal moment, not just because the lad's on top of his world but because when he slides down, his life will never be the same again.

Was this her own pivotal moment, sitting here in front of Mrs Kulman's computer, her fingers hovering above keys Mrs K had tapped? Was this to be her first step into a foreign country of emotions she should never have visited?

'Your neck of the woods,' Pru had said. Adrenalin swelled, memory jigsawed the pieces together, an accident, a sports car, a woman driver killed, a woman visiting the area. Samantha had told her Mrs Kulman had died in Bakewell. Trying to control the fizz of excitement, Alison had hustled Pru in the direction of the front door and asked what sort of car Mrs Kulman had driven.

'Car?'

'She was killed in a car crash, yes? What sort of car was it?'

Pru stopped, one trainer-clad foot on the doormat, the other outside. 'The make you mean? Something that sounds like that illness divers get if they come up too quickly.'

'Divers? Oh I see. Benz? Mercedes Benz?'

'That's the ticket.'

'But what sort?' Agitation grabbed the words and flung them in Pru's direction. 'A saloon, a sports car, what?'

Pru stepped back into the hall, blocking the light. 'No need to shout,' she said. 'It was one of those with a roof you can roll back. Loved driving around with the roof down, she did. Proper lady muck, waving to the less fortunate.'

Alison had all but bundled her off the premises then rushed to her laptop. But Bryn's arrival had meant another delay. He seemed a nice guy, as much adrift as she was, but all that stuff about keys and jazz had held her up even more, when she was itching to get online. By the time she'd sat down to log on, her muscles were in fiery tautness, her jaw aching, her chest in a vice. Fingers and thumbs were hardly co-operative but eventually, skimming over full-page adverts she found the archive of the local paper back home.

The victim of the accident was 'Mrs May Kulman [76] who had been staying in a nearby holiday cottage. Witnesses to the fatality included Mrs Joan Redcliffe [84] resident of Sheldon Lifestyle Community. 'It fair shook me up,' Mrs Redcliffe said.'

Alison had banged the desk with clenched fists. How could she have been so stupid not to have worked this out earlier? Had her brain been so addled with one thing and another that it had stopped functioning? She pictured the woman she'd seen in the Sheldon Community lounge, the woman hugging her cardigan, remembered her stare. 'Before it's too late,' she'd said to Jude. What had that meant? Had Jude known who she was and what she was doing there?

She'd grabbed her phone and was scrolling down to Jude's number when a picture of her aunt filtered through her exasperation, Jude's face ashen, her fingers trembling, the relief in her eyes when the medication started to numb memory of the accident. The phone went back into her bag. Jude deserved a holiday. They could sort all this out when she got back.

Now, alone with the desktop icons the next pieces of the puzzle were waiting. Alison took a breath and clicked on My Documents.

Nothing.

Outlook Express: nothing incoming, nothing outgoing. Deleted items, empty.

Shortcut to Internet: internet history had been deleted.

Recycle Bin: empty.

There was nothing left to try.

It was tempting to hurl the computer out of the nearest window, to make it pay for its owner's deficiencies. Mrs Kulman was dead but though the dead were beyond retribution, the potency of their possessions was never completely neutralised. Frustration had Leo, the go-between, resorting to magic, rushing to gather deadly nightshade while the music score gathered pace and tension. But potions and spells harmed only himself.

It had been stupid to expect the computer to hold the answers. Someone who had so meticulously removed all trace of herself would hardly have let her computer go for repair with personal information intact. But that must have been some time before she'd travelled north. The repair guy had apologised for the delay. Mrs Kulman hadn't known she was about to die, suicide had never been mentioned, so why had she cleared her home of everything that could witness her life there?

Alison was about to turn off the computer when she noticed the lid of the key box was jamming the drawer. Reaching to free it, she glimpsed something that seemed out of place, a different colour. Pale blue plastic amongst the metallic black and gold, a memory stick. Before logic could dish out sound advice Alison slotted it into the computer.

PASSWORD?

Now, with Leo, she was tumbling down the other side of the stack, the hay scratching the backs of her legs, the cutting block at the bottom. But there was no dishy farmer to mop up a bloody mess, just a silence only the wind can inhabit.

What was the worst sort of password to use? Your own name. She typed KULMAN, then MAY, then as many variations as she could think of.

Someone else's name perhaps? CHILTERN brought not response. Without much thought she tried DRAPER. Had she imagined a flicker after the first two letters? She tried again omitting the vowels.

The screen went blank then, against a blue background, offered a file and a folder.

The file was in diary form:
January 4th Meeting with GT
Details arranged
Costs agreed
January 11th Appointment with LH
Will drawn up
Special arrangements discussed
January 15th GT's colleague to Bakewell
January 19th Report from GT

Similar cryptic notes and initials appeared for the next couple of months then, at the beginning of February, was a copy of an email sent to Peak Cottages with an open-ended arrangement to rent one of their properties.

The last entry was a spreadsheet detailing a list of coded costs.

The folder was full of photographs. Alison gasped.

Every single shot had been taken in and around Draper's Garden Centre. Here was her mother-in-law, Lady Golf Captain's smile, pearl ear-rings, dispensing advice to a bemused-looking woman in a green sweater. Here was Malcolm standing in the doorway to one of the greenhouses, his arms full of seedling trays. And now Alison herself getting into the delivery van. At the end of the slide-show were three shots of Malcolm's father.

Something snagged at her memory, a tall woman, reddish hair? Arrived at Draper's months back. Journalist for a magazine Alison had never heard of, *Gardening A Plot*? Too smartly dressed to ring true. She'd taken lots of photographs. Malcolm had been very keen to co-operate.

Chapter 30

The Dean's secretary, straight of back, dumpy of figure, flagellated the computer keyboard with broad fingers. Her eyes, behind round glasses, gleamed with glee. Ms. Marion Fowler, her desk plaque declared in a flowery Gothic script, she had, Thomas decided, probably chosen herself. Her hair, uncompromising in the face of twenty-first century aids to coiffeur, was the colour of mouldy hay.

He pictured her in the garb of her Anglo-Saxon forebears, wimple and facebands confining chubby cheeks, plaincloth gown parcelling uncorseted curves, the whole littered with the feathers that announced her father's occupation. Unaware of the benefits her namesake descendants would bestow on mankind (William in the eighteenth century, something or other to do with the manufacture of glass. John in the mid-nineteen-hundreds, the invention of a steam plough) she would plod her way from birth to dusty death with very little to show for her efforts.

She beamed in the general direction of where Thomas sat in what always felt like a penitential chair, low slung and designed for infants, adjacent to the great man's office.

'Won't be keeping-yew long now Dr Carr,' she chirped. 'The Dean's so busy these days. Not a moment to spare, poor man.'

Thomas nodded. Pointless to mention the small matter of an appointment, invitation even, relayed by those pounding fingers via cyberspace and reinforced by snail mail.

The Faculty noticeboard gave prominence to the Edward Burra exhibition, the poster hiding most of what lay beneath, a palimpsest of culture unusual in these parts. Since Alison swept off and took her opinions with her, he hadn't felt like a return visit to the Art Gallery.

The door to the inner sanctum opened and a pennant of floral fabric appeared at the level of Thomas's shoulder. The rest of the skirt followed, along with the silver belt cinching in a shapely waist. Behind this slice of déja vu bumbled the Dean, in unctuous mood.

'Lovely to have you on board, Professor Hartman,' he said extending the hand that rocked the cradle of the Faculty.

Glancing down on Thomas, Cordelia said, 'Need a hand up do you, Tom?'

'Dr Carr?' the Dean said.

Thomas pulled back his sleeve and glanced at his watch. 'We have, sorry had, an appointment. Fifteen minutes ago?'

'So,' Thomas said when the Dean stopped to take in air, 'what it amounts to is this, the temporary post has been awarded, without interview?'

The Dean arranged his face into conciliatory mode and offered to run the situation past Thomas again. 'You see,' he explained,' there are, now how shall I put it?' He gazed out of the window beside him, hoping perhaps to interrupt the flight of a passing guardian angel. 'There are, well you know how these things work, Dr Carr, there are implications.' He cleared his throat to make way for the steely touch. 'Financial implications.'

'As I recall, Dean,' Thomas countered, steel for steel, 'financial implications, like the poor, are always with us.'

The Dean, dogged in his furrow, ploughed on. 'The post was never formally advertised, as Human Resources agreed, so it was thought, well this offer was on the table.' He gazed at the ceiling. 'As you are well aware, Medieval History has been in the melting pot for some time.' He gulped then lowered his voice. 'Professor Bruce Hartman is, temporarily, to join the Physics Department, you see, and, well there has been mention of a Nobel. A great honour for the university if that were to be achieved.' He beamed over steepled fingers.

Sir Dreadnought shook his head in sorrow, for a vanished brotherhood of arms, failure to aid a stricken comrade, a melting away of mercenaries. Thomas sighed. 'And Professor Hartman, Professor Cordelia Hartman?'

For a moment, the Dean's expression crumpled into the sort of smile bestowed on kittens and pretty ladies but the demands of leadership were soon reasserted. 'Will hold a watching brief, a part time watching brief. Her interest, and indeed expertise, in the history of the creative arts will inject a fresh approach to our endeavours.'

'And Medieval History?'

The Dean fiddled with his in-tray files then hid behind them. 'Will, of course, remain a module on offer, to our undergraduates and MA students.'

'And doctorates?' Thomas leaned over the desk.

The Dean risked a peek round the files but then retreated. 'Well, these things are always addressed on an individual basis, as you know.'

'We're to be pampered with a brace of Professors then,' Thomas said. 'Professor Cordelia, on sabbatical from Midshires, holding a watching history brief, creatively speaking, and Professor Bruce, a temporary Physics loan, with financial implications and a Nobel carrot.' He tapped his finger on the side of his nose. 'Nothing in the way of American Litter Studies then? Small mercies continue to come our way.'

A puzzled expression filtered over the Dean's features. He slotted his hands into the edges of his cardigan. 'Sarcasm, Dr Carr, has always been considered the lowest form of wit.'

'Really?' Thomas said, pushing back his chair. 'What original thoughts you do have, Dean.' He stood up. 'May I enquire about my own position?'

'This university,' announced the Dean, lubricating his tone in accordance with dictates of the latest charm offensive, 'is not in the habit of arbitrarily downgrading its senior personnel.' Without getting up, he thrust his hand across the desk. 'The Establishment Committee does not meet to discuss future staffing for another three months.'

'Nice to see-yew, Dr Carr,' purred Ms. Fowler as Thomas strode across the Faculty Office . 'Have a nice day now.'

Thomas drummed his fingers on the steering wheel. Unhorse the bastard, fight on with mace and sword, tear up the manual of chivalry, let loose the crossbow bolt, brandish the decapitated head.

The figure of Rage in Tacuinum Sanitatis, the medieval handbook of health and wellbeing, he recalled, was pictured baring his chest and rending his garments with his teeth. To Thomas, caged inside the Jensen Interceptor, his mind a tornado of fury, garment-rending sounded about right. But, as was still the case, in the fourteenth century the enemy was never far away; beside the raging render in the picture, stood a guy wagging his finger in Dean-like admonition.

When every red traffic light looked like a call to arms and road junctions segued into tournament lists, driving was not a good idea. Thomas parked the car in a village just off the bypass. An oast-house turned pub was a good sanctuary in which to calm the sinews. He ordered a cup of black coffee and allowed a curvaceous serving wench to persuade him into eating a toasted teacake. Gradually, relishing the sight of charms behind the bar, he relinquished getting mad and began to devise the getting even.

Thomas was held up at the temporary traffic lights on Netherstone High Street. Where the shops used to be was now an ugly building site. Peering through the gap in the fencing, apparently provided to keep the natives interested in all the improvements about to come their way, was Adrian Cooper. Beside him Trixie was taking an interest in the genitals of an unattached mongrel.

Just before he reached the turning for his house, Thomas stopped at the crossing and waited for the little train to chug by. The train bridge over the military canal, with steam engine puffing across it and two canoeists gliding underneath was picture postcard stuff, the kind of image to be gracing many a mantelshelf.

He thought about his own mantelshelf, the hearth that had never felt like home. With things the way they were now, he needed to be rid of that house. Cordelia, due to take up her watching brief immediately, would not be on the interview board for the Midshires post Gwenda was after. If Gwenda didn't get the position, he was in trouble.

Pastures new beckoned. American universities were always delighted to get their hands on good, solid British academics. The Dean, over his academic moon to receive notice from Thomas, would gladly waive the usual period of notice in the euphoria of washing his hands of Medieval History. Thomas grinned. As soon as probate was granted on May's will, he'd settle the bequest to the charity she'd favoured and then get right away. By the time he drove the Jensen into the garage, his future was looking rosy.

Before he got out of the car, hubris erupted in a text from Lynwood Higton. 'Thomas old lad, major cock-up with May Kulman's will. Give me a bell asap'.

Chapter 31

The Tarot was best on her own, Daphne thought. Sharing it with Pru was always a mistake. She didn't understand the meanings of the cards and spoilt the readings with ridiculous suggestions. But Pru had never seen this deck, nobody else had, not since Luca gave it to her. In its sparkly blue, drawstring bag it was waiting inside the Victorian writing box. She lifted out the small package and ran the tassels over the backs of her hand.

*

'Look at these,' Luca says. His caravan is cosy, safe. He shows her the pictures, kings and queens and people in long robes. 'Oh how pretty,' she cries. The cards slip through his fingers and cascade onto the small table. He points to a knight on a white horse, carrying a goblet. 'That's me,' he tells her, 'your knight in shining armour.' He strokes her cheek. 'And here, look, I'm fighting off the opposition.' The next card is pale, with sky and water in the same soft blue. 'Here's you.' He points. She blushes to see the naked girl kneeling by the pool. 'My Daphne sitting in a garden.' She asks him what the shape by the lady's side means, a circle fixed to a downward pointing cross, enclosed in a heart. 'It stands for love,' he says.

*

For the short time she was with Luca, she'd loved sharing the happiness and sadness of those magic Tarot figures, their triumphs and despair. They meant so much to her, were so much part of him, that when he'd given her a generous stack of notes and told her to go and get some new things for herself, she'd slipped the deck into her handbag, to keep him close while she was away.

She wouldn't think about the sneers on the faces of the other lads when she'd got back, the crash and clatter of the fairground being dismantled, the hall of mirrors in sections on the ground. She wouldn't think about that dry, faded patch of grass where his caravan had been. Someone had sent him away and all she had left of him were his Tarot pictures, and his baby.

And now that baby had turned into a monster bent on revenge, not a silky turquoise-scaled dragon monster, like the one with St. George in the church window, but a fat, ugly toad who had come to inflict reprisals. She thought about the virgin who expected St. George to rescue her, standing there with her hands in the air. Perhaps she'd had a disappointing life.

'Is there more to me than just the disappointments, pusskins?' she said, looking round for the cat. Nelson seemed to have popped out.

She was making a supreme effort, deep breathing and pulling herself together nicely when the phone rang.

'You'll never guess.' Pru said. 'How are you by the way? Only our lass has just got in touch and they want us to go over there, for Christmas would you believe?'

'Over?'

'To the States, yes. We'll go early December and stay for a month or so. You'll have to help me choose.'

'Choose?'

'One of those jumpers. They're all the rage. You've opened my eyes to fashion, Daph. And not before time, I hear you say. I saw them in the paper, the jumpers, in one of those articles by the beautiful people who tell the rest of us what fantastic lives they live in London or somesuch.'

'But?'

'We knew it was coming though, didn't we?'

'Pru, I'm sorry but I'm not really, I mean, I'm just a wee bit anxious right now.'

'Sorry love, there I go blathering on again and there's you not too well.'

Was that what Pru thought, not too well? Crisis upon crisis, one trouble heaped on another, the darkest days for over fifty years and the friend she had trusted calling it not too well?

Luca's Tarot knew the score. There it was, right in front of her eyes, the Eight of Cups, the bowed figure leaving behind everything known and setting out into the wilderness.

'But it was in the tea leaves, wasn't it?' Pru was saying. Her voice rose to a very ugly crescendo. 'The kite? A holiday Pru, that's what you said and then you counted the spare leaves on the side of the cup? Six, remember? A holiday in six months.'

Daphne picked up the Eight of Cups card and held it to her face. Now Pru was about to desert her. She was truly alone, apart from Nelson of course. Dear pusskins, it would be such a comfort to stroke him, feel his warmth on her knee, the soft fur under her fingers but you can't force these things. Love has to be earned.

She would have to drag herself out, there was hardly any food left in the kitchen. She'd find some nice sardines for poor pusskins. He knew who loved him.

When she got back she'd go for her dip. She would float in the nurturing, life-giving water, float and drift with her sisters, the sea nymphs, the only beings she could call kinfolk. Gently she put down the phone on Pru and went to find her bag.

Daphne had no memory of leaving the house but she seemed to be on the High Street. Was there something she had to buy? Go past the shops she told herself and it will come to you. But the shops were surrounded by a high wooden fence, topped with barbed wire. Above it she could see the columns of the shop she wouldn't think about, the roof of the butcher's, the mini-market name board. Somewhere a bulldozer was raising dust.

'Getting on with it, aren't they?'

It was Mr Cooper, with that poodle of Pearl's.

'Soon get a move on when they get started these boys,' Mr Cooper said. About time too in Pearl's view.'

'What's happening?' Daphne said. Had Pearl meant something was happening to her, or to the shops? Nothing was the same.

'It's the supermarket,' Mr Cooper said. He pulled the poodle away from a very nasty looking dog. 'Stop that Trixie. Naughty girl.'

'You mean our old shops have gone?'

Mr Cooper scooped the poodle off the pavement and tucked her under his arm. 'Abbas has a temporary building round the corner,' he said. 'Should get most of the stuff you want there, for the time being.'

Daphne stared at the street that wasn't her street, at the fence that had grown where her shops used to be. This was her fault, all her fault. Samantha had asked her to sign a petition to stop all this, to keep things as they were. And what had she done? Brushed her aside, that's what, gone off on the bus, ignored the one person who had shown her any true kindness. And now Mr Jenkins had lost his livelihood, the mahogany counters, the two ounces of mild Cheddar for Jim's tea, the Chopin festival. All gone. All her fault.

Mulberry House, that's where she needed to be. Warm and cosy in her flat, where she belonged. Nelson would be waiting. He'd understand how upset she was, how lonely since everything had changed. She could rely on Nelson.

But when she got there, the house stared down in disapproval. Who is this stranger on my path? You have no business here. From inside came laughter, laughter at her expense. The door didn't want her to open it, the key wouldn't turn. The laughter stopped and footsteps came down the hallway. She slid to the side of the porch, clinging to its trellis.

'Hallo?' Samantha peered round the side of the porch. 'Oh it's you, Daphne. God, you gave me a fright. I thought it was a Marsh ghost.' She turned back down the hall. The kitchen door was open, no more rent-on-Friday's, no more sizzling breakfasts for the guests, just the sickly smell of something on the cooker.

'Only Daphne,' Samantha called to The Heiress. She'd been in there with Her, laughing about Daphne. He was there too, the man who'd come to punish her, laughing with them, cooking up something. He must have told them who he was. Samantha had joined in. Telling Daphne's secrets. Laughing about Luca. She must get up the stairs, get to Nelson.

'Have a piece of fudge, Miss Chiltern?' the man called. 'Freshly made.'

The Heiress looked up then, looked up from the chair she was sitting on over by the window. Her eyes met Daphne's, cool and smiling in triumph. And, on her lap, snuggled and nuzzling and purring, was a tabby cat. It couldn't be. But it was. It was Nelson.

Chapter 32

Alison woke from a dream of making love with Malcolm. They were young and happy, cosy on a sheepskin rug in front of a log fire. Outside, snow fell like gliding lace and muffled the world beyond their window. She hugged the savour of the dream, the joy of how they were then, before sex became hedged by charts and rules and calculations. Waiting for the clench of loss to recede, she listened to the new day.

Her ears expected now to wake to the rustle of mulberry branches, the whispers of the sea; her morning eyes no longer blinked in bewilderment. This ground floor bedroom at the back of the house overlooked the garden with its mulberry tree, covered now in a lather of white blossom. The room had no view of the sea and it was shaded by Daphne's fire-escape but it was tucked away, the refuge she needed.

She'd begun to make small claims, re-arranging the furniture, moving the bed from under the window so that she could lie and watch the rectangle of light disappearing at night and returning in the morning. That was her necklace strung across the dressing table mirror, her dressing gown on the back of the door. The clothes hanging in the wardrobe were hers, not redolent of stale citrus but of recently-bought cedarwood balls in a smart, mesh bag tied with jade green ribbon. Most of the spaces her life had offered had been borrowed. This was beginning to feel her own.

The sitting room next door was lighter, more airy and comfortable and with a view out to sea but she wasn't ready yet for its public face.

Upstairs was a void above her head. She didn't go there but Bryn had made himself at home. He was moving about now and the water pipes gurgled. They'd come to an agreement about using the kitchen. He seemed a nice guy. It was good to have him around.

A couple of days ago he'd appeared with a bag full of groceries. 'Fancy some coffee fudge?' He'd delved into the bag and plonked the ingredients onto the work surface. They stood there, milk, sugar, butter, coffee essence, like a still life painting. 'I've even remembered this,' he said, returning to the bag and pulling out a cooking tray. 'I'm not sure yet what's in the cupboards.'

'You intend to stay long enough to find out, do you?' Alison had teased. He'd blushed, a nice old-fashioned blush, and apologised. 'It's just that I feel at home here,' he said. She'd been about to say she knew what he meant but she changed her mind.

Then Samantha had turned up and the pair of them had set to, under Bryn's instructions. 'Milk and sugar into a strong saucepan.' His tone was gentle, concerned for the success of these fledgling fudge makers. Alison and Samantha had taken turns to stir over a mild heat, to allow the golden, bubbled boiling to last about fifteen minutes, all the time pulling Bryn's leg about beck-and-call serving wenches. Samantha had asked if he'd learnt to make sweets at his mother's knee, spent his childhood slaving over hot stoves. He'd batted off all her questions with jokes and clowning which had them hooting with laughter.

The hilarity must surely have seeped across the hall softening the sharp corners of those empty dining tables, billowing over the lounge's uncreased cushions. It had certainly seeped under the front door and irritated Thomas.

'Forgive the interruption,' he'd said when Alison answered his knock. He sounded very far from sorry. He glared beyond her. 'I can see you're fully occupied just now.' No way could he have missed the smothered giggles and he probably heard Samantha wonder who'd rattled the good doctor's cage. He'd departed with a curt request that she ring him sometime soon, striding off down the front path, his neck poker stiff.

Back in the kitchen Bryn was pouring water into a saucer. 'Drop a little of the mixture in here,' he said. The three of them watched the tiny dollop roll itself into a ball in the water. 'Done!' Bryn had triumphed, adding the coffee essence to the saucepan, waiting a moment then beating the dark veins into the thickening mixture.

While the fudge cooled and set in its tin, they were like children waiting for Christmas, constantly jumping up to inspect the tray of sweetmeats and needing to be dissuaded from having a little prod. In the end Samantha had entertained them with affectionate tales of what she called the churchy people who crossed her path these days. Nelson had sidled round the door, spotted the space on Alison's lap and filled it with his warm, furry bulk. The sun had co-operated, sending soft shafts of pink evening light through window, kitchen and into the hall.

But then Daphne had arrived.

What would today bring? Alison knew she ought to investigate what she had found on Mrs Kulman's memory stick but something held her back. Was she afraid that finding the truth would spoil this new life she was beginning to enjoy?

She pulled on her dressing gown and padded barefoot into the kitchen. Bryn was filling the kettle. 'Sorry,' he said.

'Has anyone ever counted how many times a day you say that?' Alison said.

He closed the kettle lid and plugged in. 'Sorry?'

'That's twice already and I've only been here two minutes.'

He grinned, a big, friendly, brown-bear grin and began to click his fingers and tap his foot as the kettle hummed. Following the rhythm, Alison joined in. 'What are we tapping to?' she said

'Jimmy Yancey,' he said, picking mugs from the drying rack. 'This one's called *Yancey Stomp*.'

'Sounds like a guy who means business.'

What he was seeing on the cupboard door, Alison had no idea but it made him smile.

'Seventeen I was,' he said, 'when I first met Jimmy. I'd go round to use Gran's radiogram. The old records sound better on the old machines.'

He was well down memory lane now. Alison smiled and poured steaming water into the tea pot.

'It'll be the music box you're wanting, not me, Gran used to say. Don't worry, I won't tell your father. She had one of those really old-fashioned front rooms, the sort where the stag's still at bay over the mantelpiece and the piano lid's firmly shut to repel boarders. But fit the disc onto the green baize turntable, lower the needle and wow, the likes of Jimmy Yancey boogied into my life.' He sighed and took the mug of tea from Alison, without looking at it. 'Piano keys trilling, rivulets of sound flicking, fluttering. Bass notes anchoring the four-beat. How can your fingers help but click and your feet tap? I'd throw off the horrendous suit jacket Dad made me wear for work, fling my cufflinks into the arms of the sofa. and roll up my sleeves. And then? Surrender. I swear Jimmy looked up and winked.'

It was unexpected, Alison thought, to find poetry in a guy like Bryn but it was the poetry of passion, likely to turn up in unexpected places. He'd talked about running away. That made two of them.

Outside a gull called, then another. Above Bryn's head, the clock ticked. He looked at Alison and winked.

'Magic,' she said. But a gate had closed behind Bryn's eyes, his expression was wary, too wary to invite questions about the father, the hated jacket, the sort of work he did.

The cat edged round the door. 'Eh up, Nelson,' Bryn said. 'Hungry are you mate?'

'That's his name is it?' Alison said. 'He's been meowing around the place a lot lately. I put some milk down for him yesterday and he wolfed it as if cows had been on strike for a month.' She bent down and stroked him.' We shouldn't really feed you, should we?' she said. 'But you look famished.'

'Any sign of Miss Chiltern?' Bryn said.

'Come to think of it, no, not for a couple of days. Have you seen her?'

'She runs a mile if she sets eyes on me,' Bryn said. 'I don't know why.'

'Who knows what goes on in that mind of hers. Weird or what? I've never met anyone remotely like her.'

'And that's a fact, as her friend Pru would say.'

'You've met her then?'

'I wonder,' Bryn said, 'if she's all right, the old lady upstairs I mean.' He went out into the hall. 'Shall I knock on her door on my way past?'

Alison sighed. 'Leave it a while. Sleeping dogs and all that. She may have gone away for a couple of days.'

'Without saying anything?'

'Well she wouldn't would she? She treats me like I'm some kind of monster from the north.'

Bryn laughed. 'I'll keep an eye out though, and an ear perhaps? Is that your phone?'

Alison picked it up.

'Alison dear? It's Joan Redcliffe.'

'Joan?'

'From Sheldon Lifestyle, that's right. I have got the right number haven't I? This is Alison, Jude's niece?'

Alison steadied herself on the edge of the sink. This didn't sound good. 'Yes, Joan,' she said, 'it's me. Is something wrong?'

'I don't know how to put this. It's Jude dear, your aunt.'

Jude was due back from France today. Back to her old self, raring to go was the plan. Alison swallowed. 'Has something happened to her, Joan?'

'You'd better come soon as poss dear, Jude's in the hospital. I'm afraid she's had a stroke.'

Chapter 33

Daphne couldn't remember deciding to take a trip on the little train but here she was. It was years since she'd had a ride. The tiny carriage rocked along soothingly, the steam puffing gently past the window.

'Romney, Hythe and Dymchurch Light Railway, loco number ten,' someone in the carriage said. She couldn't be sure how far away the voice was. 'Called Dr Syn now.'

Dr Syn, The Marsh Scarecrow, Daphne thought, that evil apparition galloping round the countryside in his skeleton mask, trying to make his poor wife come back to him apparently. She'd eloped with the man she loved, poor lamb. And who could blame her?

'Twenty-eight feet in length.' The voice was young, intense. 'Eight ton, fifteen hundredweight. The Light Railway Company has yet to change to the metric measuring system.'

Sounds flowed, the swish of fabric against the seat, a rubber sole squeaking on the floor, the pulse thumping in her ear. From outside, the whisper of wind through grasses, a gull's shriek, the clacketting of train wheels. And high above her arched the calls of the water nymphs, marsh to sea, sea to marsh, sister to sister, a cocoon of song.

'What d'you think, of my sketch, Jake?' Another voice, slightly deeper, alto perhaps, quite near.

Daphne blinked and tried to see the speakers but her eyes seemed cloudy.

'I think, Mum,' the first voice said, 'that you've drawn the cab very well. The Canadian style loco has a larger cab than some others, so it gives the driver more protection in inclement weather.'

'That's a good word, inclement,' the woman said.

Daphne felt a tap on her arm and looked down on fingers with grubby nails. 'This is the last stop,' a young woman said. 'You'll need to get off now.'

'You might be allowed to stay on whilst the train goes round the reversing loop, ready for the return journey,' the intense voice explained. 'So you could go back if you want to.'

Daphne heard someone thank him. Perhaps it was her?

There was a white building. She stood with her back to it, hands behind her, feeling the rough, pebbly walls. If she went hand over hand she could find where the wall ended.

'Are you feeling all right?' someone said. 'Can we get you something to drink?'

'Come inside and sit down.'

She was sitting on a hard chair. Someone bent over her. There was a hoot, then a hiss of steam. 'I must get back,' she said and held out her ticket.

'Let us take you back to the train,' the alto voice said. 'Is there someone I can call, to meet you perhaps?'

There are times when things get a little hazy, Daphne told herself on the ride back. Silly old Daphne, too much worry that's your trouble. She closed her eyes. Dark haired babies, pennies in hems, waiting in the wings, pointing fingers. Silly old pictures.

When she got off the train she tried to nudge her mind into remembering. Where was it she had to go?

'Can I help?' The man beside her was tall and dark.

'Luca?' she said.

'Where is it you live?' Can I call you a taxi?'

Of course, that's why he hadn't come before, he hadn't known where she was. Now he was here, everything will be all right.

'There's a policeman over there,' someone said. 'The poor soul needs help.'

'It's all right,' Daphne heard herself say. 'Luca's gone to call a taxi to take us back to Mulberry House.'

Daphne climbed the stairs to her flat. There was no Luca. There was no May. No Pru. No Nelson.

In her bedroom she undressed, left her clothes in a neat pile and stepped into her swimming costume. Sliding her arms into the aqua towelling robe, she looked round at the walls, glowing soft apricot in the evening light, at the velvet green curtains, the dressing table with her brushes and combs. She touched the silk of the cream bedcover, ran her fingers along the frilled edge of the pillowcases. All these things had once been hers. She tucked the Eight of Cups card into her robe pocket and went into the sitting room, checked there were two sheets of paper in the envelope no longer behind the clock but on the Regency table, then went back down the stairs.

Once over the road, over the shingle, past the sandy belt and with Mulberry House far behind her, she walked into the sea. Here there were no more betrayals of friendship, no more sinister figures from the past, no more disappointments, only the waiting arms of her true sisters.

PART 4

The mulberry tree – a long-lived but slow-growing tree, tolerant of a range of soils and climates

Chapter 34

On his way back from giving Alison a lift to Ashford Station, Bryn discovered the sound mirrors. Before going back to the Marsh, he'd bought an expensive pair of binoculars, explaining the cash sale by a recent win on the horses. He knew he'd have to be careful not to use this explanation too often. Being without credit card or bank account had its disadvantages and drawing attention by wafting around large wads of notes was the last thing he needed.

Not far from Marine Drive he stopped at a road junction and noticed some very odd shapes on the skyline. He got as near as he could by road, parked and got out of the pick-up. This was a good opportunity to try his new purchase.

He was looking at a small island, gravelly brown and covered with tufts of stubby grasses. The shapes he'd seen from a distance were concrete structures, two tilted, shallow bowls, one about 10 metres in diameter, the other smaller, both mounted into supports. Some distance away stretched a curved wall, well over fifty metres long, a skateboarder's dream by the looks of it.

'Alison get off all right, did she? She phoned me, about going back up north.'

Samantha was coming towards him, toting a camera with the biggest lens Bryn had ever seen. 'Fascinating aren't they?' She pointed over the fence. 'The sound mirrors?'

'Sound mirrors? What the dickens are they?'

Samantha readjusted the camera lens. 'Built to provide early warning of enemy aircraft apparently. Obsolete technology.'

'It looks like a set for an early Star Wars movie,' Bryn said. 'They were forerunners of radar then?'

'S'pose so. Aren't the shapes wonderful?'

'Interesting, certainly.'

The camera shutter clicked and clicked again. 'What do you think?' She showed him one of the shots. 'I'm aiming for a hint of mystery.' She lowered the camera and looked at him. 'Rather like you.'

'Sorry?'

'You're a bit of a mystery yourself, aren't you?' Head on one side, she regarded him solemnly. 'Stranger in the night, fudge maker, chauffeur to women in distress. Where could you have come from?'

Bryn peered through the binoculars at the sound mirrors. They had the look of another world but he was getting used to that feeling. 'Alison got the train okay,' he said. 'She was right to wait until this morning. Public transport's hell at night.'

'She seemed very worried. I hope her aunt's okay. She brought her up, didn't she say? It must be odd, not knowing your parents, don't you think? Have you seen Daphne at all?'

Bit of a free player this one, Bryn thought, flitting from one variation to another with no regard for theme. Whatever was going on was beyond him. But women were beyond him, as he should have recognised long ago. He said, 'I seem to make her very jumpy. Miss Chiltern, I mean. Can't think why.'

'But you've met her before, haven't you? You mentioned it the night you arrived. She was in quite a state wasn't she, poor thing? What d'you reckon all that was about?'

'I did meet her,' Bryn said slowly, 'years ago when I was a kid. My Dad and I stayed a night at Mulberry House.'

'And you remembered it from all that time back? For no other reason? Only I got the impression,' Samantha pushed her hair out of her eyes, 'there might be more to it than that.'

Watch your back, laddo, Bryn told himself. We're off the diatonic scale here. 'Heard of cross-rhythm, have you?' he said.

Samantha unscrewed the long lens from her camera and eased it into its slot in her bag. 'Say again?'

'Cross-rhythm, something that jars with the original beat.' He looked at his feet. 'We started with sound mirrors and now it's the third degree?'

She grinned. 'Don't mind me. My Dad's always telling me to get my brain in gear before letting out the mouth clutch.'

'Maybe it's time you tried an automatic then?'

The camera was back in its case now. Samantha closed the zip and said, 'I'm sorry. Put it down to the artistic temperament.'

'Dad again?'

'Tony mostly, my husband.'

'The vicar?'

'Strange as it may seem, yes. He wasn't a vicar when he married me.'

Bryn grinned at her. 'That explains it then.' Was it really him coming out with this bantering stuff?

'Going back to Daphne,' she glanced up at him. 'She isn't answering her landline. She doesn't have a mobile. Have you seen her, since the night we made the fudge? Once I got home, I realised how upset she'd looked. If I hadn't been so busy with this assignment, I'd have gone to see her. I've phoned several times but no joy.'

Bryn remembered what Alison had said about not seeing Daphne, about how hungry Nelson had been. 'Perhaps I should have knocked on her door after all.'

'But you didn't know what sort of reception you'd get. Can't say I blame you.'

'Is there someone else who might know if she's okay?' Bryn said. 'What about that friend who came round the night I arrived? Pru, is it?'

'Good idea,' Samantha said, 'I pass her house on my way home. I'll call in.'

'Let me know how you get on, will you?' Bryn hooked the binoculars onto his shoulder. 'If help's needed, I'm on the premises.'

'What's your mobile number?' Samantha got out her phone.

Bryn hesitated. Not having the normal trappings of modern life was more complicated than he'd imagined. 'You can ring me on the Mulberry House line,' he said. 'Alison's given me the key to the office.'

Samantha gave him a funny look and opened her mouth to say something but then she seemed to change her mind and just nodded.

The girl with the coconut-ice hair was changing the Dandy Candy window display. Inside latex gloves her fingernails looked like green jelly beans trapped under ice.

It was easier this time to ignore the red and gold labels. Prossers was just a name, not quite like any other brand but just an arrangement of letters.

'Yellow and brown's the new colour scheme then?' Bryn said watching her nudge the noses of chocolate mice nearer to a row of fat-tummy jelly babies. 'With hints of green?'

The girl looked up from the diagram she was following. 'Whatever,' she said reaching for a jar of Lime Sherbets.

'Selling well, are they?' Bryn said, 'the sherbets?'

The girl's frown reminded him that sales figures were no longer his concern.

'Your own design, is it?' he said quickly. 'The window?'

She sneered down at the diagram. 'Not so's you'd notice.'

'I'll have a couple of those chocolate mice, please. When you're ready. And a large bag of liquorice allsorts.'

Bryn drove back to Mulberry house and sat on a bench overlooking the beach. He was happier here on the grass verge, a respectful distance from the shore with its unstable shingle and wavelets sliding and retreating over patches of sand. There was that awful sense of being on the brink of things, vulnerable.

'You need to conquer the fear, son,' his father used to say, though whether he was talking about the sea, the rugby scrum, stripping off in the changing room or any of the other challenges other boys took in their stride, it was impossible to pinpoint.

The bag of allsorts crinkled as he got it out of his pocket. There they all were, the layered ones waiting to be dismantled, the coconut offering to be nibbled, the tubular ones itching for an enthusiastic tongue to flatten them.

The memory of his father wanted to tell him about the origin of allsorts, about Charlie Thompson the salesman who had spilled the contents of the separate trays, creating by mistake the allsorts image. Bryn ignored him, slit open the bag and grabbed a blue, aniseed jelly. He closed his eyes and set about sucking away the sugary bobbles.

'Mum and I have been looking for round, flat pebbles.' Jake was standing at the end of the bench, his bony knees sticking into the space between the bench arm and seat. There were green splodges on his t-shirt and a rip in his jeans. 'We borrow them for a while, 'til Mum's done her paintings. Then we put them back. '

'Good plan,' Bryn said. 'Your Mum about, is she?'

'She has gone to spend a penny,' the lad said, 'though it doesn't really cost a penny. It's just a polite thing to say. We saw you sitting here and she said I could come and talk to you.'

'She said that, did she?' Maybe she hadn't had him down as a fool after all. Nice thought.

'She said that someone who was afraid of geese couldn't really be dangerous.'

Bryn winced at this stark honesty.

'She did laugh when she said it,' Jake explained, 'so it may have been a joke.'

Resisting the urge to offer the bag of allsorts, Bryn plumped for a change of subject. 'I saw the sound mirrors today,' he said. 'They're interesting aren't they?'

Jake perched on the edge of the bench, as far away from Bryn as he could manage. 'Sound mirrors, also known as acoustic early warning systems, were designed to catch the noise of approaching aircraft,' he said. 'There was a microphone attached to a metal pole in the middle of the dishes.' He slid his hands under his thighs and swung his legs. 'The wall was a later design. In the nineteen-thirties, when aircraft became faster, the mirrors weren't any good because the planes could be seen before the mirrors worked.'

'And by then radar had been developed?' Bryn said.

'Considered to have been invented by Sir Robert Alexander Watson-Watt, about nineteen thirty-nine.'

How different this was from his father's expositions, Bryn thought. Dropped to demonstrate your ignorance, his facts sat in your path like land mines. Jake's facts hid no agenda of one-upmanship, of making you feel inadequate. They were benign, neutral.

'You'd be good on the pub quiz team.' Bryn said.

'I am not old enough for a pub quiz team,' Jake said sternly.

'There seems to be a lot of reminders of the war around here,' Bryn said. 'Isn't that a Mulberry Harbour out there?'

'Mulberry House is just behind us,' Jake said, 'The lady who lived there liked Mum's paintings. She has died. She had a lot of boxes.'

'Boxes?'

Jake nodded. 'A whole van full of boxes, not a removal lorry but a two thousand and nine Ford transit van like the one that delivers Mum's canvases. It had butterflies painted all over it. '

'When did you see this?' Bryn said. 'The Mulberry House boxes.'

'Before the lady died. I was sitting in the car on Ashton Gardens waiting for Mum. She hadn't gone to spend a penny that time.'

'No?'

'She was delivering some of her paintings to the lady who sells them in her shop. She lives on Ashton Gardens, the lady with the shop.'

'And you saw Mrs Kulman?'

'I don't know anyone called Mrs Kulman. The Mulberry House lady was bringing boxes out of the garage and putting them into the butterfly van. There was a man helping her, the man with a fat wife, the lady who usually wears a dirty track suit.'

Chapter 35

Lynwood Higton wanted to meet Thomas in the aero club. 'More privacy in the clubhouse there,' he'd said. 'And I have a session on the simulator booked that morning.' Apparently, for some reason the golf club was off limits and his office wasn't an option.

Thomas had spent the past few days working on an article for *Past Issues*, a magazine edited by an Oxbridge reject only too willing to court scholastic controversy. Thomas's pitch for a series entitled *Past Usefulness? Historical Research in the Modern World*, had been welcomed with enthusiasm. They paid well and were happy for contributors to publish under a pseudonym. He'd toyed with calling himself The Green Knight, appropriate for someone mysterious and sometimes terrifying, but decided it was too near his own field to ensure anonymity. In the end he'd plumped for Albedo. Few readers would realise it was what alchemists called the cleansing, the second stage of their Great Work.

This first article, *Novelty or Nonsense?* questioned whether novelists could ever accurately convey the flavour of the age in which they wrote. Cordelia had published two papers on the subject. In a tone more sorrowful than censorious, he savaged her arguments without mentioning her name.

To keep him in the right mood, he'd printed off a portrait of the sorceress Morgan le Fay, not a bland pre-Raphaelite version but a raven-haired witch, girdled with skulls and clutching a crystal ball. Her alluring bare breasts he'd covered with a Best-before label peeled from a packet of ham.

Sir Dreadnought, ready with the winner's trophy, was standing by with reinforcements. Hadn't he pointed out more than once that Thomas needed to get his women in order? Look where the notion that nothing was ever a lady's fault had got King Arthur. Ladies who deviated from their role as kind, honourable and softly-spoken supporters forfeited their right to a knight's protection.

Thomas nodded, replaced a full stop with a semi-colon and closed down the computer. There was just time to take Nell for a quick run before setting of to meet Lynwood.

He was half way down the drive and bending to fix Nell's lead when Anna Bestwood's car pulled in.

'Sorry,' he called. 'Not a good time.'

'On the contrary,' she said, getting out of the car, 'I could do with a walk.'

Thomas pictured her spiky heels skinned by pebbles. 'So be it,' he said.

But Ms Bestwood's presence didn't feature as far as the beach. Stride for stride she matched his pace past the Edwardian terrace and 60's boxes, all the while commenting on the weather, the misunderstood profession of private investigation, her efforts to ensure her daughter was chosen Carnival Queen this year. When they got to the mismatched semi's, with Nell at the end of the extended lead nosing the remains of a dead mouse, she faced him.

'Mr Thornly took your advice.' she said, 'and consulted with Mrs Kulman's solicitor.'

That hint of efficiency was attractive, Thomas decided, a delightful nanny air, a starched insistence. 'I'm flattered to hear it,' he said.

Her eyebrows disappeared under her fringe. 'You might not think so,' she said, 'when I tell you that no progress was made with our claim for expenses incurred by the late Mrs Kulman.'

'Tell you that debts die with the debtor, did he, old Higton?'

Her expression veered from smirk to sneer. 'Mr Higton indicated that matters concerning Mrs Kulman's estate are, how did he put it, the complex side of complicated.'

'That sounds like the Higton we all know and love,' Thomas said. 'I have an appointment with him to discuss that very matter.' He looked at his watch. 'In less time than I realised. You'll have to excuse me. Good day to you.'

Her voice followed him round the corner. 'Mr Thornly asked me to tell you, Dr Carr, that he does not see this as the end of the matter.'

'Sorry to keep you, Thomas,' Lynwood Higton bustled through the door of the clubhouse. 'I've just been over the Alps, so to speak. Closest I get to the real thing, more's the pity.' His glasses were a toboggan on the slide of his nose. 'Twenty-twenty vision's long gone I'm afraid and you can't take to the air without it these days. Little lady's okay though. She gets our skyrider aloft, no problem.' He nodded at the cup on the table in front of Thomas. 'Someone told you about the victuals then? We look after ourselves nowadays.' He pointed to a state-of-the-art coffee machine. 'Jeeves there makes a good fist of it, don't you think? Should be some biscuits around somewhere or other. I'll have a decko.'

His gait across the room was stiff, unbending, like his opinions, according to The Grey Goose fraternity. He came back with his own cup and a mini packet of custard creams.

'Not a bad little set-up here,' he said, pointing to the floor-to-ceiling windows. 'Overlooking the main apron, watching the safety guys do their stuff, planes coming and going.'

'This isn't a social call, Lynwood,' Thomas said.

'Indeed not.' Lynwood checked over his shoulder for spies in the camp, then leaned across the table. 'Damned nuisance. Hence the meeting here. I'd be grateful if this didn't get out, not until the firm is well clear of any fall-out. It's all down to that idiot up north, Derbyshire was it?'

'Tell me more,' Thomas said.

'The guy's made a complete balls-up of the Last Will and Testament of the late and not very lamented May Kulman.' Lynwood stuck the edge of the biscuit packet between his teeth and yanked at the cellophane. 'Want one?'

Thomas shook his head. 'Thing is, Lynwood, I'm a bit pushed for time today.'

The solicitor slid out a custard cream, bit off a chunk and chewed. Crumbs splattered over his sweater. 'Damned tricky situation.'

'I never was sure how the Derbyshire guy got in on the act,' Thomas said. 'I thought you drew up the will yourself. '

Lynwood popped the remaining biscuit segment into his mouth and rubbed his hand over his chin. 'The original will, yes.' He held up his hand to quieten Thomas's questions. 'Hear me out, there's a good chap' He pushed his glasses up his nose. 'About eighteen months ago, May Kulman came to see me to update the will she made some years back. She was very precise about the bequests, the Mulberry House property to this Mrs Alison Draper with the stipulation about Miss Chiltern's flat, five thousand to you in gratitude for your teaching skills and for taking on the duties of executor, the rest, the considerable rest, properties and investments and what not, to this single parent charity. Nothing complicated. Done and dusted in a couple of days, signed, witnessed and deposited in our strong room.'

'Those updates, to the will,' Thomas said, 'did they change things much, from the earlier will, I mean? '

Lynwood shook his head. 'Sorry, Thomas. Client confidentiality and all that.'

'Beyond the grave?'

'Indeed so.'

Which means he can't remember, Thomas thought. Outside, a small aircraft skimmed the edge of his vision and buzzed into the clouds. The coffee machine hissed. 'So?' he said.

'So,' Lynwood said, 'Last January she called to tell me she was going away for a while, maybe for good. 'Before it's too late to put things right,' she said. She didn't want it to get out, swore me to secrecy. But one thing she was very clear about, she wanted a photocopy of her will to leave with a local solicitor, along with my details, in case.'

'In case of what?'

'In case of her demise. Make it easier for the local johnny to know whom to contact.' Lynwood rubbed his chin. 'Damned odd thing her smashing into that lorry. She was a good driver. I've wondered since if there was more to it, but sleeping dogs and all that, though I have had my doubts.' He stroked his chin. 'I left the copying to one of the juniors, who made a complete balls-up of the thing. Ink cartridge running out I suppose. Had to pretend to Mrs Draper that someone else had done the business.'

Were all solicitors disappointed barristers, Thomas wondered, aching for a captive audience, meandering around the finer legal points?

'What do you mean about doubts?' Thomas said, 'Doubts about the cause of death you mean? Is that the problem you referred to?'

Lynwood's jaw dropped. 'Good lord, no. Don't make waves like that, old man. Properly appointed inquest verdict, no question, no question at all. Even if there were a suggestion of such a thing, which there isn't, it wouldn't involve you, as the executor.'

Why the hell hadn't he left all this business to Lynwood, as the guy had offered, Thomas thought. Probate, a piece of cake had been his attitude. Any fool could fill in a couple of forms. Overconfidence, Sir Dreadnought was suggesting. No two ways about it.

'Still,' Lynwood was saying, 'at least probate hasn't been granted and the main legatee of the earlier will hasn't been informed.'

'Sorry?'

'You'll need to apply for probate on the first will to be cancelled. Start all over again. I'd like to help you out on this one, Thomas, but there it is. We're about to take to the skies, the little lady and yours t. Extended holiday, hopping around, EU countries mainly. A fitting prelude to an early but well-earned retirement.'

'You've lost me,' Thomas said. 'What's all this about cancelling the probate application?'

Lynwood sighed. 'It's what the executor has to do,' he said enunciating each word, 'when another will turns up.'

'What other will?'

'The one the Derbyshire guy unearthed last Friday. The one May Kulman made a fortnight before she died. The one she omitted to tell me about. It postdates the one I drew up.'

Thomas slammed his fists on the arms of his chair. 'A bloody balls-up indeed, Lynwood.'

'My sentiments exactly, old man. Some people should never be allowed within a mile of a legal document. The Derbyshire feller past his sell-by date perhaps? Not that you heard me say that. Professional courtesy and all.'

'You're telling me that the will we have, the will I've spent all this time on is not valid?

'Not the *last* Will and Testament, I'm afraid. Damned nuisance.'

Thomas flopped back in his chair. 'And there are changes?'

'Indeed so, not drastic, well not in one sense. It's more a question of re-distribution. I'll make sure you get your copy in due course.'

'Bloody hell, man, put me out of my misery, can't you?'

'Keep it down, Thomas old lad.' Lynwood checked for eavesdroppers. 'Mrs Draper still inherits Mulberry House with Miss Chiltern as sitting tenant. The charity now receives property to the value of one hundred thousand pounds, and you still get your five. No worries there.'

'And the rest?'

'The rest,' Lynwood paused in the manner of TV knock-out competitions. 'The rest, goes to the said Miss Daphne Chiltern.'

Chapter 36

The ward buzzed with afternoon visitors, a subdued buzz, Alison thought, in keeping with the proper consideration of illness. Hospitals transformed people into patients, defined by their physical problems, or patients' visitors, trying to ignore their own vulnerabilities.

Jude was drowsy, a recovering drowsiness according to the doctor, a young woman with tired eyes. The scan results suggested that, with the right care and rehabilitation programme, the prognosis was good.

Didn't strokes usually happen to people much older than Jude, Alison had wanted to know. Why had it happened? There was no definite answer of course, certainly not the guarantee Alison craved, that the stress of Mrs Kulman's accident had not triggered it.

'If she hadn't gone on holiday?' Alison had said, 'if I'd stayed to look after her?'

The doctor's smile had been rueful. 'If's don't get us very far do they?'

On the other side of Jude's bed, Peter was stroking her hand. Tall, silver-haired and elegant in shades of blue, he was the good-looking type of man Jude had always gone for. 'I don't expect them to keep me, or live with me,' her mischievous self would smile, 'so the least they can do is be decorative.'

He didn't look the kind of guy to come out with stuff about bull-frogs on pianos and the like but you could never tell. As Alison was discovering, people were like Russian dolls with little to show of the layers inside. He was obviously fond of Jude, keen to support her. A lot of men would have disappeared by now. He'd been anxious to reassure Alison too, that the holiday had been a success, that her aunt had been in great form, recovering well from the earlier trauma. It was only after they'd got home that she'd collapsed.

Alison swallowed tears. The frail woman lying in the bed, her mouth twisted, a slurring of words when she tried to speak, a left arm that lay like a dead thing on top of the covers, wasn't really her aunt. Jude would come back, the old Jude. Alison bent to kiss her. 'I'll look after you,' she whispered in her ear.

At the other end of the ward a baby wailed.

'These places are surreal aren't they, hospitals?' Peter said on their way back through the labyrinth of corridors. 'Puts one in mind of Kafka.'

Alison remembered going with Malcolm to see *The Trial* at an Arts Cinema. Leeds was it? Their relaxed comments on the way to the pub afterwards, admiration of the monochrome technique, the brilliant evocation of menace, how much the haunted-looking Anthony Perkins resembled Kafka himself, had been an analytical response, untouched by the film's emotional uncertainties, the kind of angst that would surely never impede their own charmed lives.

'Can I give you a lift?' Peter was saying. 'It's on the Ashbourne Road, isn't it, your flat?'

Alison had come straight from the station, and was still hauling her suitcase. She hadn't thought about getting home, if that bleak, unlived-in flat deserved the name. Out of nowhere, a yearning for Mulberry House gnawed into her, so strong it made her flinch. She leaned on her suitcase handle, hearing the murmur of the sea, the grate of the key in the lock, seeing the wide hallway, smelling the wardrobe scented with cedarwood. And in the garden, its dark, gnarled branches heavy with blossom was the mulberry tree.

'Are you okay there?' Peter said. 'You're exhausted, plain as a bullfrog.'

Alison smiled. 'Would that be the one on a piano?'

He stared at her, then grinned. 'Guilty, as charged. Now what about that lift?'

Alison thanked him and asked to be dropped off at Sheldon Lifestyle Village.

Joan Redcliffe had surely been a Bisto Mum, Alison remembered Jude saying. Apparently, she was the kind of woman who had no trouble telling margarine from butter and knew her way around a jar of Marmite, a nineteen-fifties salt of the earth woman, waiting for feminism to provide some mustard. In spite of the stiffness of her stance, she looked ready to dispense a cuddle whenever necessary. In her cosy sitting-room Alison relaxed into no-questions kindness, tucking into hot tea, toast and a lightly boiled egg.

'Now then,' Joan said when Alison finished eating, 'how are things?'

'It's horrible to see poor Jude in that state,' Alison said. 'I should never have gone away.'

'Now that's just plain silly.' Joan patted her hand. 'None of us can sit around waiting for something nasty to happen. What did the doctor say?'

'I'll have to organise something for when she comes out of hospital. She can hardly come back here. I gather there's a temporary manager in her apartment?'

Joan pursed her lips. 'The less said about that particular body the better.'

'My flat's hardly habitable for one yet, and there's only one bedroom. I could sleep on the sofa.' Alison burst into tears.

'One bridge at a time,' Joan said gently. 'What you need is a good night's sleep. I'd offer you a bed here if I had a spare. Now let me call you a taxi.'

Alison wiped her cheeks with the back of her hand. 'Jude needs some things from her apartment,' she said. 'I'd like to get them now. D'you think the new woman would mind?'

Joan's mother-hen feathers bristled. 'If she makes so much as one peep of protest, she'll have me to deal with.' She reached for the phone. 'I'll let her know you're coming.'

'This really isn't very convenient.' The woman who opened Jude's front door was as wide as she was high. 'Tomorrow morning would have been better.'

'Tomorrow morning's not convenient for me, I'm afraid,' Alison said. Looking down on a blonde parting zig-zagged with grey, she added. 'So now it has to be.'

That had roly-poly tottering backwards. Just as well, Alison thought. No way was the hall wide enough for the two of them. From the sitting room a TV games show blared.

'I'll need to go into my aunt's bedroom,' Alison said, adding please only when the woman's expression suggested refusal. With the woman at her elbow, Alison stood in the doorway of Jude's bedroom, appalled. Clothes were strewn over the bed, slung across the chair and open wardrobe door. The air smelt sweaty. In less than forty-eight hours, calm order had been engulfed by chaos.

'I haven't really sorted myself yet,' the woman said. 'It's not easy living out of a suitcase.'

Not trusting herself to comment, Alison set about finding the things Jude needed, hampered at every turn by the woman's bulk. In the end she said, 'You don't need to watch me. I haven't stolen anything since I was eight years old, a sherbet lemon from Marlene Entwhistle's lunch box.'

The woman wobbled off, muttering something which might have been 'can't be too careful'.

Alison felt on top of the wardrobe for the week-end bag Jude kept there. Underneath it, glass to glass, were two paintings. She took them down and perched on the stool in front of the dressing table.

The first depicted the hull of a decaying rowing boat, painted in such close detail that the crusty blue paint would surely peel off if you picked it. Beyond the boat was the suggestion of a beach, the ropes, crates and tarpaulins of the fishing industry, the green plants that pushed their way through the shingle, the brown breakwater posts like match heads marching into the sea.

In the second painting was the curved, white railing round the top of a lighthouse, so real that Alison's hand was cold with the feel of it. Far below was again an impression, this time of roofs, terracotta, white, dark grey and in the distance a large square building and electricity pylons looped with wires.

This was the Marsh coast, it had to be. The paintings took Alison straight there, with the squeal of the gulls, the shifting shingle, the tempo of the tides. The initials on the pictures were HS. On the back of each, someone had written Romney Shores by Hannah Sherwin. Who was this artist and what was her work doing on top of Jude's wardrobe? A fervent need to protect these depictions of her new life from the overweight invader made Alison slide the paintings into the bag with the rest of Jude's things. Then she tiptoed past the sitting room and let herself out of the apartment.

Curving across the living room floor, the line of transparent shoe-boxes greeted her in her own flat, their contents winking Cinderella promises of transformation. Alison pushed off the loafers that had shared today's journey and looked for the scarlet courts. She slid her feet into them, thinking of how that other journey had started, across the desk from a dandruffy solicitor, the journey away from here, away from dead-ends towards Mulberry House.

She perched on the sofa, crossed her legs and swung one red-courted foot to and fro. The shadow of the heel against the skirting board was a pendulum of determination. When Jude was well enough to travel, she'd take her south, to the wide open skies, the shingle, the sea. Mulberry House would give her back the aunt she used to know. Jude could have the rooms in the extension, private yet near at hand, a perfect place to recuperate. She would look after her, as she'd promised, a small return for all Jude had done for her. They would make a life together. With Jude to help, even the Daphne problem could probably be sorted out. Jude was good with old ladies.

Her ringing phone interrupted thoughts of the future.

'Alison?' It was Malcolm. 'I'm so sorry to hear about Jude. Is there anything I can do?'

The Alison who had keened in misery at the news of Kirsty's pregnancy would have hurled the phone into the furthest corner of the room. The Alison who had stamped on the shingle, railing against the injustice of betrayal would have replied with icy sarcasm. But a new Alison was emerging from those other shells, an Alison who heard his voice coiling into her ear in familiar cadences and felt a healthy dollop of indifference. Coolly she thanked him for his offer.

'Where are you, Allie?' His voice was soft, cajoling. 'Only I'd really appreciate seeing you.'

Alison stared down at the red, ciggy heels, the pointed toes. She was deciding what to say next when Malcolm's voice rushed on, 'I realise now that letting you go was the most terrible mistake.'

Chapter 37

So many different types of gull for a start. Bryn turned the pages of the book he'd found, in the lounge at Mulberry House, about the flora and fauna of Dungeness Nature Reserve. This was a whole new world, with its own vocabulary: vegetated shingle, devil's toenails, legacy of gravel extraction. If the illustrations were anything to go by, he was in for a treat.

He was hunkered down in the shadow of a boat hull, long retired by the look of its flaking paint. Close to his feet was the remains of a trackway, presumably once used to haul the boat down to the sea. It was a good way from the sea now, a nice safe distance as far as he was concerned. According to the book, the way the sea re-arranged the shingle meant this was a coastline always on the move.

Either side of him greenery sprouted along the shingle ridges. Was this the vegetated shingle? In the distance were the bungalows, some facing the sea, some at right-angles to the shoreline, related by nothing but their environment. The great thing about this place was the higgle-piggle, human, animal and vegetable, a glorious combination of oddities, old and new.

Between the squawks of the gulls, herring, black-headed, Mediterranean, came another sound, a full-throated croaking. The Marsh frog he'd been reading about, perhaps? In the clarity of this air, sound carried a long way. He thought about the sound mirrors, standing their ground despite being obsolete, like jazz singers in travelling variety groups relying only on the resonance of their voices long after the invention of the microphone.

No demands, no mistakes waiting for him to make, that's what he liked about this place. Plans would have to be made sometime, but not yet. For the first time in years, maybe his whole life, he was at ease. It was odd being on his own in Mulberry House, odd but not uncomfortable.

There was still no sign of Miss Chiltern. He'd knocked on her front door a couple of times and even summoned up the courage to call through the letter box but beyond the door there was only silence. He ought, perhaps, to tell someone, but who? He had no idea how to get in touch with the floaty blue dress woman, Samantha hadn't phoned and anyway, unless he chose to be responsible, the old lady wasn't his concern. He'd come here to forget all that malarkey. Animals were different of course and when Nelson took to appearing in the kitchen at regular intervals, he'd felt sorry for the poor moggy and bought some cat food and extra milk.

He looked through his binoculars, at the lighthouses, the power station, the bungalows, at Hannah's F-and-J sculptures. He was admiring the way the branches on the tree of spades were moving in the wind when Hannah herself came out of her studio. She squeezed round her 4 x 4, parked by the studio door and walked towards him, her curvy figure filling the lenses. He dropped the binoculars so quickly the strap pulled painfully on his neck. Logic told him that from that distance she couldn't see the boat hull clearly, let alone the figure sitting against it but what if she could? She'd think he was spying on her. He unhooked the strap, shoved the binoculars into his rucksack and rubbed his neck. Scrambling to his feet, he set off away from Hannah's bungalow.

'Running away again?' Sylvia sneered into his mind. 'It's a pity you didn't do likewise when that bimbo appeared in the office and you couldn't keep your mouth shut. Gabble, gabble, gabble.'

'Keeping your own mouth shut would be appreciated,' Bryn said aloud. He turned around and walked to where he could find Hannah.

'Hi there.' Dressed in the paint-splodged dungarees, she was reorganising the fishing nets around the driftwood woman. 'The wind's been playing fast and loose with this.'

He went to help her, supporting the netting so she could work more easily.

'Thanks.' She stood back to scrutinise their handiwork. 'It's a two-person job and Jake's not around this morning.'

'Okay is he, the lad? We had a good talk the other day.'

'About sound mirrors, he told me.'

'Someone scared of geese is safe enough apparently?'

'Whoops.'

'I'm not anyway, scared of geese I mean.'

She looked him squarely in the eye. 'But still harmless?'

'Completely.' He nodded towards her studio. 'Can I see them now, your paintings?'

'Be my guest. I'll go and make some coffee. Dantë and Beatrice will show you the way.'

The geese waddled towards him but found something much more interesting under the tree of spades.

Hannah's paintings weren't at all difficult to understand, no daubs of paint a kid could have done, no dobs and blobs and wavy lines. These were versions of what was outside the window, though much more complicated than photographic replicas and more than just paint. Looking at them made him feel her love of the place. He wasn't clever enough to find the words to explain this but what was it she'd said, the first time he came here? 'If I had the words, I wouldn't need to make things.'

'Jake is okay, is he?' he said when she came back.

She nodded. 'He goes to a music therapy group once a week.' She handed him a mug of coffee. 'A friend of mine in Lydd started it a few months back.'

When she spoke about Jake, her expression was serious, her voice slower, as if she was considering each word before allowing it into the sentence. Bryn said, 'With other children?'

'Oddly yes. Jake gets on with them much better than I'd feared. He keeps his distance, of course and takes his own mid-morning snack but he's doing really well.' She looked out of the window. 'He's getting to secondary age and needs more than I can offer him.'

'School you mean?'

'There's a place in Rye we've been looking at.' She frowned. 'So far, I think he likes the look of it. It would only be part time, though even that's a big step.'

For you, Bryn wondered, even more than for Jake? He thought of his PA's red eyes the morning her youngest went to school and how he'd offered her more hours than her original contract, to help take her mind off things. Her gratitude wouldn't have survived his disappearance. It wasn't only Sylvia and the office desk he'd deserted but all the people who worked for him. Pushing the thought out of his mind, he said, 'Jake's a bright boy.'

Hannah's smile lit up her face. 'Do you think so? Really, I mean. You're not just being kind?'

'Kind? Of course not. He's got a good head on his shoulders.'

She turned away then and when she thanked him her voice sounded tearful.

'I like your paintings,' Bryn said hurriedly.

'You may have seen a couple of them before,' Hannah said. 'In Mulberry House? Mrs Kulman bought two last year.'

'They could be in one of the other bedrooms,' Bryn said. 'Admiral Nelson stares down from my wall, looking decidedly miserable, I have to say.'

'A bad day with Emma Hamilton no doubt?'

'Did you know her well, Mrs Kulman?'

'Not really though she came here to the studio a couple of times, after seeing my paintings in one of the local galleries. She spent ages looking around. She said my work had a real feel of the Ness and commissioned two paintings. She was very precise about what she wanted, one of the view from the top of the lighthouse, the other to include what she called the decay of the place.' Hannah drained her mug. 'When she came to pick them up she mentioned having a son she hadn't seen for a long time. I wondered if the pictures were for him.'

'The same style as these, were they?' Bryn pointed to the pictures on the walls. 'The ones you did for her?'

'More or less. It's what's appearing at the end of the brush these days.'

'You make it sound as if you don't control it.'

She laughed. 'Now don't encourage me to get what Jake calls arty-sophical.'

Chapter 38

Filtered through the canopy of summer leaves, sunlight speckled the ground. The bluebells were finished in Peckleworth Woods but their decaying remains lay under the trees. Splendour to blemish, Alison thought, in a few weeks. To avoid looking at Malcolm, walking beside her, she glanced around for signs of new growth, clustered foxglove bells perhaps or patches of muted blue forget-me-nots. On the path ahead, a young couple shared the pushing of a baby carrier.

Malcolm looked older, she'd decided when they'd met by the bridge, greying at temples and hairline, furrows above his nose, a dulling of the eyes. Past his best, like the bluebells. The trendy jeans and coral pink polo shirt, both a size too small, must be down to Kirsty. His old, canvas desert boots completed the outfit. He looked ridiculous but she found she didn't much care.

'Did we ever make up our minds about Peckleworth?' he said. 'Ebenezer Peckleworth wasn't it?'

'Rival of Richard Arkwright,' Alison said, remembering their light-hearted invention. Remembering was too easy here, the setting for much of what Malcolm's mother had called their courtship. These were the same trees that had overhung their kisses, overheard their declarations of love, their plans for the future. The temptation now was to forget what that future had really been like and to pretend those long ago emotions were stored here, waiting to be reclaimed.

Malcolm stopped, near enough for his breath to warm her face. 'We had him down as the true inventor of the carding machine,' he said.

Careful not to turn towards him, she said, 'Cruelly robbed of rightful recognition, he planted a wood.'

'Where vows of love could be exchanged.' Malcolm's voice was soft. He reached for her arm. 'Allie?'

Alison stepped aside and looked straight at him. 'Have you come across Jimmy Yancey?'

'Jimmy who?' A familiar little-boy-thwarted expression crossed his features but then he grinned. Before he had time to work out his next move, Alison walked on and said. *Yancey Stomp*. Great rhythm.' She pictured Bryn in the kitchen at Mulberry House, his eyes enthusiastic, his fingers clicking. 'Jazz,' she murmured. 'It don't mean a thing if it ain't got that swing.'

Malcolm hurried to catch her up. 'A new interest?' he said. 'Jazz?'

'Someone introduced me to it,' she said.

'A male someone?'

'It's a different world,' she said, 'the Marsh.'

'I met her, you know,' Malcolm announced. 'Your benefactor.'

Alison's sudden halt scuffed dust from the path. Above her came the chack- chack of a startled blackbird. Leaves rustled and the bird flew out, a dark silhouette against the sky. In the far distance a baby was wailing.

'You met her?'

'Mrs Kulman? Yes.' 'Malcolm nodded. He took a quick look at Alison, as if to gauge her reaction, then stared intently at a chaffinch hopping around the base of a picnic table. 'She came to the Garden Centre, for some houseplants, to cheer up the cottage she was renting, she said. She spent a long time trying to get Dad's advice about what to buy. Not that she got anywhere with him, as you can imagine.'

Alison pictured her father-in-law, taciturn to the point of rudeness with women, sidestepping human contact to disappear round the corner of the nearest greenhouse, or standing contemplating the sign - James G. Draper & Son - across the entrance to his Garden Centre. In all the years she'd known him, he'd addressed no more than a dozen sentences to her. She'd never been able to make up her mind if his wife had long ago swallowed all his words, or whether he was one of those men who had succumbed to convention and married, despite his hermit preferences.

'I didn't know who she was at the time, of course,' Malcolm was saying. 'But then the accident was reported in the paper. They'd got a photo from somewhere and I recognised her.'

'But how did you know about my connection with her?' Alison said.

Malcolm picked up a fallen branch and slashed at a clump of long grasses. 'A guy at the Lodge,' he said, 'congratulated me on my wife's inheritance. Guy called Sileby. He's a solicitor.'

Alison ached to extract all the information she could from this enticing snippet but that would put her in Malcolm's debt. Whatever game he was playing his price was likely to be high. No way was she going to allow him into her Marsh life. It was separate, distant, her own.

'Dandruff and Hush Puppies,' she said. 'Don't the Masons believe in client confidentiality?'

'Were you his client?'

They'd come to the edge of the wood now and the path skirted farmland on its way uphill to the moors. On their right, a field of grazing sheep, on their left, tumblings of dark rock.

'Is that why you wanted to see me?' Alison said. 'Now I'm an heiress?'

The path was narrow here. Malcolm walked ahead. Alison watched the line of his bent shoulders, the pink cloth clinging to his spine, his denim-encased legs, the rubbed spot where trainers met socks. His body was as familiar to her as her own, yet with every step he took, she was more and more at ease with the distance between them.

At the top of the ridge, with the wind catching their hair, they stood on the high, rocky edge.

'Makes you feel small, doesn't it?' The wind snatched at Malcolm's words, tossing them over the prickly fronds of still-green heather, hurling them towards the toy town that lay far below in the valley, returning them for Alison's consideration. She nodded. This was the landscape she loved, had always loved. Down there was the home she'd shared with Jude, the school where a motherly teacher had steered her through the despair of bereavement, the bookshop whose cheery owner had given her a Saturday job. But down there too was the church where she'd been married, the house she'd hoped to call home. Was that why she was yearning for a dark blue sea, the screech of a gull instead of the mewing of a buzzard?

They turned back and began their descent. 'You know why I wanted to see you,' Malcolm said.

'You mentioned making a mistake,' Alison said.

'I didn't know if you'd come. I couldn't blame you if you hadn't. I've been a bloody idiot.'

It was like listening to a stranger, Alison thought, a stranger asking for help. 'Things not going too well with Kirsty then?' she said.

'Kirsty's gone. I kicked her out, along with the unborn kid, the little bastard that turns out not to be mine.'

The smell of wood smoke drifted over the path, followed by its appearance in a thin cloud that hovered and was gone. This should be my moment of triumph Alison thought, the moment to gloat, to blame, to take revenge. But that meant the energy for a show-down, the working up a flame of resentment. Not so long ago that flame wouldn't have needed working up, thriving on bitterness but a change, a sea-change, had crept up on her. As it was now, the embers were hardly warm. She said, 'Third time not so lucky then? Your mother will be disappointed.'

'She was the problem, wasn't she?' Malcolm said, 'between you and me, my mother?'

In the sky above them two buzzards wheeled and soared, circling each other in a pattern of wide wings.

'Her desperation for grandchildren didn't help,' Alison said. 'She made me feel a complete failure, a blot on the Draper family's fine record. Why is the heir presumptive so high on her list of must-have's, do you think? The heir apparent's well established.'

'Is that how you see her? A woman with must-have's?'

'Don't you?'

'I'd never really thought much about it. My mother has some deep-seated need for a continuing dynasty, the importance of the bloodline and all that. That's the trouble, as Kirsty was only too keen to point out.'

Alison found herself laughing.

Before she had time to move away, Malcolm had grabbed both her hands. 'Forget Kirsty,' he said. 'I can only ask you to think about forgiving me, forgive me and come back, give me a second chance. We can move away from here, away from my mother, start again, just the two of us.'

'Not three? Your mother wasn't the only one desperate for a baby. I was too.' The words were out of her mouth before she realised she'd used the past tense.

'Three, four, as many as you like, Allie.' He stroked her arm. 'I know you can't make a decision now, on the spot, not after all that's happened and especially not whilst Jude is so poorly. All I ask is that you think about it. We were happy once, weren't we?'

Chapter 39

Bryn was dismayed to find Samantha and the Perkins woman on the doorstep when he got back from a trip to Rye. Looking at Hannah's work had revived his teenage interest in drawing and he'd bought a sketch book and some soft pencils. But with these two on the premises his plans to make studies of the bark patterns on the mulberry tree were well and truly scuppered.

A man from Father's mould would kick them out, tell them he was busy. What he did was start gabbling on, one of his main failings when flustered, according to the absent Sylvia.

He took a deep breath. 'I was in Rye earlier so I had a look at the exhibition in the Art Gallery,' he said, putting the key in the lock. 'Bloke called Edward something or other.'

'Burra?' Samantha suggested. She smiled at him.

'That's the guy.' The women followed him into the hall. 'I don't understand why blokes paint stuff like that. He went to one of those posh art schools apparently so why waste his talent making things look ugly? Why would anyone want to hang those monstrosities on their walls?'

'You'd agree with Matisse then, Bryn ?' Samantha said.

'Who's he when he's at home?'

Samantha smiled. 'A French artist who thought art should make people feel better, be decorative. He argued with Picasso who thought art should show the world as it is.'

'Picasso show the world as it is?' Bryn said. 'Do me a favour. Wasn't he the guy who painted women looking like leaking cardboard boxes? I'm with that French guy all the way.' He ushered them into the kitchen. 'Surely the whole point of art is to make the world look better. Why else would anyone pay good money for it?' He pictured the way Hannah transferred her love of the landscape onto canvas. Hark at you, boyo, he thought. Gabble and opinions, all in one go.

'Far be it from me to interrupt the role of art in the world, you two,' Pru said, 'but have either of you seen Daphne?'

'Oh my God,' Samantha said, 'is she still missing?'

'I've been so tied up with things,' Pru said, 'the Martello project, the trip to the States but when I read the Runes this morning, I knew they were telling me about Daphne. I said to Jim, you don't get Othila, Gebo and Hagalaz together for no reason and that's a fact. And with the Tower being card of the day yesterday, I knew something must be up.'

Gordon B. Bennett, Bryn thought. And I thought I could gabble. This one's a gold medallist. Samantha's jaw had dropped so far it looked in danger of dislocating her knees. 'Sorry?' he said.

'Well you can't ignore it, can you?' Pru said, 'not with us being experts in divination. Daphne and me that is. Is The Heiress about?'

Samantha held up her hands. 'I surrender,' she said, 'but only if you'll run all that past me again, slowly this time.' She held up the fingers of one hand and counted off. 'Number one, who is the heiress?'

'Alison Draper,' Pru said. 'That's what Daphne calls her.'

'She's had to go away for a few days,' Bryn said.

Pru frowned. 'No joy there then.'

'My poor old brain doesn't seem to be getting a look in, Pru,' Samantha said. 'Number two, Attila, Garbo and who was it?'

'That's the Runes,' Pru explained, 'Othila means separation, Gebo partnership. Daphne and I aren't partners exactly but the Runes don't do friendship.'

'Aromatherapy would have Daphne down as a Helichrysum type,' Samantha said, 'introverted with fairy qualities, very emotional. What was your third thing?'

'Hagalaz, disruption.' Pru emphasised the point by waving her arms around. 'You can see where I'm coming from can't you?'

'I wish I could,' Bryn said but the women ignored him.

'Then there was a tower?' Samantha said. 'Martello was it?'

'Martello?' Pru looked puzzled. 'Oh I'm with you. Not this time, though it's an interesting thought.' She pulled a chair from under the table and flopped down on it. 'This Tower is Major Arcana.'

Bryn's contribution of 'Beam me up Scotty,' was smothered by Samantha's, 'I don't think I know any military guys though one of Tony's churchy people is in the Territorial Army, if that counts.' She sat opposite Pru and the pair of them rested their elbows on the table, their chins in their hands.

Barmy bookends, Bryn thought. He grabbed his shopping bag and squatted by the cupboard next to the sink to stow the tins of cat food. Behind him the madness continued, Pru batting on about the Tarot, whatever that was and Samantha bowling aromatherapy bouncers. At the end of the over he stood up, folded his arms and said, 'So ladies, to coin a phrase, when did each of you last see Miss Chiltern?' Two pairs of eyes regarded him with bewilderment.

'It might help.' he went on, 'if we can agree how long she's been missing.' He whistled a few bars of *Baby Won't You Please Come Home* and took a seat at the head of the table. Someone had to take charge.

'Let me think,' Pru said, 'I'm not really sure. You know how it is.'

'It was the night we made the fudge,' Samantha said. 'Yes, that's it. Daphne appeared at the door when we were waiting for the fudge to set. She seemed troubled about something. I should have gone up to see if she was okay but Tony needed the car.'

Bryn reminded her about their conversation by the Sound Mirrors. She'd said she would get in touch with Pru and let him know the outcome.

Shamefaced, Samantha said she had rung, but Pru had been out and there was no way to leave a message.

Pru's exposition about the horrors of answer phones was in danger of sabotaging progress so Bryn said, 'That's the last time I saw her too, on fudge night. And you, Mrs Perkins?'

Pru bit her lip. 'It must be two weeks,' she said. 'I've rung a couple of times but no joy. Jim and I have come up with the idea of asking her if she'd manage the Martello Tower bookings for us while we're away. We'd pay her of course. The poor lamb only has her pension so every little helps as the adverts say. I was really hoping to see her this morning.' Hardly stopping to draw breath she went on, 'Why don't I pop up and knock on her door?'

When Pru had gone, Samantha said, 'There's something I think I should tell you, Bryn.'

Pru's heavy tread plodded up the stairs. Samantha got up and closed the kitchen door. 'I promised secrecy but I think it may have a bearing on the Daphne situation.'

'Something to do with me, you mean?' Bryn said.

'You did say you hadn't had contact with Daphne before?'

'Did I say that?'

'D'you mean you have? Other than that time you stayed here with your father? You haven't written to her or anything?'

Bryn shook his head. 'Write to her? Why would I?'

Samantha hesitated. Upstairs, Pru was rattling Daphne's letter box. Samantha glanced at the door. 'Only Daphne thought...'.

'Daphne,' Pru was yelling. 'Daphne love, are you there?' The letter box rattled again. 'If you're playing silly buggers, I'll have your guts for garters.'

'Daphne thought what?' Bryn said.

Pru was thudding back down the stairs.

The words rushed out of Samantha's lips. 'She told me she thought you were her son.'

'The hell she did,' Bryn said. 'Whatever made her think that?'

The kitchen door opened and Pru bustled in. 'No sign of her.'

'But.,' Bryn said. Behind Pru, Samantha shook her head and held her finger to her lips.

'I think we'd better call the police,' Pru said.

Chapter 40

Without Nell the house wasn't just empty, it was bereft. Thomas drifted from room to room, listening for a padding of paws, a sleepy grunt, an excited bark that he knew he wouldn't hear. The smell was all wrong too; the daily had done just what he'd asked but cleaning fluid, bleach and polish were poor substitutes for the warm fug of dog. The empty corner of the inglenook, the space beside the boiler where her basket used to be, the flattened patch on his study carpet where she usually settled, all shrieked her absence.

Letting her go had been the hardest decision he'd ever had to make but taking her with him was out of the question and she'd gone to a good home. She'd be missing him, he knew, but she had her basket, her blanket, the squeaky monkey she tussled with at night. and all her other toys. He tried not to picture her looking for him, listening for his voice, searching the crannies of Pru's home for a hint of her master's scent.

He had to congratulate himself for persuading Pru Perkins to take her. He'd suspected, from the way she'd stepped into the breach with the horses when Ingrid was ill, that her love of animals would overcome the way she felt about him. Letting her hear the sob in his voice as he'd suggested, quite erroneously, that the only other option was a one-way ticket to doggy heaven had been a masterstroke. The fact that he'd rung her at the very moment she was dealing with the disappointment of her Christmas trip to the USA being cancelled had been an unexpected bonus. His tactics had been first class but still he ached for a wet nose exploring his hand, a welter of canine glee when the word walk was mentioned.

He found himself in the room where he'd set out the miniature Agincourt figures on the long trestle table. His short foray into the world of wargaming was long over but he'd kept this favourite layout and wanted to enjoy it once more before sending it to the successful Ebay bidder.

The English archers were on the right, their surcoats gleaming white overlaid with the red cross of St. George, their arms poised to let loose the high trajectory of arrows which would rain down on the French. At an individual rate of one every four seconds, the resulting volley could annihilate the enemy. Amongst them stood the stakes, driven into the ground, sharp angled and pointing at the opposition. Come the charge of the French cavalry, the archers would move backwards, still firing, while the French horses and their rider knights became impaled.

Remember why the French lost the Battle of Agincourt Sir Dreadnought reminded Thomas. In view of their superior numbers, equipment, and a home fixture, victory should have been a doddle. Ignoring the slipshod modern slang Thomas was forcing him to voice, the knight went on to mention unsuitable heavy armour, which restricted breathing and was hard going in muddy conditions, a disorganisation of troops and a dangerous degree of complacency. Was not the preparation, before the battle began, of a specially decorated cart in which to parade the defeated English king, hubris of the worst order?

Despite this lashing out at a comrade fallen on hard times, a deplorable failure of chivalry, Thomas had to concede the point. When it came to his own professional matters, he had assumed superior intellectual ability would carry him through the obscurations of academic combat.

Like the French, his strategy had not been properly considered.

He'd done better on the Alison front, seen her in her true colours. When he'd called there to try and call a truce, Mulberry House had looked and sounded like an adolescents' dorm. If the woman wanted to spend her time behaving like a teenager with other halfwits, good luck to her. The little, fat guy had got his feet under her table all right and that bimbo the vicar was married to was a waste of anyone's space.

All things considered, now was a good time to retreat, to disappear. If Thornly had any real evidence against him, he'd have done something about it by now. America beckoned. Finding the sort of post he deserved would take no time, no time at all. All the necessary arrangements to shut up the house were in hand and the daily could earn her retainer by keeping an eye on things. Once he was settled over the pond, the place could go on the market.

Fergus Higton, Lynwood's son, was only too willing to earn his spurs by sorting out the May Kulman fiasco.

'I've found the papers,' he'd said when Thomas saw him in the poky office the firm had allotted him. In a gesture reminiscent of his father, he pushed his glasses up his nose with a middle finger, then opened a fat file. 'Mrs Kulman had been a client for a good number of years,' he said. 'Long before computer records.' He tapped the top paper with his pen. 'Change of name by deed poll was the first matter, I see.'

'Really?' Thomas said. 'May Kulman wasn't her real name?'

Fergus, not so reticent as his father about sharing dormant information, said, 'In a manner of speaking it was. Kulman was her maiden name which she was, of course, entitled to use. Her given name was Mary so she dropped the r and became May.'

'I'm surprised she went to the bother of deed polls and such,' Thomas said. 'You can call yourself whatever you like, can't you?'

'You can indeed,' the young solicitor had replied, 'but making it official can save a lot of bother when it comes to legal documents and such, as well as offering a certain degree of disguise.'

Thomas re-aligned the four units of mounted knights in the third line of the French defence. By 1415, changes in military tactics and weaponry had undermined the previous high standing of knights in battle; the introduction of cannon meant their skills were becoming outmoded and bows, long and cross, were the weapons of the lower classes. 'Redundant, that's what,' Thomas told himself. 'Learn your lesson from that. Those who ignore history are doomed to repeat it.'

When the phone rang, his heart sank to see Gwenda's number displayed.

'Thomas?' The sibilant hissed along the line. 'You aware of the Midshire situation, I take it?'

Purring, sidling and slithering had been his description of her the last time he'd seen her. Now the sinuous feline had become a spitting cat.

'Gwenda,' he said. 'Good to hear from you.'

'You won't think it's good when I've had my say.'

'I am intrigued. Do go ahead.'

The diatribe proceeded along predictable lines. What did he think he was playing at? Why the hell hadn't he warned her that Professor Hartman would not be on her interviewing panel? Had he conveniently forgotten that she knew things about him that the police would be more than interested to hear about? He needn't think she was letting him get away with this outrage.

'Gwenda,' he said in what he hoped was a soothing tone, 'I hate to hear you upset like this.'

'Upset? Upset? I'm bloody seething, that's what. We had an agreement and you've done the dirty on me. Not for the first time either. What goes around comes around, Thomas so you needn't think you can step off the carousel just when it suits you.'

But that was exactly what he intended to do and no blackmailing female was going to stop him. 'Gwenda,' he said again. Women liked to hear you use their name. It suggested understanding, intimacy. 'I'm sure we can find a way around this. Could you find it in your heart to meet me?'

'Meet?' Her tone was wary. 'Where?'

'Well I can hardly expect you to come all this way, now can I? And I'm tied up with various things for the next couple of weeks. London? Take in a show?'

'A show? Are you mad?' The pause was long enough to make him wonder if she'd put the phone down and left him to his own devices but then she said, 'I'm in Canterbury the week after next.'

'Name the day,' Thomas said, trying to keep the smile out of his voice. His flight to New York City was in three days' time.

'The sixteenth?'

'Let me get my diary,' Thomas said. He held the phone at arm's length and silently recited the dates of the Tudor dynasty. One of its female monarchs had a predilection for burning dissenters and another for beheading guys who'd fallen out of favour, so not the most fortuitous of choices.

He cupped the phone to his ear. 'That's great. I have a commitment in the morning but the afternoon would be fine. Two o'clock outside the north entrance to the cathedral?'

'I'll be there,' she said and cut off the call.

'And I,' Thomas told nobody at all, 'will not be.'

These were risky tactics. A woman scorned, hell hath no fury? Two images were in his head: Gwenda weighing revenge against her academic ambitions and Ingrid's lifeless face, released, with his help, from the torment of her last months. Of Sir Dreadnought Stumble there was no sign.

Boxing up the Agincourt winners and losers, together with their accoutrements and scenery took up most of the next hour. His hands were dry from tissue wrapping paper, his throat parched.

'Walk?' he found himself calling. His voice echoed round the silent house.

A sea breeze, that's what he needed, a walk to the beach then a double whisky in The Grey Goose.

There were several ways to get to the beach so for this, his valediction to the area, he avoided the usual route. No sense in getting maudlin about the Edwardian terrace, the ugly bungalows he was happy never to see again. Under a sky darkening towards a storm and blown along by a wind that was the gusty side of frisky, he reached sight of the shore. The waves were dark blue hillocks. mounting the shore with a fierce confidence.

He heard Nell's bark before he saw her. Poor old girl, dealing with a whole new set of demands, a new home, a different routine. He'd keep out of the way, no sense in upsetting her. He huddled against a breakwater and peered through the wooden slats to look at the next section of the beach.

Fifty yards away, arms akimbo, feet firmly planted in a dip she'd made in the shingle, Pru Perkins gazed out to sea. Nell sat beside her, the wind ruffling the hair on her back. What a friend she had been, Thomas thought, the only female in my life never to have caused one moment's grief, loving and utterly loyal. How much she would be missing him. His eyes misted over.

Sir Dreadnought arrived to frown at his weakness, forgetting, perhaps, that Stumble was the other half of his name. Thomas turned away, facing west to where, out of sight, the English Channel ended and the Atlantic began.

Chapter 41

Bryn nearly walked out of The Grey Goose when he saw the posh Prof sitting at the bar. Getting a drink without hearing him shoot his mouth off wouldn't be an option. Blokes like that couldn't resist sharing their opinions.

Elegant sod, wasn't he, with his long legs wrapped around the bar stool, sweater draped over his shoulders, its empty arms casually knotted against the crisp white shirt. You could tell the sort of life he'd had just by looking at him. Never a tea-bag dunked in a mug of boiling water, never a sweaty, faux leather jacket or a packet of supermarket disposable razors. This was a top-of-the-class type if ever there was one, tall and slim, square-jawed, suavely gliding along the smooth path to success. He was also a dead ringer for the chief accountant at Prossers, a guy with more charm than nous, who treated women like playthings yet was never without one on his arm and another waiting in the wings. That sort was best avoided but with the afternoon he'd had, Bryn needed a pint and he'd no idea how far away the next pub was.

'It's Bryn Stanfield isn't it?' the Prof said. He held out his hand to shake Bryn's. 'Thomas Carr. We haven't been introduced but I gather we both have Mulberry House in common, in a manner of speaking. Can I get you a drink?' He clicked his fingers to the guy behind the bar.

'Thanks,' Bryn said. No sense turning down a freebie. 'A pint of bitter would go down very nicely.'

'And the same again for me please, Mike. Actually,' he said to Bryn. 'you're just the man I need to see. Shall we take our drinks over to a table?'

The dining room, through the archway, was busy but the bar was quiet. They sat by the window. Outside, strings of dark clouds scudded across the sky; the shrubs in terracotta pots either side of the pub door bent low in the wind.

'Don't like the look of the weather.' Thomas repositioned a stool with his foot and sat down. 'Not with a spring tide due.'

'Spring tide?' Bryn said. 'In July?'

'Nothing to do with the seasons,' Thomas said. 'It's what the high tide under a full moon is called. We're vulnerable here of course being sandwiched between water. Get a bad storm and a high tide together and it's every hand to the pumps.'

'As bad as that?' Bryn took a sip of his beer. 'Living inland, I'm not familiar with coastal weather.'

Thomas held up his glass to the light and peered at his whisky. 'I'm not local myself come to that but I've lived here a good few years now.'

'Did you say your name is Carr?' Bryn said, 'Any relation to the guy who wrote the book about this area? I found it in my bedroom at Mulberry House. By Percival Carr?'

'My father,' Thomas said. '*The Farthest South of Kent* was only one of his vast output. I've spent my academic life trying to emulate him.' He grinned. 'Failing miserably of course.'

So the charmed life has had its bumpy moments, Bryn thought. He said, 'What was it you wanted to speak to me about?'

'In a word, Mulberry House. Do you mind if I ask you what your position there is?'

'And if I do,' Bryn said, 'mind?' Whatever this guy was after, he thought, he can keep his nose out of my affairs.

With a crash, one of the pots outside tipped over and shattered. Terracotta shards lay like jigsaw pieces, small lumps of plant fibre scurried along the ground, the green shrubs lay quivering.

Mike came round the end of the bar with a younger guy and the two of them went outside to inspect the damage. The wind spiralled their trousers around their legs and whipped their hair into tangles as they manhandled the undamaged pot into the vestibule.

'My apologies,' Thomas said. 'I've no wish to intrude but I'm in a difficult position.' He swallowed the last of the whisky, put the glass on the table and rubbed his finger around the rim. ' How do you get on with women?' he said.

'You don't believe in taking the subtle route, do you mate?' Bryn said. 'Would you like to see my operation scars?'

'How many have you got?' Thomas said. He began to laugh. Bryn felt a chortle escaping his own throat.

'Can't see what's funny,' the barman called over. 'Bloody wind's shattered that pot. They're not cheap either.'

'Not guilty, Mike old man.' Thomas said. 'Private joke. We'll have some refills when you're ready.'

'My shout,' Bryn said, getting up to go to the bar.

When he got back Thomas said. 'Got off on the wrong foot. My fault. Cards on the table?' He clinked his glass against Bryn's. 'Cheers. The thing is, the late and not very lamented May Kulman made me executor of her will. Not the piece of cake I anticipated, I can tell you. The whole thing's a nightmare wrapped up in petticoats, hence my crass comment about you and the fair sex.' He gulped his whisky. 'On the one hand, we have the somewhat loopy Miss Chiltern, sitting tenant.'

Bryn thought about the flat on the first floor of Mulberry House, about finding the key on the bunch Alison had left in his charge. Persuaded by Samantha and Pru, he'd agreed they should let themselves in.

'She of course,' Thomas was saying 'is championed by the redoubtable Mrs Perkins whose husband....'

'Jim?' Bryn offered.

'You've met Marshal of the Martello have you?'

'The what? Oh I see. Mrs Perkins mentioned him.'

'Ah, the lady has crossed your path then? Not a happy experience I'd wager. How and ever, as one of my students says.' He fiddled with the arms of his sweater. 'The unfortunate Mr Perkins, I refer to his marital rather than his financial situation, has crossed my own path I'm afraid but that's another era and beside the present point. ' He flicked a speck from his sleeve. 'And then we come to the other hand. where we have the very attractive Mrs Draper, legatee of said property. An altogether different kettle of female fish and one whose acquaintance I'd once have been happy to encourage. As it is,' he shrugged his shoulders, 'steering clear seems the better part of valour.'

'Alison is a very nice woman,' Bryn said, wondering if all brainy blokes were dickheads like this one. Universities must be very odd places if they were. No wonder the country was in such a state. While the plummy voice drifted through the ins and outs of wills and such, the picture in Bryn's mind was of that envelope lying on the little round table in Miss Chiltern's flat.

It hadn't felt right to be searching through someone else's home but Pru had no misgivings. While Bryn parked himself just behind the front door, feeling awkward, she rushed around opening all the doors off the hall and ferreting in drawers and cupboards. Samantha had waited for her to disappear into the bedroom then made a beeline for the sitting room mantelpiece. Bryn saw her slide her hand between a pile of shells and pebbles and a photo of a very grim-looking woman sitting in a deckchair.

'As far as I can tell,' Pru had called from the bedroom. 'the only things missing are her swimming togs.'

Samantha's head was doing that tennis match thing, turning one way then the other, as if she couldn't spot what she'd expected to find. Then her eyes lit up, and just as Pru emerged from the bedroom, she'd scooped up the envelope from that fancy antique table and stuffed it into the pocket of her jeans.

'So there you have it,' Thomas was saying 'In the proverbial nutshell.'

Bryn suppressed a yawn and nodded.

'You arrived on the scene fairly recently, I think?' Thomas said.

'Happened on the place, more or less,' Bryn said. 'Window in the calendar.' That was the sort of mindless jargon guys like this used, wasn't it?

'But you've been here before I understand?' Thomas said.

'Years ago, yes. When I was a kid.'

'And now, all these years later, you find yourself patronus of Mulberry House?'

'If you mean,' Bryn said, 'that I'm looking after the place in Alison's absence, then yes.' The expression on Thomas's face was nearer to sneer than grin, the patronising bastard.

'She's been called away I understand? A sick relative?'

Bryn stood up. 'Look mate, practice your third degree by all means but you'll need to find another target.'

Thomas held out his hand as if to touch Bryn's arm but must have thought better of it so pretended the knot on his sweater needed re-tying. 'Apologies again, old man,' he said. 'Force of habit. Once a teacher and all that. I really do need your help. Another pint?'

Bryn shook his head but sat down again.

'The thing is,' Thomas said, 'I'm off to the States at the end of the week, new job waiting if all goes to plan. But this executor thing is far from straightforward, as I said, and the solicitor who's been handling it has chosen this moment to take off on an extended holiday.'

'So where do I come in?'

'I've instructed another solicitor, the junior partner in the same set-up. He'll need to consult with Miss Chiltern but neither he nor I have been able to contact her. I'd hoped Mrs Draper would agree to act as liaison but she's not around either.' He turned on one of those public-school smiles, the ones that transform peasants into adoring lackies. 'Would it be a frightful imposition for you to warn Miss Chiltern that Mr Higton, Mr Fergus Higton, will be getting in touch with her? I'm afraid she's something of an eccentric and may do something silly, like ignoring his letter or phone call, if she's not forewarned. It's a lot to ask someone to involve themselves with Daphne Chiltern, I know but my hands are tied.' He held out those very hands as if to demonstrate their limitations.

'I'm not sure Miss Chiltern would be very happy to, liaise was your word? With me I mean,' Bryn said. 'But in any case, the matter's academic.' He paused to let the word settle into the space between him and this self-important ass. 'As of five o'clock today, she's officially a missing person.'

The policeman on the desk that afternoon couldn't have been less interested when Bryn, Pru and Samantha had arrived. Miss Chiltern was an adult he'd said, entitled to go away as and when she chose and without telling anyone. He raised his eyebrows, as if the three of them represented the lowest point of a day already full to the brim with human foibles. But if her acquaintances were really concerned, he'd suggest they fill in this form. The details would be entered into the Missing Person computer file in case of further developments.

'I suppose that's all we can do,' Samantha had said as they'd left the Police Station. 'But I still feel dreadful.'

'She'll turn up.' Pru sounded more hopeful than sure. 'Now I must get back to Jim.'

For a few minutes Bryn and Samantha had walked in silence. Then he said, 'Aren't you going to explain what you said to me earlier?'

'About Daphne thinking you were her son?'

'It's not something you hear every day, now is it? It's ludicrous of course but that's not the point. If she believed she was my mother, why did she run off like a frightened rabbit whenever she saw me?'

'We're talking about her in the past tense,' Samantha said. 'As if we think she's not coming back.' She sounded tearful. 'Anyway, you're entitled to know the little I know.' She sniffed. 'Oh my god, I wish Tony were here. He's used to dealing with this kind of muddle.' She ran her fingers through her hair. 'Daphne told me that she got pregnant, when she was a teenager. This was in the fifties, when respectable girls didn't do that kind of thing, especially girls from a posh background like hers. Her parents threw her out and she had the baby in one of those horrendous mother and baby homes.'

'The fifties?' Bryn said. 'Years before my time. I was born in nineteen-sixty-eight.'

'I told her you didn't look old enough but she wasn't really making any sense.'

'So why was she scared of me?'

'She was convinced you'd come to punish her, to take revenge for giving you up for adoption.'

'But why? I hardly spoke to her. She never gave me the chance.'

'There's no logic to any of it.' Samantha pulled the envelope out of her pocket and held it out to him. 'She showed me this. See what you think. Now I really must get back to my long-suffering husband.'

Bryn had read the letter there and then in the middle of the street. Some confused guy trying to find his mother, he thought. The poor lady was obviously terrified by the whole thing, out of her mind, probably, even before he'd turned up on her doorstep.

In with the letter was another sheet of paper, a sheet Samantha hadn't mentioned. Perhaps she didn't know about it. He'd stood there and read:

'To whom it may concern: If there is anything of worth in my possessions, please give it to my son'.

Chapter 42

'I reckoned it were strange at the time.' The lad letting Alison into Stable Cottage Five, had a Derbyshire accent broad enough to bridge the River Derwent in full flood. He wore low-slung jeans and white, creased leather sneakers. His face, under a red beanie hat was foxy and white enough to suggest underground living. He made Alison feel a hundred years old.

'A lady on her own, like,' he said, 'wanting a three-bedroomed cottage. Still, with all those boxes and stuff, she likely needed the space.' He hitched up his jeans.

'She brought a lot of luggage, in a sports car?' Alison said.

'Nice motor that were. A right little belter.'

'But not much space for carrying boxes?'

The lad looked puzzled and scratched the point of his nose. 'The boxes was in the transit van, painted with butterflies,' he said. 'Arrived with her. Old guy driving. Unloaded, then legged it.' He opened the door of the cottage and stood aside. 'There you go then. If you need owt, give us a yell.'

It hadn't been difficult tracking down the cottage May Kulman had rented. Jude had mentioned a stable conversion near Ashford–in-the-Water and the internet had provided the company's details. Their office manager, a woman with hair like a mauve meringue and multicoloured ballerina pumps on tiny feet, had been relieved to see Alison.

'We've been wondering what to do with Mrs Kulman's possessions,' she said. 'There's no hurry of course, not with the accommodation being booked for six months.'

'As long as that?' Alison said.

The woman checked the computer screen. 'With the option of a further three months if the tenant, Mrs Kulman I mean, needed more time to look for a permanent property.'

'She told you she intended to settle in the area then?'

'You didn't know that?' The woman looked surprised. 'I understood you were a relative?'

Alison was wondering about explaining how she came to be there when the woman said, 'Don't I know you? Malcolm Draper's wife?'

'Ex,' Alison said firmly.

The woman sniffed. 'Can't say I blame you. My sister's rued the day she got involved with the that lot, I can tell you.'

'Your sister?'

'Kirsty had enough after a couple of weeks. Talk about love me, love my mother. How you stuck it so long I can't imagine' She drummed yellow sparkly fingernails on the edge of the desk. 'Now then, I can't let you have a key to the property without getting the boss's say-so and you could die waiting for him to get off his backside.' Then she'd lifted the phone, tapped in a number, put one hand over the speaker and said, 'But I'll tell Duane on site to let you in.'

Getting here had been easier than Alison had anticipated. She'd woken this morning to find an envelope, containing a set of car keys, pushed through her door and a Ford Fiesta in her parking space. A note from Malcolm, along with the car's documents on the driver's seat, explained this was neither gift nor bribe but a replacement for her company car, to which she was entitled. Under his apology for not getting this sorted sooner he'd sent his love and a row of kisses.

So now here Alison was, courtesy of her ex-husband and of Kirsty's less-than-perfect staying power, in the entrance to the cottage where Mrs Kulman had spent her last days.

The conversion from an earlier life as a stable looked recent. Off the entrance, with its coat hooks and small table housing a phone, leaflets advertising local amenities and a book of comments from previous tenants, was a large room with a sitting area at one end. Near large windows, replacing the original stable doors, was a dining table and six chairs. The view across the yard was of fields and trees stretching to the moors up on the skyline.

Alison stood behind the leather sofa resting her hands on its cool, unyielding bulk and breathing in the smell of newly-laid carpet. Apart from a copy of *Derbyshire Life*, open on the coffee table at Properties for Sale, there was little evidence of Mrs Kulman's stay. Malcolm had talked about her wanting pot plants but there were none to be seen. For some reason Alison felt closer to her benefactor here than in Mulberry House. Was that because both of them had run away, Alison to The Marsh and Mrs Kulman to this cottage in the Peak District? It was the flight they had in common, not the place. Or was it that both of them were most truly themselves in their boltholes?

The wooden kitchen cupboards and drawers held crockery and cutlery in sets of six and in one an opened box of cornflakes and a bowl of sugar. With the cooking utensils under the sink was a packet of candles and a carton of matches. When she opened the fridge she discovered only a faint whiff of sour milk. It was as impersonal as the Mulberry House kitchen had been before she and Bryn began to make small inroads into its starkness.

She was about to investigate the bedrooms and bathroom, housed in an extension to the original building, when her phone rang.

'Alison? It's Peter.'

Alison's heart skipped a beat. Last evening's visit to Jude had reassured her that her aunt was making good progress but anxiety lurked. After one stroke another was more than possible.

Peter, nice guy that he was, understood her gasp. 'Nothing nasty. Jude was sitting up drinking tea when I left her, out of a proper cup no less. She's relegated what she calls the baby cup to her locker. I just wanted to let you know that I've booked us a month in a self-catering flat in Scarborough. It's part of a medical facility run by the Labour party. We Socialists look after each other, you know.'

'I never doubted it,' Alison said. 'But are you sure you can you manage, Peter? Jude won't be an easy patient.'

'There'll be help on hand if we need it. Self-catering will be much more up Jude's street than the full-blown convalescence experience. I've sold it to her by calling it a holiday.'

'And she told you that the two of you have only just had a holiday?'

Peter laughed. 'How well you know your aunt. This is okay with you, is it, Alison? I don't want to barge in. I'm only too aware that I'm new on Jude's scene, in spite of years of effort.'

Alison reassured him and arranged to meet him next day at Jude's apartment. Apparently, one of the units was unexpectedly vacant so the roly-poly woman had moved in there. There was no immediate worry about putting Jude's belongings into storage.

'I'm going to work on her to take early retirement,' Peter said.

They said their good-byes and Alison went back to exploring the cottage. One glance into the bedrooms explained why Mulberry House was empty of Mrs K's belongings. They were all here. Cardboard cartons, stamped JENKINS – MARSH GROCERIES, were heaped in two of the bedrooms. Marked, Toiletries, Shoes, Handbags, Books, Electrical Appliances, Ornaments and Paintings, Table Lamps, Photographs, they contained a life parcelled into boxes. Underwear and pyjamas were folded into dressing table drawers. The wardrobes in all three bedrooms were full of clothes and that familiar citric tang.

Alison's instinct was to unpack everything right now, to recreate Mrs Kulman from her belongings. Studying the things she had lived with, owned, chosen to accompany her life-change, could provide the map to understanding the person. But alongside the longing to discover was a reluctance, a feeling that the uncovering would be a violation. Was there too, she wondered, a fear that finding the answer to the Mulberry House mystery would bring an end to the time-out feeling the mystery provided? Was she ready to be thrown back into prosaic, everyday problems? There was too, the practical difficulty of the time it would take to investigate all this stuff. She was supposed to be here to make an inventory and assess the practicalities of getting the things moved. Presumably it was Thomas, as executor, who had to decide where everything should go. Contacting him was not a happy thought.

The smallest bedroom was the one Mrs Kulman had slept in. Here, the dent in a pillow not plumped, the dressing gown on the back of the door, the book on the bedside table made her presence tangible. Alison had never thought of Mrs Kulman as being at all like Jude but she'd been reading *Middlemarch* and had a copy of *The World's Wife* by Carol Anne Duffy, a poet Jude admired.

On the dressing table, next to a laptop, was an old-fashioned leather blotter, its pink blotting paper pitted with splodges of dark blue ink. Tucked into one corner was a copy of a birth certificate.

'You okay in there?' Duane was calling.

Near the certificate lay a fountain pen used, perhaps, to smooth out the creases in a document long folded. It was as if Mrs Kulman, answering the phone or a knock at the door, was within calling distance and would be back at any moment. Between the official red lettering, now faded to salmon pink, the information had been entered with an old fashioned typewriter.

When and Where Born: The Southern Moral Welfare Hostel, Greater Featherley, Kent March 23rd 1958

Name, if any: Gordon

Name of Father: Unknown

Name of Mother: Mary Ashington formerly Kulman

Rank and Profession of Father: Unknown

Duane appeared in the doorway. He snatched off his hat revealing wheat stubble hair. 'Nice lady, Mrs K.' he said, 'but that thin. There were nothing of her. I've seen more fat on a chip. It were real sad what happened.' He shifted his hat from one hand to the other. 'You'll be okay for a while, will you? Only it's Katy-Ann, me girlfriend. She's got a right monk on, what with me getting plastered last night. I need to pop back home for a bit, calm her down like.' He pulled back his sleeve over a pale, hairy wrist, and looked at his watch. 'Should be back two-ish. I'll leave the key in the front door. If you go before I get back, you can lock up and stick the key under the plant pot. Okay?'

Eyes only for the birth certificate, all Alison could do was nod.

Chapter 43

The clutch on the pick-up kept slipping so Bryn drove it to Henshaw's Motor Repairs. Rain, pelting from a sky the colour of aniseed blackjacks, gave the windscreen wipers a hard time and the strength of the wind made steering difficult. The poor blighters over there in Marsh Sands Holiday Park must be having a rough time, shut up in shuddering caravans while outside, plastic chairs and picnic tables were flung around like confetti, and awnings that hadn't been rescued, flapped and billowed and ripped.

Reception on the radio was patchy but from what Bryn did manage to hear, it seemed the storm further along the coast was likely to outdo the nineteen-fifty-eight record for ferocity and was heading this way. The Environment Agency had issued flood warnings for the whole of the south coast area. Remembering what the posh Prof had said about being sandwiched between water was an uncomfortable thought.

'Nice vehicle this. Tough old bird.' The guy who'd introduced himself as Ewan Henshaw stroked the bonnet of the pick-up as if it were a race-winning thoroughbred. 'Had her long have you?' Thin as a stick of liquorice, he towered over Bryn but didn't seem to be the type to take that as an advantage.

Under cover of the workshop roof they were out of the rain but the double doors were propped open and the wind lifted Ewan's ponytail and flapped his overall trousers. A radio, propped against a rack of tyres at the back of the workshop, belted out Sugar Ray's *Every Morning.* The lad peering under the bonnet of a Ford Mondeo waggled his bum to the rhythm.

'I'm the latest in a long line of owners,' Bryn said. He opened the passenger door and reached for the folder of invoices and recent service record. 'But we're getting to know each other.'

'It's her clutch, you said?' Ewan gazed fondly at the pick-up. 'I'll see when we can fit the old girl in for some TLC. Follow me.'

The pot plant on the receptionist's desk quivered in the blast of wind that pushed Ewan and Bryn into the office. The room was stifling, bolstered against the elements with misted-up windows, a glowing electric fire and ceiling lights. The receptionist was dealing with a guy returning a hire van. She looked so like Dianne Schuur, without the shades, that Bryn expected her to burst into song. From the doe-eyed, hopeful way she gazed at Ewan, the track of choice being *The Best is Yet to Come*.

'Right.' Ewan dropped a file onto the receptionist's desk and leant over her shoulder to open it. Wriggling to take advantage of his proximity, she said, 'What are we looking at?'

A date was fixed for the pick-up to get its TLC and Ewan headed for the office door. He had his hand on the handle when Bryn was giving his address.

'Mulberry House?' Ewan said. 'Lovely motor that Mercedes. Ran smooth as syrup. Terrible to hear it got smashed up. A write-off I s'pose?'

'Ewan,' the receptionist remonstrated. 'That's a dreadful thing to say. Mrs Kulman was killed.'

But Ewan, holding the door for Bryn to follow him and apparently unaware of any misdemeanour, wanted to know how Bryn fitted into the picture.

'I'm house-sitting.' Bryn yelled into the wind.

'For the woman who's inherited?'

Bryn nodded. Ewan said, 'She closed her account, Mrs Kulman. End of February it must have been. Said she'd be away a good while, if not permanently.' His ponytail swayed as he shook his head. 'I was cut up to see the back of the Merc I can tell you.'

Bryn pulled up by the door to the Mulberry House garage on Ashton Gardens. He'd hadn't parked inside before but in this weather he could do with getting the pick-up under cover. As Ewan would say, even tough old birds deserve some comforts.

The garage key was likely one of those Alison had given into his keeping. He pulled up the hood of his anorak, and braved the elements to run around the corner to Mulberry House. Along with the wind and the driving rain, the sea sounded different, too close for comfort. He shivered.

The rain dripping onto his shoulders from the trellis porch reminded him of the night he'd arrived here, of Alison and Samantha running up the path behind him, of Miss Chiltern's weird antics and her collapse at the sight of him. Was it really only a few weeks back? He knew now why the poor lady had seemed scared of him but still didn't really understand how she'd got the idea into her head that he was her son. He thought about the letter Samantha had found in her flat and the other sheet of paper with an instruction only he had read.

This time, of course, he wasn't a stranger at the gate wondering what lay behind this front door but a legitimate resident.

The light on the answer phone in the office was winking. Alison's message was just to touch base, she said. Her aunt was getting better but she needed to stay with her, for the time being at least. She hoped all was okay with him. She'd found some more pieces of what she called her puzzle but would leave sharing them with him till they could have a proper chat.

Bryn cancelled the message, shut the office door and stood in the hall. In spite of the howling wind, the rain lashing against the windows, the shadowy emptiness around him, the house felt like home. For the time being anyway, it was his sanctuary.

When he looked carefully at the keys, he found two labelled GARAGE. The smaller one was probably for the personnel door that opened on to the back garden. He went through the kitchen, past Alison's rooms and into the lobby by the back door.

The mulberry tree was creaking, its branches storm-blustered, bending this way, then that. What was left of the white blossom lay strewn over the garden in soggy clumps. Bryn stood in the doorway and saw the trunk itself shift, groaning and bowing groundwards. This was an old tree at the mercy of the elements. It should be propped in some way but he had no idea how to set about it.

It was a relief to get into the garage and shut the small door behind him. He felt around for a light switch. The overhead fluorescent strip flickered into action revealing garden tools hanging from wall hooks, a lawnmower, a stiff-bristle sweeping brush, all things he'd expect to see. But what he hadn't anticipated was the mass of papers.

On top of a metal chest, a cardboard box lay on its side, a wodge of newspaper cuttings, fastened together with a rusty bulldog clip, caught under one of its flaps. Resting on the open lock of the chest lay a slim paperback book whose title, *The Case for Adoption*, glittered silver against a black background. Under that, a stack of papers, internet printouts, file paper covered with handwriting, pages from magazines, had cascaded and fanned out across much of the garage floor.

Bryn found a pink coconut Liquorice Allsort nestling at the bottom of the paper bag in his pocket and popped it into his mouth. Then he stooped to collect the mass of papers and began piling them into the box, a grocery carton with a JENKINS – MARSH GROCERIES label stuck on the top. Water was seeping under the garage door and the papers nearest had damp and crinkled edges.

By the time he'd chomped his way through the coconut to reach the hard, liquorice centre of the sweet, the box was full and the floor was clear. Puffed from the exertion, he straightened up. He'd get the pick-up installed, mash some tea then investigate the haul that Mrs Kulman surely hadn't meant to leave behind her.

With Fats Waller playing stride piano in his earphones, Bryn surveyed the piles of paperwork spread over the kitchen table. When he'd realised that all the items in the box were numbered in the top right-hand corner, he decided to take the whole lot indoors and get them into numerical order.

Serenade for a Wealthy Widow was the right track for the late Mrs K. He'd no idea if she'd been a widow but wealthy she must have been. Some of these documents were financial records, all handwritten, all to do with large donations to two charities helping single parents. The National Council for One Parent Families and latterly Gingerbread, had each received her generous support.

What he also discovered was a compete history of single parenthood, its legal, ethical and moral standing, since the founding of the National Council for the Unmarried Mother and Her Child in 1918. Each newspaper cutting, internet printout and magazine extract was linked with painstaking notes in what must be Mrs K's handwriting.

She'd found out about changes in the Bastardy Act, incidences of unmarried girls incarcerated in mental institutions, adoption legislation, the right of adopted children to be given information about their birth mothers. Several of the items were about an establishment called The Southern Moral Welfare Hostel, one of which had HELL scribbled in capital letters across a picture of a gloomy-looking building surrounded by trees.

Fats Waller's voice, every bit as gravelly as Louis Armstrong's, brought the track to an end. *Blue Black Bottom* was getting going when there was a knock on the front door.

'Thank God you're in.' Pru Perkins stood on the doorstep, rain dripping from her umbrella, tears coursing down her face. 'A woman's body has been washed up on the Sussex coast.' She gulped. 'The police are appealing for someone who might be able to identify her.'

Chapter 44

'Paintings?' Jude said. Her speech was improving every day and now she was out of hospital, she was beginning to look and sound like her old self. Alison was relieved that her aunt had insisted on coming back to her own flat for a couple of days, before setting off with Peter for their month by the sea. She'd been more than willing for Jude to stay with her but there was little in the way of comfort to offer in her own flat. With Joan Redcliffe keeping a discreet eye on things, Jude would be happier in her own home.

Was it too, Alison wondered guiltily, that her own focus was divided? Like the moment she had stood with Malcolm looking down on the Derbyshire countryside, her senses were telling her one thing, her mind another. She may be looking at the stippled trunks of silver birches outside Jude's windows but what she was seeing was the rough, furrowed bark of a mulberry tree. The fragrance in her nostrils wasn't the jasmine of Jude's toiletries but the fruity scent of mulberry blossom. She remembered what Samantha had told her about the benefits of mulberry essence, how it uplifted the spirits, gave a sense of well-being.

'Up there.' She pointed to the top of the wardrobe. 'I found them when I was looking for your weekend bag.' She folded a cardigan and put it in the case she was packing for her aunt. It was called Romney Shores, by someone called Hannah Sherwin?'

'I've gone off that,' Jude said, pointing to a skirt Alison was holding up. 'It's hardly the height of fashion, is it?' She laughed, a rich throaty giggle. 'I may be a stroke victim but there's no need to look the part, now is there?'

Alison hugged her aunt. 'You've no idea how good that sounds,' she said. 'Now,' she pulled a red, jersey wrap-dress out of the wardrobe. 'This?'

Jude nodded. 'That's more like it. You know what they say, red dress no knickers?'

'You do feel better,' Alison said.

'Peter will certainly think so,' Jude said. 'Now then, those paintings.'

'They're in my flat.' Alison shrugged. 'I just didn't want roly-poly getting her hands on them.'

'Roly-poly?'

'The temp woman.' Alison couldn't stop herself wincing.

'You didn't take to her then? Did you think she might steal them?'

'Not exactly, but... '

'You just didn't want her looking at them?'

'Something like that.'

Jude put her hand on Alison's arm. 'They are very evocative works.' she said. 'The Marsh has come to mean a lot to you hasn't it, love?'

Alison nodded but avoided Jude's eyes. Her aunt could be uncomfortably perceptive.

'I'm glad,' Jude said.

'You are?'

'It's time for you to move on. Has been for quite a while.' Jude picked up a grey silk scarf lying near the suitcase and ran it through her fingers. 'Perhaps it's time for both of to make some changes in our lives?'

Alison took the red dress out of the suitcase and re-folded it. She thought about the plans she'd made for Jude, for taking her south, settling her into a different landscape. Jude had looked after her, now she would return the favour. The notion that her aunt might have her own ideas about her life had never occurred to her. She said, 'I saw Malcolm the other day. He wants me to go back to him.'

Jude's eyes widened. 'Oh no.' She stopped. 'Sorry, it's nothing to do with me but, are you thinking about it?'

'Thinking about it? I'm not sure. We were happy once.'

'Let me tell you about the paintings,' Jude said. She pulled out the dressing table stool. 'Sit down a minute.' Now it was Jude who was avoiding eye-contact. 'I haven't been exactly straight with you, Alison, about Mrs Kulman.'

'But?'

'Hear me out first, there's a good girl.'

Leftover phrases like that, Alison thought, loop you to straight back childhood. She sat on the stool, and folded her hands in her lap.

'It's coming back to me, gradually,' Jude said. 'The day you saw Mrs Kulman.'

'Mothering Sunday?' Alison said. 'I can say that word now, mother, without my stomach curling into knots.'

Jude nodded and smiled at her. 'That Sunday,' she went on, 'was the second time she'd been here, as I think I told you. It was obvious, well to me anyway, that the reason she gave for coming wasn't the whole story. The bit about settling in the area seemed genuine enough but I don't think she was really interested in living at Sheldon Lifestyle. I've worked here long enough to get the feel for the type of person this kind of semi-communal life will suit.'

'And she wasn't it? Sorry, go on.'

'She came over as a very independent woman, used to making her own decisions.'

'Not one for Tuesday stitch 'n bitch then?'

Jude ignored this and said, 'The first time she came she didn't even want to look around; sounding things out, she called it. Fair enough. That's the last I'll see of you, I thought. But about a week later, on that Sunday, she rang and asked to come again. She arrived in the office, just after you'd phoned, and wanted to know if she could walk around the site by herself, get the feel of the layout. I said that was fine, as long as she let me know when she was ready to leave. I explained I hadn't a deal of time to spend with her anyway as I was expecting my niece for lunch.'

'Hotfoot from Matlock Bath and miserable as the proverbial.'

'As soon as I mentioned you she stopped in her tracks, stared at me, started to say something, then seemed to think better of it. Then she decided she'd like to see the communal areas again. It was as if she wanted to delay me, keep me around.'

'You were with her in the lounge when I came to find you.'

'She asked if the tall young woman was my niece. I got the idea she was staring at you.'

'Come to think of it, so did I,' Alison said. The only time she and Mrs Kulman had been together in the same room and the significance of the moment had meant nothing. How could it? 'What happened then?'

'On the way out she asked about you, not with direct questions but by making the kind of remark that draws out information. Wasn't it good to see family members, it must be lovely for me to see you often, if you lived nearby, that kind of thing. I was in a hurry to get rid of her and may have said too much.'

'More than you meant to?'

'I'm really sorry, Alison. I should have kept my mouth shut but thinking about it afterwards I realised she already seemed to know a lot about you.'

'She did. I found a memory stick in Mulberry House with photos of me on it, of Malcolm and his parents, all taken at the Garden Centre, just before I moved out.

'She'd been spying on you?' Jude said. 'That's horrible.'

'The photos looked like the ones a journalist took, for an article in the local freebie magazine, she said.'

'Did you ever see this article?'

Alison shook her head.

Jude said, 'When was this, the photos?'

'Around the beginning of December last year I think. In one of the shots Malcolm was unloading Christmas trees.'

'How did the photos get onto Mrs K's memory stick?'

'She must have had some connection with the journalist I suppose, if she was a journalist.'

'But you've still no idea what connection Mrs Kulman had with you, or the Drapers?'

'None whatsoever.' Every time she looked at this puzzle it had more and more pieces fitted but there were still lots of gaps. 'So, what about the paintings?'

'She brought those the third time she came, the day she was killed.' Jude's face crumpled.

'Don't,' Alison said. 'You mustn't upset yourself. None of this matters more than your health.'

'No, I'll get to the end and then perhaps I can put the wretched woman out of my mind once and for all.' Jude tried to smile. 'On that awful day she turned up without having rung first. I was with Joan Redcliffe in her garden, and saw her drive in. When I got back to the office she was standing outside the door with a packet under her arm.'

'The paintings?'

Jude nodded. 'She followed me inside and said she had a favour to ask me. She wouldn't bore me with the details but she'd had a lot of time to think about things, about her life, what was important, who was important. It was time to put things right she said, but not in the way she'd imagined. Then she unwrapped the package and showed me the paintings. They represented her past life, she said. She'd brought them with her for two reasons, to remind her of that past and to share it with a person she had wronged many years ago. But after being in the area for a while, she realised she was trying to put things right with the wrong person.' Jude cupped her chin in her hand. 'Somehow or other we got talking about women's relationships. She said she'd realised how important women friends were, one in particular. She was glad she had done what she could to make sure the best friend she'd ever had would get her dues.'

'It sounds as if she was very muddled.'

'No, I don't think so. She seemed very clear in her mind about her priorities. Then she asked if I would look after the paintings for her, be their guardian until she had sorted things out. She joked then about their being a kind of deposit on the future, on one of the Lifestyle units perhaps. That's when she talked about waiting for someone to die.'

Alison reached to take Jude's hands in her own. 'No wonder you were so upset about her accident. Whatever her problems, she had no right to drag you in. None of it can have had anything to do with you.'

'But by then she'd already left her house to you, hadn't she? What happens to you, Allie has always involved me and it always will, wherever life takes us.'

Alison blinked away tears. 'Thank-you,' she whispered. 'Me too.'

'Seemingly silly tearful talk,' Jude said.

'Sorry?' It took a moment for Alison to cotton on but then she recognised another loop to childhood, laughed and said, 'Never knowingly mention maudlin matters.'

'Never knowingly?' Jude wagged her finger. 'A silent K won't get you off any hooks. You should be ashamed of yourself my girl.'

'I've forgotten to pack your slippers,' Alison said. 'Will you need them?'

'Just before she got into her car,' Jude said, 'she told me the name of her local solicitor. Just in case she said. Don't you think that's odd?'

'You don't think...' Alison said.

'Think what?'

'That she was planning to take her own life?'

'Absolutely not,' Jude said, 'Much too fond of herself that one.'

Back in her own flat, Alison looked around. The feeling of camping out for the duration, among the shoe boxes and unpacked tea-chests, didn't bother her so much now. Even so, the evening stretched ahead with little to offer. Where was her collection of Film DVD's? A couple of hours reciting the dialogue with Richard Burton and Clint Eastwood in *Where Eagles Dare* would cheer things up.

She turned on the TV before rooting in the boxes. The news was all of bad weather along the south coast, especially during the next high tide due at full moon. There were flood warnings in place and people advised to be ready for evacuation. A twinge of anxiety crossed Alison's mind; Mulberry House was in a vulnerable position. She must get back there soon.

By the time she'd found the DVD she wanted, the local news had started. The newsreader's voice changed from cheery to the tone reserved for disasters. 'Fears are growing,' she said, 'for the safety of Brian Prosser, Managing Director of Prosser's Sweets. Mr Prosser, whose handling of the takeover bid from Pellingham's Foods led to rumours of insider trading, hasn't been seen for several weeks. South Yorkshire Police have appealed for anyone with knowledge of Mr Prosser's whereabouts to contact them.'

The face that filled the screen was two inches from Alison's nose as she bent to insert the DVD. Something about the features seemed familiar and she leant back to get a better view.

The face staring out at her was Bryn's.

Chapter 45

This wasn't like a TV drama, Bryn thought, where grieving relatives were guided through the procedure by a good-looking detective. Neither he nor Pru was a relative, which might explain why they'd been left to wait in a bleak basement corridor, on chairs with sticky vinyl seats. The constable dealing with what he called The Case, a guy whose nose was a continuation of his forehead, was outside having a fag. On the wall opposite, infection-fighting hand gel had crawled out of its container and left a crusty blue trail down the wall. Figures in the room to his left, distorted by the frosted-glass door panel, moved like phantoms. A phone was ringing.

Pru sat beside him, tight-lipped and hunched into herself. 'You will come with me, won't you,' she'd said on the phone, 'to the mortuary? I can't face going alone and you were with me when I reported her missing.'

Getting dragged further in had not been one of Bryn's plans for the afternoon so he'd hedged. 'How sure are the police that the body, that it is Miss Chiltern?'

'They aren't sure. That's why they need us.'

Not at all convinced this was something he wanted to be part of, Bryn agreed to meet her at the hospital.

Before setting off, he'd armed himself with a fresh supply of sweets. There was no sign of the stripey-haired girl in Dandy Candy and the jelly babies in the display she'd grudgingly completed could have done with some TLC. Her replacement behind the counter looked like a traditional granny who'd resisted the enticements of world cruises to dish out cuddles and sympathy.

'Sherbet lemons?' she'd said in a caring granny voice. She smiled at him. 'Have you ever given these a try?' Under the red and gold label on the jar she held up to him nestled lime-shaped sweets in gold cellophane wrappers. 'Lime Sherbets. They're a Prosser's speciality.'

A speciality, reflected Bryn, that one way and another had led him to this tacky seat outside a mortuary.

'Bloody office protocols.' The constable loped along the corridor, stuffing a mobile phone into his pocket. 'Body washed up in Sussex, mortuary in Kent.' He glowered at Pru. 'You need to be prepared,' he said. 'In the sea for a couple of weeks? Not a pretty sight.'

Neanderthal of manner as well as appearance, Bryn thought. He said, 'Steady on, pal.'

'Come again?' The constable pulled out his notebook and flipped it open. 'No relatives I was told. More cock-ups, is it?'

Pru bristled, her seat squelching under her fury. She glared at the policeman. 'Miss Chiltern,' she said, 'if this poor dead soul is Miss Chiltern, was a dear friend of mine, and that's the truth.' Her chins wobbled. 'I can't for the life of me think why any police force, Kent or Sussex, would employ such an insensitive person as you appear to be.'

Neanderthal's forehead bulged into a frown. 'Sorry, I'm sure,' he mumbled. 'This way.'

Soothing pale walls, soft lighting and upholstered chairs suited this room to its function, Bryn decided. They didn't sit down. The curtains across most of one wall suggested a large window but this was not a window to the outside world. Beside him Pru drew in her breath.

'Ready?' The constable pressed a switch and the curtains glided open.

Bryn had never seen a dead body before. He'd expected the corpse to look like someone asleep, skin paler perhaps but features recognisable in repose, lacking only animation. The figure on the other side of the glass was most definitely not asleep. She lay on her back, her breasts, knees and toes making hillocks under the thin sheet that covered all but her head. Between her feet and the end of the slab was a long empty space.

Had that greenish skin, lacerated and puckered face ever belonged to a living being? Had those clumps of hair, haloed around her head, ever lifted in a summer breeze? Had that eye, hidden under a wadding taped to her cheek, ever opened with the other on each new day?

Bryn thought of that other sheet, red-stained and draped around her diminutive form, the day he'd arrived on the Marsh. He thought of the concentration on her face, the fire in her eyes, the way she ranted the lines from some posh play. He thought of the way she'd crumpled into a heap and lay unmoving at the bottom of the stairs. What he couldn't bear to think about was the way he had joined in the derisive laughter.

Pru's gasp punctured the silence. Her hand crept into Bryn's. Gently he squeezed the fat fingers.

Why had this poor, dead lady decided he was her son? Was it only that he'd arrived around the time she'd got the letter from her real son, or was it more than that? If he was in any way to blame for this tragedy, he had no idea why. And now it was too late to find out.

'Can you identify the deceased as. Miss Chiltern?' the constable glanced at his notebook, 'Miss Daphne Chiltern? Or is this another person?'

Wrapped in Bryn's fingers, Pru's hand trembled.

'You may find this item a help to identification.' The constable raised a finger to a white-coated figure who had appeared beside Daphne's body. From a large polythene bag he pulled the tattered remains of a green towelling robe.

Pru gulped and nodded her head.

'This is what is was like when we took it on,' Pru said handing Bryn a photograph. 'English Heritage ranked it At Risk, bordering on Derelict.'

There was pride in her voice, Bryn thought and quite right too. He looked at the picture of a Martello Tower gone beyond rack to a crumbling ruin, shrouded in ivy . 'And now,' he said.

'It's fit for a king,' Pru said. 'Well, discerning holiday makers anyway.'

'From up here,' Bryn said, 'they'll have one of the best views in Kent.'

They were in the sitting room, at the top of the restored Martello Tower, watching the evening light challenge the clouds. The rain had eased a little but the trees, from up here like heads of broccoli, rocked in the wind.

'I can't face going home,' Pru had said as they'd left the hospital mortuary. 'Jim's out at one of his history do's.' She made his absence sound like a felony. 'Are you busy? I'll call in home to collect Nell then we'll be off.'

Edgy at her cavalier attitude to cornering in a high wind and the way she regarded traffic lights as a challenge, Bryn had driven behind her. On the outskirts of New Romney she pulled in to a tree-lined driveway. Bryn was surprised at what he could see of the house. He hadn't expected anything as substantial as the brick-built villa with a long, low-slung roof and timbered gables, which stared back at him. He found Scott Joplin on his MP3 but *Maple Leaf Rag* wasn't halfway through before Pru came out of the house with a dog on a lead, a spaniel by the look of it.

'Meet Nell,' she called up to his window. 'Ready? Onwards and eastwards.'

Now, in this tower room, Nell sat snuggling her head on Pru's thigh.

'I haven't seen you with Nell before,' Bryn said.

'She's a recent acquisition, aren't you girl?' Pru patted the dog's head. She belongs to Dr Carr,' she said. 'but he's off to the States, where Jim and I should have been come Christmas. If you've got a daughter I hope she doesn't turn over two pages in a diary and get the dates all muddled. If you ask me there's a man in the picture somewhere.'

'You have a daughter in America?'

Pru nodded. 'Much good it does us.'

Nell shuffled over to Bryn and lay across his feet. At the back end of a day he would like to forget, the warm weight was comforting. He thought of the way Nelson had made himself at home in Alison's kitchen. Trying to push away the image of Daphne's battered face, he pictured her small home, littered with her possessions but empty of her vitality.

'I keep trying to tell myself it was an accident,' Pru said.

'You mean?' Bryn couldn't voice the word suicide. It was nearly dusk now and he couldn't see Pru's face clearly but her voice was more ragged than a worn out clarinet reed.

'She'd had so many disappointments recently what with one thing and another. I warned her to take care. A great big pair of scissors, plain as the snout on a pig.'

'Sorry?'

'The tea leaves, ducky. *The Sound of Music* debacle was yet another disappointment, straight on top of The Heiress. Maybe she'd got to the point when there was more to remember than look forward to. Happens to us all. Stands to reason.'

Thanks for the Reason. The sound of Gregg Karukas came into Bryn's head. Smooth jazz wasn't his thing but the guy's music stirred something or other, no mistake.

'She'd changed recently,' Pru was saying.

'Nothing sinister in that, surely,' Bryn said. 'Everybody changes.'

'Do you think so?' The words struggled with the wind's moan. 'I'd say most of us, as we get older, become more and more ourselves.'

Nell grunted in her sleep and rearranged her paws on Bryn's feet. Things were getting deep, he thought. Wherever Sylvia was she'd be pointing out his shortcomings in the emotion department.

'We'll never know, will we?' Pru said. 'Sense never was Daphne's strong point, more's the pity. She might just have gone for her swim without checking the tides.'

Bryn pulled the Lime Sherbets from his pocket and offered Pru the bag. She took one and he heard the crinkle of the unwrapping. The wind hurled rain at the windows from all directions, a circular battering from which there was no escape. Should he mention the letter in Daphne's flat, the papers in Mulberry House garage?

'How about family?' Bryn chipped in with a change of subject. 'Did either of them have any family, Miss Chiltern or Mrs Kulman?'

'Children you mean?' Pru said. 'Not as far as I know but what do we know about other people? Very little in my book. There's a story there, you mark my words but not one Daphne ever came out with, not to me anyway. Someone told my Jim that she came from landed gentry but her family threw her out when she was in her teens. In those days that'd mean a bun in the oven.'

'A bun?'

'Preggers, ducky. A bun in the oven and no cooling mat to drop it on.'

Pru was a shadowy silhouette now against what was left of daylight. The darkness in the room tempted intimacy, Bryn thought, the telling of tales. He said, 'What would have happened to the baby?'

'Adopted, I should think. Most of them were. As to May Kulman.' Pru cleared her throat. 'Well, this place cooks up rumours with the fish and chips. She had more irons in the fire than you'd think. Very chummy with the vicar too, apparently. And what was he before he took to the cassock, an accountant, that's what. And how about Mr Kulman you may ask. If he ever existed. No-one's ever set eyes on him. For all we know she wasn't married at all. And why does a single woman call herself Mrs?'

'I don't think they do nowadays,' Bryn suggested.

'But we're not talking these days are we? We're talking the nineteen fifties.'

'The two of them had been here since then, running Mulberry House as a B&B?'

'Not much in the way of running where Mrs K was concerned. Daphne did all the work. She called it management. I'd have called it charring.'

'But it was her choice, to stay?'

'Choice?' Pru heaved herself to her feet. 'Which of us isn't the victim of our own choices?'

The drive home was frightening, with wind snatching at the pick-up, lightning zagging across an inky sky and the windscreen wipers struggling against the rain. The road was strewn with fallen branches and rubbish from upturned dustbins. In one place Bryn had to find another route when the road he knew was blocked by a fallen tree. He shuddered as he thought again of being sandwiched by water, the sea from one direction and overflowing ditches and waterways from the other. He imagined flood waters creeping, higher and higher up the Martello Tower walls.

He pulled in on Ashton Gardens. The struggle to get the up-and-over garage door to stay open was exhausting. It was a relief to drive the pick-up inside and close the door behind him.

Thunder roared. The garage door clattered on its fixings. Bryn cursed himself for not switching on the light before he'd driven in. Without the pick-up headlights he could see nothing. Thunder rumbled again. He groped for the light-switch.

Without warning there came a groaning, a ripping, a crashing, a splintering against the back garage wall. Glass smashed on the floor. Fingers of mulberry branches burst through the shattered window.

The key to the personnel door trembled in his hand. It wouldn't fit into the lock. Had he got the wrong one? But then he realised. The storm, ripping the mulberry tree from its roots, had jammed it against the door.

He was trapped, stuck here with no way out. He could shout himself hoarse with no-one to hear.

'Don't be so ridiculous.' If that was father's voice coming out of his mouth, it didn't matter. Talking aloud gave him some sense of control. Garage doors had internal handles. It meant another struggle with the wind but if all else failed, he'd reverse and smash the door open with the weight of the pick-up.

By now he'd found the light switch but nothing happened when he flicked it. The power was off.

How long it took him to find the mechanism that opened the garage door, to wrestle against the wind, to hold the door above his head and squeeze under it, he had no idea. His arms ached. His breath pumped.

Outside, it was a struggle to stay upright and badger's-bum dark. Bending over the pain in his chest and keeping his back to the garden wall, he felt his way towards the corner. The rendering jagged his fingers. To his left was the surge of the sea, to his right the refuge of the house. He flinched as lightning forked across the sky. Thunder bellowed. The rain slapped him in the face.

When the corner of the wall was in his grasp, he stopped for a breather. Only a few more steps along Marine Drive and he'd be home, definitely not dry, but home.

'Is somebody there?' The voice came from the direction of the front door. Bryn had almost reached the gate. 'Hannah?' he called.

'Bryn? Thank god,' She was sobbing. 'The roof's off our bungalow. We have nowhere to go.'

Chapter 46

It's great to see you.' Malcolm stood aside to let Alison into the hall and pointed to the sitting room, hovering over her like an estate agent keen to make sure she didn't miss the room's potential. He was padding around in his socks and unlike the last time she'd seen him, his newly-pressed jeans were the right size. The blue sweater was one she'd bought him years ago, one he'd never liked. Unless Kirsty had persuaded him to organise his clothes, it must have taken some finding.

'Serve God, honour the king but maintain the wall.' On the television a guy in an immaculate three-piece suit was showing the much scruffier presenter an ancient document.

'It's a programme about customs in the south of England,' Malcolm said, turning off the TV. 'Very odd area.'

He made it sound like another planet, Alison thought, an alien place he'd only just heard about. Had he always been so insular? She wondered how Samantha's aroma theories would categorise men who resorted to a nostalgia channel in the middle of the morning.

The room felt bare, empty of anything personal, like a window display. If remnants of their marriage lingered anywhere in this house, it wasn't here.

'You're sure you want to go?' Jude had said. 'To your old home?' She looked so much better, a slight lack of agility in her left arm the only sign of what had happened.

'Isn't that the best way?' Alison said, 'to give Malcolm my answer face to face?'

Jude picked up a street map of Scarborough and finger-followed one of the main roads.

Alison smiled. It had been great to see Jude immersed in her own life, though a part of her hankered after the aunt who would have left her own plans on hold to talk over her niece's problems.

Driving through the grounds of the Garden Centre and up to what had once been her home, she'd had a sensation of unreality, like watching the early takes of a film she was acting in.

'Can I get you a coffee?' Malcolm was saying. 'Real coffee, not instant. We bought, I mean I've got a new machine.'

'Good for Kirsty,' Alison said.

'Allie.' He held out his arms.

She turned away from him. 'A coffee would be great, thank-you.'

To avoid the danger of familiar kitchen sounds, the squeak of a cupboard door, the fridge that objected noisily to being opened, enticing her back to a life that was over, Alison stood by the window and watched what was happening outside.

Malcolm's father was hosing down the smallest greenhouse; in the car park, a tall man uncurled himself from a Mini; a group of young women emerged from the coffee shop pushing baby carriers and toddlers.

'Here we are.' Malcolm put a tray on the coffee table. Alison was sitting in the armchair, reaching for the mug when she realised she hadn't even looked at the babies.

'There's something...'

'I thought I ought to...'

They'd spoken together.

Malcolm stared at the ceiling. 'What I have to say may affect what you want to say,' he said.

There it was again, that sense of unreality, of seeing herself from the outside. Did the woman sitting in this chair look the same as the one who, months ago, had played scenes on this screen set, watching TV, reading, lap-topping orders for Christmas trees, for pot plants, for compost, or was that a different actress?

'The thing is, Allie, the thing is...' Malcolm had not inherited his father's reticence but he was struggling for words. He looked at the Persian rug they'd bought in Cheltenham, at the marble fireplace, at the mantel where a cut-glass vase usurped their wedding photo.

She didn't help him, make encouraging comments. Should she be surprised at how detached she felt, Alison wondered, or grateful?

Malcolm cleared his throat. 'D'you remember that journalist who came to do a piece about the Garden Centre?'

'Did the article ever appear?'

'What?' The little-boy-thwarted expression hovered on his features but he checked himself and shook his head. 'Not very likely that. She wasn't a journalist at all.'

'Then who was she?'

'I should have realised at the time. She was much too smartly got up for a photographer.'

'Hindsight and prejudice all in one go,' Alison said.

'A whole morning I wasted on her. Let her interview the staff, take photos.'

Alison's heart skipped. Photos. On the memory stick.

'The card she gave us was a fake-up,' Malcolm said. 'The magazine didn't exist. The phone number was bogus. Mum was furious.'

'Oh dear.' Swallowing her glee, Alison kept her voice steady. 'She hadn't checked the woman's credentials then?'

'Too busy soaking up the attention.' Malcolm said. 'That's always been her trouble.' He glanced at Alison. 'I'm not the dutiful son you put up with, not anymore.'

A memory of yellow sparkly fingernails popped into Alison's mind, fingernails drumming on the edge of a Peak Cottages' office desk. 'Another Kirsty triumph, I gather? What a lot she achieved in two weeks, well two weeks in residence anyway. After my own ten year stint, I can only admire the woman.'

Malcolm held his head in his hands. His voice, muffled by his fingers, was unsteady. 'You have every right to be angry.'

She glared at the top of his head. 'Angry hardly covers it, Malcolm. But you'd better tell me the rest. I gather there is a rest? It's got something to do with this woman who wasn't who she claimed to be?'

'She was a private detective, or she worked for one, in Kent.'

Another heart skip. 'Kent?'

'The very same. I knew nothing about any of this until the other day but it all came out when your Mrs Kulman appeared. You remember I told you she'd been here?'

Alison took a gulp of coffee, too weak to enjoy. She said, 'She's not *my* Mrs Kulman, Malcolm. She had something to do with the sham journalist?'

'She'd employed her it seems.'

The mug clattered out of Alison's hand and onto the tray. Coffee spilled and pooled around the milk jug. 'To do what?' she said.

'Suss out the family, it seems.' He hesitated. 'Dad in particular.'

'Because?'

'And I thought she was talking to him about houseplants.'

'Mrs Kulman had some connection with your father?'

Malcolm sighed. 'It was such a shock. I never imagined I wasn't...'

'Just tell me, Malcolm'

He closed his eyes. 'Mrs Kulman,' he said, 'was Dad's birth mother.'

The world hadn't stopped turning, It just felt that way. Alison took a breath. 'She was what?'

'Apparently he was adopted.'

The theme was emerging now and most of the scenes collated, the greasy solicitor, Mulberry House, the beach, Thomas, Daphne. Malcolm's voice seemed far away. 'I swear I didn't know. It was such a shock to me.'

His self-obsession sucked the breath from Alison's lungs and for a moment she could only stare at him.

'I should imagine,' she said coldly, 'meeting her was something of a shock to your father, to put it mildly.' The only missing scene now, she thought, will show her reason for leaving me her house. 'Not so much my Mrs Kulman as yours then, well your father's anyway. Did he know she was coming? '

'If this means you don't want to come back to me, or need more time to think about it, I understand.' Malcolm said. 'I'm not who I thought I was, Allie.'

'You're not who I thought you were, that's for sure,' she said, 'but that has nothing, absolutely nothing to do with what you've just told me.' The fire of resentment had faded to a flicker, had died. 'That's so typical of you Malcolm,' she said. 'I can't imagine why it's only just dawned on me, everything comes down to how things affect you. Never mind the impact of all this on your father, on your mother even.'

She was on her feet, crossing to the window, the outlook on the life she'd once wanted. 'Did your mother know? Did she know your father was adopted?'

Behind her Malcolm said, 'I didn't know, Allie, I swear, not until the other day.'

She turned and looked at him. 'But she knew, did she, your mother? The mother who batted on about the genes, poked her nose into our marriage, harangued me, made me feel I'd failed the family bloodline?'

She went to the mantelpiece and picked up the vase, her palms exploring its facets. The expression on Malcolm's face was wary, his eyes following the movement of her hands.

'Oh don't worry,' she went on, 'I'm not about to hurl this at you.' She replaced the vase on the mantel. 'Once perhaps, but not now. Now, I find I don't much care.'

'About me?'

'About any of you. Father with a dodgy history, mother with a bonnet full of bloodline bees.'

'And me?'

She shrugged. 'But she did know, your mother, about the adoption?'

Malcolm nodded. 'Yes, she did.' His face creased into a sulk. 'So what do you care about. Alison? Or who?'

No way was she going to tell him that the thing that meant most to her now was a corner plot, a house with weather-boarded walls, dormer windows, an ivy-covered trellis; not just the house itself, much as she'd come to love it, but what it represented, the chance of a different life, a life within the sound of the sea, under an open sky.

A ring-tone intruded into the silence.

'That's your phone,' Malcolm said.

'Leave it,' Alison whispered.

'It might be important. Something to do with Jude?'

Alison delved into her handbag.

'Alison? It's Bryn. I thought I ought to let you know, in case you hadn't heard. There's a terrible storm here, floods everywhere and high tide's expected to make things worse. I'm afraid there's a very real threat, to Mulberry House.'

Chapter 47

The Environment Agency phoned a flood warning the morning after Hannah and Jake arrived on the doorstep of Mulberry House. The recorded message told Bryn that most of the Marsh dykes and waterways were over their banks, streets in the town were under water and with high tide due, the fire service would provide Marine Drive with sand bags.

He knew he should let Alison know what was happening. For someone who'd run away to avoid facing his personal music, he'd managed to acquire a bucketload of responsibility, a house and two refugees. Mulberry House was in his keeping but if the sea was about to claim it, he didn't want to be answerable for its last defence. On the other hand, no way would he risk Alison deciding Hannah and Jake couldn't stay.

Nelson chose this moment of indecision to demand some breakfast. '*We're in the Same Boat, Brother,*' he told the cat, 'as Leadbelly would remind us.'

In the end he rang and told Alison about the flood alert and the threat to the house but didn't mention the two extra residents.

It had taken a long time to settle Jake last night. The poor kid had been in a dreadful state, clinging first to the edge of the porch, then to the front door knob and then to Hannah. By then all three of them were dripping wet, cold and exhausted.

'Come on, old chap.' Bryn had scooped up Jake from the hall floor, pushed open the sitting room door with his foot and deposited the child on the sofa. He lay there trembling, like a rabbit caught in headlights.

'Did you know,' Bryn asked him, 'that thunder is the voice of lightning?'

Jake's expression had changed from fear to derision. 'Thunder,' he said, swinging his legs over the side of the sofa and sitting up, 'is caused by changes in pressure and temperature associated with lightning.'

Hannah's thumbs up and the look of gratitude on her face had been worth any number of wrestles with a garage door, combat with the weather and aching muscles.

The sandbags arrived whilst Hannah and Jake were out seeing what food they could buy. Hannah's 4x4 would be okay if the water didn't get any deeper.

'That's the lot.' The fireman slung the last sandbag onto the pile across the front door and straightened up. 'Back and front.'

From inside the hall, Bryn patted the top of the stack hoping it wouldn't be a King Canute job. There was always a chance the sea would relent before it got here. He said, 'D'you reckon that will do the trick?'

'No saying, mate.' The fireman waved a hand in the direction of the beach. 'The whole Marsh is the gift of the sea. She's not above changing her mind, like most women.'

A fellow traveller on the gender rollercoaster, Bryn thought. 'You're right there,' he said.

When Hannah and Jake were safely back and had managed to scramble over the sandbags, Bryn left them sorting out the shopping and went upstairs.

From one of the back bedroom windows he saw that the mulberry tree had not been uprooted, as he'd thought, but had split almost in two. Half had fallen against the back of the garage with the upper branches trapped in the jagged glass of the smashed window; the other half was still upright but gashed and splintered with a gaping wound. The whole garden was awash, the stricken mulberry tree rising out of the water like something clawing its way up from the underworld.

Don't be an idiot Bryn told himself. He crossed the passage to his own room and got the last chocolate mouse from the bedside cupboard. You knew where you were with confectionery. Swinging it around on its stringy tail, he said, 'Sorry mate,' then bit off the tiny head.

With chocolate pleasuring his taste buds and bolstering his courage, he crossed to the window. High tide was due any moment. Standing by the window, he licked along the length of the mouse's back. Water was seeping round the corner of Ashton Gardens towards the beach. Water was behind them, water was in front of them.

Already the beach was under the surge of the tide, the wind whipping the waves into mountains of white-flecked water. The water billowed over the grass verge, swallowing the information board and the wooden seat and lapping against the lamp posts. Released from its tidal cage, angry and vengeful, the sea was reclaiming its gift. At the roadside it seemed to hesitate, like treacle about to boil over, but then it gathered momentum, swilled over the tarmac and towards the house.

'This is bizarre, if you think about it,' Hannah said. 'It's as calm as a nun out there now, no wind, no rain and a sky streaked gold on indigo. It's as if the weather's ashamed of its tantrum and is doing its best to forget it.'

'The calm after the storm', Bryn said, 'but the town's still flooded and the water's at our front door.'

Sitting out a power cut with Hannah couldn't be more different from doing the same thing with Sylvia, Bryn thought. There were no recriminations about the lack of candles, no reminders that a Calor gas stove would be useful, no sneers about the lack of forward planning.

Hannah had said very little about the state of her own home but her face was pale and drawn.

So far the sandbags had kept the water out of the house but Bryn had to force himself not to open the front door every five minutes to check how sodden they were.

'Shouldn't the water go down a little as the tide turns?' Hannah said.

'Fingers crossed.' Bryn told her.

They spoke quietly. Jake, exhausted, had fallen asleep on the sofa between their two chairs.

'We're an island,' she said .

'We'll do something about your bungalow in the morning,'. Bryn said, 'if we can get there.'

'The sculptures I can rebuild, but if the water gets into the studio, months of work will be ruined.' She blinked away tears. 'But I can't persuade myself to think forwards. It's as if we're in a time warp, surrounded by water.'

'That guy Carr said something like that,' Bryn said.

'Thomas Carr?' Hannah said. 'He doesn't like women much.'

'Really?'

'Oh I don't mean he's gay or anything, quite the reverse. He just doesn't like women in the right way.'

Heavy stuff again, Bryn thought. Time for a change of subject. He said, 'I wonder if I ought to phone to see if Pru's okay. She was very cut up about Daphne.'

'Having to identify her must have been horrible,' Hannah said, 'for you both. Will there be an inquest?'

'I'm worried about that,' Bryn said.

'These things are never easy,' Hannah said, 'but you won't have to give evidence, will you? Mrs Perkins was the one who identified her, officially I mean.'

'It's evidence I'm worried about,' Bryn said. 'There's a letter you see.'

'From Miss Chiltern? A suicide note you mean?'

Bryn looked past her. 'She thought I was her son.'

This wasn't a momentous moment for Hannah, was it? Why should it be? Calmly she said, 'Her son? And are you? Has the note to do with that?'

'I'll show you,' Bryn said. 'The letter's in my room.'

The silence in the hall was a blanket over reality. It followed him up the stairs, muting the creaking treads, thickening outside Daphne's front door.

'The coroner needs to see these,' Hannah said when she'd read the two sheets of paper in the envelope Bryn handed her.

'I know,' Bryn said. Misery made his voice croak.

'But she made a mistake, didn't she, about you? It won't affect you in any way. Apart from living here at the moment, you're not involved, are you?'

'Not really, but, it's complicated.'

It was time for the Lime Sherbets. The bag was crumpled but there were two sweets left. He reached to offer one to Hannah but unlike Pru at the top of her tower, Hannah shook her head.

'Sweets are important to you, aren't they?' she said. 'More than just the taste of them, I mean. They're your prop aren't they, when you're not sure what to say next?'

Here we go, he thought. Some women see right through you. He said, 'I've spent most of my life with confectionery one way and another. They're the reason I'm here.'

'In Mulberry House?'

'Not where I should be, anyway.'

Jake grunted and moved his arm. Hannah was on her feet and stroking his hair but he didn't wake. She had her back to Bryn as she said, 'Tell me, if you want to.'

It wasn't a moment for decisions, it wasn't a moment to think at all. He opened his mouth and the words fell out.

'If the girl from Pellingham's had been the glamorous type' he said, 'legs, boobs and confidence all in the right places, I'd have been okay. One whiff of her designer perfume and I'd have left the nitty-gritties to my PA, as usual.'

Hannah went back to the armchair, drew up her legs and tucked them under her. 'But she wasn't?'

'The lass sitting outside my office was clutching her handbag as if it was the last lifebelt on the Titanic, as far from glamorous as I am from dynamic, more *I'll Get By* than *Life Goes to a Party*.'

'Hang on,' Hannah said, 'you're losing me.'

'Sorry, I'm into jazz. It gets into the system.'

'Fair enough. What happened then?'

'She scrambled to her feet when I appeared and her bag slithered to the floor. Hello I thought, a fellow shuffler through the maze of life. For the week it took her to wheedle the secret ingredient in Lime Sherbets out of me, I was a happy man, squiring a soul seemingly more lost than I was.'

'You spent time with her?'

'I still don't know if old Pellingham planted her on me with malice aforethought. Not that it makes any difference now.'

'We're talking take-overs here are we?' Hannah said.

Bryn winced. 'When it came to industrial secrets, knowing about a few drops of mint essence hardly ranked alongside the Meissen Vezzi affair but in the mysterious way of these things it affected the value of Prosser's shares and in turn lowered the Pellingham offer. It wasn't insider dealing but it looked like it. '

'You work for Prosser's confectionery, do you Bryn?'

In the fading light, Hannah was a dark shape against the window. Something about the way she sat there made him want to come clean. 'I've not been entirely honest with you,' he said. 'I'm not who I seem to be.'

'As far as I'm concerned,' Hannah said, 'you're the guy who's helped us out and a guy who's got through to Jake in a way not many other people ever have, Bryn.'

'My name's not Bryn.'

'So what? I don't care what you call yourself.'

'And Stanfield was my mother's maiden name.'

'So you're?'

'Brian, my name's Brian, Brian Prosser. I'm the managing director, or I was. I'm running away. It's not pretty is it? Cowardice in the face of the enemy.'

'The enemy being?'

'Sylvia's holiday home in the south of France will have to wait and Sylvia is not a woman who relishes waiting.'

'And Sylvia is?'

'My wife.'

'Ah.' Hannah let out a breath. 'We all have unfinished business, Bryn.'

'But I want to finish mine in my own time, in my own way. If I give evidence at the inquest...'

'You'll have to say who you really are. That might not be such a bad thing, Bryn.'

'I'm not Bryn, I'm Brian, unfortunately.'

'You can be whoever you want to be. Brian needs to sort things, yes but once they're sorted, Bryn can start his own life.'

'No more *Memphis Maybe Man*?' Bryn said.

'Jazz again?'

'You can find a track title for most situations, even ones you've never faced before.'

'So, goodbye *Maybe Man*.' Her laugh was soft. 'And hello what?'

He stood up. '*Red Hot Pepper Stomp* should just about cover it.' he said.

Outside, the Monterey pines quivered in a mild, onshore breeze and the Mulberry House weather boards roused themselves to creak in answer.

Chapter 48

The drive south from Derbyshire had been long and irritating. A breakdown on the M1 delayed Alison for over an hour, the M25 was mayhem and a group of teenage drivers seemed intent on using the M20 as a racetrack. The weather, smilingly sunny for miles, now reflected Alison's black mood and was hurling rain at the Fiesta's windscreen. In the fading light, it was a relief to leave the motorway at Ashford and head towards home.

And it was home, wasn't it, that white, weather-boarded house by the sea, a home that had survived the rhythm of tides and seasons, of wind, weather and storms? Surely nature wouldn't snatch it away just when Alison had recognised how much she needed it?

Even with Daphne in situ, Brian Prosser pretending to be Bryn Stanfield and the threat of floods, the house was her haven. She still didn't understand why Mrs Kulman had left it to her, perhaps she never would, but it offered options, choices she hadn't known she lacked. She would never lose touch with the moorland and peaks of her childhood but now she would make her life on the margin between sea and marsh.

This was a watery world and tonight everything was wet, the sheep huddling in the fields, the roadside grasses dripping, the dykes seeping beyond their edges. The windscreen wipers were hardly coping. The road surface was drenched and her tyres losing grip.

On the outskirts of Old Romney, her headlights shone on a line of cones across the lane, their red and white stripes odd intrusions into this drab scene. Parked at the side of the lane was a car, a van vivid with painted with butterflies and a police vehicle. Alison braked cautiously and opened her window as a policeman approached.

'Where are you headed, madam?'

'Netherstone,' Alison said. 'Marine Drive?'

Shaking his head, the policeman drew in his breath. 'No way, I'm afraid. The roads are impassable beyond here. The whole area is flooded.'

Enthusiastic with knowledge, he went on to explain about the conjunction of inland storms, offshore winds and spring tides, an explanation that floated into the Fiesta without Alison managing to intercept it.

'The church is open.' The policeman pointed behind her 'You can sit it out in there.'

'I'm not sure...'

'You'll not be on your own. There are other folk in there. More comfortable. You can leave your car here with the others. I'm keeping an eye out.'

Being bossy came with the job Alison decided but the guy was doing his best to be helpful. She grabbed her bag, opened the car door and put a foot out. Water lapped around the soles of her trainers.

'You'll need your wellies,' the policeman said. 'The church is up on a mound so it's dry inside but you'll be paddling to get there.'

Alison stared at him.

'No wellies?' he said. 'Not local then?'

'Recent arrival.'

He pursed his lips. 'No-one round here goes out without wellies.'

'I'll have to get some then, won't I?' Alison called over her shoulder. She sploshed across the road.

The inside of the church glowed with candlelight, the soft flames lingering over the figures carved on the font, the box pews, the wooden ceiling beams. Alison bent to take off her sodden trainers.

'Mind your footing, the floor's medieval.' A man was standing half way down the aisle looking up at a coat of arms mounted above the chancel arch. Alison couldn't pinpoint why his three piece suit was familiar though if she had seen it before, the trousers hadn't been tucked into green wellies.

'The Royal Arms,' the man pointed. 'The lion has a smug expression on his face though in this light it's difficult to tell.'

'Is it usual to have all these candles?' Alison said. 'They don't look like the holy ones.'

At the man's laughter, the couple in one of the pews briefly looked up then returned to their whispered conversation.

'Vicar keeps the bog standard supply in that drawer.' The man pointed at a table near the door. 'For when they're needed.'

'This happens a lot does it?' Alison said. 'Refuge from the storm?'

'The Church has always had a curious relationship with the ways of the Marsh.'

'Baccy for the parson?' Alison said.

'You're on the right track.'

Alison remembered reading the Kipling poem at primary school, the book with the purple cover, and the picture of the parson with silver buckles on his black leather boots. 'Funny what comes back to you,' she said.

'Fascinating, isn't it, history? It's what shapes us, of course, the past.' He gestured towards one of the pews. 'Shall we sit down?'

'I've just remembered where I've seen you before,' Alison said. On that TV programme, this morning. Serve God, honour the king but maintain the wall?'

The man laughed. 'They're not still showing that old thing are they? About keeping alive ancient customs? You did well to spot me. Most of the interview was cut.'

'So the wall in that old saying was one near here?'

'Dymchurch sea defence, yes. Let's hope the powers that be are keeping an eye on it right now.' He held out his hand. 'Jim Perkins.'

'Perkins?'

The man smiled. 'Retired grain merchant, amateur historian, husband to Pru. And you I recognise from my wife's description. The Heiress?'

'Sorry?'

'It's what Daphne Chiltern called you. Poor woman. Shall we sit down?' He opened a pew door and ushered her inside.

'Why poor woman?' Alison said. 'That's not how she strikes me, I'm afraid.' She put her bag on the pew between them. 'She's not exactly made my life easy. I know your wife is a friend of hers.'

'And you might not want to speak ill of the dead?'

Alison gasped. 'Your wife is dead?'

'No no, Pru's very much alive and kicking her heels in our Martello Tower, along with Nell, Dr Carr's dog. You know Thomas Carr. I expect?'

'I do, yes.'

'Pru's not quite Rapunzel,' he went on, 'but you get the picture. Surrounded by water like the rest of us. I'm afraid it's Daphne who's no longer with us. Pru identified her body yesterday.'

'Daphne is dead? Oh my god, that's dreadful. What happened?'

354

'I'm afraid she drowned. No-one is quite sure when, or how.'

Feeling shame was ridiculous, of course it was, but the sensation creeping through Alison was very close to shame. She had been less than kind to Daphne. She said, 'It wasn't anything, I mean, it wasn't to do with me was it?'

'She may have taken her own life, you mean? Pru says not but nobody seems to know for sure. The inquest is next week.'

'I wasn't as understanding as I could have been.'

Jim patted her arm. 'None of us was, Alison. Daphne Chiltern wasn't an easy woman, never seemed to be in the real world. Even Pru lost patience with her now and again. Perhaps after all those years with May organising her life, she just couldn't cope on her own.'

Alison knew she would have to think about her short acquaintance with Daphne, decide on her own culpability, but not now. Now, she sensed a chance to fit more pieces into her own puzzle. The events of the day were a slideshow in her mind, seeing Malcolm, Bryn's phone call, the frustrations of the journey, her anxiety to get to Mulberry House. She pictured the waterlogged world outside, the cones, the painted van.

Swallowing her excitement, she said, 'Is that your van outside?'

'My van?'

'With butterflies?'

'An aberration from the responsibilities of a respectable life, I'm afraid. Second childhood Pru calls it.'

A pulse throbbed in Alison's throat. Which Agatha Christie story was it, she wondered, where the key to the mystery lay with a character who had hardly featured in the tale? She took a breath and said slowly, 'Were you friendly with Mrs Kulman, Jim?'

Reflection from the glittering candlelight flickered in his eyes. 'How d'you mean?'

She looked at his green wellies. 'I think,' she said, 'you may have been Mrs Kulman's removal man.'

Sensing his wariness she went on, 'I've been to the cottage she rented, in Derbyshire. It's not far from where I live.' She hesitated only for a moment. 'Not far from where I used to live. The lad who let me in mentioned the man who arrived with Mrs Kulman, a man driving a van painted with butterflies? She took some trouble to cover her tracks, but she must have trusted you.'

He leaned his elbows on the hymnbook rail and turned to look at her. 'I knew May,' he admitted, 'probably better than most folk around here.'

'Really?' Alison said. 'When I spoke with your wife, she seemed as much in the dark as I am, about my connection with Mrs Kulman, I mean. Are you telling me that was all an act?'

Jim shook his head. 'Not at all. What you see is what you get with Pru. No artifice there, I'm pleased to say. As far as Pru's concerned, May was just another member of the Chamber of Commerce.' He grinned. 'But May and I were on the same wavelength. Friends. We got on.'

Sometimes, Alison thought, the only way to get where you want to be is to take the direct route. 'My parents died when I was very young.' she said. 'Did Mrs Kulman know them?'

Jim opened a hymn book and flicked through the pages as if he were searching for the right answer.

'I'm not asking you to break confidences,' Alison said. 'But...'

'You're looking for reasons?' Jim's voice was low.
'Yes.'

One of the candles on the window sill above them fluttered and went out. A thin plume of smoke drifted over their heads.

Jim cleared his throat. 'You think May knew your family?

'Did she? If so....'

'It could explain why she left her house to you?'

'Perhaps. I don't know. I don't really know anything, but I think you do, Jim.'

Sensing his reluctance to travel this road with her, Alison fought to keep impatience out of her voice. She leaned towards him and said quietly, 'I have absolutely no idea why she left me her house, though I do know about her connection with my ex-husband's family.'

'You do? How come?'

'A memory stick with photos, a cottage in Derbyshire, a birth certificate, for starters.'

He sighed. 'You know your father-in-law was her son?'

Alison nodded. 'I found out this morning, from my ex.'

Was it really still the same day? The journey from morning to now was longer than could be counted in hours.

'I saw her,'Alison said, 'Mrs Kulman, sometime before the accident. I didn't know who she was. She was visiting the retirement village my aunt manages.'

'She was trying to see you.'

'But why? Wasn't it her son she was looking for?'

'I think,' Jim said. 'I'd better start from the beginning.' He leaned back in his seat, glanced at the couple further down the aisle then closed his eyes.

The story he began was about Mary, a young woman in the nineteen fifties, a woman unhappily married to a man much older, a friend of her father's.

Ashington, Alison thought

There was a love affair, the young man, an employee of her husband's, about to do his national service. Only when he'd gone did Mary realise she'd fallen pregnant. The way things were with her husband, she could not pretend the child was his. Abortion was illegal, her father was a member of a strict religious sect and refused to help her. With no money of her own, and little opportunity to earn any, eventually she confessed to her husband.

'Did he help her?' Alison said.

Jim shook his head. 'He threw her out. Her mother gave her all her own savings without her husband knowing but she was too afraid of him to do anything more. The minister of their chapel gave Mary the address of an institution, a home for fallen women was how he described it. The child, a boy, was born there. She called him...'

'Gordon?' Alison said. She pictured a birth certificate tucked into the corner of a blotter. More pieces were fitting into the jigsaw but there were still gaps. Her rib cage ached with trapped breath.

'That's where she met Daphne,' Jim went on. 'At the home. Daphne had a son too.'

Another undiscovered layer of Daphne's story, Alison thought. 'What happened to him?' she said.

'The pair of them were pressured into letting their babies go for adoption.'

Alison stared. 'Adoption? That's appalling.'

How could any woman carry a child, feel it growing inside her, give birth and then hand the baby over to someone else? It was unthinkable. Could anyone forgive a mother who did that?

'It's how things were then,' Jim said. 'Not the best of times, I'm afraid though one woman's loss was another's gain.'

Alison frowned. 'How d'you mean? Oh I see, the couples adopting the babies?'

An image of Malcolm's face popped into her mind. 'Adoption?' he'd said, 'No way.' Wondering what he'd say now, if she made it a stipulation of returning to their marriage, was an unworthy but intriguing thought.

There was so much more to both Daphne and Mrs Kulman than she'd ever imagined. She'd seen them only in relation to her own life, the problems each of them had posed her. Knowing about their own struggles made them feel much nearer, more like herself.

'The money Mary's mother had given her,' Jim was saying, 'was enough for a mortgage deposit. She bought a house.'

'Mulberry House?'

Jim tucked his tie further into his waistcoat. 'She invited Daphne to come with her, a new start.' He paused, looked down at his hands then said, 'By then Mary had dropped the r from her first name and gone back to her maiden surname. The B&B did well. May found she was a dab hand at investments. She went into property in a big way.'

'So Mulberry House wasn't her only asset?'

'Not by a long way.'

'Did Daphne know that?'

Jim shook his head. 'Daphne created the world as she wanted it to be. She wouldn't have taken any interest in May's wider life.'

'And things went on like that for a very long time?' Alison said. 'What happened to change them? Why did Mrs Kulman decide to leave Kent, to look for Gordon? He's not called that now, by the way.'

'A TV programme apparently triggered her decision,' Jim said. 'It was about the effect on children of being adopted. I'm not really sure why it made such an impact on her but it made her reassess things. She planned it all very carefully, intended to sort things out with Daphne before making things final.'

'I'm not exactly clear about the timing,' Alison said, 'but at some point she decided not to leave Mulberry House to her son?'

'Before she went up north, she'd done some digging. Hired a private detective to visit, ask questions, take photos.'

'A private investigator? I know about her. The pretence she came up with irritated the hell out of my ex-husband.'

Jim nodded. 'Not a very nice man, I understand? Handsome yes, but what you see isn't what you get?'

Alison could only stare. 'You do know a lot about all this, don't you?'

Jim grinned and pulled down the edges of his waistcoat. 'It's a long drive from here to Derbyshire, Alison. Lots of comfort stops and cups of tea. May wanted to do the right thing, she told me, talk to her son and put right the wrong she felt she'd done him so many years before.'

'Some things are better left, perhaps,' Alison said.

'As she discovered. The photos had shown her a family working together, the kind of set-up she felt she ought to have provided for Gordon. The four of you, your in-laws, Malcolm and yourself, looked like a good team.'

'Don't tell me she thought we were playing happy families. I've seen those photos...'

'You've seen them? May thought she'd removed everything and anything that would give the clue to where she'd gone.'

'As I said, there was a memory stick.'

Jim raised his eyebrows. 'She'd have been furious with herself.'

'Why,' Alison said, 'did she clear everything out of Mulberry House, make things so mysterious?'

Jim laughed. 'The lure of drama? Who knows. We all have our own ways of spicing things up perhaps?'

'So,' Alison said, 'having got the detective's report and the photos, she goes to Derbyshire. A couple of recce trips first, which was when I saw her?'

'Her decision to leave the south altogether seemed sudden to me. Very unlike May but people are like fractals, don't you find, layer beneath layer? The more you find out about them, the more there is to find. On that first trip she hadn't spoken to any of you, just wandered around the Garden Centre, watching. Only after the big move north did she approach your father-in-law.'

'She wouldn't have got far with him,'

'She was appalled. Phoned me in an awful state. They were wrong 'uns, the pair of them, she said, her son and her grandson. She'd taken two paintings with her, representing her life since she'd let her son go. She'd planned to give them to him, to her son, as a kind of token that she meant to put things right. She made it sound like some sort of test. In the end, a test she never made.'

'The paintings on top of Jude's wardrobe.' Alison said.

Jim frowned. 'You've seen those too?'

'Scenes of the marsh by a local artist, Hannah something?'

'Sherwin, Hannah Sherwin. Unusual compositions, very atmospheric?'

'She asked Jude, my aunt, to take care of them for her. For the time being she said.'

'She hadn't even shown them to her son, of course. She wanted them out of her way, until she decided what to do. Her son, was an ignorant boor, she told me, and his son was eyeing up everything in a skirt when he had a wonderful wife working her socks off for the bastard. Arrogant pigs she called them, like all men. Every single man in her life had let her down, she said. The only decent one on the planet was my good self apparently.'

He replaced the hymn book, lining it up with the others on the rack. 'It was women who needed the breaks in life, she'd decided. She heard, from your aunt, I think, that you were cutting the ties with those bloody men, as she called them, going it alone. May was in a position to make sure there was something waiting for the lass, as she called you, after she'd gone. You'd make good use of it she said.'

'But she didn't know me at all, did she?' Would she have tried to know me, Alison wondered, if she'd lived? It sounded as though her inheritance of Mulberry House was the result of a whim, an impulse.

'She spoke about the sisterhood of women' Jim was saying. 'that she'd put things right as far as Daphne was concerned. I'm not sure I really understood it all.'

'Jude, my aunt, may have had some hand in that,' Alison said, 'She's ardently feminist and nicely persuasive. Would she have come back here, to Kent, do you think, Mrs Kulman? If she hadn't been killed? Sorted things out, as she said? '

The church door banged open and the policeman appeared. 'Good news, folks,' he said. 'The rain's given up and apparently the tide has turned.'

Chapter 49

Only the back row of the crematorium chapel was empty. Nearly a full house for Daphne's last scene, Alison thought. She'd have liked that. On top of the coffin, Daphne's photographed profile smiled beside a spray of pink roses. Wreathes of summer flowers lay propped against the sides of the supporting trestle, filling the room with the scent of blossom.

Pru and Jim's sartorial choices demonstrated the attraction of opposites, Alison decided, an odd assortment of ill-fitting brown garments beside a black, three piece suit of immaculate cut. On the other side of the aisle, Samantha, demure in pale grey, dabbed the corners of her eyes with a tissue and reached for her husband's hand.

Alison had hesitated in front of her wardrobe that morning. Her status in Daphne's life, created by the idiosyncrasies of Mrs Kulman's will, was ill-defined. She wasn't sure she ought to go to the funeral at all. She knew the navy blue dress she'd eventually chosen was only an indication of how she ought to feel. She had a vague memory of Shakespeare saying something about the outward show masking what lay beneath.

'We are here this morning, ladies and gentlemen, to honour the life of a dear friend.' The guy holding wide his arms from the reading desk had not chosen funereal gear for this appearance. His quiff of gingery hair, goatee beard, bright green jacket and red shirt gave him the look of an exotic bird. 'For those of you who haven't had the privilege of enjoying the artistic scene in these parts, my name is Harvey Trevelian, a longstanding admirer of Daphne's talents.' His quiff trembled as he gestured towards the coffin. 'Daphne's friends,' he looked first at Pru and then at Samantha, 'know that she followed her own spiritual path.' The glance at Samantha's husband was apologetic. 'Hence our decision to say goodbye to her without recourse to organised religion.'

On Alison's right, the middle-aged man who had slipped in at the last moment, was frowning at his brown suede boots, as if he'd not meant to wear them with his black suit.

She looked at the back of Bryn's bowed head and wondered what had made him act as one of the coffin bearers. Had he felt some kind of obligation to do Daphne a last service?

He'd looked wary at the inquest, giving his real name and keeping his voice so low that the coroner had asked him to speak up. Samantha's evidence had corroborated his account of finding the letter from Daphne's son, and the note from her in the same envelope. As neither document was dated, the coroner concluded there was no proof they had any bearing on her state of mind. He had brought in a verdict of Accidental Death.

Pru, with a swirl of brown skirt, joined members of the choral society at the front of the chapel. After the first few notes of a *Climb Every Mountain* she cast anxious, sidelong glances at the tenors.

Alison swallowed a giggle and concentrated on the large wall-hanging beside her. Its mixture of embroidery and appliqué reminded her of the knight in Thomas Carr's sitting room. Here, under a bridge of brown felt bricks, embroidered fish swam in formation through threaded blue and white ribbons. Alison thought of all the watery aspects of life here on the Marsh, of the sea, of the Mulberry Harbour, marsh witches and mermaids. And mixed in with these images were the smells of aromatherapy, of fudge in a warm kitchen. She thought of the Art of Fugue, of the morning wind whispering in the branches of the mulberry tree.

She could understand why Mrs Kulman had left instructions that her own last rites be as brief as was legal. After discovering her son was not the person she'd hoped he'd be, family ties wouldn't have been top of her agenda. Why the woman had been foolish enough to have those expectations in the first place was completely illogical.

Alison sighed, knowing that Mrs Kulman wasn't the only one with illogical high hopes. Her own unfulfilled expectations of others had caused her the most pain. From now on she'd try to take Jude's advice and write her own lines.

From what Jim Perkins had said, Mrs Kulman had been a determined woman who knew her own mind but wasn't afraid to change it. All that feminist stuff about supporting women would have gone down well with Jude. But why hadn't the principals that had led to the will in Alison's favour extended to looking after Daphne? Jim had suggested she'd meant to sort things out with her friend but she hadn't got round to it.

Alison glanced at the coffin. Perhaps that poor woman hadn't been strong enough to live with thinking May had let her down.

'And now,' Harvey Trevelian lowered his voice, 'I suggest we each take a few moments to remember Daphne in our own way.'

The man beside Alison was the only person to kneel as well as bowing his head in a gesture of respect. Something about his profile, and the way his hair clustered around his head made her feel she might have seen him before. And then she realised. The identical profile and similar cluster of hair was pictured only feet away, in the photograph on top of Daphne's coffin.

Outside the chapel, the mourners stood in small groups, some inspecting the floral tributes arranged around a splashing fountain in the middle of the courtyard, others chatting with less reserve than the chapel environment had demanded. The middle-aged man in the suede boots was shaking hands with Bryn.

Alison had planned to slip away as quickly as possible, hopefully unnoticed, but the one-way system of leaving the chapel by another door meant she was one of the last to leave. She sidled between a cloister arch and a group of choir ladies, searching for the quickest way to the exit.

'Mrs Draper?' The man beside her was pushing his glasses up his nose. 'I'm Fergus Higton, the solicitor acting on Dr Carr's instructions.'

'Another to add to my collection,' Alison said.

'Would this be a convenient moment for a word?'

He looked about her own age but his manner suggested the days when women knew their place. Jude would have him sliced into little pieces and fed to the nearest shark. Without waiting for her reply, he took her elbow and led her into the corner of the cloister. From here, the next funeral party could be seen lining up behind another coffin. 'Ah,' he said, 'in the midst of life.'

'Mr Higton,' Alison summoned her assertive voice, 'I'm afraid this isn't a convenient time, not convenient at all. If there is a good reason why you need to speak with me, perhaps we could make an appointment for you to call me at Mulberry House?'

'Ah, Mulberry House, the thorn in all our sides,' Fergus said. 'Dr Carr would be the first to agree, I know.'

'I was surprised not to see him at the funeral,' Alison said, 'as executor of Mrs Kulman's will.'

'To which will do you refer?'

His smugness was infuriating. She said, 'How do you mean?'

'Unfortunately the solicitor you saw in, wherever it is you live, had been given the wrong document, or had lost the new one. Staff can be sadly lacking in loyalty these days.'

'Dandruff and scruffy shoes hardly merit loyalty perhaps?'

He looked at her as if she were speaking a foreign language which might be dangerously contagious.

'Nonetheless, another will has surfaced,' he said, 'post-dating by a few days the one Dr Carr spoke to you about. Lawyers are greatly impeded when clients do not know their own minds.'

'Dreadfully inconvenient for you,' Alison said.

He took a step backwards. 'Probate is pending for a set of different bequests.'

Fear clawed into Alison's gut. 'You mean the house isn't mine after all?' she said.

'Not at all, not at all Mrs Draper. I should have said the disposition of the bequests differs. Mulberry House remains yours entirely, as before, the amount going to Dr Carr remains, the charity named receives a smaller amount, but the residue, a considerable estate, was left to Miss Chiltern.'

'Daphne? But she's dead.''

'Indeed she is, indeed, indeed. A sad business. But the note she left indicates her wishes for her own assets.'

'I understood that document wasn't witnessed.'

Fergus rubbed his chin. 'That complicates matters of course though I don't doubt her wishes will be upheld by the court of probate.'

'Which means?'

'Which means I have an urgent need to locate Miss Chiltern's son. I have written to the address on his letter but received no reply. Have you any idea where he might be found?"

Bryn and the middle aged man were scrutinising the cards on the wreathes.

'I think,' Alison said pointing, 'the man with the suede boots might be able to help.'

Alison was reluctant to go straight back to Mulberry House. Bryn, she couldn't think of him as Brian, had arranged to help Hannah and Jake move back to their bungalow as soon as the funeral was over and it would take them some time to pack up. It had been great to help them out but now their home was habitable, she was glad they were going back. She wanted to arrive at Mulberry House when, for the first time, she would be the only person there.

Mrs Kulman had wanted her to have the house and the sea had stopped just short of snatching it from her. She needed not just to enjoy it by herself for the couple of hours before Bryn came back but somehow to set about laying Daphne's ghost.

She drove towards Thomas's house. Everywhere were signs of the recent floods, tide marks, mud and scatterings of shingle that had been washed up from the beach. The sea had left its mark.

It was odd that Thomas hadn't come to say goodbye to Daphne. Despite his annoyance and irritation, she knew he saw himself as a knight in armour shiny enough to ensure courtesy and correct behaviour. According to Bryn, he'd not turned up for the semi-final of the Pub Quiz League so he was persona very much non grata in The Grey Goose. Jim Perkins had said Pru was looking after Thomas's dog but he hadn't said why.

The last time she'd come this way she'd been on foot, newly arrived and adrift, a failed wife and would-be mother, confused about who she was and what she wanted. She thought about that first evening on the beach when she'd seen herself at the mercy of an endless line of hurdles. They hadn't gone away but she felt herself squaring up to the ones still in sight.

She'd even kitted herself out with a pair of wellies, blue ones with a bright, floral decoration. The shoe shop assistant's corkscrew curls had looked familiar.

'You'll recognise me from the mini-mart,' the woman said. 'Closed down now. I was lucky to get this new job.' She'd smiled at Alison and nodded at the wellies. 'Good idea those. All Marshies need wellies.'

The For Sale sign outside Thomas's house was a shock. Leaning against a white MG parked by the gate was a small woman with purple hair, spiky above an angry expression.

'Another one of his victims, are you?' she said when Alison got out of the car. 'He's buggered off, the bastard. America according to the neighbour.'

Alison pointed at the sale sign. 'For good and all by the looks of it.'

'Smarmy arse, that he is,' the woman said. 'Promises, promises but no can do when the chips are down.'

'You know him well, do you?' Alison said.

'As well as it gets,' the woman said. 'Wined, dined, bedded. One minute, yes Gwenda, the job's yours, buggering off the next.' She glared at Alison. 'You know he killed his wife, do you? That'll douse your ardour.'

Alison laughed. 'Hang on,' she said, 'ardour and Thomas Carr have never appeared in the same room as far as I'm concerned.'

'You must be the first then. Not had much time to work on you perhaps?'

'What do you mean about his wife?' Alison said. 'Are you saying the police were involved?'

The woman's face twisted into a snarl. 'Only briefly,' she said. 'But that was down to yours truly. You'll be my alibi

Gwenda darling, won't you, he says. Tell them I was with you. And there I was, stupid besotted cow, going along with it. When all the time he was having his wicked way.'

'Wicked way?'

'Stuffing pills down her throat, that's what.' She slammed her fist into the For Sale board. 'Dumped me after that. Just for a time, darling, he says. Soon as the dust's settled we'll get together again. I left my husband for him, you know.'

'Men,' Alison said.

'And what did the bastard do when I asked for a small favour in return? Bugger off to the other side of the bloody Atlantic.'

'Bastard indeed,' Alison agreed.

The woman glared at her. 'You can say that again,' she said. Picking up the bag she'd flung onto the grass verge, she got into the MG, slammed the door and revved the engine.

Chapter 50

'Reckon there's any truth in it?' Bryn said. 'What the purple spikes woman said about Dr Carr?' How are the mighty fallen, he thought. Posh bloke has feet of clay.

Alison shrugged. 'Who knows? There must be more to it than what she told me. Doctors and death certificates and so on. Nothing to do with us though, is it?'

They were sitting in the Mulberry House kitchen, the remains of their breakfast on the table. Bryn's bags were packed and waiting in the hall.

'You'll be okay, will you, on your own here?' he said. Alison looked so much happier now that her aunt was better, more *Jazz on a Summer's Day* than *Lady Sings the Blues*.

Alison nodded. 'I've a lot to organise,' she said. 'Now that Jude has decided to throw in her lot with the man in her life, I'll have the time to get this place organised.'

'Organised for what, do you know?'

'The B&B trade, perhaps?.'

'There's a demand, certainly,' Bryn said. 'As well as the tourist trade, when the supermarket people have finished mopping up their site, the place will be crawling with workmen looking for accommodation.'

'What about the protests?' Alison said. 'Upsetting the locals is the last thing I need.'

Bryn laughed. 'Now it's been agreed to preserve the facade of the original shops, that's all died down. It's amazing how quickly people change their minds when it comes to extra jobs for the area.'

'What about the man who ran the self-service place?'

'Abbas? He's applied for the supermarket's management scheme, apparently. The butcher's on a world cruise and the other guy, Jenkins is it, is purveying his coffee beans and fancy cheeses in one of the posh Shires.'

'Watch it,' Alison laughed, 'your northern prejudices are on the prowl.'

Bryn grinned at her, stacked up the crockery and carried it to the draining board. 'D'you mind if I ask you something?'

Alison opened the cupboard to put away the cereal packets. 'Depends what sort of something,' she said.

'Sorry.'

'I thought we'd agreed,' Alison wagged her finger, 'no more apologising.'

She was right, Bryn thought, watching her run hot water into the bowl, it was time to stop all that nonsense. 'About seeing me,' he said, 'on TV that time?'

'Why I didn't shop you, you mean?'

Bryn nodded.

'Enough on my own plate, perhaps? I knew you'd sort it out, sooner or later.' She turned off the tap. 'My turn now,' she said, 'to ask you something.'

'Fire away.'

'Did you realise who I was? When you first arrived here?'

Bryn frowned. What did she mean?

'Draper?' she said. 'Did you connect me with the Garden Centre? You didn't live far away, did you?'

'Oh I see. No, sorry, too caught up with confectionery to bother with plants and such.'

'And what about Daphne's son. Was it you who let him know she'd died?'

Bryn nodded. 'It seemed the right thing to do. It wasn't my fault she thought I was her son but something made me feel responsible, as if I had an obligation to her and to that poor guy. He was trying to find her.'

'What's he like? His face seemed familiar but that might have been because he's so like Daphne.'

'You may have seen him on the box. He's an actor. Not big time apparently but what he describes as a good steady living.'

'Ironic that,' Alison said, 'given Daphne's theatrical ambitions.' She rinsed a plate and put it to drain. 'She made quite an impression on both of us, didn't she, one way and another? I'm not proud of the way I treated her.'

'You shouldn't feel like that. Daphne was a very unusual person.' Finding words to describe that poor woman was impossible. He remembered the hunted look in her eyes when he'd arrived, the ridiculous costume and later, her tiny body on a mortuary slab.

Alison was looking over her shoulder at him, a squaring-up sort of look. 'Eccentric is the word most people use about her,' she said. She lowered a mug into the bubbly water and scrubbed it with the brush. 'I had this idea, after the funeral, of trying to, well, face her I suppose. I went up to her flat thinking I might be able to lay her ghost.'

'And did you?'

She smiled.' There wasn't a ghost, well none I could find. If it was lurking under all that chaos, it didn't choose to come out.'

'What will you do with her stuff?'

'Help her son to sort it out I expect. When did you say he was coming?'

'Sometime next month. I wrote it in the office diary.' Bryn said. He grabbed the tea towel and started to dry a plate.

'A dishwasher's high on my list,' Alison said. 'God knows how Daphne managed without one all those years.'

'Pru Perkins reckons she was Mrs K's skivvy,' Bryn said. He put the plate away and picked up a mug. 'What d'you think she was really like, Mrs K?'

Alison sighed. 'I've really no idea,' she said. 'My rules for summing up people have taken a battering recently, and that's the ones who are still with us.'

'I'm not too good with rules,' Bryn said. 'Never was. Square peg in a business hole, me.'

'You're out of the hole now though aren't you, or soon will be?' She left the washing up and went to the window. 'The insurance money for the flood damage will cover most of the renovations I need to make,' she said, 'though I'm not sure if the poor old mulberry tree will survive.'

They'd found a local tree surgeon to make a start on sorting out the tree, sawing off the branches that had smashed through the garage window and shoring up the rest. The tree bloke had advised leaving things for the time being, though the remaining growth made a sorry sight.

'I've been talking to Jim Perkins about that,' Bryn said. 'Horticulture's among his many talents. A lot of the tree is still rooted, he says, so it might survive. And if we plant a cutting in the autumn, there's every hope of starting again.'

'We?' Alison smiled at him.

Bryn felt himself colour up. 'Brian Prosser needs sorting. It'll take a while but Bryn will be back.'

'What about Hannah?'

'Hannah and Jake will be here when I get back to the Marsh,' he said. 'After that, we'll see.'

They finished the washing up and then Alison helped him carry out his stuff. The lock on the garden garage door hadn't been repaired so they left the house by the front door. Beside the hallstand was a pair of fancy wellington boots.

'Where have they come from?' Bryn said.

Alison winked at him. 'They're my new wellies,' she said. 'Every Marshy needs wellies. Come on, let's get you on the road.'

Outside, the air was soft, the sky covered in candy-floss clouds. Bryn glanced at the sea, glimmering like warm syrup. When he came back, he thought, he might treat his toes to a paddle.

In the garage, he heaved a couple of boxes into the back of the pick-up. For a bloke who'd reckoned to live without possessions, there was more stuff than he'd realised.

He backed into Ashton Gardens, careful not to hit Alison's Fiesta. She closed the garage door and came to stand under his window.

'Bye Bryn.' she said. 'Come back soon.'

'Not goodbye,' he said, 'auf wiedersehen.'

Hark at you boyo, he thought, poncy foreign stuff now. He checked the supply of sweets in the glove compartment. He had a long way to go.

The weeks he'd spent on the Marsh had been a forgetting, a self-induced memory loss into which his past had intruded only in fragments. Those fragments had to be put back together again. Only then could he turn the strange amnesia into a reality.

With Humphrey Lyttelton's *Travellin' Blues* on the player, he pulled away, waving to Alison out of the window. Before he got to the end of the street, he looked in the rear view mirror and saw her rounding the corner into Marine Drive and towards Mulberry House.

'One of the main features of the Kent Marsh settlements is the unchanging nature of their shape. House styles come and go and in many parts of the area nineteen-sixties, inter-war and Edwardian homes enjoy a close proximity but the underlying skeleton of the place remains the same. A returning eighteenth century smuggler would recognise the alignment of the streets and the continuing presence of the churches whose facilities he once employed.

This is land leased from the sea, perched on the edges of a watery world. At any moment the ocean may demand its rent. Changes that do occur arrive with a history to appreciate, a legacy to uphold.

It was pleasing to note therefore, that when the trustees of The Daphne Chiltern Foundation for the Arts [headquarters Mulberry House, Netherstone] investigated accommodation for their gallery, theatre and art school, they were able to find new uses for existing buildings and to build new ones in keeping with the treasured ambience of the area.'

[*Buildings in the Farthest South of Kent* (revised edition) by Dr Thomas Carr published 2014.]

Acknowledgements

I am grateful to:

Steve Shaw for support throughout the project and many hours of proof-reading.

Members of Chesterfield Saturday Writers' Group and Moorside Writers' Group for their encouragement and generous sharing of individual expertise.

Philip Hanwell for sharing his great knowledge and love of classical music.

Bernetta Moseley for photographs of Romney Marsh and other helpful materials.

Tom Blyth of Bannister Publications for help and guidance with printing and publication.

Any mistakes and inaccuracies within the story are entirely my own.

I hope residents of The Peak District and of Romney Marsh - both places of wild beauty - will forgive the way I have mixed real and invented places in creating the settings for this story.